C000148589

FIFTEEN WORDS

Monika Jephcott Thomas

Clink Street

London | New York

Published by Clink Street Publishing 2016

Copyright © 2016

First edition.

The author asserts the moral right under the Copyright, Designs and Patents Act 1988 to be identified as the author of this work.

All rights reserved. No part of this publication may be reproduced, stored in a retrieval system or transmitted, in any form or by any means without the prior consent of the author, nor be otherwise circulated in any form of binding or cover other than that with which it is published and without a similar condition being imposed on the subsequent purchaser.

Although the novel is inspired by family history the book is a work of fiction. Names, characters, business, organisations, places and events are either the product of the author's imagination or are used fictitiously. Any resemblance to actual persons, living or dead, events and locales is totally coincidential.

ISBN: 978-1-911110-95-8 paperback
978-1-911110-96-5 ebook

To my parents who encouraged me to be myself

Preface

He was poisoned. Someone had poisoned him.

'It might have been an accident,' Erika offered rather lamely.

'An accident?' Edgar snapped. 'How does a man accidentally ingest enough cyanide to do that?' He gestured to the puddle of wine on the floor as if the professor was still there re-enacting his convulsions for the benefit of their education.

'The Gestapo warned him not to speak out against their euthanasia program,' Horst stated quietly from behind his hand.

'Warned! They threatened him. And he wasn't intimidated. So they've tried to bump him off. These are the kind of people that are running our country.' Edgar looked from Horst to Erika.

Erika dropped her eyes to the floor and watched as one of the café staff mopped the red wine from it.

Max looked at the revolver in his hand. It was the first time he had taken it from its holster since that terrifying train journey through Romania close to the Southern Front. Yet this time he felt he was actually going to have to pull the trigger. The question was, would he be aiming at the Russians surrounding the city or at himself?

The gun was a Walther P38, not dissimilar to his father's Luger P08, but a cheaper version massed produced for the German army now that the financial cost of war was spiralling out of control. Max turned the gun over in his hands, juggling it with thoughts of his father putting that Luger to his own forearm when Max was just a boy and pulling the trigger. Papa had shattered just about every bone in his wrist, but it was the only way he could make sure he did not have to serve in the German army in the Great War.

'There was nothing *great* about it,' Papa had grumbled the day Max had announced his intention to join up. But his father had reluctantly chewed up his bitterness for the Nazis and his fears for his son and swallowed them with a mouthful of recently rationed hard bread and tinned pork. He had to admire his son for forging a career for himself as a doctor. 'What would this country do without people like him?' he whispered to his wife as they both stared at the ceiling that night in bed, wide-eyed in the gloom with parental concern. 'Our people will be broken soon, just like they were before, and it will be his job to try and put them back together again, God help him!'

Max had wanted to be a doctor since he was sixteen. He had known he *had* to be a doctor since he was sixteen. Since the time Tante Bertel had taken him to the theatre. Then, he was so engrossed in the play before him (on the edge of his seat as Polly Peachum cried for her lover and Macheath was about to be hung on the gallows; the ominous music from the orchestra seemingly emanating from his own swelling chest) that Max thought the mighty crash which rocked the floor beneath him, was the result of a wonderful choreography between pyrotechnical effects, timpani and cymbals. But as the screams from the street dominoed through the audience and even reached the actors, Max realised this was not part of the show. Some of the audience were frozen to their seats, fearful of what the screams outside portended. Others, who Max could only assume were not as enamoured with *The Threepenny Opera* as he was, hurried their friends and partners into the street with a strange excitement on their faces for the greater spectacle which awaited them outside the theatre.

'There's been an accident. A terrible accident. A tram. A lorry...' one disembodied screech reached Max and his aunt from over the heads of the stampeding theatregoers.

'Tante,' Max could not control the quivering in his voice. 'What should we do?'

'Let's go!' Bertel declared in a tone of such confidence she might well have been trying to compensate for her nephew's obvious lack of it. 'We need to help!'

Max followed Bertel into a street strewn with beer and bodies. For a second, he told himself that there had been a riotous party and everyone had collapsed on the ground from too much drinking. But the blood and dismemberment told another story; one which he could not deny when he saw the double-decker tram torn apart as if it was made of paper and the lorry from the Kronen brewery on its side, its contents soaking the road with a boozy stench.

Bertel grabbed Max by the sleeve and, with an intrepidity which he could only marvel at, she marched through the chaos towards the cigar shop opposite the theatre, where a ladder leant against the awning.

'Help me carry this!' she ordered Max. 'We are going to use it as a stretcher. We're going to lay each casualty on it in turn and carry them to the hospital, understand?'

Max nodded his head furiously. From the moment Bertel had opened her mouth he was hanging on her every word, determined not to let her down, determined to infect himself with her courage.

The hospital was only two hundred metres away. Yet after hauling four casualties there and watching Bertel's stern but comforting way of telling each that they would be OK, despite their screams and horrific injuries, Max felt weaker and more useless than ever.

'I should have been able to do more,' he told himself when he finally got home and hid in the lavatory, trying to get the sound of that screaming to quieten down; desperate for a sense of solitude after all the crowds, the bumping of elbows, the tripping over bodies. 'I will never be so useless again.'

So *Dr* Max Portner weighed the pistol in his palms, red and cracked from the late winter frosts. He noted the secret code *480* on the slide, which had replaced the old Walther Arms banner decorating previous models for fear the Allies could identify weapon production sites from such markings and bomb them. But that was the least of his fears and those of his fellow Germans right now in Breslau, the city surrounded as it was by the Sixth Army of the First Ukrainian Front. The city had been under siege now for over seventy days. Max had tended to so many wounded and dying soldiers in that time he knew there couldn't be many left to protect the great military fortress Hitler had decreed the city to become against the advancing Russians.

A plane roared overhead. Max shoved his pistol back into its holster and threw himself instinctively into one of the bomb craters in the garden which they had begun using as latrines. The last thing on his mind was the gallons of other people's shit he was now crouched trembling in. When the bombs didn't come he dared to look up and, since the plane was so low, he managed to identify one of his own, a Luftwaffe aircraft dropping another load of supplies. These air drops used to bring him a sense of hope, but the city was on its knees now and he doubted they would survive until tomorrow. Doubted they *should* survive if all he'd heard about the POW camps was true.

'Erika,' he whispered to himself, craning his neck up to track the plane, 'If only...'

His unarticulated wish stuck in his extended throat as his eyes took in the sight of the plane exploding – a direct hit from one of the Russian anti-aircraft guns positioned around the city. His heart sank to its lowest point yet, but his eyes found strange solace in the bizarre beauty of the billowing clouds of smoke and flame, sending now useless pieces of medical equipment and food hurtling to the earth. Some of it even reached the garden where he was rooted in the ground agog.

And then it began to snow.

As if nature was attempting to cool down the infernal destruction and pacify the angry explosion marring its skies. The flakes were big, some too big to be snow Max gradually realised as he blinked at the smaller ones adorning his lashes. He held out his hand to catch one of the false flakes. It was part of a letter. Pages and pages, some quite intact began to flutter down into the garden. He clambered out of the cesspit and began, as instinctively as he had protected himself from the bombs by diving into a stinking toilet, to gather up the mail which the plane had also been trying to deliver along with supplies. Letters from loved ones to their men on the front. His fists were soon full of the treasure, the only thing salvageable from this final nail in the coffin of Breslau. Somewhere in the frosted corners of his mind he wished there was a letter from Erika among them and yet, like a player in one of Hitler's fundraising lotteries, he never believed for a minute that he held the winning ticket.

The burning plane was gone now. The white winter sky was victorious again. Max expected a phalanx of white-coated Russians to emerge from it any second, swarming over his hospital. He waited. But as it didn't come – yet – he wedged his bounty of letters under part of a broken bedframe to stop the wind stealing them and washed as much shit from his skin as he could with the burning cold water from the barrel which had been set up to catch the rain. He was careful to use the cracked bowl to decant the water. Careful not to let the dirty liquid cascading off of him fall back into the barrel. This was, after all, all the water they had; water for sterilising surgical instruments and for cleaning the gaping wounds of soldiers.

The cold water on his cracked skin felt like a punishment rather than a remedy. The shit didn't seem that bad by comparison. He hurried inside – as far as the carcass of the monastery could be called inside – to dry off and see if there was any likelihood of them bringing any survivors from the exploded plane.

No one came.

He stood looking out of one of the grand arches that used to be a window at the front of this monastery they had commandeered as a field hospital. He stood there rather recklessly since most of the staff and patients in this hospital now spent their time below ground in the cellars, one of the few features of the building left intact, and a far safer place to be if the next plane that cast a shadow on this place was a Russian one.

He had felt awkward when they had first arrived. Felt he was bringing death and havoc to a place of peace and meditation, but, as their trucks wheezed and heaved into the driveway a year earlier in March of '44, he saw from the rubble, which used to be the church, that death and havoc had already beaten them to it.

The monks had been welcoming enough and had donned the Red Cross arm bands to denote their role as nursing assistants enthusiastically, but the nuns, who also cared for the sick, did so with much more disdain behind their eyes, Max thought. And he didn't blame them. The Nazis had ordered the convent to house thirty prostitutes alongside the Sisters. These girls could serve the men in ways the nuns could only wonder at. And the Nazis could have housed them anywhere in the city. But they chose the convent just to offend the nuns. To underline their contempt for all things religious. After all, how could you be devoted to the Führer if you were wasting your time devoting yourself to some insubstantial God?

Max was here as a doctor, not a Nazi. He had never supported the party and he couldn't help but wish Erika could see what he saw now. Then perhaps the vestiges of faith she had in the government would explode with the same strange beauty and completeness as the plane had over the monastery garden.

The plane. The letters! He'd forgotten in his haste to get dry (though he still felt damp) and in his concern for the survivors, who did not survive.

He hurried back through the shell of the monastery out to the garden. If he didn't know it was medically impossible, he would have believed he could feel his heart melting into his stomach.

He prayed the letters had not been ripped out from under their unsightly paperweight by the insidious winds. He had no idea why but he felt terribly attached to these shreds of communication. He needed them to still be there. He would hate himself if he had been so stupid as to let them blow away.

Shielded by the garden wall, the papers were where he'd left them under the slats of the broken bed. The massage of relief his entire being felt then told him he did know why he felt so attached to these bits of paper after all. Because he knew how he would feel if Erika's words were among them. How warmed, how hugged, how caressed he would be. How connected. As connected as his fingers interlaced with hers moments before their first kiss, or just like they used to be beneath the blanket he brought down from his room to keep them warm as they read together wedged into the old armchair she had in her room in their student digs in Freiburg.

At night the landing strip looked as beautiful to Max as Freiburg Cathedral used to during mass. But here on the airfield – which Hitler had destroyed a large swathe of the city centre to create – there was no great gothic architecture arching above him like the ribcage of a prehistoric whale; no stained glass windows afire with colours which glowed from a mysterious fuel; no spine-stroking, soul-squeezing music pumping from the feet and fingers of his great friend Edgar on the organ. No, all this bald patch of ground in the middle of Breslau had in common with his beloved cathedral were the candles.

A hundred candles in tin can lanterns, fifty on each side of the otherwise dark landing-strip to guide the plywood gliders bringing food, ammunition and medical supplies under cover of the night. It almost managed to take his breath away now as much as it did on that first night he worked this shift so many months ago. Their own little vigil, one which he hoped was being matched somewhere by his wife staring into the heart of a candle as if it was a portal to the ones that twinkled before him. This was his church now. His pew a cot inside the bunker which peeped out just above the ground near the airfield.

Edgar, his best friend, fellow medical graduate and favourite musician from Freiburg had folded his long body onto the cot next to Max. A soldier and two monks were also in the bunker waiting to get the supplies off the expected plane and then to extinguish the hundred candles, like some greedy centenarians eager to eat their birthday cake, before the Russians spotted their landing strip and turned it into unusable craters.

'What's in the bag, buddy?' Edgar nodded at the extra backpack Max had brought tonight, using the English (or rather the US) word to address his friend as he always did, to demonstrate his love of all things American as much as his contempt of the government's efforts to suppress them. He could see paper sprouting from the side with the broken clasp and was suddenly filled with the crazy idea it might be sheet music. Forbidden swing music from the USA, which Max had acquired for him as a wonderful present. But where the hell would Max get swing music these days? Edgar couldn't remember the last time he had heard any, let alone played some.

'Take a look,' Max smiled. 'And you,' he said to the soldier. 'They're letters I rescued from the plane that came down yesterday. There might be something for you in there.'

Max watched as the soldier tore into the bag and rifled through the pages as he would devour some Silesian Streuselkuchen should he ever get to taste some again. God's best invention on earth that plum crumble cake! Max told his nose that that's what he smelt now instead of the mildew fermenting on the bunker walls.

Edgar waited patiently for his turn with the letters. He wasn't in as much of a rush as the soldier because he could almost guarantee there would be nothing for him in there. He didn't have a wife like Max did, not even a girlfriend. He preferred to *keep his options open*. He was still in his mid-twenties after all. As was Max. He loved both Max and Erika dearly, but their desire to bind themselves together so soon in life, in a life that was doing everything it could possibly do to keep them apart, to destroy one of them and leave the other in wretched grief for the rest of their days, was simply beyond Edgar.

'Was there anything from In...?'

Was that a crack of thunder? Or a Russian anti-aircraft gun?

The first they knew of the glider landing was the sound, like a tree being felled. It had been hit by the Russians and smashed on the landing strip, sending its crew sprawling over the field and swiping many of those celestial candles from their places, extinguishing some whilst the others turned into devilish little firelighters, setting aflame parts of the plane that weren't already in splinters.

A switch flicked in Max. As it did in Edgar. Max was no longer an extra pair of hands to get supplies off the plane, he was the doctor in charge of saving the five airmen strewn about out there beyond the bunker. The concrete bunker that could keep them safe from further gunfire. What was the point in leaving it then? The airmen must be in as many pieces as their plane. Surely they were beyond saving, weren't they? These thoughts of a sixteen-year-old Max inevitably raced through his head at a time like this. Thoughts chased and kicked out by images of his aunt Bertel crackling with initiative and puffed with resourcefulness. And that was why Max found himself outside the bunker seconds after the candle flames had begun to taste the plane.

'Bring the cots!' he bellowed. Bellowing was never his strong point, but he would not be heard over the continuing gunfire otherwise.

Edgar, who had his arms outstretched as he ran behind Max, as if to grab him and drag him back into the sensible safety of the bunker, quickly followed his friend's order and directed the monks to carry one cot between them whilst he grabbed the other with the soldier whose name he thought was Thomas. It was difficult to remember all the soldiers' names that came through here. And it didn't pay to get too friendly with any of them. They might not be around for long or they might be delivered back to you in a terrible state of dismemberment. Edgar felt it was much better to just stay tight with his little medical team: Max, Horst, Dolf and Lutz. Just the five of them. They were there to help the wounded and the sick and they'd all be home again by Christmas. At least that's what they kept telling themselves. Just like they had the year before when they'd been posted here, and the year before that on the Western Front.

Edgar and Thomas scampered towards the silhouette of Max,

all of them stooped like old men as bullets whipped the air above them. The silhouette waved one arm at Edgar emphatically in the negative. It seems there were only four airmen to save now. The silhouette fled to the left and Edgar followed. With no signal from Max over the second airman, save the flashing of the firelight in his round glasses, Edgar knew this one was alive and he directed Thomas to haul him onto the cot.

Max could not be so sure about the third airman at first. His eyes were shut tight and he appeared to have two mouths. Both wide open. One above the other. The first where a mouth should be. The second below it and slightly to the right, a gaping red cavity where the man's chin should be. He felt for signs of life. It was almost impossible to distinguish the man's weak pulse beneath his own raging blood thumping through his fingers and booming in his ears. He allowed the monks to arrive anyway, allowed them to drag him onto the cot.

'Maxillo-facial wound,' he said, more to himself than the untrained monks as he began flicking through the annals of his two-year qualified mind, preparing himself for the surgery to come. If they ever made it back to the bunker alive, that is, let alone the hospital.

The fourth airman was dead as the first. You didn't need to be a doctor to know this. Bodies without their heads are universally acknowledged to be kaput. And the fifth? His roars of agony were a good sign. He was very much alive. Max began to haul him towards the bunker, but the guy was a lump. Luckily for both Max and the lump, Edgar and Thomas were back from depositing their first rescue and the three of them carried the lardy loudmouth back to the bunker. He appeared to have a femoral fracture and multiple shrapnel wounds. However, Max couldn't help but find himself annoyed by this airman. Not by the noise he was making, but by his corpulence. He knew he shouldn't, but supplies were so low these days Max couldn't remember the last time he had a decent meal. His trousers were clinging for dear life to his now bony hips and, although the nuns had cultivated some delicious fruit in the garden, both the bombing and the winter had put pay to any more of that.

He looked at Edgar – his tall friend who was looking skinnier by the day too – struggling at the other end of the cot and felt a strange desire to laugh.

'And we thought being a student was tough!' he wanted to blurt out to Edgar, but right then keeping their cargo and themselves in one piece was far more pressing.

Triage was simple back inside the bunker: the two quiet airmen were seen to first, one by Edgar the other by Max with the monks assisting. Thomas was ordered to reassure the portly pilot that his fracture and wounds would be seen to as soon as possible and that he was going to be just...

Bullets ricocheted off the side of the bunker and the pilot actually quietened momentarily. Thomas peeked through the spyhole.

'Shit!' he announced to the rest. 'They are on the airfield. They are close.'

All the chaos outside suddenly hushed, which had a calming effect on the chaos inside too, and now only German words spoken in a Russian accent were being fired at the bunker.

'What are they saying?' Max hissed with his hands still working at packing the gaping wound on his patient's face.

'They say they've got grenades. And they'll use them on us. Unless we surrender now.'

The doctors looked to the soldier for military instruction in this matter, but Thomas looked like he might need a doctor soon himself.

Max waited for as many long seconds as he could for the soldier to spring into action, but he could see it wasn't going to happen. He saw his own hands were shaking as he pressed on his patient's face, so welcomed the excuse his idea gave him to use his hands for something else.

'Thomas, come here and apply pressure, as I am.'

Thomas gladly did as he was told. Max grabbed the portable telephone and tried to keep his voice from quivering as he spoke into it.

'We need artillery support now on the airfield. Fire on the area around the bunker... No, not *on* the bunker. That is where we are. *Around* it. That's where Ivan is.'

'Bloody hell, Max,' Edgar whispered still splinting his patient's snapped wrist. 'Are you sure about that? What if they miss and hit us?'

'What if they do nothing? Then we get blown up by grenades or go out there and surrender and get shot by Ivan anyway.'

'After they've tortured us,' Thomas added.

Edgar was about to voice his approval of Max's plan, given this concise but persuasive argument, but the swift arrival of his army's shells pounding the ground around them silenced him and everyone else. Except the pilot who was convinced now more than ever his life was ending and screamed with every shell that rocked the bunker.

Max crouched on the ground beside his patient and Thomas. He took strength from the soldier's manifest fear – his pale face, his cartoon-wide eyes, his shivering frame – just as his aunt had done from him at the theatre when he was sixteen, although to this day he never knew that. (If my nephew is terrified then I have to be strong, Tante Bertel had told herself.) If this soldier is weakening I have to be strong, Max reasoned. He took over packing the facial wound again, but kept low, both knees on the ground to steady himself every time the bunker felt like it would be destroyed. Both knees on the ground in the manner of prayer.

The ground was rocked ten times in quick succession. Then again and again… and again.

And again.

Each time the gap lengthened in between explosions. Like the gap between lightning and thunder Max used to count when he was a child. The gap got longer each time and he knew the thunder was getting further away and it would be safe to come out from under the covers soon.

The Russians had fled.

Then Lutz was frantically rapping on the door, their only remaining truck with a puddle of petrol in its fuel tank, waiting outside to rush them all back to the hospital. When everyone was out Max grabbed his bag to follow but was halted by Thomas, waiting at the entrance looking more like a soldier again.

'Sir?' he said and nodded to one of the dark corners where Max's backpack of letters had been flung when the glider had crashed.

Max knew Thomas wanted to appear to be looking out for the chief doctor's belongings, when in fact he was desperate to have another opportunity to leaf through the contents of the bag, just in case there was something from his Maria to comfort him tonight when he would no doubt be plagued by nightmares of near death and images of terrible wounds and shocking dismemberment, which he could usually blame on an active imagination if he hadn't seen them for real just now. Why did this bloody doctor have to run out on the airfield in the first place and subject him to all that? So they saved three lives, but they could have all been killed? He was the military representation in the bunker that night, why did he even listen to Dr Portner? Why didn't Dr Portner listen to him?

Thomas found the remains of a letter from Maria in the bag that night and caressed the charred paper in his bed as if it were the smooth, clean, white skin on her guitar shaped body.

My Darling Little Sweetheart,

Just a few lines, Thomas, hoping that my letter finds you in the best of health. I am very well myself at present and so is my family.

Well, Lovey, you see your Maria is faithfully thinking of you, no one else, only you. You know I love you so much, my Little Husband and I'll never love anybody else. If you get killed I'll stay with no one but our little baby, when you give me one.

I dreamt about you last night. I dreamt you got married to someone else. I hope to see you very

Erika smoothed her dress over her pregnant belly. Six months pregnant, but she felt nearly full term, her slim body heavy with the new life inside her; her slim body weighed down by the absence of her soulmate Max, by the chaos of her country and now by the fact that she must leave her mother behind in Neurode.

As Max's father struggled to unload the last of the luggage from the sledge, Erika held onto her zaftig mother in a final embrace. Mother held mother who held baby inside her. Erika the daughter, felt she was being ripped from her mother's womb all over again, but Erika the doctor told herself not to be so silly. Told herself to banish all those thoughts of turning Herr Portner away and staying here in Neurode with her own family. Told herself that it made sense to go with him to Bernried, where the support and facilities for her new baby would be so much better. Told herself to go now before it was too late, before the authorities clamped down even further on the movements of civilians.

Despite it being the logical balm to both women's sadness at parting, there was no chance of her mother coming too.

'The only way I'll be leaving that factory is in a coffin,' Erika's mother had declared – valiantly enough, but it did nothing for Erika's fear that that was exactly how her mother would be leaving the place. Yet she could also understand the extent to which her mama was invested in the business both her parents had worked so hard to build up from nothing. Together. Erika got it. She got it now she had Max in her life. Now they were building a life together too. Or they were, until the Nazis embroiled him in their futile war and broke up her happy home.

The news was changing by the hour, they had to leave now, Herr Portner urged her. So she stretched out these seconds in her mother's fleshy grasp as impossibly as her own skin had stretched to accommodate her growing child, which, despite her scientific knowledge of the elasticity of the epidermis and the stages of development of the human foetus, never ceased to fill her with a visceral wonder. And, as they boarded the 06:16 to Mittelsteine, Erika toyed with the notion that although every metre of this journey took her further from her mother it would also bring her closer to the possibility of seeing Max again and the blossoming of their new little family.

Should Max ever make it back to Bernried, that is.

Erika allowed the slamming of the train door to chop that rogue thought out of the carriage; to leave it shivering on the platform and let it freeze to death in the black sleety mess where boots trampled over it – the boots of those desperate to find a place on this train, since the next wouldn't be for twelve hours at least.

She hardly noticed the others in the carriage, despite being elbow to elbow, toe to toe, nose to nose almost, with them. Her field of vision was hazy with longing, fatigue and loss; as hazy as the morning light trying to reach her through the icy windows dripping with the condensed breath of nervous passengers. She hardly noticed after a while how slow the train was, how often it ground to a halt so that it was two hours late getting into Mittelsteine. She allowed herself to be ushered off the train by Max's father. Heard him asking someone about the train to Braunau and heard the reply:

'It's already gone, sir. But there's another.'

'Oh good. When?' The brighter note in Karl's voice fired Erika's eyes back into focus, but only to see his face droop when doused with the news:

'16:25, sir.'

It was now 08:45.

Bless Karl Portner, Erika thought. He was a pinball there on the platform, bouncing between their luggage, the station staff and her, trying to look after everything, trying to keep her from harm. She had to pull herself together. She had to help him. Help herself. She might be pregnant but she wasn't hopeless. She was a doctor, for God's sake! The textbook on how to assist with birth was not stuffed in her rucksack for *her* information. She knew very well what to do if someone was giving birth, but she also knew how she'd be in no position to assist when the baby was pushing itself unstoppably out of her.

'The NSV.' She lay her hand gently on Karl's which seemed to be permanently clasped to the sleeve of her coat no matter what he was doing; no matter even if he was hauling their heavy suitcases about the station, he seemed to be under strict orders not to let her go. She imagined those orders were Max's and a smile almost thawed her face. But Karl's response was surprisingly frosty.

'The NSV? What use have they been so far? People's Welfare, my foot!'

He continued to fuss over the luggage, very occasionally using both hands on the big cases. She could see how the wrist of his left hand was giving him some pain, but there wasn't much even she could do to remedy that. It would always be weaker than the other since he shot it to avoid military service. His cynicism for the NSV matched his disdain for anything Hitler's government proposed. And then more rogue thoughts buffeted her about with the crowds in the station. There was no strict order from Max to his father to keep a hand on her at all times. Karl was simply keeping his weak wrist out of harm's way when lugging about the cases. He probably didn't even care for Erika that much either, she was just the vessel, the thing carrying the cargo that was truly precious to him – his soon to be born grandchild.

Erika allowed a shiver to shoot up her spine and shake those absurd thoughts from her head. 'Let's go to the NSV office. There must be one nearby. And let's *demand* some help, Karl.'

Her father-in-law seemed to appreciate this more belligerent tack and it wasn't long before they found the office and indeed demanded some assistance under the terms of the Mother and Child Care Programme the NSV purported to promote.

'We have to wait for over seven hours until the next train out of here.' Karl leant over the desk, the little fog which he made as he spoke (which everyone made in this weather) was fired in the face of the non-administering and un-assisting administrative assistant. 'The least you can do is give her a place to lie down while she waits.' He thought about banging his right fist on the table for emphasis, to wake up this feckless robot, but then he thought better of it. He didn't need two damaged wrists when trying to haul Erika and her ridiculous amounts of luggage across the country.

The door to the street opened behind them.

'Where would you propose she lay down?' the robot monotonised, gesturing around the tiny office.

'A woman in her condition...' Karl began, but was stopped in his tracks by a deep and surprisingly calm voice speaking to Erika.

'A woman in your condition should be lying down indeed!' said the nurse examining Erika with crystalline eyes. 'Unfortunately, you can see we are rather limited on resources here, to say the least.'

Erika almost collapsed with relief at the sight of the nurse. Not really because she was in the presence of another health care professional, but because this woman reminded her, physically at least, of her own mother. It was all she could to do not to wrap herself in the nurse's beautiful marshmallow arms right there in the draughty little office with the secretary looking blankly on. Especially when she cooed:

'But my apartment is just around the corner. Literally two minutes' walk. You are welcome to lay down there until your train leaves.'

The nurse sang everything she said. Her words came like lullabies and Erika knew she would be well rested wherever this woman called home.

The apartment was simple, sparsely furnished, but immaculate, just as Erika had predicted. When Karl was sure she was comfortable, he went off to find a church that was holding High Mass. Erika marvelled at his devotion, even now after her own conversion, but it seemed his faith was more likely to get them through this odyssey now than the crumbling infrastructure of the country whose government she had put her own conviction in with such surety for so long.

'Now,' said the nurse, tucking Erika into her own bed where the sheets smelled as if they had just been laundered, 'I have to go back to work, but I'll come back later and check up on you, OK?' She smiled, smoothing a lock of Erika's black hair behind her ear, which made Erika feel like a little girl again. She loved it.

The nurse chattered on in a whisper for a minute and Erika dropped quickly and gently into the space between reality and dream, where the nurse's voice became that of Fräulein Toni, her nanny when she was four.

And then she was with Fräulein Toni slowly walking the length of her parents' living room in the fading light. Sometimes hand in hand. Sometimes Fräulein Toni carried her. But she was getting too big to be carried by anyone, so her nanny only did it if she wanted to whisper a story right into her ear or for the extra dramatic effect a squeeze in her strong arms could make. To have a living room where they could walk in this way made Erika think it must have been a very large living room in a very big house. Or perhaps it was just that she was a little girl and so everything seemed enormous – even a cupboard could take on the gigantic proportions of a mountain in the fairy tales Fräulein Toni told so well. As they trod the floorboards on which this cupboard-mountain stood it shook a little and the Chinese vases which adorned it clinked together adding a perfectly eerie accompaniment to the tales of evil queens and poison apples in *Schneewittchen*, of cannibalistic old ladies in *Hänsel und Gretel* and of cruel-hearted stepsisters and golden slippers in *Aschenputtel*.

Erika loved *Aschenputtel* more than any other story Fräulein Toni told her. She loved the love story. She could endure all the abuse and hardships along with poor 'Ash Fool' because she knew Ash Fool's mother was watching over her from heaven, dropping beautiful gowns and slippers in her lap and making sure that eventually, no matter how unlikely it seemed, the prince would find her and they'd live happily ever after.

Adolf Hitler loved *Aschenputtel* too. He loved the story of racial purity. A story which could show children how the aliens will never succeed in crushing the pure blooded heroine. And how the prince, with an unspoilt instinct could distinguish between the repellent intruders and the true unadulterated beauty – no matter what dirty tricks and grotesque acts the aliens employ to try and avoid detection. Cutting off their toes and slicing at their heels to try and fit into the golden slipper! Their evil ways will find them out and their eyes will be plucked out by the beaks of the same white doves that gently dropped the sumptuous gowns and footwear into our heroine's lap.

Erika woke as her baby kicked her insides. Her heart was racing and she found herself muttering, 'I loved the love story, I just loved the love story,' as she blinked images of toes being sliced off and eyes being plucked out from her cloudy mind.

She looked at the clock on the mantelpiece. It was the shape of Napoleon's hat.

Tick tick tick tick.

It ticked loudly, as if it was taunting her about how little time she had to rest before they had to be on the move again.

Half past three.

It ticked loudly like that irritating cheap watch Max had bought from the market in Freiburg when they were students. She hated that watch, but she would give anything to be irritated by it right now if it was strapped to the wrist of her husband.

There was a knocking at the door. It was Karl. Erika hauled herself out of bed and shuffled across the room in the fading light to let him in.

'How was the Mass?'

'Really rather good,' he said looking a lot less flustered than he had been this morning, but the tension soon began to crawl back over his brow as he tried to gather up all their things and get them to the station on time.

'Just before you go...' The nurse appeared at the open door like a fairy godmother. 'I must check you over first. Make sure you're OK to travel.'

Erika glanced at Karl and saw him bite his lip and look at his watch and flap his arms with impatience.

Tick tick tick tick, the hat shaped clock laughed.

But Erika knew he was as concerned about her health as the nurse was, it was just that he had a different idea of how her health might be protected and that involved not missing any of these trains and getting her home to his wife as soon as possible.

The nurse was satisfied and Karl thanked her as he tried to get himself and Erika's luggage through the narrow door, like Laurel or Hardy in a *Dick und Doof* movie. Erika hugged the nurse to emphasise her gratitude and to stock up on embraces, as it were, for she feared without her mother and her beloved Max around she would be starved of physical affection for a while, at a time when she needed it most. Not that Karl and Martha were cold. Far from it, they were clearly doing everything they could to help their daughter-in-law, but they weren't her parents and they weren't Max.

The station was swarming with people, so much so that Erika stopped in the street as they approached, doubtful that they could actually get through the entrance.

'What's wrong?' Karl said, 'Are you feeling ill?'

'No, but are you sure we'll make it? I mean, look at all these people, Karl.'

'Don't worry, come on, we'll make it. I guarantee it,' he grinned as if he knew a secret passageway to the train. And in a way he did, but for now they had to push their way through the gasping, tutting, huffing hoards, the anxious, despondent, distracted droves. Women with lips pressed tightly together, men in uniform and blood soaked bandages. For a split second she thought one such man was Max. Her heart leapt. It wasn't him. Her heart sank. She didn't know what would be better: to see him now seriously wounded, or to know he was all right but not see him again for another six months. All the faces crowding her vision were as pale as the winter sky except for the red rings around their tired eyes. Yet they moved so fast. Survival now depended on haste. Get to the store too late and the goods would be sold out, get to the stop too late and the streetcar would be gone or the seat taken by someone else, get to work too late and risk having your wages slashed, get home as quick as possible before the air raid siren goes off. And besides all these things you had to keep moving, keep busy, because then there was no time for reflection or brooding – that would kill you faster than the lack of vitamins.

'There's so many refugees they've laid on an extra train,' Karl said over his shoulder using Erika's luggage as a battering ram against the crowds. 'Mind would you, there's a pregnant woman coming through!' he shouted and bashed around with all the impunity a pregnant woman in tow affords you.

Nevertheless, Erika still had to edge forward slowly with her arms around her swollen belly like a cage to protect it from the throng. She saw Karl had stopped, had put down all the luggage and was now talking to a train guard who looked to Erika remarkably like a rat in a uniform. The rat and her father-in-law huddled conspiratorially for a minute until Karl turned to Erika jubilantly saying, 'I told you we'd make it!' He winked and Erika watched amazed as the rat scurried back and forth to the train with her luggage, finding a special space for it in the goods wagon before ushering Karl and helping her to two seats which miraculously appeared in the front carriage of the train to Halbstadt. And not a moment too soon, as the rat bared his yellow teeth at them by way of a farewell and hopped back onto the platform before the train shuddered to life and groaned under the unprecedented weight of the passengers it carried out of Braunau.

Erika looked at Karl for an explanation for this unparalleled level of customer service.

'Cigarettes,' he beamed. 'I came armed with enough to grease more palms too should we need it along the way.'

Erika smiled at Karl and gave his arm a grateful squeeze. She looked back at all the pale frustrated faces bustling about on the crowded platform as they pulled away. *You had to keep moving, keep busy, because then there was no time for reflection or brooding – that would kill you faster than the lack of vitamins.* She had made it onto the train, but that meant for the next God knows how many hours she had nothing else to do but reflect and brood. Brood about her husband, stew over where he was, what he was doing. She prayed he was safe. Funny, she thought, even before I converted, when I believed religion was nonsense, I would still pray to God when I wanted something badly enough, when I was scared enough. She prayed he wasn't wounded, hoped he never had to go too near the fighting, that he was ensconced in some field hospital somewhere far back from the enemy lines. And then she found herself praying he wasn't having too much of a good time either. She knew only too well how it was when men got together. And it was all men on the front. Apart from the whores. And the nurses, whom he would be working in very close contact with. And they'd probably all be

23

swooning at his prowess on the operating table. He wouldn't! She told herself. He wasn't the type. Normally. But what was normal about the war? No! She let the jerking train shake this ridiculous paranoia from her head and, trance like, she watched the scene of their first meeting play out on the knees of the woman sitting opposite her.

It was the 18th of April 1939 when she had registered at the medical faculty of the University of Freiburg. She had found herself a lovely spacious student pad with a conservatory, just like a winter garden, where she could grow things all year round whatever the weather outside. That was what told her it was the place for her. She was to share the house with a chemist and another medical student. On the first evening there, the medical student invited them all to go dancing at the Rheinterrassen. Socialising was never a problem for Erika and this evening would make meeting new people a breeze.

Only one out of all the male students there didn't ask her to dance that night, which made her curious about him. He was slim, blonde, wore round black-rimmed glasses, and had a high forehead, which she told herself promised great wisdom despite having no medical evidence to back it up, and a firm and chiselled chin which she would always find enticing. It was only later, when they had moved on to the Kakadu Bar, with its plush red décor and soft music that the curiosity finally got too much for her to resist. She got some information on him from her housemate, then went over and said, rather brashly, due to the volume of port sloshing around inside her:

'Every other boy here has asked me to dance tonight. Every other boy has flirted with me, except you.'

'Well,' the boy, already painted red by the seedy lighting just got redder, 'I'm not really one for dancing... nor for flirting.' He jabbed his glasses further up his nose.

'Oh.'

'Not that you aren't attractive,' he stuttered. 'I mean, I understand why all the men here would want to flirt with you, it's just that I'm not that confident, I suppose.'

'Oh really? Well, my friend Edith over there tells me you're tipped to be top of the class in all subjects this year so you can't tell me you're not confident.'

'Ah,' he raised a finger, almost confidently. 'Confidence in medicine is not the same as confidence in situations like this.'

'Like what? What is this?'

'This. Parties, chatting. Women.'

'Why not?'

'Well, there are hundreds of text books that tell you exactly what to do when it comes to medicine. All you have to do is memorise the facts.'

'All you have to do!' Erika mumbled to her glass as a vision of the impossible task of her studies ahead almost sobered her up. But before it could, she parried, 'But there's plenty of books that tell you what to do in these situations too.'

'Really?'

'Of course.'

'Like what?'

'*Romeo and Juliet,*' she grinned.

'Yeah, but look how that ends.'

'*Gone with the Wind.*'

He hadn't read it, so couldn't comment. He chose to nod politely instead.

'*Madame Bovary.*'

'That's the one about the woman who reads too many books about love and ends up ruining her life, isn't it?'

She slapped him gently on his chest, '*Pride and Prejudice,*' and kept her hand there as she mischievously reeled off more of the world's most famous love stories.

He was captivated. Her dark eyes were so full of adventure, her high cheekbones bursting with mischief, and, with all he already knew about anatomy, it was the perfect example to him of why there had to be more to life than flesh, blood and bone. Why he believed in God.

'I'm Erika, by the way.'

'Max.'

'I know.'

They shook hands which seemed an absurd gesture since they had been almost nose to nose and cheek to cheek for the last few wonderful minutes.

'So are we having that dance or what?'

As he told her, he wasn't confident on the dancefloor, but he started to enjoy it, knowing that many of the other blokes in the room were looking at him enviously. Then that made him feel vulnerable and he stepped on her toe.

'Sorry,' he said.

'It's OK,' she laughed.

What if these other men came now and stole her away from him with their social confidence, their Rhett Butler boldness, their Mr Darcy dash? It's not as if he was totally unaccustomed to *parties, chatting, women*, but with Erika the gears of his heart had shifted, the parameters of his world widened, the focus he had always had on his studies was now disturbed and suddenly everything got a lot more complicated. Deliciously complicated.

The first thing Max saw next morning was his breath forming brief little clouds above his face.

It must be even colder than yesterday, was his first thought. And we're still here, was his second.

He got out of bed still clothed in his uniform, encrusted in places with shit from the pit he'd dived into a couple of days before, but taking off anything was increasingly difficult in these temperatures.

However, today, Jenny will wash my tunic and trousers for me. She's good like that, he thought, emerging from the basement to see a sky so blue for a moment you could kid yourself that it was the middle of summer.

He checked he had all the necessary items in his medical bag and set off without bothering to take some bread from the stores for his breakfast. The girls at the convent always seemed somehow to have more provisions than they did at the hospital and were always willing to share it with Max in return for his services.

He walked down the street. Or rather he stepped his way carefully through the rubble which once was the houses standing on either side of the road. It made what would have been a five-minute walk into fifteen.

The white marble edifice of the convent stood intact at the end of the street, apart from its windows now boarded up. Even the fragile looking crucifix on top of the façade was still there proud and erect. Max liked to think it was because it was a house of God that it had survived the blasts which had levelled much of the rest of Breslau.

But then, was not the monastery a house of God too? And look at the state of that.

He could almost hear Erika's voice saying these words and it irked him. And it made him squirm that it irked him. After all, wouldn't she have a point if she said that? Perhaps the convent was not immune from the Russian bombs because of its religious spirit, but because of the sense of sexual abandonment that now inhabited it. Perhaps he was wrong to encourage Erika to convert to Catholicism. Perhaps

27

her irreligious scientific approach was the right approach. Wasn't there actually something very scientific about prostitution anyway? About paying for an itch to be scratched when the itch arose and bypassing all the complicated and destructive emotions that go with love and marriage? The Nazis knew this was an important service to keep their soldier's morale up. Perhaps *that* was why the convent was still standing. Because the Nazi's devoted all their defences to protecting it? More than the airfield, the energy supplies, more than the transport network? Well, it seemed like that sometimes anyway. The Nazis housed the prostitutes in the convent to insult the nuns, that was all. If the convent and all the whores inside it had been blown to bits last night they would have drafted in more from Dresden and housed them somewhere else.

'There is no need for religion in the new Germany,' Erika had said to Max.

Yet she had wanted nothing more than to be married to him. Marriage! A *religious* construct.

He knocked on the door of the convent envious of the sky for having such clarity today.

Bolts were yanked and the door scraped open enough so a face framed in a wimple could be seen.

'Dr Portner,' Sister Hilda smiled politely. She was younger than most of the nuns and so could still muster a smile for him, unjaded by life, young enough not to remember the Great War before this one.

'Is that our Puff Direktor?' Another very young woman elbowed Sister Hilda aside. This one was not clad in nun's costume, in fact she was clad in surprisingly little for the time of year. But she smiled and she laughed and she welcomed him in a way which grabbed Max's attention away from her covered counterpart Hilda, who now looked ill at the way this girl had just described him as the boss of their brothel. This girl's name was Trudi.

Max couldn't resist seeing the girls in the convent as bizarre pairs. Trudi and Hilda were the very young pair, both novices if you like. Jenny and Sister Agnes were a pair – slightly more mature, both very industrious, but industrious about very different things. And

Beatrix, the actual boss of the girls, as far as Max could work out, was the obvious complement to the stern faced Mother Superior, Sarah.

Mother Sarah would not show herself on a day like today. A day when all thirty of the girls would be examined and tested by Dr Portner. There was a festive atmosphere among the girls whenever he called, as if he was Santa Claus delivering presents. All the girls scampered around and shoved each other eager to get their gift first: the all clear from the doctor.

'Girls, girls!' bellowed Beatrix, sitting on a wooden chair in the hallway, the only lady not scampering about, although trying to lounge as she did on such a utilitarian object was one of the greatest challenges of her day. 'Let the poor man breathe and bring him something to eat first.'

Just as Max had predicted, the hospitality of the girls knew no bounds. Breakfast would be served.

'He'll need something to line his stomach,' cackled Beatrix, 'before delving about in all your nether regions'.

Suddenly Max wasn't so hungry any more. But Jenny was there with bread and a sweet preserve probably borrowed from the nuns' stores. And since Jenny was serving the breakfast, she got to be examined first, which she was only too aware of.

*

'How do I look?' Jenny asked.

Max knew she meant was she clear of infection. But he also knew she used an inappropriately seductive tone to suggest something else since he was looking directly at her genitals at the time. He maintained utter professionalism throughout the examination. It wasn't hard for him. Looking at the human anatomy in a disinterested and scientific manner was what he was trained to do.

'There seems to be no sign of infection. You can...'

Get dressed. Cover up. Whatever he wanted to say he just couldn't manage it for some reason, as if he would sound like some disrespectful client of hers at the end of sex if he did, so he just waved a hand towards her hitched up dress. Which made him feel even worse.

The only time Max failed to look at Jenny professionally was when he spoke to her face after these examinations. When she asked him how he was doing, how he was coping, as if he was the patient now, or even as if he was just a friend of hers. And then he would have to ask her something which made him feel even more vulnerable in her presence.

'I was wondering Jenny, after I've done here if you, er, wouldn't mind...'

A smile began to smoulder on Jenny's face.

Why was he stuttering so much?

'I mean, if it's not too much trouble. If you're free I mean, er...'

Jenny knew what he wanted to ask, but had to enjoy the sweet sight of his shyness a little more before letting him off the hook.

'Not free to, er, you know, I mean, if you have the time just t-t-to...'

'To wash your clothes?' she put him out of his misery at last.

'To wash my clothes. Exactly. If it's not too much trouble.' He visibly relaxed.

And Jenny saw it. So she felt the overwhelming need to see him stiffen again, so to speak, and she reached out to caress his collar as if she needed to assess just how much washing was necessary to get this uniform spotless again.

'I better get at least a few of the other girls checked out first,' he quickly added, in case she was about to start stripping him right then and there. Not that she ever had, or ever would. She would always make sure he had some privacy in the cell they used to examine the girls, usually before he had given the first one the all clear or given her the necessary treatment for gonorrhoea, so there was plenty of time to start drying his clothes, bringing him the spare uniform a client once left behind, so she said.

'But what was he wearing when he left?' Max would often ask.

Jenny would never give him a straight answer, just smother a smile and dance her slender eyebrows about. Sometimes she would linger at the door after this, toying with him a little more, knowing he wouldn't dare begin to undress before she had left the room. She wallowed in the awkwardness of the moment. But not out of malice towards him. She just wanted to be around him and his gentleness for as long as possible. She wasn't used to it. Oh, she was used to hearing the soldiers tell her that they loved her and call her by their wives' names in the heat of the moment, she even put up with the rough angry ones working out their frustrations on her, but they were paying. They were customers. Regardless of getting a free examination, she found herself happily donating her time and effort to Max. Breakfast, washing, concern.

'We heard about the plane crash the other night,' she said when his clothes were drying and he was appropriately dressed in the spare uniform, drinking coffee – no doubt left behind by another grateful customer.

'Who told you?'

'Thomas. When he was here with Trudi.'

I suppose the letter from his wife wasn't enough to comfort him then, Max thought with a bitterness that surprised even himself.

'Oh,' he said filling his mouth with hot coffee to avoid voicing his thoughts.

'He said you took over.'

'Well, someone had to and it certainly wasn't going to be him.'

The little cockroach, Max thought swallowing more coffee and bile. Bad-mouthing me to a load of prostitutes because he was too spineless to do his job. And too spineless to be faithful in marriage come to think of it, if his little visit to Trudi is anything to go by. And I helped him sort through the letters as well! Granted we only found half a note, but at least he got something.

'It sounded like you were very brave,' Jenny said without a hint of playfulness this time.

'I was just doing my job,' Max said with a modesty that sounded ridiculous even to his unassuming soul.

Jenny gestured for him to stay where he was as she clip-clopped down the hall to her cell, returning moments later clutching a small picture, which she pressed into his palm.

The picture was by no means new. It was curling at the edges, the

31

back was stained with something brown and the image itself was faded. It was an image of the baby Jesus held by a Black Madonna. At first he thought she had "borrowed" it from the nuns, as she had his breakfast marmalade, but from the way she said:

'I want you to have this. If you keep this with you all the time it will keep you safe and protected. Will you do that?'

He knew it was hers and that it had kept her safe and protected for many years already. And that's why he replied:

'I can't take this. What about you?'

He wondered if the nuns knew that their antitheses, their nemeses, or one of them at least, was a Madonna-toting Catholic too.

'I'm all right. No need to worry about me. I live a charmed life, I do,' she laughed.

She laughed so hard it echoed down the hall, but he caught the look in her eyes at the same time which didn't hold the same conviction about her invincibility as her voice. Nevertheless he knew it would be futile to try and refuse the gift. And he was deeply moved by it. So he held it reverently admiring it for a while before slipping it into his pocket.

Yet the moment he pocketed it he felt as though he'd been unfaithful to Erika. Not only had he accepted a gift from another woman, he'd accepted a gift from a prostitute. How would he ever explain that to her when she asked where he'd got it? He'd probably lie in order not to hurt her feelings. Say some dying soldier had given it to him or something like that. Not that there was anything to be hurt about. It's not like he was sleeping with Jenny. She was just a patient. A friend even, but nothing more. A very pretty friend with incredibly slender eyebrows and a petite hourglass figure, sure... He poured the still very hot coffee down his throat to punish himself for noticing. Now he was angry at Erika for being suspicious when she wasn't; she couldn't be yet, and she had no knowledge of the picture. Now he was angry at himself for being angry with her.

Now his commanding officer was marching down the hallway followed by Beatrix, sweeping the marble floor with the hem of the feather-trimmed dressing gown she wore so flamboyantly in the hope he might notice.

'Right this way, officer,' Beatrix croaked pointlessly as he clearly knew where he was going.

'Heil Hitler!' the officer barked

''Tler!' Max mumbled as he stood and saluted.

'I wanted to come and tell you personally, Dr Portner, that having been informed by Private Thomas Huber…'

Oh, not content with bad-mouthing me to the girls, he's been crying to the CO now too! Max paled at the injustice of it all. Just because he had more balls than that silly little private.

'… of your immense bravery and initiative on the night of Thursday last at the landing strip, you and Dr Edgar Klein will be awarded the Iron Cross, Second Class.'

Jenny squealed with delight and clapped a clap which brought Max back from his trance where thoughts of injustice entangled themselves with words of commendation.

'I beg your pardon, sir?' he asked.

'I told you!' cried Jenny. 'We all said how brave you were.'

Even Thomas, it seemed.

The CO rather impatiently repeated himself and Max thanked him before he turned on his heels and hurried out of the convent, pursued by Beatrix again. Jenny could not stand on ceremony a moment longer and threw her arms around him and kissed his cheek.

'Well done!' she beamed at him as she pulled away again.

'Thank you,' he said, fishing in his pocket to make sure the picture was still there.

It was. And he caressed it gratefully and secretly with his thumb.

They had to change trains at Halbstadt, but this time there was no room for them in the passenger carriages. They had to ride with their luggage in the goods wagon to Trautenau, but Karl produced some chocolate this time for the female guards who worked on the wagon and in return they made sure he and Erika had as comfortable a ride as possible among the mountains of things people were travelling with. Not just suitcases, but enormous framed pictures, grandfather clocks, furniture, boxes of possessions, the entire life of the non-Germans (and those who thought they were German until the government said otherwise) who were now refugees fleeing from the country they had called home all their lives.

On the train from Trautenau to Alt-Backa, they found space in the passenger carriages again. Some girls from the Hitler Youth employment programme fell over themselves to help Karl and Erika into their carriage. Karl's masculinity and his repulsion at their swastika armbands tempted him to refuse their offers, but the aching in his wrist overruled him and he found their fussing almost amusing in his relief.

As the train pulled out of the station Erika answered the girls' clucky questions about her bump, when it was due, what she wanted to call it if it was a boy, if it was a girl.

'If it's a girl I thought about Netta,' she said. 'If it's a boy, Max. Definitely Max.'

She found their enthusiasm something of a tonic and remembered the way she used to hold court like this with her own Hitler Youth group when she was a teenager.

She felt her heart swell in her chest as she recalled singing through the streets of her village, leading the other young girls in her group, swastika banners held high. They would play sports in the fields, then make campfires, discuss the traditions and costumes of Germany and tell stories from the myths of the Norse people. The Youth Movement for Young Women gave Erika a way out of the gilded cage her parents had painstakingly forged for her. You're the daughter of a textile factory owner, but you mustn't venture out of the garden and across to the factory to mix with the labourers! We are such successful parents and that is why we do not have any time to spend with you, but you must not go looking for adventure outside the grounds of the villa.

The factory chimney dominated the entire village. To the adults there it was dominating enough – threatening their rest day with shadows of the working week ahead; or swelling their pride as a breadwinner for the family; or undermining their confidence in the future of farming; or corroborating their conviction in the rise of the cities, the urbanisation of the people. As the posters on her classroom wall said:

In 1870, Germany had two farmers for every city-dweller. In 1930, there were four city dwellers for every two farmers. In 1870, two-thirds of the population lived in the countryside. By 1930, the proportion was reversed.

Apartment buildings are the breeding ground of misery. They are fertile soil for Bolshevism. No soil, bad air, little sun, disease, unemployment and hunger, misery, moral decline, high death rate.

But to little Erika, what she saw when she looked at that chimney through the bars of the villa gate was a veritable enchanted castle, the scaly neck of a rearing dragon, or Rapunzel's doorless home. The gates of the factory opened into a world where Schneewittchen's dwarves and the pointed-eared, winged Wichtelmänner toiled, creating all the wonderful fabrics her father boasted of. On one side of the factory gates was the porter's lodge manned by the one-armed Herr Weiser, or rather, the lair where the deformed troll dwelt, she told herself on that impulsive day when she found her bare feet darting from the villa gate, hopping across the dirt track and tip-toeing under his window. But concentrating more on not being spotted than where she was putting her feet, she stepped on a shard of broken glass. Being barefoot, the shard sunk deep into her skin and, had she not slapped a hand across her mouth, her yelp of pain would have surely alerted the porter to her presence. But there was no way she would be able to hide her bleeding foot from her mother as she scampered back to the villa. Blood red footprints led her mother straight to Erika, who was punished for disobeying her parents.

'If only I was a doctor,' she had thought as she sat locked in her bedroom, 'I could have fixed my own foot before they ever found out.'

When she was thirteen the Youth Movement handed her the key to escape her eternal house arrest. It was every boy and girl's duty to join the Hitler Youth. And there was even an opportunity for Erika to organise and lead a group of girls of her own, enhancing her education and promoting national pride. Her parents would never argue with that. And she got to escape the villa for training camps in Hassitz. She found herself loved and valued by the other rural girls. She adored looking after them, feasted on the feedback, a novelty to her. Starved of cinema or theatre or anything remotely fun, she brought the girls sports and stories of life way beyond the villages. Stories of a proud people with strong traditions, of a people without space. She read all these things in the book which was delivered to her every month from the leader of the Movement, Baldur von Schirach himself. A book of songs, lectures, and stories which she would absorb lying on her front, feet in the air, legs twisting around each other in the zoetrope light of a log fire.

On a Youth Movement hiking trip to the Allgäu Alps, it wasn't the thinning air at such altitudes which left her breathless, but the majestic landscapes they traversed like something from the Nordic sagas with which she entertained the other girls by campfire light in the evenings. If these mythical landscapes really could exist, she thought, then so could the powerful Aryan race that originated in such places.

There she met Hans, a boy in a hiking group from a nearby Swiss boarding school. He was tall, quiet and gentle. He looked every bit the handsome Aryan ideal. All the way to the summit of

Walmendinger Horn, they talked – when their lungs allowed them – of the beauty around them, the millions of years of history it had presided over and what might be in store for it in the future. When they got to the summit, two thousand feet above sea level, she pulled a booklet she had been given by the Hitler Youth from her backpack and enthusiastically pointed him to the parts which appealed to her scientific sensibilities:

From the study of genetics, we have learned that the individual human being is inextricably bound to his ancestors through his birth and inheritance. The great genetic river of a people can suffer many impurities and injuries along the way. These can occur in two ways. First, diseased genes can develop within the bloodstream of a people. If a people is to remain strong and healthy, these cannot be allowed to be passed on. The purpose of our current genetic policy is to prevent the passing on of such diseased genes and to promote healthy blood. A people's bloodstream, however, can also be injured by mixing it with alien blood from foreign races. Our racial policy is designed to prevent this from happening.

The past era either entirely ignored human inequality, or else acted contrary to its better knowledge. During the colonisation of Paraguay in the nineteenth century, for example, the Jesuits permitted white settlers to marry native Indian women. Perhaps they thought that the native population would thus be raised to the level of the whites. But these mixed marriages produced unhappy bastards who were neither white nor native. In most cases, they inherited the bad characteristics of both groups, lacking spiritual stability. In our time, too, certain people occasionally lacked a feeling for racial honour. The numerous bastards resulting from relations with the black occupation forces in the Rhine region, or those that came from relations between Jews and Germans, are tragic examples.

Hans closed the book and turned the red cover over in his

reddening hands, stroking the canvas binding and caressing the embossed letters as if they might serve better than his mittens up here in the dipping temperatures.

'Be careful, Erika, please.'

He spoke in such gentle tones that the frigid winds almost whisked the words away over the ridge before she had a chance to register them.

She thought for a moment he was talking about the smooth outcrop of rock on which they sat, legs dangling into the heavens below. But she had no fear of heights and, as he continued, she realised he was not worried for her physical safety here.

'Some diseases may well be genetic. But that's why we have doctors to heal the sick and scientists who can help the doctors find better remedies. I'm not sure that anyone has proved that spiritual stability and honour can be passed down in the blood. Are these not things the people around us instil in us, our parents and leaders?'

Erika looked out across the ridge and felt a little vertigo for the first time in her life.

'Yet your leaders simply kill anyone with a different view to them. Does that sound honourable or stable?'

'If you're referring to the Röhm-Putsch...'

'The Night of the Long Knives,' Hans gave the alternative moniker.

'That was a necessary response,' Erika said to the eagle levitating below them scanning the pass for prey, 'to a coup which would have seen our government unlawfully executed themselves'.

'Who told you there was ever a coup planned? This book?'

Hans was stroking it again and Erika registered that his hands did so unconsciously in an effort to find something pleasing about it at least on the outside, if there was nothing attractive to him within. She snatched back the book.

They sat legs dangling into the abyss below.

'I like you, Erika. I like you because you are clever and strong. Just take care of yourself and look around you at all the other sides of the story before you make up your mind.'

Erika felt patronised. At least that's what she told herself she felt.

It was much easier to comprehend and describe than the swirling emotions this lad had stirred in her. So she hoisted herself up onto her feet and climbed back onto the plateau.

'Erika!' Hans' voice was weak against the wind again as he called after her, but she ignored him. She didn't look back down to the outcrop preferring now the company of her peers who were finishing their packed lunches and were ready to be led by her, happily, unquestioningly.

Just a few minutes later, as Erika and the girls were about to set off again, the Alps began to bellow, shriek and weep. Some of the girls rushed to the edge of the plateau to see what this eerie sound was, but Erika was rooted to the spot by it. It was the sound of adolescent boys crying for their classmate.

'He's down there! He's fallen! He must have slipped! Hans! Hans! Oh, God! Oh, God! Oh, God!'

Erika replayed the last few minutes in her mind and was wracked with the sound of Hans calling after her transmuting into the noise of him crying for help. When she eventually shuffled over to the young crowd, which wailed in a way beyond its years, she saw, as they did, that there was no trace left of Hans on the outcrop, except for one mitten they all recognised as his.

The eagle rode the thermals, circling the ridge, waiting for confirmation that the large creature that had just landed there was dead and fair game for scavenging.

In her tent that night, Erika cried as quietly as she could. She needed to be strong for the others. But something else kept putting an icy hand over her mouth to subdue her distress too. That something had a gusty voice which confirmed that things were in fact as simple as the posters on the classroom wall drew them, things were as elementary as her Hitler Youth literature laid out for her. And to prove it was so, to prove it was Nature's way, things had been made very simple for her again, now the voice of dissension had been eliminated up here by Nature, where Nature reigned supreme.

There was a screaming of metal on metal and her eyes snapped open. The girls were gone and Karl was gently shaking her telling her they had to get off the train.

Max hurried back to the hospital. There were patients that needed his care. He needed to lend a hand. Couldn't leave Edgar and Lutz on their own all morning. And of course he couldn't wait to tell them about his Iron Cross. Oh, and also there was the small matter of possibly getting bombed on the way back to keep him moving quickly. He nearly twisted his ankle a couple of times clambering over the rubble without concentrating properly. He couldn't wait to tell Erika too. He would write to her that night and hope the Red Cross could take his letter out of the city and back to Kunzendorf when they passed through.

'I'm going to have to sort through the rest of those letters first,' he exhaled the words to himself as he hustled, 'just in case there's actually something from her'.

He had only got part of the way through half of them the other night when Thomas had called out 'Got it!' and held Maria's letter up from his pile, so Max had stopped. He had told other soldiers in the unit, his patients and his medical colleagues to go through them when they could, but he had not found the time himself yet. Perhaps because he knew how deflated he'd be if he didn't find anything from Erika. But that might not be because she hadn't written, he told himself, her letter may have not survived the explosion. Many didn't and of the many others, only a few shreds remained. Without the address at the top or the signature at the end for many soldiers it was a guessing game to recognise the handwriting or identify their loved ones from the turns of phrase they favoured. And so he would enjoy the game tonight, he promised himself. He would know it was her the moment he saw it because her handwriting was identical to his. This had been a great advantage when she had been struggling with Physics so badly in the second year of medical school. He had taken the exam for her and they both passed with flying colours. Max hadn't felt great about deceiving the faculty but knew he'd have felt a whole lot worse if she had failed the course and had to move away.

These thoughts kept him distracted as he entered the monastery shell through the archway and one of its bricks shattered and flung itself at Max's face. A bullet had hit it inches from his head. He threw himself to the floor, blinking brick dust from his eyes and scrambled across the floor in his clean uniform heading to the basement. Now the air was being sliced with bullet after bullet and the remains of the monastery rained down in little pieces over him.

He was shocked. Bombing had become part and parcel of this war. The constant bumblebee buzz of bomber planes in the distance were a feature of the night you got used to eventually. But being shot at was still a relative novelty for the doctor. Especially here in his hospital where he'd hoped the huge red cross on the roof acted as a kind of talisman warding off advancing Russians.

The bullets were coming from all angles now which meant, Max hoped, some of them were from his own unit firing back. He heard his own involuntary grunts of fear every time the air was whipped near him, every time he thought he'd been hit for sure this time. He finally reached the basement door and found it to be locked. Of course. They had heard the gunfire below and had begun barricading themselves in.

'Edgar! Lutz! It's Max. Let me in!' he hammered on the door with a force he didn't know he possessed and one that would leave his hand feeling bruised for days afterwards – although that would be the least of his troubles.

It seemed as if a rifle had been fired close by his head, but it was just the sound of the bolts on the other side of the door being undone quickly. The door opened and Max almost fell in on whoever it was standing there, but not before he had caught a glimpse of the garden and the field behind it, covered with snow still, transforming itself from a flat white expanse to the ghostly shapes of soldiers in white snow vests and hoods. The place was crawling with them. Russian soldiers, well prepared for a winter war. This is it, he thought to himself, they're upon us, God help us.

He fell into the basement only to be faced with more white coats. His heart almost stopped right then. They had already been here. Laid a trap for him.

'Good God, buddy, we thought you were...' It was Edgar who was clad in white. Of course, medical garb. And Lutz in his white coat too, bolting the door behind him. Horst and Dolf were not in white yet, as they had been rudely awakened by the attack and were still stumbling around trying to work out if they were in the grip of a nightmare or not. The nuns and monks fussed around the maze of beds audibly praying for themselves and their charges. Sister Agnes was among them this morning. She glanced across at Max as he entered. Her face was thunder. *This is the final indignation*, it seemed to roar. *You bring your whores and your war upon us. And now we are to be captured by the Russians too.*

The fact that in Max's mind she was the stiff and puritanical yin to Jenny's yang only made him suddenly fear for the convent and all its inhabitants, stiff or not, yin or yang.

The Walther P38 was back in Max's hand. His colleagues held their revolvers too. They all looked absurd holding guns. They should have retractors or swabs or scalpels. They weren't soldiers. All of the soldiers were lying in beds around them incapacitated, useless. The few that remained active of their unit could now be heard shouting above their heads 'Retreat! Retreat!'

'If they fall back,' Horst said, 'perhaps the Russians will follow and pass over us.'

Horst, usually the joker in their pack, was trying to convince himself more than anyone else in the room, so that was when Max knew it was over for them.

'And then what?' Edgar grumbled. 'We jump in the truck with no petrol and escape?' Where to?'

It was painful to hear, but Edgar had a point. The city had been surrounded for nearly three months now. They had no resources left. Really the only option now was surrender or be killed. And none of them were sure whether they even had a say in that any more.

The familiar crescendo of a plane had Max grabbing the backpack of letters along with his medical bag which he still had with him from this morning. The ground started shaking as bombs fell in the street. The basement door turned into spears hurtling across the room. The blast wave sent the nuns' headgear and the men's hats whizzing off their heads. It would have been comical to witness if some of the nuns were not now impaled on shards of the door. The ceiling was ripped from the basement, allowing the sunlight to flood in but the eyes of everyone inside were filled with a darkening dust.

'Max! Max!' he heard Edgar calling his name and was instantly galvanised by the knowledge that his friend was alive.

'Get the patients above ground,' he called back. Although the distinction between above and below was fast becoming blurred.

The floor was crunchy with the shattered glass from the patients' drips. Those that could walk were already being helped by Horst and Lutz to clamber out of the basement, barefoot and in their pyjamas. They limped, slipped and slid across the icy grounds, falling on top of one another absurdly, heading who knows where.

Max and Edgar fumbled around the remains of the basement, assessing those still in their beds, trying to reassure the monk sitting on a bench with a thick piece of the ceiling crushing his lap like a diabolical desk.

'Doctor, help me!' he cried out.

'Edgar?' Max asked hopelessly.

'I'll see what I can do,' Edgar remained for a while knowing the masonry was too heavy to move and even if they ever did move it the resulting reperfusion in the legs would send potassium, phosphate and urate leaking into the circulation killing the monk before they could amputate. How ironic, scoffed Edgar to himself, I know about crush syndrome because of Bywater's findings published in the *British* Medical Journal; findings he'd made during our blitz on London a few years back.

Max began clearing rubble from a pile, out of which stuck a nun's legs. He soon stopped. Her head was pressed flat like a flower in a book. He helped another nun up to the street and saw how the blast had slung around the sandstone monuments and headstones in the church yard. How it had denuded the resting bones beneath, exposing them to the harsh existence of their descendants. He saw the intact wall of the house opposite where the Nazis had painted:

We will never surrender

And then his heart leapt as he saw soldiers, German soldiers from his unit, familiar faces, emerging from the clouds of dust. Only to find their arms raised, their weapons gone, and the white cloaked Russians prodding them from behind with the barrels of their Tokarevs.

The Russians were shouting commands. One of the German soldiers translated, though there wasn't much need. If any one of them put a foot in the wrong direction they would be bashed with the barrel of a gun, shepherded into the correct formation.

'Can you see Dolf?' Max whispered to Edgar, 'Did he make it out?'

'I don't think so,' Edgar said before getting a whack with the butt of a gun in his back.

The loss of Dolf shook Max harder than anything else had up to that point. Here they were defeated by the Russians, but at least his team of five were still together. After everything they were still there to support each other, help others, work through this, survive. But no, one of them hadn't survived. The team was crumbling at last and he felt like one of his patients who had lost a limb now trying to stand where their captors told them to without stumbling.

'Get up!' a Soviet soldier bawled at the one-legged patient on the ground, whose remaining foot was bleeding from the glass and blue from the cold.

Edgar dared to move to help his patient up and got another whack for his troubles.

'Get up! Get up! Get up!' the Russian screamed.

The soldier in pyjamas looked up at his adversary with a knitted brow that said, 'Can't you see? That is the one thing on earth right now I cannot do for you.'

And the Russian knew it was the one thing on earth the patient couldn't do. It was the perfect opportunity to show the rest of these fascists what would happen to them if they disobeyed orders.

The Russian shot the man in the face.

Max's medical muscles twitched needing to spring into action to

45

fix the man, but he was beyond fixing, and had Max been so bold as to move he would have been shot in the face too. And then what good would he be to the rest of the unit? He told himself over and over again. It was not cowardice, now they were prisoners of war, to stay alive. It was the best thing he could do for his fellow Germans. It was the only thing he could do for Erika.

Another Soviet, not the trigger-happy one thankfully, approached Edgar.

Edgar, not wanting another smack, kept his eyes front. The Soviet circled him, like a Siberian tiger picking up a scent, the scent of one who would dare to help the man in pyjamas, the scent of a doctor. He yanked the backpack from Edgar. It had medical equipment in it. Bingo! He confiscated that and turned to Max. Max felt the muscles in his lumbar strain as the soldier ripped his bags from his back too. One contained the letters. It might as well have been used toilet paper for all the Russian cared. The other contained his medical equipment and some food he'd been hoarding too. The soldier took this one and left the bag of letters in the mud at Max's feet.

Max pushed his hand into his pocket. It was the bruised one and as the bruise was pinched by the lining of his trousers it made him feel sick, but he ploughed on, delving in to find the picture of the Black Madonna and Jesus, the one Jenny had given him for protection.

But it wasn't there.

His hand was throbbing with pain as it fished frantically around for the picture. He tried his other pocket. And then he realised. He was wearing the spare uniform when she had given it to him. He had put it in the pocket of the spare uniform whilst his own was drying and no doubt it was still in there.

'If you keep this with you all the time it will keep you safe and protected. Will you do that?' she'd said.

And he'd already failed to do so. And now look what had happened!

But then, at least, he told himself, she might have found it again. And so she still has it to keep herself safe.

He looked down the street in which they were all held now at gunpoint. Blinking through the dust which was beginning to settle, allowing the bright cold sun to illuminate everything again.

The convent was gone. Blown to bits finally like everything else in the street.

So much for religion, Max sneered inwardly.

Karl's wrist was pinching and throbbing. Its disability was a memento he carried with him eternally. A memento of the strength of his convictions. A memento of his youthful recklessness. Would he have put a gun to his own arm now if called up to fight for the Nazis? Probably not. Age was a strict governess. But he would still had to have found a way – albeit a less permanent one – of avoiding conscription. Yet if the governess of age was so bloody sensible, why was he at four o'clock on a freezing January morning dragging himself from station to station all around the country with his pregnant daughter-in-law and her tonnes of luggage? Women, he thought, do they have a gene that makes them incapable of travelling light? Of course the reason why I am at four o'clock on a freezing January morning dragging myself at my age from station to station all around the country with my pregnant daughter-in-law and her tonnes of luggage, he said to himself as someone knocked Erika's valise from his weakening grip, is that my young fit son is not available to do so because he wasn't bold enough to shoot himself in the wrist. Another case dropped from his grasp and hit the platform with a resounding slap. He took it as a slap across his own face for that last remark about Max. In fact, he was proud of Max. He knew his son was simply following his vocation as a doctor and doing that at a time of war when you did not support the government took more conviction than perhaps even Karl had when he was his age.

Erika was trying to crouch to pick up the cases that had fallen, but the strain on her back was severe now and you didn't have to be a doctor to know she might not be able to get up again if she got herself too near the floor.

'I've got it, I've got it,' Karl used his damaged hand to shoo Erika back upright whilst he put one last great effort in with his good hand and gathered up the valise and the suitcase somehow keeping the portmanteau and the satchel under his armpits.

He waddled to the waiting room pregnant with luggage and

found a corner in which to let it all fall again, this time intentionally. As he stacked the luggage neatly, he turned to look for Erika. She was waddling too and looking rather yellow, but that might have been just the glow from the lanterns in the crowded room.

It wasn't.

The room was so warm, what with the lanterns and the number of bodies crammed into it, that it should have been a joy after the icy conditions outside, but the heat wrapped itself round Erika's face like a horse blanket and she couldn't breathe. She felt nauseous and looked desperately around for somewhere to sit. But, with no enthusiastic girls from the Hitler Youth on hand to demonstrate their community spirit, the seats remained full and the faces in them turned carefully away to look at the floor, their newspapers or their fingernails, if necessary. Anything to avoid catching the eye of the pregnant woman and her father, or whatever he was. Erika was furious, which didn't help her light-headedness. If she vomited right there and then over these ignoramuses' feet it would serve them right. No wonder the country was going to shit, she thought. This is not what they taught us in the Youth Movement.

'Are you all right?' Karl hurried back to her.

'I can't stay in here. I'm sorry, Karl. I've got to get out.'

Karl ushered her out and looked back at the pyramid of luggage in the corner. His heart sank at the thought of hauling it back out again. For a moment he hesitated at the threshold like a man torn between two mistresses. Or rather, like Odysseus caught between Scylla and Charybdis, he thought, because of all the people that could be with her now, I have no idea how to deal with a pregnant woman. My wife would know what to do. Even Max would know, medically at least.

Erika knew perfectly well what to do with a pregnant woman, but that didn't stop her cursing her gender as Karl pushed through the crowds with his good arm, whilst she clutched at his damaged one.

'We'll see if we can find another NSV office. There must be one around here somewhere,' he said.

She resented being seen as the woman among her fellow

graduates, rather than the doctor. She was as much as a doctor as the rest of them, but here she was stuck on the home front, lugging this fat lump of a body around a disintegrating rail network, all because of a small anatomical difference between them that made the men men and the women women. OK, not so small in Max's case, she smiled naughtily to herself and felt especially wanton as Max's father was right there next to her ranting at another NSV administrator. She was glad she had managed to joke herself out of this bad mood. The sofa she was sitting on, that she put her elephantine ankles up on, helped dissolve her resentment and her nausea too.

'I'll go back and look after the luggage,' Karl was saying, 'then I'll come back and get you when the train is about to go'.

She nodded and smiled gratefully at him, but she couldn't help wishing she had a woman here with her. Sometimes, empathy was even more valuable than a determined man armed with cigarettes and chocolate. When the men were called up, she was left behind without even a fellow female doctor to bemoan the situation with. She sometimes thought she would have liked it if there was at least one other girl in their little gang at Freiburg, but females were very much in the minority at medical school and, besides, she rather enjoyed the status of being the only girl in the group, privy to all the lads' laddishness when they forgot, as they so readily did, that there was a lady present, and yet equally she was revered by them as a precious island of femininity set in this testosterone sea. She didn't even mind the attention it got her from the lecturers, even if it did blow her cover occasionally. Professor Lang had called out to her as she sat down to her final lecture at Innsbruck in the spring term:

'Fräulein Kollegin, I have not seen *you* very often this term.'

Erika had blushed a little, but it was well hidden beneath her unusually tanned skin. Because the professor was right. She had barely attended a lecture of his all term. As the German system allowed students to change universities on a term by term basis, she and Max had chosen Innsbruck just for the spring term not because of Lang's expertise in physiological chemistry, as they told the faculty, but because of the university's close proximity to some of the best ski slopes in the country.

She closed her eyes, ignoring the rather dubious scent of the upholstery beneath her head there in the NSV office. The secretary found a blanket, with an equally curious odour, but Erika allowed herself to be covered in it and imagined it was the one Max used to bring down from his room in their digs. She imagined she was snuggled against her love under the blanket and soon found herself looking around her draughty room at her friends who had all gathered for gossip and coffee before they went off to the lecture theatre.

Edgar was there. Dearest Edgar Klein. Such a wonderfully ironic surname since he was usually the tallest person in the room. Best friend to both Erika and Max. They were all in the same exam group. Brilliant at his studies and an equally brilliant musician, his determination to succeed in life left Erika sometimes inspired, sometimes depressed that she wasn't as dedicated.

'You are as dedicated,' Edgar said, tapping out some rhythm on his knees which sounded to Erika like some new swing beat from the USA. Typical Edgar: anything the government banned was likely to get him interested. Which is why he couldn't keep still this afternoon, the anticipation of the lecture was such. Erika tried her hardest not to be infected by this delicious dissentient, 'You *are* as dedicated. It's just I haven't got the gorgeous Max as my boyfriend to distract me from my studies,' he lisped and lolled in a camp enough manner to generate the laugh he required from the rest of the gang.

'Sometimes I wonder about you, Edgar, you play the part of a lady too well.' That was Kurt, or Babyface as he was called only by the people in this room – his nearest and dearest. He acquired his nickname not just because of the incredibly smooth and hairless skin he still had at twenty-one, but because of his unwavering desire to specialise in paediatrics.

'Well, at least I can grow a beard,' Edgar retorted, with a surprising lack of intellect, Erika thought. She caught him blushing as he got up and danced and tapped his way nonchalantly to the window. Why the rush of blood to the head? Erika asked herself. Embarrassed by his lack of wit, or had Babyface hit a nerve when he drew attention to Edgar's skill at effeminacy?

'What's so special about Friedrich Hass anyway?' said Horst who sensed a slight modulation in the subject matter was in order.

'What's so special about Friedrich Hass?' Edgar turned from the window where he'd drawn a thick cross in the condensation, like an arrow slit in battlements. 'Not only is he a great pathologist and a great speaker, but his research on the role of hypoxia in congenital malformations is seminal.'

'But it's not hypoxia that's got you itching to see him talk today, is it?' Max piped up from the blanket under which he wedged himself into the armchair with Erika, trying to keep warm.

'No, of course not. He's speaking on the Oath of Hippocrates and apparently the Gestapo have already warned him not to touch on euthanasia.'

'Really?' said Horst, still playing dumb, though in fact he just liked to push people's buttons and watch them go. It was so much more comforting than silence for him, Erika observed, though *she* liked nothing more these days than lying under this blanket with Max and exhaling wordless shivers with him. She squeezed Max's hand under the cover and he reciprocated.

'Yes, Horst, really,' Edgar enjoyed showing his exasperation. '*Are* you a medical student or just some Rheinlander who's lost his way to the vineyards?'

Despite appearances, Horst and Edgar loved each other as much as Erika loved every one of these boys in her room that day.

Edgar went back to his arrow slit in the window and peered through it. 'We should get going,' he said, chewing his bottom lip. 'People are flocking in already. Come on!'

He headed for the door. Babyface and Horst warmed their mouths and insides on the still hot coffee they were forced to down too soon whilst Erika and Max examined each other's faces, reading excitement to get to the controversial lecture, but also comprehending a desire to stay under the quilt as long as possible before they had to leave the warmth they had kindled there.

'Come on, Max and Dorothea, that means you too!' Edgar called dramatically, enjoying, no doubt, his voice, echoing down the bare stairwell.

'Dorothea?' Horst feigned ignorance again. 'But her name's Erika.'

Edgar didn't rise on this occasion, he was almost through the front door and already out of earshot, so Babyface, proud to get the reference, piped up, 'Max and Dorothea are the lovers in that...'

'... poem, I know,' Horst gave one of Kurt's irresistible baby cheeks two quick light slaps with his chunky hand and set off after Edgar with a whoop which also made the most of the acoustics in the stairwell. Spurred on by all this energy, Max and Erika darted out from their quilted nest, she grabbing her purple coat, since Max had told her how lovely she looked in it just a few days ago, and they chased the others out of the house.

Five coffee cups stood in various locations around the room and in various states of emptiness, but all still steaming. The vapours hurried to the window to fill with condensation the gap made by Edgar's arrow slit, which was already changing shape, now spreading to resemble the solid even red cross of the humanitarian services, now dripping to resemble a bleeding crucifix.

They were lucky to get a seat at all, let alone five in a row. But the sunlight streaming down from the high window pointed the way to the perfect spot for them. The hall was full of the sound of sensible shoes flamencoing against the wooden floor of the rakes, as students sought the best place to sit. Erika looked down to see that the first layer of this year's snow had clung to their shoes, eager not to miss out on the gathering, and had left little white cakes on the floor as its contribution to the party. She tap-danced the rest from her soles as a thousand other shoes noisily took their places. Erika loved the sound. The sound of excitement, the sound of an eagerness to know and learn. But mostly she loved the fact that it was not the sound of high-heeled dress shoes and the swish of ball gowns on marble floors; the kind of sound her parents wanted her to be familiar with.

High society, they thought, was the echelon their daughter should be part of, since she was the progeny of a textile factory owner and his wife. Her father pulled strings whilst her mother pulled her hair into styles Erika felt silly in, and they managed to find her a place away from their tiny village of Kunzendorf, where boys like Richard the carpenter's son were all too accessible. She was sent to Berlin to study at the Lettehaus and live with Frau von Geröllheimer in the hope that some of the noblewoman's impeccable manners would rub off on the "wayward" Erika.

Frau von Geröllheimer was an overbearing and stiff old hag, Erika thought, but even she felt compelled to give the old lady a kiss when she managed to get Erika into the parliament building during the Chancellor's birthday celebrations.

The flat, plain, functional building was that day rippling with red. The street was draped with red. Red seemed to rain and reign as the government flags adorned everything. And Erika was of course in red too. A long and bustled ball gown, which in combination with the reams of other red material everywhere that day had her feeling almost part of that high society her parents insisted was their right. She was directed through a corridor lined with red carpets, hung with red tapestries and punctuated with high backed red chairs against the wall every fifteen feet or so.

What on earth are those chairs there for? Erika couldn't help wondering as she hurried up the stairs. Why would anyone want to sit in a corridor? There aren't even any rooms off it to wait outside. Perhaps these weren't the kind of practical questions a lady of high society should be asking herself. Rather she should be concentrating on her footing and her dress in order not to—

Erika trod on the hem of her gown and tripped herself up. She fell and her hands slapped the cold smooth marble of the Mosaic Room just before her face did, announcing her faux pas to the entire assemblage. All the guests briefly turned to see if the clapping sound was meant to indicate some new direction in the evening's proceedings, but as soon as they saw it was just some girl making a fool of herself, they went back to their small talk and schmoozing. Erika was mortified, of course, and swore at her parents inwardly over and over again for sending her to Frau von Geröllheimer in the first place, but before too much silent profanity had passed her lips, there was more clapping, this time of hands on hands rather than hands on stone, and not from her but from one of the stewards – the parade was beginning.

Erika was ushered to the enormous window at which Frau von Geröllheimer had reserved her a space and she caught her breath. Not just because of the celestial spectacle of a thousand flaming torches marching past in the street below, held by deputations from all over Germany, but by the fact that on the balcony which jutted out right next to her window stood the Chancellor himself. Their Führer. Her leader. She felt tiny and gigantic all at once. She blushed and she blanched. There he was! In the flesh. This was the first time she had ever seen him in real life, but she felt like she knew him, she had seen his image on so many posters and read his words in so many magazines. He had saved the country from utter ruin after the Great War. Saved the economy and so kept her parents' factory from going under. He had led the National Socialists to power, despite all the ridicule and disdain. He is not about high society, Erika thought, though she stood under a chandelier as big as her bedroom. He is about a new Germany united and equal, strong in the face of alien oppressors. The tired, the happy, the doubter, the fat, the thin, the rich, the soldier – the song went – they are all equal before God's sun.

The Russians made them march in pairs out to the end of the street and off towards the airstrip. When they eventually got there they told them to keep going.

'Where are they taking us?' a soldier in front of Max hissed to his mate.

'Russia, I suppose,' his mate replied.

'Then why are we heading south?'

Max, like a schoolmaster among children on an excursion, counted around seventy people left in his unit. It was hard to get an exact figure being in the midst of all those bobbing heads and faltering feet himself. He was sure there were other units still in the city, some may still be resisting the Soviets, but all of them he was sure were greatly depleted like his.

After hours of marching he was strangely glad not to have his heavy medic's bag any longer, although he was concerned that neither Edgar nor himself had any medical equipment now. He still carried the backpack of letters though and for him it was the lightest bag of gold any man had ever carried. Some of the soldiers were even struggling now under the weight of their sixty kilo packs and the patients from his hospital were not able to keep up.

A shot rang out from the rear. Every one of the prisoners' instinct was to stop and look behind them but the soldiers guarding them ordered them to keep going. Max knew, as well as the others, it was a patient who was too weak to walk any more.

Another shot. Another patient.

And another. And another.

Max felt his eyes fill with tears. He was livid at the contempt this signified his captors had for the infirm when he had made it his mission in life to mend and cure them.

'Oh God!' the soldier in front of him cried. Max couldn't be sure if he cried for the patients being shot or for himself as his trousers dripped with urine.

All that coffee this morning with Jenny was having the laxative effect it was fast becoming associated with in some medical journals. He thought about asking one of the Russians if they could stop for a break, appeal to their better nature, but then another shot rang out from behind them and he realised shitting himself would be the least of his worries. But he settled on urinating, like his comrade in front, just to ease the pressure on his bowel, buy a few more hours, he hoped.

He looked at Edgar as he did it. To lock eyes with him perhaps. To keep Edgar from looking down and seeing him do it. Edgar smiled at him in the way Max had seen him smile at the monk crushed under the masonry. Horst and Lutz were behind him. They probably saw, he thought, but what could he do about that now?

Night came and they were still being marched around the burning city. They were clearly not heading for Russia. Perhaps this bunch of Ivans had no idea what they were doing. Perhaps they were awaiting orders from elsewhere and were just killing time – and killing Germans – until then.

Knowing his food hoard was in his backpack now languishing on the bed of the truck which rumbled along beside the captors (where one shift of Russians rested whilst the others prowled among the prisoners) made Max think about food more than he otherwise would. By now all the Germans were hungry and he saw the lad in front of him signal to his partner, who then delved into the lad's backpack and found some dried bacon to munch on. He then returned the favour and the lad rummaged quietly in his partner's pack until he came up with a chunk of bread. This way they didn't have to take off their packs or stop marching. This way, in the darkness, they could feed themselves without Ivan noticing. The lad drew the short straw though. He got the bread. His mate got the bacon. I'd rather have bacon any day, Max thought to himself. He was salivating. He could taste the meat in his own mouth right then. He looked at Edgar. Edgar was without a bag too.

His stomach growled.

So did a Soviet somewhere up ahead. 'No food!' he shouted in German and the sound of a rifle butt striking a body punched its way through the darkness towards Max. He felt at once jealous of the lad and his bread and relieved he did not have any food that could get him in trouble.

An hour passed. It felt like an hour. Max looked at his watch – the cheap one on his wrist, which he'd bought in Freiburg for five deutschmarks. He was surprised it was still intact. He felt under his coat for his quality pocket watch, the one he used for all things work related. It was still there. It had been a few minutes since he last looked, not an hour at all.

He felt someone prod him in the back and began to tremble. He hadn't been eating, drinking, talking, not recently anyway. They had taken all his equipment and supplies, so what the hell had he done to deserve such attention now? He kept marching, kept his eyes on the road. The prodding came again. This time accompanied with a little hiss. He threw a glance over his shoulder. There was no Russian there. It was Horst.

'Take it!' he hissed again.

Max reached behind and grabbed whatever it was his friend was telling him to take. It was a piece of bread. Edgar was getting the same from Lutz. He bit into it gratefully. It was hard and cold, but Max instructed his brain to tell his taste buds it was warm and soft, fresh from the oven and oozing with butter melting all over it.

And so it was.

When dawn came the next day they were marching between the pink sunrise and the constant sunset red of Breslau burning. Men started to slow, flounder, complain of pain. Max could feel his own feet blistering despite his heavy duty ski boots – hardly standard issue, but he was so glad now that Erika had loved skiing so much even though he was useless at it. These boots would last him much longer than the regular ones the other soldiers wore.

From all the friction and sweat of marching, his buttocks were beginning to get sore. He knew if this carried on he wouldn't be able to walk much further, no matter how good his boots, and they all knew the fate of those that couldn't go on. He started scanning the ground for a solution.

A spent rifle cartridge, a burnt book, a sock, a stone...

He had a tub of Vaseline in his medic's pack.

'Oh my kingdom for some Vaseline!' he chuckled mirthlessly to Edgar.

Edgar just winced in empathy.

… a broken wine glass, the frames of some spectacles, a cork…

He lunged and swiped the cork from the ground without even disturbing his comrades' step behind him.

It was the cork from a bottle of champagne. He turned it over between his fingertips examining it for a moment. A big fat cork from a big expensive bottle of booze. Who had been celebrating? What had they been celebrating? And when? A long time ago, he imagined. Perhaps a few years back when some Nazi supporters had heard about France surrendering. Or the damage done to Coventry in England. He couldn't imagine what anyone could have been celebrating in more recent times round here.

Satisfied it was good for the job, he slipped the cork down his trousers and inserted it between his buttocks. It kept his cheeks from rubbing together beautifully. It can plug up my arse whilst it's there too, Max thought with the hilarity induced by such relief, stop that shit from coming out.

But the others weren't so lucky. Some of the men were stopping, crippled by sores, begging the Russians to let them rest.

They were shot.

'If I could just get to my bag,' Max said desperately over his shoulder to Horst, his relief short lived by the terror of more of his unit being murdered, 'we could pass some ointments and pain relief around.'

He thought about just asking for it, demanding it back even.

Another soldier fell from exhaustion. He was shot. Max thought again.

Sometime during the next night Thomas broke rank from his place behind Lutz. He had heard Max wishing for his bag and he knew exactly where it was. They all did. It had been staring at them, taunting them under the bench on the back of the truck for days now. The food in it had been eaten by its new owners, but they had not required any of the medical supplies yet, so it remained there half forgotten.

'What the hell…?' Max heard Horst say through gritted teeth and squinted past Edgar into the dark to see the diminutive figure of Thomas – Maria's Little Sweetheart, her Lovey, her Little Husband – skipping quietly to the slow moving truck, plucking the bag from the back, right under an Ivan sleeping on the bench, and falling back into line with all the grace of a cat.

'What do you need, sir?' Thomas's voice was breathless, not from fear, but from the thrill of success.

Max looked over his shoulder and could see in the light from the smouldering city Thomas's face brimming with pride, delighted at being able, at last, to follow the example of the brave doctor in the bunker, return the favour and assist him for once.

'What do you need, sir?'

Max looked again at Thomas with utter despair. He couldn't help it, but he wished he hadn't. He wished that look of pride and accomplishment had been the last thing on Thomas's face, but Thomas saw the look in Max's eye and he mirrored it. The look that said, there's an Ivan right behind you and…

The shots sounded louder at night. Everyone jumped. Thomas – Maria's Little Sweetheart, her Lovey, her Little Husband – fell and the bag was returned to the truck, a little further inside this time.

They marched on. Well, not so much marching anymore, but shuffling. They crossed the river Oder on the bridge which was littered with the debris of a fierce battle – a battle the Germans had lost, a quick scan over the corpses there told Max that.

'Halt!'

Like wind-up toys the men at the back continued shuffling into those who had stopped up ahead already.

Halt? Thought Max, are they messing with us? It had been so long since they had been allowed to stop that he doubted it could be true, doubted stopping was ever something any of them would do again in their lives, no matter how painful moving had become.

But no, stop they had. He craned his neck about to see what was happening up front.

He saw his CO – the one that had delivered him the news of

his Iron Cross at the convent, the one Beatrix had been flaunting herself so unsuccessfully in front of – he saw him taking off his long warm leather coat. The Soviets had ordered him to hand it over. They were ordering everyone to hand over their topcoats, their watches and their laces. What the hell did they want with laces?

Max started to shiver and he thought it was his body's anticipation of being without an overcoat, but it wasn't. It was fear. He was trembling again because he believed that they were asking them to hand over their belongings only now because it was time to die.

A Russian appeared at his side. Took his coat, demanded his watch. Max found solace in handing over the five deutschmark piece of tat on his wrist and keeping his pocket watch inside his tunic. Ivan looked at the wristwatch with disdain.

Tick tick tick tick.

The watch ticked so loudly, you could even hear it here on the bridge with the wind rushing through your ears. Max always hated that about it. But what did you expect for five deutschmarks? Ivan chucked the watch back at him in disgust and demanded his laces.

You can have my trousers, Max thought as he bent down and got a good whiff of himself, why don't you have my trousers, you bastard, they're full of shit now anyway.

The Russian took the laces and moved on to Horst behind.

Time started to speed up here on the bridge. Max had a strange desire to stay here forever, not just because it was such a relief to be standing still, but because what was coming next, he felt certain, was a bleak death.

'Look!' Edgar nudged Max. He was pointing to the road on the other side of the bridge.

Hundreds of German soldiers were being marched towards them. Just as tattered and sore as their own sparse unit. The sum of what was left of Hitler's great fortress against the Bolshevists. Six days and nights they had been herded about and Max counted around twenty of his group left from the seventy or so that started this futile trek. More empty trucks arrived beyond the bridge and Max knew then that this wasn't their time to die. They were being loaded up and shipped on somewhere else. He saw that some of his comrades ahead of him had realised this wasn't the end of the line too, realised they would be needing something to replace the stuff Ivan had just taken from them after all, so they were crouching down and stripping the coats from the corpses, pulling off boots from stiff-ankled feet. Max spotted a motorbike lying in the dirt with a leather jacket still wrapped around the handle bars where the owner had hung it before they were attacked. He was glad he didn't have to take it from a dead man. Looking at the rest of his unit stripping the bodies, they seemed to him to have acquired his detached clinical attitude to cadavers. As he swiped the jacket and hurried back to his place in line, one of his lace-less boots slipped off. He cursed his captors silently and ferreted around in his tunic for his pocket watch. He unclasped the chain from it and slipped it through the offending boot.

'They are some extravagant laces,' Edgar mumbled, half worried for his friend if the Russians saw him with a silver chain fastening his boot, half jealous that he had nothing to tighten his own yet.

Max looked at the boot. It did look absurdly decadent now. So he scraped up a hand full of mud from the damp ground and smeared the chain until it was camouflaged.

'Get up!' Edgar tugged at Max's collar.

Their captors were coming down the line again, telling them to get moving, herding them onto the trucks.

An image of Erika smoothing down the lapels of his brand new uniform when he and Edgar were first posted to the Western Front on the Rhine flashed behind his eyes. They had come back after a few months almost as neat as the day they had left, although their insides had begun to be dishevelled in ways they could never repair.

On their way to the Rhine they had bounced about involuntarily in the back of the truck that took them from the base across to the front line. They looked at each other's shiny faces mildly amused by the discomfort for the first twenty miles or so, then they began to focus on the world outside. Until then Edgar and Max had been not only cocooned from real life in the small pond of a student's existence, but cocooned from the war in the untouched city of Freiburg. Now the quaintness of the country they thought they knew began to crumble before their eyes. First it was just a few houses here and there reduced to rubble from rogue bombs, an improvised grave or two by the side of the road, but then the truck had to slalom around the dead horses and cows and they were driving through a whole town destroyed by the firestorms that had raged there. And another. And another. Where once the landscape was town separated from town by great plains of picturesque countryside, the towns were now plains of debris and the countryside populated by dust-covered trees. There were no towns and no rural beauty anymore, just hours and hours when all they saw was wasteland. Max and Edgar watched it all from the back of the truck and as the roads got progressively worse, full of craters from the bombing, they were bounced around so furiously their heads hit the ceiling of the truck, that initial amusement long gone. What would have been a relatively short journey took hours longer as detours had to be made around blocked roads and detonated bridges being frantically rebuilt by German engineers. The sights silenced Max's mind as a great snowfall does a city. They joined convoys hundreds of trucks long; passed through colossal collections of military equipment. Where does it all come from, Max wondered, all this gear, and all these men?

They slept in a big empty house that night. Found themselves blankets and mattresses and fell asleep easily. But before he did Max wondered who had owned the house. It must have been some very wealthy people, but where were they now? Had they donated it? Or had they been kicked out? Half an hour later and Max's eyes snapped open at the sound of artillery. All the new recruits got up drowsily and looked out of the windows. The sky was full of Christmas trees. Intense cascades of light pouring down the darkness, green and red flares, incendiary sticks fizzing through the sky and landing on the timbered buildings of the Rhenish towns, getting the firestorms going.

Max was aware that for the first time in his life he was in immediate danger of death, but strangely he didn't feel scared. He had to admit, if only to himself, it was a titillating feeling not without a thrill. He studied Edgar's face at the window illuminated by the fireworks outside to check he wasn't peculiar in enjoying this buzz.

Their field hospital was set up in a museum less than a mile away from the Eastern bank of the Rhine where the fighting was raging.

The fighting was raging.

People said that about fighting. That it was raging. It was just something you said. Max didn't realise until the day they arrived at the front that that was exactly what happened. The air was full of rage down there. Rage from the sergeants at their incompetent units, rage from the enemy towards the Nazis invading their home, rage from the wounded toward the foreigners that maimed them, toward their leaders for conscripting them, toward themselves for being so careless. That titillating thrill was soon stamped into the mud on the bank, drowned in the black river, blasted into the air with the grey matter from an uncovered head.

Max and Edgar quickly exchanged their peaked caps for metal helmets and kept their gas masks with them at all times.

They were doctors now. It wasn't as if they hadn't seen a lot of blood, some horrible injuries or the insides of people before. It's just that they hadn't seen the insides exploding from men running towards them; they hadn't had to assess and treat patients whilst French soldiers shot at them from the ominous concrete ulcers of the Maginot Line. The French had been forced to build a city of bunkers on their side of the Rhine, a futuristic looking canker on what used to be some beautiful lowlands. As the German's tried to advance across the river the gun slots of the Line would spew out round after round at the bridge or the boats. Max and Edgar were told it was their job to rescue the wounded from the water and treat them back at the relative safety of the field hospital. They were presented with long poles made of bamboo with metal hooks lashed to the end as if they were about to head out on some bizarre Oriental fishing trip.

'You can use them to get the men nearest the bank out of the water,' stuttered their troop commander as he hurried away back towards the museum.

'Where's he going?' Edgar asked. 'Shouldn't he be leading the attack?'

'Commander Kohl?' a private piped up. 'You must be joking. Right now he'll be hiding himself in his office pretending he has some urgent phone calls to make to Berlin. And funnily enough those calls will last just until today's attack stops. If it ever stops.'

'Oh, marvellous,' Edgar scoffed.

'Yep. He's the talk of the town, our brave Commander Kohl.'

'I'm sure,' Edgar said, 'that very tiny part of town where cowardice is revered, eh?'

The private and Edgar shared a nervous laugh.

In this new paradigm Max was groping around in, he wasn't sure what constituted cowardice. He had no idea what bravery was here. In a nightmare like the one he watched from the river bank, just staying may well be described as brave. But he had a pretty good idea of what bravery wasn't, he thought, looking at Commander Kohl's military VW car scuttling off to the museum.

'OK,' Max exhaled and looked at his tall friend holding his long hooked pole like an affable Grim Reaper. 'Let's get to work.'

Some of the fish they caught that day were vocal in their gratitude for the assistance in getting out of the water since their broken limbs made it difficult to swim. Others were silent, inert. Bloated blue bodies that had been dead for hours.

Little wooden rowing boats crammed with soldiers were constantly pushing off from the bank and trying to make it to the other side, trying to force the French back. Occasionally one boat would make it, but for every one that did, three or four would be sunk.

Seeing this, Max had to draw on his memories of Tante Bertel and douse his fears with the aura of her courage that night outside the theatre when he was sixteen.

'We need a boat,' he said slinging his bamboo pole to ground. 'We need to get to the casualties in the middle of the river, or they'll be dead by the time they reach the shore.'

Edgar looked at the rain of artillery pouring over the water. Thought about how rowing into that was suicidal. Saw how Max was already commandeering a boat. And went to support his friend.

As Edgar and Max rowed out into the Rhine, the Germans pounded the Maginot Line with artillery fire over the doctors' wide-eyed heads. This caused the French to go on the defensive, slide its gun slots shut for a while. A rare vacuum of peace followed, pierced only by the occasional cry for help from the water and the rocking-chair creak of the wooden boat. For those few seconds the raging stopped and the doctors looked at each other like victims of shell shock. Max saw Erika sitting where Edgar was. The churned up waters of the Rhine became the mirror smooth surface of Lake Schluchsee where they spent their gleaming summers together.

'Help,' Erika cried. 'Get me out of here!'

'Help,' a soldier cried. 'Get me out of here!'

The desperate shouts of men yanked him quickly back from the green conifer clad hillsides around the lake to the sepia scab of his present and the young doctors began to fill their boat with as many casualties as they could before rowing back to shore.

'Are we in danger of sinking ourselves with all these men in here?' Edgar asked, pulling in another anyway.

'Yes we are,' Max shouted over the racket of resumed artillery fire, straining to pull in a gored gunner who had fallen from the sky. 'But the fewer times we have to come back out here the better, don't you think?'

'I'm with you there, buddy.'

Back on the bank, as they unloaded their catch Max watched an officer bellow in the ear of an infantryman sitting in the mud with his back against the boat he was supposed to be getting into. The soldier was a teenager still, but looked even younger as he bawled with his fists at his mouth, tears making clean streaks on his dirty face.

'You will get in this boat and you will fight for your country or you will be shot for disobeying orders, do you hear me, soldier?'

'I can't do it. I can't go out there,' the kid howled.

Max thought about rushing over, diagnosing him with a medical condition and piling him into the truck with the rest of the casualties, but an explosion on the felled bridge nearby sent a more pressing casualty his way.

Raging.

Raging red like an enormous newborn baby, stripped of his clothes by the blast, stripped of his skin by the fire, screaming having just been slapped by the midwife of war. If this soldier survived he would be reborn like everyone around him – perhaps the red colour would calm eventually but the rage never would.

Max and Edgar may have returned from the Western Front with a promotion to NCO for their bravery in the river that day; they may have returned with the added tinsel to denote the promotion on their freshly laundered uniforms; they may have smiled as they greeted Erika at Freiburg station, their exteriors all shiny and re-varnished, but underneath the rot had already set in.

What would she say if she saw me now, in a corpse's jacket, my pocket watch broken to lace up my boots, shit in my trousers?

Max flushed with embarrassment as if she was standing right there on the bridge before him.

An image of Jenny brushing off the shoulders of his tunic and feeling the cuffs to make sure once again they were properly dry before she let him leave the convent a week ago blew through his mind and was carried on the wind down the Oder and all the way out to the glacial Baltic Sea before he had even registered it.

'Take care,' Erika had ordered Edgar before they left for the Rhine, 'of him and you. And if you come back dead, I'll kill you'.

Fifteen words. Most of which made no sense. And yet they said it all.

He had felt his insides torn then when he had first left her yet she was only a few hundred miles away in Freiburg. This time was worse, all the way over in Breslau on the other side of the country. And now he was being taken away to God knows where. Another country most probably and he had no way of telling her. In the truck he clutched the bag of letters to his chest as he used to clutch his teddy bear when he was a child. He didn't dare continue his search through it yet, just in case these vindictive Soviets thought it was something worth stealing, like his doctor's bag. Luckily they had no idea these letters were, to him and his men, far more medicinal than any ointment or drug ever could be.

E rika had tried to imagine that the sunlight streaming down on their row in the lecture hall was warming. But it was November.

She shivered.

All the light did was blind them, so they had to squint and shield their eyes for the first few minutes of Professor Hass's lecture until the Earth shifted a little more in a favourable direction.

As the sunlight moved on, Erika could appreciate the vision that was Hass: complementing the frost in his hair and on the lawn outside he wore a white linen suit, a colour men rarely wore in the USA let alone the musty halls of German universities. And isn't white usually a colour associated with summer, thought Erika, imagining herself in her favourite summer dress and Max in the tennis shorts she liked to see his hairy calves emerging from, extending and flexing as they carried their paddle boat uphill all the way to Lake Schluchsee, a hellish haul in summer heat, but worth every second when they spent the rest of those burnished days out on the water, just the two of them? OK, there were many other couples, groups and families out on the lake in those days too, but if she lay back and put her feet up on the bow in just the right spot to block them out, her point of view told her this was their own private lake as was the conifer-clad land beyond where they reigned supreme.

She shivered.

As bright as that sunlight was, it could not warm the earth any longer. Hass, she thought therefore, must be like one of those arctic animals whose fur miraculously changes from tawny brown to snowy white as the winter comes, to camouflage themselves from predators. But what predators could someone as erudite and esteemed as Professor Hass have to fear? And if he really did want to be inconspicuous, why was he so openly challenging the government's euthanasia program:

'Hippocrates himself states that: *With regard to healing the sick,*

I will devise and order for them the best diet, according to my judgment and means; and I will take care that they suffer no hurt or damage. Nor shall any man's entreaty prevail upon me to administer poison to anyone. And that, ladies and gentlemen,' the professor wagged a baton-like finger at his audience, 'as far as I am concerned anyway, includes administering poison to the man who himself entreaties me to do so. *Neither* the father of modern medicine, which we are all here to practise, are we not, continues, *neither will I counsel any man to do so. Moreover, I will give no sort of medicine to any pregnant woman, with a view to destroying the child.* Because no human has the right to say which life is worth living and which is not. No human has that right. None. Even though there are some who wield power in certain political circles today who indulge in the misguided belief that they also wield the power of God.'

Hass raised his frosty eyebrows and twisted his lips comically as a cue for the audience to snigger knowingly before they broke out in applause which ricocheted off the timber belly of the hall in a way which moved Erika.

But she hadn't chuckled when everyone else around her did; when she felt Max's abdominal oblique muscles gently punch her own, as if they were trying to fuse with hers and carry the neurological charge that signalled laughter to another body. Even Edgar's cartoon guffaw designed to tell the entire hall how in tune he was with the professor, couldn't get her giggling. Erika applauded politely as she would a pianist having played Stravinsky – appreciating the technical skill involved in producing such sounds, but not sure she liked what she heard. She looked down at the floor in case Professor Hass could somehow pick out her doubt in the sea of fans before him. The pretty cakes of snow were gone. Only grey puddles lingered, hazardous now to her footing.

The 'certain circles' of politics Hass had mocked were obviously the National Socialists. The party that had raised her country from its knees. The party that had shown her that science was the path which led to her country's prosperity, not religion. It was a simple matter of genetics and economics. But the more she studied and the older she got, the more complicated it all seemed. Her stomach growled, but not all the pangs there were for food. One was of longing for her school days, brightly coloured posters on the classroom wall helped it all seem so clear to her. She could still see one now. Two frames below the title:

𝕮osts for the genetically ill – 𝕾ocial consequences

In the left hand frame the greens and ochre of farmland had been painted with two imposing buildings drawn to loom over the tops of the pear-shaped trees. The right hand frame was printed in equally idyllic colours, but the two unfriendly buildings were gone and now the fields were studded with perfect little houses, lots and lots of houses stretching off into the distance. The words under the left frame read:

𝕬n institution that houses 130 feeble minded costs about 104,000 𝕽eichsmarks a year.

The words under the right frame read:

𝕿he same amount of money is enough to build 17 houses for healthy working class families.

The sentence at the bottom of the poster in bold red typeface concluded:

𝕿he genetically ill are a burden for the people.

She shivered.

Max felt her shiver and put his arm around her shoulders. She was happy they walked this way down the rakes which seemed precipitous to her now.

Professor Hass would be, no doubt, having a post-lecture drink in the café, so Edgar encouraged his friends to follow him there and linger, as so many other students intended to do, in the hope of engaging their professor in further discussion on the subjects he had dazzled them with so far this afternoon.

The café was as packed as the lecture theatre had been, but they managed to buy a glass of wine each and gradually shuffle their way across the crowded floor. Each of them filled the gap left by the other as they moved forward led by Edgar, who, being taller than most, kept his features fully trained on Hass, barely registering the irritation with which his body nudged its way past shoulders and his large feet trod on the shoes of others who dared to stand between him and the Maestro.

Hass was already engaged in lively debate with some third-year biochemists and Professor Stöhr, who was draping one of his nail-varnished hands over Hass's shoulder and caressing his glass of port seductively with one finger of the other.

'Well,' squeaked Stöhr, 'I am but a lowly lecturer of physiology.'

Hass, who didn't look too comfortable with Stöhr's proximity, made a vocal attempt to reject Stöhr's modesty and tried to accompany it with a move that would unhook Stöhr's hand from his shoulder, but Stöhr clung on limpet-like, saying:

'No, Friedrich, it's true. Only physiology is my thing, but in that, at least, I can claim to be...' the stroking of the port glass was becoming obscene, '... expert.'

There were a few chuckles and whoops from the rowdy company who comprehended the full intent of Stöhr's unceasing innuendoes. Edgar looked over his shoulder, found Erika, shook his head and raised his eyes to the heavens to show her his impatience with the flippancy of Stöhr at a time like this, though Erika couldn't help feeling Edgar was just feeling a little upstaged by the outrageous professor.

'And so,' Stöhr continued, 'not even daring to add my insignificant little opinions to the debate, all I can do is encourage us all to raise a glass, which is incidentally the other field in which my talents lie'. Stöhr, like a seasoned cabaret performer of the Nollendorfplatz, left the appropriate pause so the audience could pour their heckles and hoots into it, then went on, 'No, seriously, we must raise a glass to the bold, challenging, stimulating,' this word was laced with enough sauce to make Hass visibly redden against his white outfit, 'and brave ideas we've been treated to this afternoon'.

That final adjective of Stöhr's, however, was stripped of all excess, flamboyance and flippancy, and in doing so it stuck out more than the rest.

Brave, repeated Erika to herself. Brave.

Stöhr finished his speech by holding his port aloft and crying:

'To Professor Hass!'

'Professor Hass!' Half the students toasted their idol, the other half frowned at this threat to the political stability and future glory of their homeland, but either way everyone was united in taking another warming draught of their booze.

'Well,' Hass cleared his throat. 'Well, well. What can I say? I am sure we'll all remember,' he cleared his throat again, 'I'm sure we'll all remember Professor's Stöhr words today, long after my lecture has faded from all memory'.

Stöhr clapped his hand to his chest with utter delight at what he took to be the highest flattery. Now free of the hand, Erika thought Hass would make a break from Stöhr's clutches, but surprisingly, clearing his throat yet again, he put his own free hand out to grab at Stöhr's knitted waistcoat. Stöhr was both at once excited and shocked by the gesture, but he soon realised, as the rest of the budding medics surrounding him did, that Hass was not well.

In fact Hass was more than not well. His ruddy skin, intensified by wine and Stöhr's innuendos, was now rapidly becoming as pale as his suit and he sank to the floor gasping for breath.

Stöhr transformed in that moment from a cabaret master of ceremonies into the distinguished doctor that he was and immediately went about trying to diagnose the problem.

He ripped at Hass's collar to loosen it and put his ear to his colleague's mouth to listen for breath.

'Dyspnoea,' he announced, 'pallor,' he grabbed the patient's wrist, 'very slow pulse'.

'Hypoxia?' an eager student offered.

'Ha! Look what all that research on hypoxia did for him?' one of Hass's young detractors sniggered from somewhere behind Erika. She felt sick and moved away from him towards the edge of the circle that now surrounded Stöhr and Hass.

'Friedrich! Friedrich!' Stöhr rubbed his knuckles into Hass's sternum, trying to get a response.

Erika thought Hass was bleeding until she realised it was his dropped red wine spreading out around his head. She grabbed for Max's hand, but he was already pushing away through the crowd and out of the café. Her instinct was quickly becoming to follow Max wherever he went, but he was so fast now that she grabbed out for an alternative hitching post in this unexpected storm and found Horst.

'What's wrong with him?' she whispered trying to cling to her boulder-like friend's tight sleeve.

'Is it a heart attack?' Horst answered out loud in order to answer Erika and attempt to assist his teacher all at once.

Stöhr had no doubt considered this himself many long seconds ago, but as Hass began convulsing he said through gritted teeth:

'Most definitely not, it seems.'

Stöhr held his colleague's head steady and took a long hard sniff at Hass's mouth, much to Erika's surprise.

'Almonds,' he announced to his students, 'I smell almonds.'

'Then it's cyanide,' Edgar piped up. 'Someone's bloody well poisoned him.'

'Get out of the way. Get out of the way!'

Erika and the rest of her peers turned at the rare sound of Max Portner raising his voice. He was dragging a cylinder of oxygen with one hand and a stretcher with the other. The crowd parted obediently and rather ashamedly that they had not done anything more than simply guess at diagnoses for the last few minutes.

'Come on, you,' Stöhr jabbed a painted nail at Babyface. 'Help Portner get him onto the stretcher, for God's sake. Unfortunately, Herr Portner,' Stöhr gave Max an appreciative pat on the shoulder, 'his cells cannot do anything with this oxygen right now. It's cyanide. So what does he need?' Stöhr asked, delving into one of the many pockets in his waistcoat.

'Amyl nitrate?' Max answered tentatively lowering the Professor onto the stretcher.

'Correct,' said Stöhr producing a little bottle of the same and holding it under Hass's nose. 'Now let's go!'

Max and Babyface carried Hass, now limp again, out to the Medical Centre with Stöhr scampering alongside the stretcher all the time waving his bottle of amyl nitrate in Hass's face.

'Dear Lord,' Edgar sat on the edge of a table in the fast emptying café and looked at Erika and Horst. 'He was poisoned. Someone poisoned him.'

'It might have been an accident,' Erika offered rather lamely.

'An accident?' Edgar snapped. 'How does a man accidentally ingest enough cyanide to do that?' he gestured to the puddle of wine on the floor as if Hass was still there re-enacting his symptoms for the benefit of their education.

'The Gestapo warned him not to speak out against their euthanasia program,' Horst stated quietly from behind his hand.

'Warned! They *threatened* him. And he wasn't intimidated. So they've tried to bump him off. These are the kind of people that are running our country,' Edgar looked from Horst to Erika.

Erika dropped her eyes to the floor and watched as one of the café staff mopped the red wine from it. Her head burned as an Alpine wind of doubt roared through her ears.

The door of the café opened.

'How is he?' Edgar asked.

Erika was saved for now by the return of Max. As he answered Edgar he gravitated towards Erika and she felt her uncertainty ebb away again.

'It's difficult to say. It was obviously a large dose of cyanide to produce such acute symptoms, but they're treating him with methylene blue right now. It was lucky that Stöhr had that amyl nitrate on him.'

'Yeah! Who carries around amyl nitrate anyway? What was Stöhr doing with that in his pocket?' Horst asked looking mischievously at Edgar.

Edgar squinted at Horst – unamused at his reference to the amyl nitrate that Edgar owned and, like Stöhr, used as a drug during sex – and deftly changed the subject. 'Where's Babyface?'

'He's hanging around in the Medical Centre in case he can help more.'

'To get Brownie points from Stöhr, you mean,' Edgar sneered, but he didn't have a problem with Babyface's diligence. He was still reacting to Horst's gibe.

'Brownie points?' Max asked.

'He's saying,' Horst was happy to answer, 'that Babyface is brown-nosing Stöhr.'

'Brown-nosing?'

'It's more of that US slang Edgar likes to assimilate, isn't it. It means to be a sycophant. To kiss someone's arse, you see?'

Max's eyes widened as the full force of the imagery dawned on him.

'Yes, well,' Edgar mumbled, 'I wish I lived in the US. They don't stop you from listening to whatever music you like, they don't make Jewish professionals disappear and they don't try and bump off academics that speak out against government policy. Did I say government? Sorry, I meant the dictatorship.'

Max was standing close to Erika now and a question from her physiology exam came rumbling through her head:

What is the process by which neutrophils and other white blood cells are attracted to an inflammatory site?

Phagocytosis? No, she often made that mistake, but Max had reminded her, phagocytosis is the process by which a cell engulfs a solid particle, the process by which neutrophils ingest bacteria. But in order to find the bacteria in the first place they rely on the process of chemotaxis, using the chemicals released by the bacteria and damaged tissue to attract them to the site. Max gravitated towards her, she felt, like a white blood cell to an inflammatory site.

'Well, I'm going to Mass this evening,' Max announced, 'to say a prayer for Professor Hass.'

'I'll be there. I'm on the organ tonight,' Edgar said looking at Horst, daring him to have other plans.

'I'll be there, of course,' Horst punctuated his statement with a tut.

Erika felt Max's fingers on her palm, feeling for hers.

She couldn't shake the image. Max had gravitated towards her, she felt, like a white blood cell to a site of infection. He was the white cell. She was the infection. Everyone else around her seemed so sure of their convictions: that the National Socialists were unhealthy for Germany. As sure as she was, most of the time, that they were the cure.

The friends dispersed.

Are you coming tonight? said the hand in hers all the way back to their digs.

Erika collected the coffee cups. Someone had used her copy of *Dubliners* as a coaster. It must have been Horst, she thought. Edgar reveres art too much to disrespect a book in this way. Babyface was sitting on the bed, she recalled, and would have used the nightstand. Horst always had more time for the factual. He would devour volumes of medical history, but a few short stories? He didn't have the concentration for it, he said. She washed up the cups, wiped the ring from the cover of the book and made a fresh pot of coffee. Then she and Max wedged themselves back into the armchair together under his blanket.

'Shall I make us some dinner soon?' she asked.

'Mmm.'

Are you coming tonight?

'You were so brilliant today, racing off like that to get the equipment when the rest of us were standing around like idiots.' Palms together she pushed her hands between his leg and hers to warm them.

'Mmm.'

Are you coming tonight?

'I know he's a doctor, of course, but he's such a clown that I never really thought of Stöhr as being an *actual* doctor until I saw him work on Hass today.' She tucked the blanket maternally around his neck and made a pillow for herself with the end on his shoulder.

'Mmm.'

Are you coming tonight?

She couldn't ignore the question any longer. Its tacit roar made her ears ache.

She took as deep a breath as her ribcage would allow her to, squeezed there between him and the fraying upholstery, and said,

'Your faith is so important to you, Max, I know that. But so is my belief that there is no need for religion in the new Germany.'

They both stared across the room to the gap under the door as Erika had done with Hans across the Alps from their perch on the edge of Walmendinger Horn.

'We are students of medicine,' she continued, 'students of science. We already know that physics and chemistry is what makes the world go round, not superstition'.

She felt him twitch beneath the blanket and wished she had used a slightly less abrasive word, yet in the same moment she wanted to slap him for putting his life in the hands of those who believed a work of fiction, which described simply impossible events, to be true. That was simply stupid!

'Hitler's minister for church affairs says there *is* a place for religion,' Max mumbled sarcastically. 'A true Christianity represented by the Nazis with Hitler as the herald of a new revelation.'

He snorted knowing as well as Erika did that there was no place for Catholics in this new religion. Hitler despised them as much as her Protestant family had when she was growing up, which made her rejection of the church twice as appealing. She had already been brought up to hate Catholics. To hate the code she'd been brought up to adhere to was and is the rite of passage of every teenager, and the Hitler Youth had been there to provide her with the alternative.

And yet still the question hung in the little mists that formed when his warm breath met the cold without.

Are you coming tonight?

Candlelight made the surface of the great gothic arches, which yawned all about the cathedral, ripple impossibly. The stained glass rose window was as far away from Erika as it was possible to be since she sat on the end of the pew closest to the entrance and the window hovered high above the golden altar. But despite this, or perhaps because of it, to Erika it had all the allure of a precious piece of jewellery set with the rarest sapphires.

Sat right beside Max, she had never felt so far away from him in all the months they had been together. Thick clouds of incense filled

77

the piece of sky the cathedral had swallowed, and they billowed about Erika's head making her feel faint. She sat near the entrance so that she could feel the air coming in through the open door, so it could revive her. She suffered from low blood pressure and the incense never helped. At least, that was the scientific explanation of events she gave herself.

The organ, at the hands of Edgar, boomed, toying with her spine. She loved the music. She loved it even more because it was played by her great friend. She loved the way it made her feel like a bird soaring over the Alps, the way it made her ache for Max. But she knew it was only an illusion, the wonderful magical way all art has of firing our emotions. The skill is, she told herself, not to make any decisions whilst in the grip of the trick, because when the music stops, when the book is closed, when you leave the theatre, you might not feel as passionately about your choices as you did when your body was awash with these vibrations of light and sound.

The service itself left her cold. She didn't understand a word of it, read as it was throughout in Latin. She began to feel herself swoon. That damn incense! She was going to vomit if she didn't get out in the fresh air at once. She squeezed Max's hand in the hope it would signify that she wasn't rushing away from the service per se, then headed for the door. The cool air outside put its chilly hand down her throat and turned her inside out – she vomited on the steps of the beautiful cathedral.

She was vomiting all right, but now it was on the floor of the NSV office as she leaned over the edge of the sofa on which she'd been sleeping. The secretary ran at her fecklessly with a waste paper bin and she heard Karl's voice somewhere in the distance muttering, 'Oh God, is this normal?'

Karl danced around Erika's little puddle of vomit and apologised profusely to the NSV secretary who looked as if she wanted to suck her own face off with indignation. 'But if we don't catch this train…' The sentence could not be finished because the consequences of not catching the train were too unbearable for Karl to even articulate let alone experience.

'With the help of my trusty cigarettes the luggage is already safely on board,' Karl said, trying to inject a little light-heartedness into his own tension, anything to gee Erika up. 'But the train is about to leave. Will you be able to make it?'

Erika felt better for having been sick, but could have happily laid on the stinking couch for the rest of the morning. The sun was up now though and she took some solace from that as she hurried as fast as she could behind Karl. 'I'll make it,' she smiled. She had to. For Karl more than herself. She couldn't imagine how frustrated he would be if they missed this train.

'Good,' he said, 'because there's not another for fifteen hours'.

As they entered the station Erika felt another wave of nausea wash over her. She stopped and bowed her head, hands out in front for balance and protection from the crowds. The feeling soon passed and she raised her head to see Karl almost hopping about with the tension of it all.

Tick tick tick tick.

A whistle sounded. Karl beckoned to Erika with epileptic energy. She hurried after him to the platform where their train and their luggage were getting ready to leave them. The guard was at one end waving his flag at the driver, signalling him to go. There was a clunk as the engine took the strain on its chain of carriages. Karl grabbed Erika's hand with his left and mounted the ledge outside the nearest compartment door as the train began to move.

'Step up!' he yelled at her.

The train continued gradually building momentum.

Erika put one foot on the ledge and found herself hopping along beside the train as Karl tried to haul her up. Karl had a firm grip on the compartment door with his good hand but Erika's weight was the last straw for the camel's back of his exhausted left wrist and he yelped.

The yelp told Erika she would end up on her back on the platform if she didn't stop relying on Karl to rescue her. With her free hand she grabbed the compartment door too and ripped herself clear of Karl's well-meaning molestations. She now had two hands to hold on with and she yanked herself up onto the ledge next to her father-in-law.

Karl and Erika looked at each other for a second, the fear on each other's faces laced with delight at their success. Until Karl tried to open the door.

It was locked.

Or it seemed to be locked. Erika looked in through the window. The compartment was full of people and she came face to face with a mother breastfeeding her baby. A soldier was standing with his back to door holding it firmly shut, as he had been since they boarded to gallantly preserve the mother's dignity. Erika couldn't be sure whether his chivalry was so fierce towards the mother that he would keep two other passengers hanging on the outside of an accelerating train till the child was full, or whether he was just unaware of their presence. Karl knocked on the window. Erika even saw the mother's lips move as she said something to the soldier. But he didn't budge. The baby suckled on. Quickly, like everyone else in the country, hurrying up in case he missed out or the supplies dried up.

Karl shouted an expletive which, coming from him, would have made Erika laugh and blush had she not been clinging on for dear life to the outside of a train that was now moving out of the station at some speed.

'Oi, boss!' a voice came riding on the growing wind from behind Karl. It belonged to a young chap sticking his head out the door of the next compartment. 'Come in this way.'

Karl looked at the chap. Looked back at Erika as if to say, 'Shall we?' Erika glowered back at Karl with more than a hint of sarcasm in her features that said, 'No, I'm fine here thanks!' And they quickly began to edge along the outside of the speeding train. Karl put one hand out to help Erika along but she slapped it away. If she had time to think at all she thought he wouldn't consider it a rude gesture in the circumstances as they both needed two hands to clamp themselves to whatever railings and bars made themselves available to them on their precarious shuffle along to the next compartment. Memories of her climbing holidays in the Alps chugged through her muscles and she later found herself, ironically, praising God for some aspects of the Hitler Youth Movement, the parts that promoted physical fitness at least. For the first time in a few months she didn't think about the fact that she was pregnant in so much as she didn't feel the tiredness, the cramps, the sickness. She was being pumped full of adrenaline, the magical hormone that put everything else the body was going through on hold when it was in charge. And now it really was a time for adrenaline to be in charge. Karl had reached the next compartment and the young chap opened the door ready to receive them.

They will have to close that if we reach the tunnel before I'm in, Erika thought to herself.

Because indeed there was a tunnel up ahead and they were closing in on it fast. She saw Karl disappear into the carriage and then she did think about the physiognomy of her pregnancy, despite the adrenaline. She thought about how far she stuck out from the side of the train because of her belly and how that meant flattening herself against the side of it as they roared through the tunnel was not an option. She would be churned up between the bricks and the train if she wasn't inside by then.

Tick tick tick tick.

'Come on, Miss,' the young chap beckoned frantically, just as Karl had done to her at the station entrance a few minutes before. She was sick of being beckoned at like a dog. She was sick of waddling like a duck. She inhaled her frustrations, like the steam engine consumed coal, turning them into kinetic energy to power herself along with her arms for the last few metres. Things suddenly got very dark as the bright blue winter sky was blocked out now by the looming tunnel. Her feet side stepped along the ledge as fast as possible, too fast for their own good and she slipped.

She felt herself fall.

'How appropriate!' Edgar sneered as they were ordered off the trucks and onto a cattle train.

Max would have laughed if it wasn't so true. If he didn't feel like an animal being herded about and shoved into a pen.

The train heaved itself out of the station with its sorry cargo and was soon rolling out of Germany and into Poland. The two lads who had marched ahead of him through Breslau were soon thick as thieves with another two in their wagon, one poking his head through the slats in the high window and reporting back to the others what he could see of the rest of the train.

'There's guards hanging out of the front wagon on the right, so when the train bends to the left they disappear from view.'

'Which means they can't see us either, correct?' said the lad who got the bacon days ago.

'Correct,' said his mate, 'so the next time it bends to the left we can jump clear. You in?' he said to the other two.

They nodded.

Max watched as other eyes in the wagon widened with fear and excitement at what was about to ensue. Some of them, he thought, looked like they wanted to be invited to jump too. Others were more circumspect, waiting to see if these four actually pulled off the escape before they bothered trying it for themselves. Others were petrified that they would botch it and attract the attention of the guards. Then who knows how many of them would pay the price?

The four stood under the window waiting. Everyone else sat on the floor waiting. Waiting for the next bend in the track. And eventually it came.

Everyone felt the train begin to lurch as it rounded the bend to the left. The four lads wobbled on their feet for a second then hoisted up bacon boy so he could kick out the wooden slats from across the window. They came away easily from this tired old train and in a heart pounding moment he was through and falling into Poland. The second was hoisted up and gone. And the third. The fourth was the tallest, which is why he elected himself to bring up the rear, but nevertheless he started to scramble at the wall of the wagon like a trapped cat as the train began to straighten and time ran out.

Tick tick tick tick.

Max thought he heard his five deutschmark watch filling the wagon with its irritating sound. He felt himself get up and catch the lad's lace-less boot in his hand and push upwards for all he was worth. The lad disappeared through the window with the sound of his knees and shins peeling themselves against the wood.

And then he was gone.

Except for one boot which Max still held in his hand like a bizarre souvenir. More like incriminating evidence of his complicity in this breakout! But instead of tossing it away he stuffed it in his bag along with the letters, fast becoming aware of how valuable a commodity clothing would be.

The train eventually stopped. Stopped for hours. Way down the line, miles and miles from where the four lads had made their escape. They had done it. A silent celebration of sorts went on behind the men's eyes for their daring comrades, which soon changed back to the more familiar fear as the sound of guards moving towards their wagon reached them through the broken window.

It was this window that told the guards something was amiss. They hauled open the heavy door and began counting the men inside, as they had in all the other wagons. Max closed his eyes. He thought he might give something away if they were open. Thought they might keep flicking towards his bag and alert the guards to the evidence of his aiding and abetting the fugitives. With his reasonable Russian skills, he heard the guards report the number to their commander who stood impatiently outside on the tracks. He heard the commander curse. He didn't understand all he said, but got the gist:

'... strict orders to arrive with the same number of prisoners as we started with.'

'Yes, sir.'

'So go and find four prisoners!'

'But, sir, they may be a hundred miles away by now.'

'I don't care if they're the *same* prisoners, I said just find me four more prisoners.'

And so the soldiers hurried off to the nearby village and within minutes had returned with four dumfounded Polish men whom they shoved into the cart.

'There was nothing *great* about it,' Papa had grumbled the day Max had announced his intention to join up, referring to the Great War, which he had blown his wrist to bits to avoid. Some would have called that cowardice. Max realised now it was the bravest thing he could have done. And he was starting to wish he'd done something similar. Was there anything great about this Second World War either? Apart from the sheer scale of the destruction? Allied soldiers bombing hospitals. Even the symbol of the Red Cross seemed to hold no respect any longer. And now Allied soldiers made prisoners of the Polish, the very people they were fighting against Hitler with, just to make up the numbers in a POW cattle train.

Max closed his eyes again. It felt so good to do so. To block out the expressions of distress and fear all around him. And he was tired. So tired. He fell asleep in seconds.

The train rumbled on.

For weeks.

It smelt worse in that wagon than it ever had when it transported cattle. More men died of their injuries or malnutrition and the four doctors – Max, Horst, Edgar and Lutz – could do nothing about it. It was all they could do to keep themselves alive. When the corpses were discovered by the guards they were thrown out into the fields and replaced by more terrified and confused civilians. It was spring now but the temperature kept dropping and the landscape became white again, like Breslau in the winter, but without the buildings, without the streets. Max would often stand to stretch his legs and to peek out at the world, and he marvelled at just how far the steppes stretched off into the distance and how hours later the scenery hadn't changed – it had just got even colder, so they knew they were heading north. The thermometer on the wall of the cart read minus thirty degrees centigrade. They didn't need a map to tell them they were in Siberia now. He wrapped himself tighter in his motorbike jacket and settled down to sort through more of the letters.

He found one for Horst from his parents back in Dortmund where both Max and Horst grew up. Horst read parts of the first page out loud and when he finished they rifled through the rest of the letters hoping to find more. They found the last page but there was a lot missing in the middle. Nevertheless Max loved hearing about the family's farm life back in Dortmund as it was so full of references to places and people he knew so well too. They wrote about a wedding at the local church, the church where Horst got married to Eva and where he and Max became altar boys when they were nine years old.

'Remember when we had to do funerals in the cemetery?' Max chuckled. 'And we had to pass by the priest's garden to get there. And that big cherry tree in his garden hung over the path.'

'Oh yeah.' Horst's eyes glazed with the memory. 'And we used the crucifix we had to carry as a ladder to get up and nick the cherries.'

'We'd fill our pockets and our mouths and then get a wallop from Father Bruno because we had bright red stains all over our white cassocks.'

Bright red stains on white. They had seen so many bright red stains on white over the past few years – white snow, or white sheets, or their white doctor's coats – and they both tried hard not to let those recent memories contaminate this one from their youth. Max was so glad he and Horst had come all this way together. They had always been brothers in spirit but it was official now. It had been official since early '43 when Max's younger brother, Sepp, had been killed by a bullet to his lung immediately after arriving at the Eastern Front to fight. Like Papa, Sepp had been fiercely anti-Nazi. He had even been removed from school at the age of twelve for voicing his opinions so frankly. Papa had to send him to a private school in order for him to finish his education. Sepp loved to study, loved to play music, he was desperate to sit his exams, but the authorities said he was only allowed to if he joined up immediately after. He was eighteen. Had been at the front for a matter of days. And he was dead. Max had just arrived in Breslau. Horst was still in Freiburg and had written him a letter from there when he heard the news:

I know it is not the same, but would you be my adopted brother, brother?

Max had kept that letter always. It was as precious to him as his wedding ring.

'Does anyone know a Ruth?' Max announced holding up a badly singed scrap of pink notepaper.

'Me! That's for me!' A private from the remains of the other unit who shared this wagon stood up among his crossed legged pals like a kid receiving a school prize.

Max tried not to read too much of the letters he sorted through, tried to respect the privacy of the men, but sometimes it was the only way to find out who it was for, if the writer had a tendency to use the recipient's name a lot in each paragraph, as in this letter which was clearly to a soldier named Tim:

wait until you come home although knowing all the time in my heart that I was untrue. When you went away and I told you that I loved you best, I really meant it Tim, but such a lot seems to have happened since then. I really thought that I had forgotten Charlie in my love for you and during the past nine months have been fighting against his love for me, wishing and longing for your return, but it is no use Tim I cannot help loving Charlie best. I suppose it is because he was first. At first I made up my mind to fight it down and be true to you and if you still wish to keep me to my promise under the circumstances I will do so.

Don't take this too much to heart Tim. I am not worth it but don't think me altogether heartless. I would not hurt you dear unless I could help it, but unfortunately we cannot control our own feelings. Will you believe me when I say that I am very sorry, for I am, more so than perhaps you think. Anyway, forgive me if you can, and I trust that you will still let us be friends, whatever happens. Have not had the courage to tell your Mother yet, perhaps you will do so. Write back as soon as you can to say

you forgive me Tim, shall wait impatiently for your answer.
One word about Charlie before I finish. He would have

In this case Max couldn't help himself. He could have stopped reading after the first paragraph of the only surviving page and been sure it was for someone called Tim, but he kept going until the scorched end. He put his head close to Horst's and whispered, 'Who's this?' tapping at the name on the paper rather than saying it out loud.

'Not sure. Someone from the other unit, I suppose.'

Edgar was close enough to hear the question and was already devouring the letter over Max's shoulder.

'I know who that is. The sergeant. Over there.' Edgar pointed subtly to the other side of the wagon.

Max examined the epaulettes on the man's shoulder to confirm he was looking at a sergeant.

'Poor fool.' Edgar felt genuinely sorry for the man, but he couldn't help but feel it was the universe corroborating his own belief yet again that there was only one type of lover: a foolish one.

Max felt a surprising embryo of rage developing in his solar plexus for this bloody woman who was being unfaithful to Tim. He hoped Tim's mother found out very soon and gave her hell for it. She sounded like she'd be a formidable and protective mother if the writer hadn't had the courage to tell her yet. But courage clearly wasn't the writer's strong point. Max despised her weakness. It wasn't just because Charlie was "first", as she so immaturely put it, it was because he was *there*. At home for some reason. Instead of being at the front risking life and limb for his country like Tim, Max thought with an unusual level of patriotism. Her inability to wait for him disgusted him. Or more accurately her inability to wait for Tim made Max wonder if Erika would ever get tired of waiting for him. He could have gone home on leave in a month or two and seen her but, now he was a POW, how long would it be? What if Erika met a nice man back in Kunzendorf? A nice man like Charlie (who Max hated as inexplicably as he hated Tim's girlfriend).

Max looked at Tim across the heads of the forty or so men

between them. Some of those heads had lice, some the signs of ringworm. Tim looked to be one of the healthiest soldiers among them all. His eyes looked bright, hopeful. The love of a woman could do that, Max thought, as he recalled the first time he had kissed Erika.

It wasn't until the leaving ball in July. Three months after that first conversation in the Kakadu Bar. Max was so desperate to kiss her by then, but he struggled to find the courage. Erika was never backwards in coming forwards, he thought, so why doesn't *she* initiate it? If he only knew how the butterflies swarmed in Erika's stomach he might have taken more confidence from that. She was as paralysed as he was because none of those other flirtations had ever meant as much to her has Max. At the end of the ball they walked back to the house and he sat on the stairs outside her door, the stairs that led to his room above. She stood in front of him, leaning her knees on his, exploring his hand with hers as they chatted about their friends, about the ball, the dancing. Neither of them could tell you what was said then, but both could recall the sensuous ballet their hands performed like it was yesterday.

'Kiss me kiss me kiss me!' she thought.

'Kiss me kiss me kiss me!' he thought.

But it was too important for both of them. They were petrified that the physical manifestation of their love would somehow contaminate the spiritual and intellectual elements which had served them so well until now; which they were afraid could not be surpassed. They were both doctors – well, they would be one day soon – and the biochemical mechanics of attraction held no mystery for them anymore. But this connection between them was evidently more than physical. Beyond any of their scientific knowledge, and therefore to be venerated.

But the evening had finally run its course. Short of a kiss, there was nothing more to be said or done.

'Goodnight,' she said.

'Goodnight,' he said.

She sloped off down the short corridor between the stairs and her door, allowing her hand to linger on the banister as she went. He watched her go. Watched the hand begin to trail off behind her too.

Then he grabbed it.

She froze. Looking in the direction of her room. Her hand held out behind her like a ballerina.

And he found himself kissing her palm.

She melted. Feeling anything but as balanced as a ballerina, she turned back, steadied herself with her free hand and watched him through the banister. Once, twice he kissed her hand then held her palm to his face and inhaled, clamping it to his mouth with his own trembling hand on top. She moved back to stand in front of him, and stroked his hair, kissed his head. They were now a wonderful pile of hands and heads. Bowed heads, like supplicants. Praying for a future together.

Give me all the medicines in the world, Max thought, but none of them can do what love can do, and he slowly folded Tim's letter and pushed it into his pocket.

'What are you doing?' Edgar said with a perverse hint of disappointment in his voice.

'Nothing,' Max said although inwardly he told himself he was acting as a doctor in the best interests of a patient.

Horst whispered, 'He should know. I'd want to know.'

'No you wouldn't,' Max mumbled. 'Not here. Not yet.'

Horst didn't argue. He just began leafing through the pile again. Calling out names, perhaps before Max could intercept any more.

Max turned to his ration instead and was just about to attempt to sink his teeth into the bread they were given each day – dipped in boiling fat and left to dry so that when it finally reached them it was like eating a stone – when his adopted brother uttered words of ambrosia for him to feast on instead.

'Are there letters that *you've* written too in here?' Horst said.

'Why do you ask?' Max said, though he knew the answer. At least he prayed that he knew what was coming.

'Isn't that your handwriting?' Horst handed some pages over with a shivering hand.

Max tried not to snatch. 'No,' he gasped weakly. 'It's Erika's. We have the same handwriting.'

'Max and Dorothea,' Edgar piped up. He and Horst grinned at each other, watching as Max devoured the words on the page as any one of them would have done a plate full of wurst and potatoes right then.

S he felt herself fall.

She felt hands claw into her aching forearms. She felt a strong grip hoist her into the compartment. She heard a woman scream as the tunnel smacked the open door from its hinges.

'Erika!' Karl was beside her, but he was beside himself too.

'My God! That was close, eh, Miss?' the chap was smiling down at her as he offered a hand and offered her his seat.

There was a mixture of excitement and indignation from the other passengers in the compartment after the drama of Karl and Erika's entrance. Excitement first for the obvious reasons which soon settled into quiet indignation at the fact that they all now had to sit in a compartment with no door on it with the January air whipping their legs and faces as the train hurtled on obliviously.

'Could be worse,' said the chap who had introduced himself as Benjamin. 'Could be raining or snowing.'

Erika giggled at Benjamin's apparently unquenchable optimism. Karl was snoring away in the seat next to him, exhausted, his *nerves frayed somewhat*, as he had put it before dozing off.

Erika should have been exhausted too and no doubt she would ache tomorrow after using muscles she hadn't known she still possessed, but the *fresh* breeze, to use one of Benjamin's positive adjectives, rushing through the carriage kept her alert.

'Where are you travelling from, Erika?' he asked.

'From Kunzendorf in Neurode. It's where I grew up. Where my parents still live, but we all thought it would be better for me to spend some time with my husband's parents,' she nodded at Karl, 'in Bernried, since the baby is coming soon'.

'I see.'

'And you?'

'I'm travelling from Freiburg. Trying to get to my family in Berlin.'

'Freiburg?' Erika was so excited to hear about the town she had so many fond memories of. It was, after all, where she had grown to love Max. 'I went to university there.'

'Really?'

'Yes, I only went back to Neurode a couple of years ago.'

'How funny to think we may have passed in the street there or sat in the same café inches away from each other before today and yet we only properly meet when you're hanging on to the outside of a speeding train somewhere outside Reichenberg.'

Erika blushed. She wasn't sure why. At how ridiculous she must have looked clinging on to the train like that? Or at the romantic way Benjamin painted their missed meetings in Freiburg? She tried to distract them both from her blushes by asking about the university town. It worked. For the first time since he'd helped her off the floor of the carriage she saw the cold breeze threaten to blow out the candle of optimism which shone from behind Benjamin's eyes.

'It's a bit of a mess I'm afraid, which is why I left. It was bombed in November. The 27th to be precise.'

Erika was stunned. Benjamin noted her reaction.

'I know,' he sighed. 'Why Freiburg? We thought it was safe from the French with the Black Forest to the east. And it was. But we also thought, what with there being no industry in the town to speak of, the British planes would leave it alone. But it seems nowhere is safe any longer. They are even bombing civilians too now.'

'Oh God,' Erika said.

'It was a bit foggy on the 27th,' Benjamin explained, 'but it had cleared by the evening and the town was all silver in the moonlight. That helped the bombers no end. I heard the bells on the cathedral chime eight o'clock. I was reading in my room. Two minutes later the early warning sirens sounded, but so did the crashing of the first bombs. I went down into the cellar with the rest of the people who lived in my house. It was what I always imagined it would be like in an earthquake. The cellar shifted about and rattled in ghostly ways. Then there was this banshee wail above us, all the ladies began to scream, there was a shattering and hissing and sweeping of air from the southern basement windows which deafened us all and left us groping about blind in a cloud of dust. The neighbours broke open the hole in the cellar wall to find out if we were still alive. I wasn't sure at first. We all looked like windswept trees on a hillside, all twisted in the same direction from the blast. Twenty-five minutes later and it was all over. Except for the time delay bombs which kept going off through the night. The city was in flames. We eventually headed for the caves on Schlossberg hill for protection from the bombers and from the raging fires. You were taking your life in your hands to work your way through Kaiserstrasse; we had to climb over high piles of stone, beams, iron, wire mesh. It was like a new world, a desert of debris, if you like. Brick and splinters covered the cathedral square ankle deep, but guess what?'

'What?' Erika could barely speak through her sadness.

'The cathedral was completely intact. The house behind it swept away. The entire ring of buildings around the square collapsed, but the cathedral was totally untouched. How wonderful is that?' he smiled, his buoyancy back. Perhaps that was the genesis of Benjamin's positivism, Erika thought, if he didn't have it already, because the sight of the cathedral towering over the destruction might just be enough to instil such an attitude in her too.

'That's really wonderful,' she agreed, but then found herself adding greedily, 'And the university?'

'Ah.' He put a consoling hand on her arm in advance of the news. 'Not so intact I'm afraid. I remember passing the Medical Centre there. It was engulfed in black smoke. Doctors and nurses rushing about outside spreading blankets on the ground. I heard women screaming and men groaning and I just wanted to get away from there. But then I remember hearing the crying of babies. The sound of new-borns, you know? And it made me linger a while. Because, I know this might sound weird to say, but it was a pleasant sound. Because that's what babies are meant to do, isn't it. Cry, I mean. It's when they're quiet that you should worry.'

Erika nodded and Benjamin's hand, which had slowly retracted to a more modest distance, was now back clasping her forearm.

'Oh God, I'm sorry. I hope I'm not upsetting you talking about babies when...'

'No, no, you're right. I'm sure it was a good thing to hear.'

'It was, but I'm afraid I was moving on again soon. I had to try and walk in the middle of the street because flames were shooting out of every window on both sides of the road and joining together overhead. Trees were throwing down their glowing branches at you as if they were alive, but then the tarmac was getting soft and made walking slow going like one of those dreams where you run and run but don't get anywhere.'

'But you weren't hurt yourself, were you?' Erika began to look her new friend over with a doctor's eye.

'I wasn't, no, but so many were. I heard of people trapped in the swimming pool who kept jumping in the water with their clothes on to escape the intense heat as the ceramic tiles all around them heated up like an oven, until the roof collapsed on them. I saw someone being dragged out of the river, half their body was one giant wound with shreds of clothing stuck to it. And then I walked passed the cinema where the wall had collapsed. Inside I could see all these moviegoers sitting in their seats, all looking quite calm, as if they'd just fallen asleep watching a very boring film, but I keep remembering their faces, just their faces because they were all cherry red. It was quite a sight.'

'Carbon monoxide poisoning,' Erika said recalling her studies.

'I beg your pardon?'

'They were all poisoned by carbon monoxide, I suppose. The red colour of their faces is a sure sign.'

'How do you know?' he asked, amused and intrigued by her knowledge, rather than threatened by it as some men might be.

'I'm a doctor. That's what I was studying at Freiburg.'

'A doctor, eh? Beautiful *and* clever! Wow!'

That hand was there again. Erika patted it with her own as she laughed modestly at Benjamin's compliments. She didn't feel it was anything to be ashamed of. Who would not enjoy such compliments, she told herself, especially when they felt as bloated and unattractive as she had these past few weeks, though her eyes kept bouncing around the compartment making sure Karl was still very much asleep.

Horst, Lutz and Edgar watched as Max poured over the fragments of Erika's letter. A letter which he had carried with him all this time without even knowing it. A link to his beloved he didn't know he had, which is why he savoured each word, each phrase, each linguistic mannerism of hers even more than he would have done if it was delivered intact in that air drop all those weeks ago. He lamented each missing page, each singed edge. Not only was it a tantalising gap in the drama of her own story, but as ever he was desperate to feel he knew what she felt about him one hundred per cent. The good and the bad. He hated it when there was bad, but he always made it his mission to try and put it right, after he had recovered from the knife which, knowing there was bad, drove into his guts. Then, when he knew she was head over heels in love with him again, unreservedly so, he could luxuriate in the good, feel Rhett Butler bold and Mr Darcy dashing like the other boys at the Rheinterrassen, fizzing with the confidence he only usually had in the classroom or on the ward.

What if she met a Charlie, like Tim's lover had? The thought bubbled up again like gastric reflux.

At least Papa was with her, he reassured himself as he read on. She wasn't likely to go off with another man right under Papa's nose. And she's on her way to my folks for some reason, he thought, smiling at the picture of his wife living with them like their very own daughter. Perhaps something had happened to her home in Kunzendorf. To her parents. God, please make them OK, he prayed.

The cattle train shuddered over some uneven rails as if trying to shake Max back to his current reality. For a moment it succeeded. He found nothing bad in the letter, nothing to concern him about her feelings for him, but if he did... he started to panic about how he could possibly put things right. He couldn't go down to her room with his blanket and snuggle up on the armchair, he couldn't revise Latin with her in her bed, they couldn't go hiking or skiing, or go out dancing, or just have a cathartic argument, as she called it, or a debate as he preferred to describe it. All he could do was write her a letter. He'd done that before. She loved literature, she loved words, letters worked a treat, but this time he had no idea if the letter would ever get to her. If the Russians had any intention of providing a postal service for their POWs. Somehow he doubted it. He read on.

He read about his father, who must have gone to get her from Neurode. The first page was missing so he had to assume that. About their arduous journey by train. About his father bribing the guards with cigarettes and chocolate. About her feeling ill for some reason. Probably her blood pressure, he thought. About the crowds and the conditions on the trains. He looked up at the faces of filth and famine around him, breathed in the stench and tried very hard not to think of Erika as being a little overdramatic. At least she could get off whenever she wanted!

The cattle train stopped as he read about his father and her hanging on to the outside of a moving train near Reichenberg when the pages ran out. He began sorting through the rest of the pages in the backpack. At first in an orderly way then gradually more and more frantically, creating an autumn of paper over his knees and the knees of his colleagues who were crammed up next to him.

'Woh, woh there, brother,' Horst put a hand on Max's flailing arms. 'Let us help you.'

'There must be more, there must be,' he said to no one in particular.

Edgar looked at his distracted buddy with pity. There but by the grace of God go I, his bachelor's face said. He tried to share his pity with Horst. But Horst wasn't having any of it.

'Let's just try and help him, eh!' Horst snapped at Edgar and handed him a pile of letters to look through.

Edgar handed some to Lutz with a gesture that said: for God's sake, Lutz, let's just try and help him, eh!

'Do you think I could have a look through when you're done?' a soldier called out.

It was Tim.

'Of course,' Lutz nodded.

And then the door was yanked open and the four doctors sat

there blinking in the low Siberian sunlight like four little boys caught having a midnight feast.

'What is this?' one of the guards bellowed in German snatching up some of the pages littered around Max.

'Letters, just letters,' Horst answered.

'Take them!' the guard said to the others who began confiscating the lot. Except for the letter from Tim's girlfriend which Max still had in his pocket. And the page he was holding from Erika which now subtly joined it.

'Hey,' Tim shouted and got to his feet on foal-like legs after so long sat down. 'You can't take them, they're from our loved...'

Max believed the letters were as precious as Tim did. He had rescued them, carried them and protected them for this long, but he also knew what the response would be from the Russians if he tried to fight for them now. The little piece of Erika he stuffed into his pocket and the words he had already read reminded him of the necessity of self-preservation. So as Tim stood, Max closed his eyes, as you do before a squeezed balloon, anticipating the inevitable.

The bullet passed through Tim and out through the back of the wagon letting a beam of sunlight in, which worked as a grim sundial for days to come.

Tim's mates had to catch his body as it fell and sit with it biting down on their grief as the guards continued addressing the doctors as if nothing had happened. Max thanked God Tim died without seeing the letter in his pocket; that he died believing he was adored. It was believing that which gave him the strength to stand up against the guards like that Max told himself later as he battled with the notion that it was thinking there might yet be a letter from his lover in the pile that propelled Tim to stand. If Max had given him the letter when he found it, he might not be dead now, but sitting in the corner of the stinking wagon nursing his broken heart. When it came to Erika, Max wasn't sure which would be worse.

'We need doctors and isolation unit,' one of the Soviets said in rudimentary German.

'Really?' Edgar mumbled sardonically. 'You'd never have guessed.'

Max was glad to have Edgar with him at times like these; his vociferous, forthright, talented, jazz-loving friend, to pierce the enemy and the atmosphere with his sharp wit and sarcastic riffs.

'You,' the guard pointed at Max, 'will be chief doctor.'

Max was only too pleased to do what he had been craving since this awful journey had begun, since the first man was shot outside the monastery back in Breslau.

'And you choose two doctors to assist.'

'OK,' Max said. 'Actually there are three other doctors here.' He spoke brightly as he offered even more resources than the Soviets had planned for.

'No. Two.'

Max gestured limply to his three colleagues.

'Choose!' the guard was becoming impatient.

It wouldn't surprise Max if he blew one of them away thereby doing the choosing for him.

'OK, OK!' There was no contest, even though it killed him to have to leave one of his men behind, knowing that his living conditions were about to get just that little bit better by virtue of the fact that he was now officially the camp doctor. Horst was his brother. Edgar was his best friend. Luckily both were as good a doctor as Lutz, if not better.

Lutz gave Max a lipless smile of resignation, though his aura was sick with abandonment. He knew what was coming. He couldn't blame Max.

'Sorry,' Max mumbled and pointed to Edgar and Horst as he cranked himself to his feet. 'Sorry,' he mouthed again at Lutz, his faced contorted with regret.

Then, for the first time in a long time, Max focused on the world outside the train. They were in a station. And there were trucks lined up outside it waiting to take the prisoners further up and further in to this eternal winter land.

The three newly reappointed doctors clambered down from the wagon and were directed to the truck at the back of the convoy.

'This is isolation truck. Put all prisoners with infectious diseases here and deal with them.'

'May we have our medical bags back then?'

The guard who appeared to be in charge said something to a subordinate, who went off supposedly to fetch the bags, but was stopped in his tracks by a rabble of his comrades cheering and slapping each other's backs.

'What's that all about?' Horst nudged Max since he had the best Russian of all of them.

Max tuned in to the shouts and cheers, as did their guard. 'It's over. The war is over. Germany surrendered. We surrendered. It's over, Horst!' He began to hug his brother, but the guard prodded them up into the isolation truck.

'No time. We must go. Up! Up!'

'But it's over,' Max said to his captor. 'The war is over.'

'So?' The guard looked miserable.

Any spark of celebration in the three Germans lads was immediately quashed and they soon mirrored his expression. The war may have ceased, but nothing had changed for any of them. It was clear from the guard's demeanour that neither he nor they would be going home any time soon.

Had Breslau resisted the siege for just days longer they all might be in an occupied country right now, but at least it would be their homeland. As they hauled themselves slowly, incredulously into the truck outside some anonymous station in some hinterland of Russia, this fact dug more viciously into their guts than the barrel of any Tokarev had so far on this rancid journey.

'How much further do we have to travel?' Edgar pouted, having to rephrase himself a few times before the guard understood.

'Nine days. Perhaps.'

'With Soviet efficiency call it two weeks then,' Edgar said under his breath.

And he wasn't wrong. The three doctors tried hopelessly amidst the constant pitch, roll and yaw of the truck, with no appropriate medicines, to treat diarrhoea, typhoid and cholera among other diseases. With a half cup of water per day per man, the patients and the doctors were dehydrated even before these desiccating conditions infested the population. Max asked his patients to do what he and his fellow doctors did with their ration of water: swill the water around in their mouths in an attempt to alleviate the thirst, then spit it into their hands and wash their faces, and use whatever few drops were left to "clean" their genitals. The cold had its advantages. Condensation on the windows quickly froze and the men could take it in turns to lick the ice from the glass. Max had some anti-lice preparation in his medical bag. He made sure Horst, Edgar and himself used this on themselves so as not to catch lice from the dead. In those two dire weeks the doctors recorded the deaths of fifty-six men. All of them had to be dumped from the back of the truck.

Then finally they stopped. In a labour camp called Hunsfeld. And a perverse kind of Christmas came to this wonderless wonderland at last.

From the incessantly shuddering and pitching world of the back of a truck, the utterly desolate stillness of the camp was a kind of gift. From sleeping among the corpses and the diseased, the doctors' new quarters with the kitchen workforce were almost cause for celebration. Not having to eat regular prison food but sharing the kitchen staff's "special" meals was as close to a festive feast as they were likely to get. The Russians it seemed were concerned above all that their food supply was not contaminated, so the doctors were ordered to check the cooks' health constantly and examine their clothing for signs of fleas. Max, Horst and Edgar would therefore be among the cooks before breakfast and dinner warming themselves over boiling vats of some liquid of dubious origin which had potatoes and animal fat in it. But the potatoes would all sink to the bottom and the fat would all float on the top. The doctors would watch as the cooks would skim off this fat, as if in some altruistic concern for the state of the prisoners' arteries, when in fact they would keep all that tasty, energy-packed lard for themselves. Then they would ladle up the liquid and chuck it into the bowls teetering on the shivering malnourished hands of the prisoners, hardly ever digging deep enough to catch a potato from the depths, thereby leaving a bounty of vegetables for themselves when the vats were 'empty.' On the rare occasions a prisoner's spoon ran aground on a potato hiding under the surface of his soup he would stay very quiet about it, lest his friends turn into jealous enemies.

Max, Edgar and Horst though were allowed to share in the spoils of the cooks, who were grateful to the doctors for keeping them in such good health.

'I don't think it's anything we are doing that's keeping them healthy,' Max whispered to Edgar as they gorged on their fat-covered potatoes, huddled around the dwindling fire on which the food had been cooked.

'Not with our meagre medicinal supplies. No, it's this diet alone that does it, but no one needs to know that, do they?' Edgar winked and nearly choked on the chunk of tuber in his mouth as the sound of a bowl being returned to the counter with unusual ferocity had them all turning their toasted faces from the fire.

It was Lutz who had returned his bowl. Lutz who had wanted them to see him watching them enjoy themselves whilst he finished another day laying brick with mortar that froze before you had a chance to get it off your trowel, from before sunrise to after sunset, after which he sucked at this diarrhoea these cooks passed off as soup whilst his erstwhile colleagues warmed themselves and nourished themselves and occasionally rubbed anti-lice powder into the hair of one of the dirty Ivans running this hell hole. His gaunt face barely had the muscle tone to describe bitterness, but his eyes bit Max's skin more than the frost ever had so far.

And that was why Max found his appetite had suddenly waned. Why Edgar's and Horst's did too, and why they pooled their leftovers and invented a reason that night to visit the hut where Lutz and hundreds of other prisoners languished. The reason they gave the guards was long and in Latin. It sounded good, scary, like something that needed investigation. They couldn't have said they suspected an outbreak of cholera or typhoid – those diseases were like the common cold here.

They moved among the drowsy inmates – who were all exhausted enough to be sleeping but cold enough to be kept awake, so to be drowsy was the best state of repose they could manage during the night – examining those that looked particularly ill, administering what little they could, until they found the true subject of their quest.

Those scathing eyes of Lutz's were wide open by the time they found him on his top bunk deep inside the hut. The doctors huddled round, trying to block the view of any prying neighbours and delivered their gift of cold, fat-soaked potatoes. It was hardly gold, frankincense and myrrh, but then they were only three doctors not three magi and Lutz was hardly the baby Jesus in a manger. Besides, what use was gold and frankincense here, when a decent meal was all that was desired and needed?

There was no need for too many words either. And too many words could get them all in trouble, so they left shortly after Lutz had gratefully received his gift and whispered his thanks. Max glanced back over his shoulder as they left and made out the silhouette sitting up sharing his food with the kid on the bunk next to his. It was foolish to try and keep something like food a secret in this overcrowded hut, he reasoned, and good to have an ally or two, he told himself, thereby excusing his own conspiracy with the cooks as well as comforting himself that Lutz still had a companion here.

Before dawn the next morning the prisoners were woken by the banging of a hammer on railings as ever, but today there was more to rouse them than just that offensive sound. There was also the commotion outside in the sickly glow of the only lamp that burned all night outside the hut where Max had left Lutz feasting the night before. And in that weak light the lantern vomited into the air, Lutz was being made to vomit too. He was being punched repeatedly in the stomach in order, the guard who was enjoying the show announced to all the gathering prisoners, to expel the valuable food this greedy cretin had stolen last night.

The three doctors stood with anyone else that gave a damn about Lutz, disgusted by their own impotence but knowing that so much as a yelp of disapproval in the guard's direction would mean the same punishment for them. Max searched the crowd for the kid that had shared the food last night with his friend – he was glad to feel the need to use his eyes for anything else than seeing Lutz tortured like this – and sure enough the kid was almost seizing with fear that he had been reported for sharing the contraband too, but as yet he seemed to be in the clear. So Max employed his eyes to study the rest of the prisoners and try and deduce which of them had betrayed a fellow prisoner by the look of guilt or triumph on their faces. But most looked like they just wanted to go back inside where it was a degree or two warmer only by virtue of the protection from the wind. Perhaps the guards themselves had discovered Lutz. Perhaps Lutz was not experienced enough with contraband to hide the evidence very well. Either way Max was wracked with guilt.

'He didn't steal it. We gave it to him,' Max mumbled more to himself than to Horst stood next to him, but Horst heard and intervened on his brother's thought process.

'It doesn't matter, they'll still punish him for eating it. And us for giving it.'

'No, no, no,' Max's voice was starting to reach other ears easily in the vacuum of a Siberian predawn.

'Now now, Max,' Edgar said through gritted teeth, 'what's the point of getting us killed too?'

'The point is, it's wrong,' Max's voice was now raised, his body moving towards the guards. 'He did not steal the food.'

The beating stopped. A gun was aimed at Max who continued, 'We... I gave him the food. When we went to investigate the, er, illness spreading round the prisoners, we assessed this man as, erm, desperately in need of nourishment. No one stole anything. It was medicine. Doctor's orders.'

Not a sound, save for the whimpering of Lutz from the frozen earth and the desperate sucking of teeth as Edgar and Horst watched not one but two of their friends about to be killed.

The guard who had been so vocal about Lutz's misdemeanours a few moments ago was now mute too. He examined the doctor before him; the doctor whom he was pretty sure had asked for this snivelling Nazi on the floor at his feet to be part of his medical team all those weeks ago at the train station. So perhaps it was true. Perhaps the chief doctor did bring the food for him, but the guard doubted it was because it was for urgent medicinal reasons. They were friends, that was why he had brought the food. If he had brought it at all. If the Nazi snake at his feet hadn't stolen it. Either way, the guard's frozen morning brain reasoned, what I am about to do will punish them both perfectly then.

The guard released the safety catch on the automatic rifle he was pointing at Max and simply said:

'No.'

He turned the gun to Lutz and fired a few rounds into the little ball of human curled up there.

Besides, he was gasping for a coffee and had wasted enough time out here already this morning. He smiled – yes smiled! – at Max and went back to his hut while a long oscillating moan began emanating from the quivering kid's lithe body. The shock of hearing this from someone else stopped Max from producing an identical sound and instead made him focus on the kid. Max had no idea why now would seem like the appropriate time to assign someone new duties – perhaps it was because he wished he'd thought of it before and gave the job to Lutz; perhaps it was a paranoia that the kid would somehow point the finger at Max even though he had pointed it at himself just now whilst staring down the barrel of a gun; or perhaps it was just an overwhelming need to make something slightly better about this whole terrible mess – but he hurried after the guard and told him he needed someone young, strong and fit to help out with carrying stretchers and other such errands and he wondered if he could employ the young boy there.

'The whining one?' the guard said impatient to get inside.

'Yes.'

'If *that* you are calling strong, be my guest.' He turned to go in, but stopped himself. 'Oh, and when trucks arrive today prepare one for isolation, as before.'

'We're moving?'

The guard thought that was perfectly obvious so didn't waste his breath with an answer. He disappeared inside and Max hurried over to the kid.

'Hey, hey, sh, sh,' he said. 'What's your name?'

'Bubi,' the kid said with an accent which Max recognised as Polish.

'How old are you?'

'Sixteen.'

'I was sixteen when I first realised I wanted to be a doctor.' He forced a smile over his quivering jaw. 'Now, I need your help as my assistant, OK?'

Bubi nodded hopelessly.

'And your first errand is to go and fetch a stretcher from the medical hut. And then you're going to have to be strong, inside I mean, and help me carry our... your friend Lutz back there, understand?' Max tried to mimic the tone of his aunt, as far as his memory would allow, from all those years ago outside the theatre as they dealt with the casualties from the road traffic accident. He tried to instil in Bubi the same confidence that his aunt had instilled in him as they had carried each broken wailing tram passenger into the hospital on that ladder whilst his shoes, soaked in sugary beer from the Kronen lorry, had stuck to the clean smooth floors of the emergency ward – although it was clear from the way the Tokarev had churned up Lutz's silent body that Bubi's first casualty was beyond saving.

This leg of her interminable odyssey across country was the only one Erika had not wished was over the moment it had begun. She chatted easily with Benjamin, but whenever there was a lull in the conversation – when, for example, the blaring of the train through a tunnel, which was amplified terribly by the lack of a door on their compartment, made it impossible for them to be heard, or the young couple squeezed in next to Karl reignited their petty but vicious argument with each other – Erika's mind would hurry back to Freiburg. But not the unimaginable Freiburg her new travelling companion had described, but the beautiful mediaeval town she had skipped through with her lover on the night she found out she had passed her Latin exam. They celebrated that night with Edgar, Babyface and Horst. They ran through the streets, all the tension of the last few days finding an outlet in their bursts of energy.

'I hate Latin. What does Latin have to do with medicine anyway?' she had pouted less than a week before.

'Er... *febris flava, febris militarius, bis in die, pro re nata, biceps brachii*,' Max had said flexing his like a circus strong man. '*Quadriceps femoris*.' He stroked her thigh. '*Trapezius*.' He squeezed her shoulders. 'So tense!' he laughed. 'We'll have to massage that properly after study. '*Pectoralis major*,' he said laying his hand gently on her breast, where she was happy for it to remain, but he slid it down the bed and underneath her. '*Gluteus maximus...*'

'OK,' she giggled wriggling away from him, as far as you could wriggle away in a single bed, 'I get your point.' But she quickly moved back into his arms when the cold air outside the blankets pierced her skin all the way to the foreign sounding muscles beneath. 'But I'm never going to pass the test. I've got two days to cram all this... stuff.'

'Well, together we'll do it, no problem.'

'You've got your own studies to worry about,' she huffed. 'I'll just have to manage on my own.' Although she had no intention of managing on her own as she waited for the magic words from Max.

'I'm doing nothing for the next two days, except helping you to cram this Latin and that's final, OK?'

Her trapeziuses relaxed instantly. The news was even more effective than his warm hands on her skin and told her everything she was longing to know about their growing relationship.

'*Trapezii.*'

'What?'

'*Trapezius, trapezii.*'

Before the day was out he had drummed it into her that the plural of *trapezius* was *trapezii* and two days later she passed the test.

So here they were running through Freiburg hand in hand, jumping over the Bächle, the little brooks that cut through the cobbles in the centre of town.

'Who made these Bächle and what for?' Erika breathlessly asked no one in particular.

'The Bürgermeister had them built in mediaeval times,' Edgar began, as he and the others caught up. She might have known he'd have the answer. 'In the hope that one day two young lovers would enjoy prancing about the town and skipping over them.'

Erika dipped the toe of her shoe in the Bächle and flicked the running water at Edgar. He tried to retaliate, but his bombardment turned into a terribly brief rain shower that hit nothing but the ground, Erika having sprinted away already, disappearing with Max up Rosastrasse and into the basement beneath the Golden Bear.

None of them had any idea there was a basement bar under the inn until they were invited to tonight's poetry reading. It was the perfect spot for such an event.

'Crowded.' Babyface's baby face aged with despair as they tumbled into the bar with a hundred students already sitting on the floor and at the few tables available.

'Intimate,' Erika preferred to describe it. 'We'll be able to hear every word,' she smiled at Max.

Edgar made as if to stick his finger down his throat and she slapped his arm, as expected.

'My God, careful, you nearly made me stick my finger down there for real,' Edgar giggled and stumbled comically towards the bar clutching some swing sheet music under one arm in case the opportunity arose for a jamboree, or *jam* as Edgar would say, emulating his jazz heroes from America. He began ordering drinks, familiar with everyone's preferences.

'I didn't want a beer,' Horst said as Edgar passed it back to him over the heads of shorter customers.

Edgar froze. With the folder of music under one arm and the beer held aloft Erika thought he looked like some alcoholic statue of liberty. Before Edgar could say the words: *You always order beer. Don't mess with me!* as his sour face surely indicated he was about to, Horst – mouth wide open, tongue out like a happily exercised Alsatian – guffawed and shouted over the noise:

'Gotcha!'

Edgar pushed the beer into Horst's hand and turned his head back to the bar quickly, to complete the order as well as to hide his relieved amusement from his sparring partner. Each of them gratefully received their drinks from Edgar's long arm before it was Max's turn to take the lead and find them a decent place to sit.

After only one near miss of treading on someone's fingers, he managed to lead them all to a space right over by the area demarcated as a stage for the performers, where none of the other recent arrivals had dared to attempt to reach and so the bar and the stairs up to the street were fast becoming impassable.

'Where's Edgar?' Babyface asked once they were all comfortably – or as comfortably as they were going to get for now – ensconced on the floor.

They all looked back in the direction of the bar to see Edgar gesturing up and down his body and shrugging his shoulders.

'What's he saying?' Max asked.

'He's saying,' Horst translated the sign language, 'he's too tall to fit in here, which is true, so he's going to stay over there, which is fine by him, because he's closer to the bar'.

Erika was briefly disappointed, not so much that Edgar was left out, but that they weren't all together, especially since this was part of her end of exam celebrations, as far as she was concerned anyway. But when she saw Edgar already engaged in banter with other students she'd never met, she knew to get on with just enjoying the company around her, as he certainly was.

The first poet took the stage... well, the space in front of one of the supporting pillars where a chair had been set. The audience hushed themselves. The poet muttered in rhyming couplets about loss, wealth and pride, using images of roses which, though Erika knew were derivative, she couldn't help but be moved by them. As the poet finished his reading to limp applause and tip-toed deflated to the bar, conversation erupted again all around. Whether it was praise or criticism, ridicule or defence, the poet's images had at least the power to spark some lively chatter, particularly about an apparently controversial organisation called The White Rose.

Erika felt emboldened after her glass of port to ask someone she didn't know – but really ought to have, having been in such close proximity to her for the last half hour – what this White Rose was all about.

'Oh, wow, haven't you heard? I mean, right, they are a terribly brave group of students from Munich Uni, who've been campaigning against the government. Sending out leaflets all over the country, like this,' the girl squirmed around until she had enough room among the bodies surrounding her to delve into her pocket, pull out a piece of once-white paper dense with black type on both sides and begin to unfold it.

'Hey, Gitte,' a young man with bloodshot eyes barked across to her, 'make sure you don't lose that! It's the only one we have'.

'OK,' she whined, giving it now completely over to Erika's hands, whereas before her nagging boyfriend spoke she had no intention of letting it go.

Erika read:

Isn't it true that every honest German is ashamed of his government these days? Who among us has any conception of the dimensions of shame that will befall us and our children when one day the veil has fallen from our eyes and the most horrible of crimes – crimes that

**infinitely outdistance every human measure –
reach the light of day?**

She stopped reading and decided to notice instead the way the title **PAMPHLET OF THE WHITE ROSE** was skewed like a badly hung picture. It all looked so thrown together compared to the beautifully presented pamphlets and booklets sent to her by the Youth Movement. She felt Max's chin rest itself on her shoulder and quickly handed the leaflet back to Gitte.

'Terribly brave,' Gitte said.

She couldn't bring herself to agree so she heard herself saying, 'Thanks,' and turned to see what the excitement pulsing through the audience was all about.

'Oh my God,' Babyface was saying to Max, 'did you know he was coming?'

'Who's he?' Erika whispered just in case it was very unhip not to know who he was, this middle aged, lipless, hollow eyed gent with the weight of the world on his eyebrows and hair of dissipating black smoke.

'It's Reinhold Schneider, the poet and novelist.' Babyface's baby face shone more than ever. 'His stuff has been banned by the government. He's red hot right now.'

Erika looked at Max's profile as he admired the star only inches away handing out copies of his latest work.

'*Did* you know he was coming?' she said into Max's ear.

He nodded, too star-struck to speak, or too ashamed perhaps. Because, what with the White Rose leaflet and now Herr Schneider, Erika did not feel like the centre of a celebration, but more like a character in the James Joyce book she was reading – Tom Kernan, to be exact, the alcoholic confronted by three of his friends and persuaded to take part in a religious retreat to help him change his ways. She would have got up and walked out, if it wasn't such a difficult thing to do. The room was heaving now and Schneider was ready to start.

'Our forces continue to push into France. It won't be long before they reach Paris,' the poet announced. 'Parisians will see our tanks rumble past their Arc de Triomphe and down the Champs Elysees to the Place de la Concorde. Curfews will be announced. The red lights of The Moulin Rouge, the life and colour of Montmartre will be extinguished. Swing music, the *music of the nigger, the kike, jungle music* will be banned.' There were a few confident boos from the audience and much awed shuffling, 'Sound familiar?'

The boos got louder and multiplied. Erika knew they weren't for Schneider, who raised his hand for quiet. The audience quickly obeyed.

'The first piece I'd like to read you tonight is called *Only Those Who Pray.*'

Erika had heard enough. There was rapturous applause after Schneider's introduction and Erika used it to cover her flight to the exit. The fact that most pairs of hands in the room were being pounded against each other right then, saved many fingers from being trodden on as she stepped out with far less care than she used coming in.

'Only those who pray may still be able

To stop the sword over our heads...'

She'd only heard fifteen words – what could you understand in just fifteen words? – but she kept on going, squeezing herself through the crowd by the exit and all the way up through the throng on the stairs until she was vomited out on the street from that throat of disunity.

She feasted on the air outside, of such a superior quality to that sweaty, hot, pretentious atmosphere in the bowels of the inn. She knew it wouldn't be long before Max emerged too to find out what was wrong with her, to check if she was feeling ill, or whether her low blood pressure was causing her to feel faint again. So in the meantime she stood hugging herself and tapping out a jazzy rhythm with her sensible shoes on the cobbles designed to convey to the small group engaged in lively debate and the couple kissing and the other few individuals apparently waiting for someone that she was perfectly happy where she was and in no way felt awkward about idly hanging around out here when the rest of the country – Nazi or otherwise – seemed to be enjoying themselves indoors.

Although there was no doubt that Max would come out soon,

after a few minutes she found herself looking for a railing or piece of wall to lean against, to help her feel less "all at sea". But such a lifebuoy was hard to come by. The couple had commandeered the railings outside the inn and the front of every other shop in this street was dominated by windows. It didn't feel safe to lean against a pane of glass. Knowing her luck, she thought, the glass would crack, the shopkeeper would call the police when he heard the commotion from his flat upstairs and she'd feel even more ostracised than she already did. Erika hugged herself tighter and moved across the road to stand under the awning outside the cigar shop.

Max still hadn't arrived. But given the difficulty she had getting out of that overfilled basement she had to allow him extra time.

She found a slither of wall between the window full of cigar boxes and the slim alleyway next to the shop and leant there against a poster recruiting air raid wardens.

She heard a deep giggle coming from the alley – another couple, no doubt smooching down there – and, although for a second she felt like a peeping Tom, she refused to move now she'd found such a perfect piece of wall. Besides, Max would be out any second now.

Perhaps he was waiting until Schneider had finished his poem. It looked like little more than a sonnet when she had seen the papers being handed out, but she could have been mistaken, of course. Perhaps it was several stanzas long and there was no way Max would be so rude as to get up and clamber over all those bodies right in the middle of it.

She watched as some of those waiting individuals became couples and were swallowed up by the basement. 'How can they get any more people in there?' she muttered to herself.

The deep giggling in the alley was accompanied by some nasal sighs and Erika knew the couple's sole purpose now was to emphasis her own solitude and the unlikeliness that she and her boyfriend would be giggling down an alley any time soon.

Max! What the hell?

Perhaps Schneider was reading part of an epic work, she told herself. Or perhaps Max had trod on someone's fingers as he rushed out to find her, and the injured party – a burly man no doubt with plenty of beer inside him – had stood up and started threatening Max and causing a scene, which had completely upstaged Schneider and his puritanical poems. She liked the image of the star being eclipsed in this manner, but then she thought, if this were true, Max might right now be being beaten up by this imaginary thug. She stepped away from the wall and made to cross the street back to the basement, but before her foot landed on the cobbles she reassured herself, that Horst and Edgar, and to a lesser extent Babyface (but only because he just wasn't as physically imposing as his friends) would be there to protect Max.

Then an animalistic snort came from the alley behind her. She recognised the sound. It was clearly Edgar, which ruined her theory about who was available to protect Max and only served to make her more worried that, despite his beefy stature just Horst would be there to defend him.

Hang on! Edgar was in the alley? With whom? For a moment this scintillating bit of gossip and intrigue obliterated all concerns for Max from her mind. She stepped back to her place by the poster and listened. Now she *was* a peeping Tom! But, of course, just at that moment things became much quieter and she had nothing to focus on again but the absence of Max.

'Schneider must be reading an entire bloody epic then!' she sneered to herself deciding right then to take off home without anyone to walk her.

'Erika!' But then there he was, 'Erika!' Calling to her, waving and wiping the condensation from his round glasses, apparently unassailed by any lout with Max's footprint on the back of his huge hand, and therefore fair game, thought Erika, for a good tongue-lashing from her. 'Are you all right?' he said ducking under the awning and putting a hand on her *deltoideus*. She hated the fact that the Latin name for her shoulder muscle flashed through her mind right then. 'Are you sick?' he asked.

'Yes, I'm sick,' she said shrugging off his hand. 'Sick of being treated like an idiot.'

'Who's treating you like an idiot?'

'You.'

Max put his glasses back on to see if that made things any clearer to him.

'How am I doing that?'

'With your White Rose friends and your anti-government poetry nights.'

'They're not my friends. I'd never heard of the White Rose until I read the name on that pamphlet you had. And it's not an anti-government poetry night, it's just a poetry night where people should be able to express themselves artistically and voice their opinions, whatever they are, freely.'

'What rubbish!'

'How is that rubbish?' Max seemed hurt by that remark so Erika stuck her finger in the wound and gauged around.

'So if I got up and read a poem about all the great things the Nazis have done for this country you're saying I wouldn't be booed off the stage and hounded out of the bar?'

'You don't write poetry,' Max could give as good as he got.

'How do you know?'

'Well... Do you?' Max seemed genuinely interested to know.

Erika stuttered and spluttered until her body reluctantly ejected the word, 'No.'

She thought she saw him swallow a smile.

'But if I did,' she went on, 'those people in there would have me silenced, which is exactly what they accuse the Nazis of doing.'

Max didn't respond. Because she was right, obviously, she told herself. But she hated it when he went quiet, when he refused to answer back. What excuse did she have to rip into him if he gave her no ammunition? But then she remembered she already had some unused grenades.

'You knew Schneider was performing tonight, didn't you? And you brought me here, knowing it would upset me, on *my* celebration night.'

'Oh, so this is all really about the fact that you're not the centre of attention for once.'

'For once? What's that supposed to mean? How am I the centre of attention when I sit in *your* cathedral? How am I the centre of attention when I listen to *your* heroes lecture…? And anyway don't try and change the subject. You knew he was performing tonight, didn't you?'

'Yes, but I thought it would be good for you.'

'Good for me? What do you think I am: one of those patients in the medical centre needing a walk around the gardens? Am I ill?'

'No, of course not, of course I don't think that.'

'Bloody Hell!' she mumbled. 'Trust me to fall in love with a…' She stopped herself from spitting on his religion. She waited for the question: *With a what? With a what?* But it never came.

He took off his glasses again, as if he'd had all the clarity he could handle for one evening, and she saw his eyes were moist.

'Do you think you love me?' he asked quietly.

'What?'

'You said you fell in love. Have you really?'

She was thrown for a moment. That wasn't the question he was supposed to ask. That wasn't the retaliation she expected. So she retraced her steps through the melee of the last few seconds but found it to be true. She *had* said she loved him. On top of that, increased production of neurotransmitters, of the kind Von Euler was proposing, had clearly caused her hands to sweat, her cheeks to flush, and her heart to race, as if she had smoked a whole cigarette by herself. And the production of the chemical enteramine, which some radical researchers had proposed was responsible for mood, was high in Erika; in very similar levels, in fact, to that found in some mentally ill patients. So she had to conclude that indeed she did love him.

'Yes,' she said sulkily, sensing a warm unexpected resolution to this battle.

But his answer came like an instant snow drift, deadening all sound and sensation: 'And I love you too. Which means you're going to have to convince me of your faith. Or I have to convince you of mine. Otherwise we'll have to separate.'

'You OK, guys?' Horst, skipping over the Bächle, was crossing the street towards them. 'Has anyone seen Edgar?'

Erika wagged her thumb loosely in the direction of the alley, but kept her eyes on Max as he hid his behind the refracting and reflecting lenses of his specs.

'What's he doing down there?' Horst didn't wait for an answer, but strode into the darkness calling out his friend's name.

'Jesus!' Edgar's voice came howling from the gloom.

'Jesus yourself!' Horst appeared again looking appalled.

As if he was a plunger, Horst appeared to have unblocked the alley and out poured Edgar buttoning his trousers and a very embarrassed looking first year psychology student wiping his lips with the back of his hand.

'What the hell do you think you're doing?' Edgar roared, his voice ricocheting off the shop fronts and cobbles.

'What the hell do you think *you're* doing?' Horst matched him, as if his ambition was to be the incarnation of his friend's echo.

'Is a man not entitled to any privacy these days?' Edgar almost grinned.

'In his own home, certainly, but you're in the middle of the bloody street, man.'

'Well, I am now, thanks to you.'

The psychology student hurried back to the basement and dived into the more liberal waters below.

'And let's face it, Horst, your problem is not *where* I do it, is it? It's *who* I do it with. Isn't it?'

'No, it is not, it's just that I wish you'd use a little more discretion. For your sake. I'm worried about you.'

'How touching.'

'Mate, did you miss the Night of the Long Knives? The execution of Röhm because he was a homosexual? The bonfires of books from the Institute of Sex Research in the Opernplatz?'

'That was nearly ten years ago. I was a kid. So were you. Times have changed.'

'Yes, they have. They've got worse. Now it's not just the homosexuals that are disappearing to God knows where, it's the spastics, the Jews and the blacks, in fact it's anyone who the Gestapo doesn't like the look of. I don't care who you do it with, just be careful who sees you, Edgar.'

A light went on in the flat above the cigar shop.

'Down there,' Edgar jabbed a finger at the alley, 'no one could see us, but now you've opened your mouth it seems the whole city knows my business. Thanks a lot!' He marched across the road and sank into the basement too.

'Damn him!' Horst followed him inside.

Erika and Max stood unable to look each other in the face now. After the bellowing of the boys the street seemed eerily quiet with just the muffled chatter from the inn and the water running through the Bächle sounding to Erika like something melting.

A mere four weeks they had spent at Hunsfeld. Much less time than it had taken to get there from Breslau. And now they were off again, all that bouncing about in the back of a truck had Max feeling nauseous and praying:

'Please, God, can we just stay in one place for a change?!'

'Be careful what you pray for,' Edgar muttered. 'I'm starting to believe our God might have a bit of a sick sense of humour.'

'Perhaps they're taking us home,' Horst said, not believing it for a second, but hoping for some entertaining reactions from Edgar at least.

Nothing came.

When they finally stopped it wasn't home. Not in the way Horst had meant anyway. It was a camp called Gegesha on the border between Russia and Eastern Finland. The centre piece of which was a long hut, a hundred metres long and thirty metres wide, Max guessed, made of wooden logs, of which two-thirds were below ground level. As they were herded towards this massive toadstool poking through the earth Max checked his five deutschmark watch.

Tick tick tick tick.

Perhaps the cheap piece of rubbish had finally given up the ghost. After all, it said midday and it was dark. He checked his quality pocket watch.

Midday too.

'It seems we're in the Arctic Circle, boys,' he mumbled to his colleagues.

No special arrangements for the doctors and their little Polish protégé here. They were ordered to find a place with the other nine thousand nine hundred and ninety six prisoners in the subterranean log hut on bunks with barely enough room to squeeze between them which meant you got to know the nocturnal habits of your neighbours all too well.

Max was cursed with a top bunk, which meant you were closer to the part of the hut that was above ground. On his first night he was pelted with razor-edged raindrops blown in by the raving winds through the gaps in the logs as he lay on his bunk trying in vain to get some sleep.

They were woken... No, not woken since most had not got to sleep yet. They were ordered out of their beds as usual before dawn... No, not dawn since they would not see the sun again for nearly five months. They were ordered out of their beds as usual at five o'clock in the morning and the medical team were instructed to follow a guard who spoke incredibly good German and was, Max, had to admit, strikingly good looking. Perhaps it was not just his chiselled faced, piercing blue eyes and blonde hair – an Aryan look which would have Hitler himself scratching at his black hair with confusion – but the sheer confidence that speaking the language of his captives so well gave him. There was not much it seemed that they could say when he was in earshot which he didn't catch, which had rarely been the case so far with other guards.

As this guard led them through a gate in the perimeter fence, through which they would always be counted in and out by the sentries there, one of them hovering above in a lookout post, Tokarev trained on them, Max became aware of a sound he had not heard for many years. The sleeping dragon sound of the sea. Until that point he had no idea that Gegesha Camp was situated on the coast. But it was hardly the seaside of his summer holidays with Erika on Rügen Island; squinting in the primary coloured dazzle, the back of your throat warmed by the sun beaming in through your mouth agape with laughter and love. This new picture was scratched out in charcoals, backwashed in diesel coloured waves.

'Welcome to your new camp hospital, gentlemen,' the guard grinned.

A wooden walkway stretched from where they stood on the edge of the gravel shore fifteen metres to a single storey wooden structure standing on stilts out in the grey water.

'This is their idea of quarantine, I suppose,' Edgar sneered, not yet familiar with the need to curb his tongue around this linguistically gifted guard.

'Yes it is,' said the guard ushering them onto the bridge. He, however, stayed on shore as a vampire would stay out of the sun and Max realised it was the Russians' fear of being contaminated with their captives' diseases that had led them to build this ivory tower, the one place in the entire camp the prisoners could be free of Ivan.

Oh my, thought Max, this place is going to be awfully popular when they find out.

The guard went on, 'And you are expected to maintain the highest standards of clinical cleanliness here at all times.'

'Well, I am sure we will be given the highest level of clinical resources to achieve that aim,' Edgar said, this time fully intending the guard to hear and understand.

Max stepped onto the walkway feeling a little like he was walking the plank. The building ahead of him was about a tenth of the size of their barracks, so it was no surprise to hear that the Soviets thought it could house about a tenth of the number of men that the barracks could.

'A maximum – and I stress this is a maximum not the norm – a maximum of nine percent of the camp's population is permitted to be ill at any one time. The rest must be fit to work. Any more than nine percent and the doctor will be held responsible and he will be put in solitary confinement or sentenced to hard labour.'

Max assumed that meant him, the chief doctor. Horst wondered if it meant the doctor who admitted the patient who tipped the sickness figures into the red. They all decided right then to keep as close an eye on their admission figures as Ivan would be.

*

The hospital started filling up fast. With the usual diseases, cold- and labour-related injuries as well as a fair share of fakers who were expelled as quickly as possible as the sickness figures rose dangerously near the nine per cent mark. As Edgar's sarcasm had foretold, the resources with which to achieve low sickness figures were very limited and any attempt at prevention as opposed to simply curing was seen by the Soviets as some kind of dissension among the doctors. But prevention was a must, not just to keep the figures below the magic number but to keep men from dying unnecessary and painful deaths.

'How are those fingers today, Paul?' Max's question was almost rhetorical.

Paul's index and middle finger on his left hand which had done him proud for all of his forty-six years so far were now, to Max, the colour of pain. His training, his exposure to the pulsing red soup inside us, meant to Max all the shades of red the body could produce were indications of life and the possibility of repair, but there was something about the majestically rich purple and green Paul's frostbitten fingers were inflated with and the layers of skin like choux pastry which fringed them that was so far from the norm that Max could barely conceal his distaste. And it wasn't an injury caused by another human being, caused by a man-made weapon tearing into flesh and bone, or even a piece of poorly maintained machinery cutting short a labourer's career. It was simply nature telling him in big purple and green neon signs that this part of the world was no place for humans, no place for humans without the appropriate equipment anyway.

'They don't feel too bad today, doctor,' Paul smiled prodding at the puffed up purple digits in a way which made Max wince. 'In fact I just can't feel them at all.'

'Well, we've given it plenty of time to see if we can recover them.'

'I'm not sure massaging them in snow and dunking them in cold water was ever going to help.'

'I know it seems crazy when all you want to do is warm them up, but if you heat severe frostbite up too fast the damage will be even greater and the tissue will never be recoverable. But, having said that, it's been weeks now, hasn't it. I think it's safe to say we've done all we can.'

'So what do we do now?'

'Well, now the non-viable tissue is clearly demarcated I think it's time we removed the fingers before they become gangrenous and it spreads into the hand and the rest of your body.'

'Oh, really?'

Paul was one of Max's favourite patients. Even when you tell him you're about to amputate his fingers he says *oh really* in the way a child does when he's told he can't go to see his favourite cousin due to the weather.

'I'm afraid so.'

'When?'

'Now. I mean, as soon as we've, er, prepared the instruments.' Max glanced out towards the shore then shared an embarrassed look with Horst who was carefully weighing up half gram portions of aspirin from the half pound ration they had been given by the Russians. Aspirin for pain and coal for diarrhoea – that was the level of resources they were working with. They had nothing to use as anaesthetic and certainly no proper instruments for amputating fingers. Hence Max's stalling.

'Where's Bubi?' he hissed over Horst's shoulder.

'Perhaps he got caught.'

'Oh no, surely not,' Max bit at his cuticles imagining the worst for his new little friend and for all his frostbitten patients too.

'The locksmith's isn't that far. It's only on the other side of the...'

'Dr Portner, sir!' A breathless Bubi burst into the building.

'Are you all right? Did you get it?' Max led Bubi to a quiet corner by the fireplace.

'Yes, yes,' the lad said ferreting about in the lining at the back of his jacket where he had concealed the locksmith's kind but contraband donation: a pair of well used pliers.

'Excellent, well done, son. No one questioned you?'

'No, I just told the guards I was running late this morning because I had the shits, and they said, well, you're going to the right place then, aren't you.'

Bubi laughed. Max almost did too, but his mind was already racing ahead in preparation for the surgery he was about to perform. He threw the metal pliers in the fire. That was as much sterilisation as they were going to get here. *The highest standards of clinical cleanliness* the dashing guard had insisted. Don't make me laugh, Max thought. When he had asked for something to clean the hospital floor with he was told to chuck a bucket of water over it, which after a few minutes froze, producing a new clean surface, sure, but it had them all tottering about the place like novice ice skaters.

'Horst, can you assist on this amputation please?'

'Of course. Bubi, do you want to take over here for a while? I've done the aspirin. All you have to do is break up that lump of coal and grind it down into a fine powder.'

'No problem,' Bubi said as eagerly as ever, sitting down in front of the little black meteor on the table and grabbing the small crowbar next to it.

Max retrieved the pliers from the fire. Horst swept up a generous helping of aspirin and they both approached the patient's bed.

'OK, Paul,' Max said as gently and apologetically as possible without losing the necessary confidence you would need to hear in the voice of the person about to hack off two of your fingers with a pair of pliers, 'let's do this, eh?'

'You're the boss,' Paul chuckled weakly offering up his colourful hand whilst his feet wiggled around under the blanket in anticipation of the pain to come.

Bubi put the crowbar to the lump of coke and pushed down. Nothing. It was clearly going to need a little more force than that to break off a piece.

'You can bite down on this if you like,' Horst offered Paul a strip of leather, once part of the left boot of a previous patient, who no longer needed it.

Bubi found a solid looking lump of wood, part of the leg of a broken chair. It would make the perfect hammer.

'We're going to need more light,' Max said stepping carefully across to the fireplace and lighting a small bunch of tapers in it. When he propped them up in an old tin can by Paul's bed things were a little clearer.

'*They* look like state of the art surgical implements!' Paul nodded nervously at the pliers.

'Only the best for you, Paul,' Max smiled.

Bubi stood up to get a better angle on the coal, nearly slipped on the icy floor and sat down again.

'OK. It'll be over before you can count to three,' Max said.

'Good, coz I'll only be able to count that far – on this hand anyway,' Paul chuckled nervously.

'OK, here we go.'

Bubi brought his improvised wooden hammer down on the crowbar—

CRACK

—and a piece sheared off—

CRACK

—and another.

That was the hard part done. Now he could enjoy grinding it up into dust in the pestle and mortar. There was something so satisfying to him about doing this. He saw himself as the coal doctor, transforming something so abrasive and harsh into something so pleasant to the touch, and something that could heal too. Bubi was also becoming expert at blocking out the sound of human suffering.

'I have to go away,' he said when she opened the door.

At first she didn't register, she was too embarrassed about the possibility of him divining that the morsel of dry bread and small jar of Rhenish apple chutney, which sat on the box that doubled as a table, was all she could afford to dine on that night. Embarrassed that she had spent all her ample monthly allowance from her parents on a new dress. But who needed food when you had love? And she had not just bought this dress because it was so very delicious to her eye. She had intended that it would be to Max's too. It was silk rayon with a heart-shaped neckline and a bow on the waist. Short sleeves with a shirred bust and bodice. But the most important feature of all was the colour. It was sapphire blue. When she saw the dress it was the colour that convinced her she had to have it. And that he would love it. She wore it to Mass one day and stared at the blue rose window over the altar throughout, hoping that Max would make the connection too.

She put the lid on the jar and stashed it in the cupboard with the bread, wiping the crumbs from the top of the box saying, 'Just a little snack before I go to feed the rats in the lab. I get hungry watching them eat otherwise.' She let out a rather limp laugh as his words settled on her cerebral cortex like snow. 'What did you say?'

'I have to go away.'

That's what she thought he said.

He had to go away.

It wasn't the first time he had to go away. He had to go away to Innsbruck in the spring term last year. In fact it was her idea. He had to go to get the best teaching in the country for physiological chemistry. She followed him. For the skiing. He'd had to go away to Freiburg when the war began and the University of Bonn decided to close because of it. She decided to go to Freiburg too. Edgar and Horst also in fact. And that was where they met Babyface. But there was something about the way he said he had to go away now which

125

told her that, this time, going with him was not an option. She felt herself shaking, heard herself saying things like:

'You can't. I mean, you don't have to. I've been trying so hard to see things your way. I've been attending the groups with the Reverend Schäufele, you know that. I like his style I really do. His take on theology and philosophy is getting through. It really is.'

'Woh, woh, woh!' Max held up his hands in surrender. 'It's OK, I'm not going away because of you,' he smiled and took both her wringing hands in his.

'Well, where are you going then?'

'To the front. I've been ordered to join the campaign against France.'

'The what?'

'The front...'

'I heard what you said,' she snapped, 'and exactly how is that OK?'

'I thought you'd be pleased,' he said throwing himself in the armchair, 'Me going off to defend the nation against the Bolshevist sympathisers.'

'That's not funny, Max,' she said feeling the need to pull the bread back out of the cupboard and chew on it furiously.

'I'm sorry,' he patted the arm of the chair. She didn't go to him. 'It's not like I have a choice anyway. And I'm not really fighting. I'm going to take care of the wounded. Whatever we believe, you can't deny that there will be hundreds of injured soldiers needing our help.'

The war had been raging around the borders of their country for nearly a year, but, apart from forcing them to choose another university to carry on their studies, it hadn't really touched them. Erika could think of it as an old Nordic battle – like the ones she used to tell her girls in the Youth camps – where other types of Germans, mythical ones, fought and worked on behalf of the ordinary German, like her, like Max, who were busy building the future of their new nation through the sharpening of their intellects, through the acquiring of knowledge. They would be doctors who could heal the sick, the TB and cholera sufferers, deliver babies, set broken bones even. But to patch up soldiers pierced with bullets, shattered by landmines, broken wilfully by other human beings – that wasn't part of her plan. She was writing a dissertation on the biochemical valency of amino acids in loaves of wholemeal bread for God's sake! Every day she had to weigh the six rats in the lab in a shoebox, feed them wholemeal bread treated with amino acids, and then analyse their faeces and urine. Every now and then, a rat would escape and Erika would have to go hunting around the lab for it, but that was about as dramatic as life got for her these days and that was the way she liked it, thank you very much!

'Will it be dangerous?' she asked with all the naivety she could muster.

'Well, I'm sure it will be more dangerous for the poor bastards with guns being shot at by the French. Besides, I'll have big bad Edgar to look after me.'

'He's going to?'

'Yes.'

It was April. She always hated April from then on.

When she saw them in their uniforms she felt a rush of blood through her body which she'd always expected was reserved for her wedding day. The wedding somewhere in the future where the groom was Max and the best man was Edgar. They looked so handsome in their thigh-length boots, their brass buttoned tunics, majestically detailed on the shoulders and collar in gold, and their dramatically lofty peaked caps. But there was something about them that had her stomach churning. And though she knew the mechanics of that was just the production of adrenalin causing a reduction in blood flow to the stomach in order to send more blood to the muscles, she could not immediately identify what it was about them that made her endocrine system produce this flight or fight chemical in the first place.

'Take care,' she ordered Edgar, 'of him and you. And if you come back dead, I'll kill you'.

Fifteen words. Most of which made no sense. And yet they said it all.

None for Max. But she hoped her embrace would be more

eloquent. With her face buried in his neck she drew long and hard on his scent and was angered by the smell of the new uniform adulterating her drug.

She pulled away and realised how her eyes were constantly drawn to the Wehrmachtsadler on their chests and on their caps, the emblem of the National Socialists – her party – the swastika in the claws of the eagle, boastfully showing off its great wingspan. She should have been proud to see them sporting this symbol. But all she could see was the bird of prey circling in the skies before her and Hans, as they sat on Walmendinger Horn, moments before she... he fell to his death.

'Come on, Erika, we have to go,' Max said.

'Come on, Erika, we have to go,' Karl said, 'We're here. We're at Bernried. We made it.'

As she hurried her half-sleeping self off the train Erika clutched the scrap of paper in her hand the way a baby does an adult finger and it was only as she stood outside the station waiting for Karl to find something on which to drag her luggage all the way home, that she unfurled her hand and the paper within which read:

Changed at Böhmisch-Leina, didn't want to wake you. Such a pleasure. Another time I hope.

She cherished the words from Benjamin as she would have done a note from Max, because here she was six months without a word. Was he alive or dead? Was he suffering? Had he been bowled over by someone new, one of those nurses or prostitutes even? She felt an instant connection to Benjamin. They had passed some delightful hours in conversation considering the circumstances. Had she missed out on the chance of knowing him further, if her husband turned cad? Another time, he hoped. How would they ever find each other again to have *another time* in this vast disintegrating country? Max a cad? How ridiculous a thought was that? Of all the men least likely to misbehave, Max was top of the list. Then where the hell was he?

Karl appeared slipping about in the grey slush of old snow pulling a small handcart.

'Quick,' he panted, 'Let's get all your luggage onto here. That way I can pull it home.'

'Where did you get this?' Erika asked as they filled it with her luggage.

'Oh, I, er, found it,' he mumbled before almost shouting out, 'We made it! We made it, Erika! For a moment there I thought we never would. Thank God, eh? Thank God.'

Through her aching muscles and cramping womb she managed to appreciate the wonder that was her father-in-law, who, having spent days travelling to meet her then hauled Erika and her cursed luggage all the way back across the country with his crippled hand purely to keep her and her child safe, give them both the best chance of life in this dying nation. Edgar had once said rather mischievously that if you wanted to see what your spouse would be like in the future you only had to look to their parents. She was doing just that right now and feeling more convinced than ever that she had married the right man.

'Yes, thank God,' she said screwing up the scrap of paper and letting it fall into the sleet which within seconds had blotted the words into an unintelligible smudge the shape of a distant memory.

When word spread that no Ivan would ever set foot in the hospital for fear of catching something, sick prisoners began arriving not just with their ailments but usually with an electronic component or a tool stolen from the cement factory, or spent rifle cartridges stuffed with oats from the stables which were meant to feed the horses. The space beneath the beds in the hospital became storage for all manner of booty and Max had no fear that it would ever be discovered. Here, fifteen feet out in the Barents Sea, a prisoner was king of his own little plot of freedom, albeit a dark, freezing, infected, isolated plot of freedom.

Edgar watched as two of his young patients sat by the fireplace. One, who had sawn through his thigh instead of the tree he was supposed to be cutting down, was bashing some of those cartridges of oats until he'd made a powder from which the chaff could easily be blown away. Left with the grey flowers, he cooked them over the fire in a tin can with some water and salt.

'I'm glad we're not vets,' Edgar said, his stomach growling.

'What makes you say that?' Max was distracted by the Wanzen infesting every bit of degraded skin on the dying captain he leant over, no matter how often he tried to clean the bugs away.

'Well those horses will be in a terrible way before long since the men are stealing all their oats.'

'Ivan doesn't mind,' the private in the bed next to the infested captain piped up. 'When the horses collapse they slaughter them and share the meat around.'

Even the thought of such a precious delicacy as horsemeat could not get Max salivating given his current view of maggot-ridden human flesh. Edgar on the other hand had his eye on some of that gruel being prepared on the fire.

'Hey, Peter, what are you doing?' he said to the patient who was merely observing the cooking.

'Nothing,' Peter said quite accurately.

'What have we told you about warming your feet on the fireplace?'

'Ah, come on, doctor, my toes are like ice,' Peter groaned his eyes fixed on the soon to be ready porridge.

'Actually your toes are on fire,' Edgar sighed rather annoyed that he would now have to wait for a taste of that porridge since for the next few minutes he would be dealing with Peter's toes again, so necrotic from the frostbite that he could not even feel the flames take hold.

'Shit!' Peter seemed to forget about porridge for a moment. 'Do something!'

'I will do something, I'll chuck you out of this hospital if you keep refusing to listen to medical advice.' Edgar hurried as fast as he could on that rink of a floor, and brought a bowl of fresh snow for Peter to dunk his smouldering purple toes into, his cement bag socks having fallen away in cinders already. 'Good job there's no shortage of this stuff round here,' Edgar pouted. 'Frostbite or burns the prescription is the same anyway: snow.'

A howl outside on the shore had everyone in the hospital thinking there were wolves attacking until Max, having peered out into the perennial gloom, called over to his colleague, 'Ed, it seems we have a new arrival.'

The two doctors ran out across the bridge to where the Russian guards had dumped the prisoner who was writhing in the gravel, his trousers around his ankles and his legs and shirt bathed in blood so bright red it seemed to be the only colour in this otherwise monochrome world.

'Can you tell us your name?'

'Dieter,' the man cried, 'my name is Dieter and you have to help me, *please*'.

'What happened, Dieter? Where is all this blood from?'

'OW, it hurts so mu-OW, you have to help m-OW. You have to save it.'

As Bubi sprinted out of the hospital with a stretcher the medics examined the exposed legs and eventually, despite the lack of lighting, focused on the source of Dieter's haemorrhaging.

With a mixture of horror, wonder and a deeply suppressed urge to laugh Edgar declared, 'His penis has exploded.'

After a roof-raising amount of howling, a huge amount of wound packing and the application of a few vascular clamps made from parts of a wire fence by an ex-engineer from Heidelberg, who slept in the bunk next to Max, Dieter was a lot calmer.

'So how did this happen?' Max asked, trying hard not to be entertained by the sheer novelty of the situation. After all, this was something he had never encountered before and made a stark contrast to the endless stream of typhoid, yellow fever, frostbite and lacerations.

'I work at the factory that makes cement bags.'

Max made a grateful sound – after all, most men nowadays had an extra layer of clothing made from some of those stolen cement bags.

'And we discovered recently that the Russian electricians that fix the machines when they break down get paid a good overtime rate. The more the machines break down, the more overtime they have to do, the happier they are. So we struck a deal with them. We would make the machines fail and they would give us some bread in return for all that overtime.'

'Some bread,' Max mused looking at Dieter's lips cracked and swollen with scurvy. You need more than bread. We all do, he thought. 'And how do you make the machines fail, short of ripping out wires which I guess the guards would soon get wise to?'

'Exactly. That was too obvious. So that's where my secret weapon came in. See, I have this weird ability to piss quite a distance, so I could stand out of sight and piss into the machine causing it to short circuit.'

'Oh.'

'Yeah. It was all going so well for weeks. And then this afternoon – boom – it kind of backfired.'

'So I see,' Max chewed at his own vitamin deficient lips for a moment then called out, 'Peter, when you were working in the woods...'

'Before he mistook his thigh for a tree trunk, you mean,' Edgar couldn't resist.

'Thank you!' Peter, toes no longer aflame, stuck out his tongue at Edgar and then gave Max his full attention, 'Yes, Dr Portner?'

Dr Portner continued, 'You must be surrounded by conifers, are you not?'

'Of course.'

'Pine needles everywhere then?'

'Absolutely.'

'And do you see any berries growing?'

'Those little red ones.'

'Cranberries?'

'I think so.'

On his way back to the barracks that night Max stopped at the kitchens to sweet talk the cooks into letting him have a couple of the empty barrels that had contained salted fish. Like the kitchen staff in Hunsfeld, they were more than happy to have the doctors keeping a special eye on their health, so Max arrived back at the barracks with two barrels which he set up by the door, announcing to all the men that whenever they worked in the forest they were now obliged to bring back a pocket full of pine needles, dumping them in one barrel where they would infuse with water, and a pocket full of cranberries, dumping them in the other. Then before leaving the barracks every morning each man was to take a drink of the pine needle water and munch on a handful of berries thereby preventing them all from getting sick with scurvy.

'And keeping our sickness figures down, you genius.' Edgar playfully prodded Max from his bunk below. 'How did you even know pine needles were a good source of vitamin C?'

'I don't know, I seem to remember reading something about it in a book I picked up in the monastery back in Breslau,' Max said to the damp wooden roof above him where scenes of crashing planes, being bombed, treating sexually transmitted diseases to prostitutes in convents and retrieving dismembered bodies from candlelit airfields flickered among the shadows like a perverse kind of idyll compared to his current reality. He turned his head on the pillow to the left and then the right. Like being in the house of mirrors at Freiburg funfair, his own image repeated hundreds of times stretched off into the distance both ways, hundreds of "sleeping" men whose sleep could only ever be described in inverted commas up here in the draughty upper bunks. He took a handful of earth from his own little collection and stuffed it into some of the particularly offensive gaps between the logs in the wall. He knew the wind or the rain would have washed his makeshift mortar away by the morning, but that didn't stop him reapplying it every night. For now at least.

'Hey, Dr Portner.' It was Paul, his head and shoulders just rising above the edge of the bunk. In the half-light from the two fireplaces at each end of the hut, Paul's clavicles resembled wire coat hangers on which someone had hung an old skin suit.

'Hello, Paul, how's the hand doing?'

Paul held the nicely healing stumps on his left hand up for inspection. 'I guess my chances of a glittering career as a concert pianist are somewhat reduced now, but otherwise everything's fine,' he grinned. 'In fact,' he brought his face close to Max and whispered, 'everything's more than fine. I was just coming to say thanks for saving my life and goodbye'.

'Goodbye?'

'Yes. I'm being released tomorrow.'

'Released?'

'Yes. Deggendorf here I come!'

'But how?' Max tried to sound happy for Paul and suffocate the rising envy by letting his face sink into his grimy emaciated pillow as they talked.

'Well, I've been here a long time now. You know I was here way before you lot arrived. And in the end I realised if you start making all the right pro-communist sounds for long enough they start to believe you, think you're converted. So I just wanted to say thanks for looking after me so well and if I can return the favour in any way, ever, you just let me know, OK?'

'OK,' Max whispered, sitting himself up at last so he could shake Paul's hand, the intact one, vigorously to demonstrate the goodwill he couldn't articulate in words right then.

Max watched Paul saunter back to his bunk – it was the relaxed walk of one who knows his awful circumstances are about to be reversed for ever, which makes the awful something almost to be savoured for once. Max grabbed a little more dirt from his stash and punched it into a taunting gap in the wall. Would he still have the energy to do this every night if he had been here as long as Paul, he wondered? Would he still have the resourcefulness and desire to help his patients after so long, after losing so many to such usually curable ailments? Paul was free to go. That should have given him hope, but it just made him conscious of how long he had been away from home.

Tick tick tick tick.

He searched among the shadows in the roof for images of Erika. He saw slender eyebrows and a petite hourglass figure and realised he was seeing parts of Jenny. The last female he had seen, the most recent in his memory. He had learnt so much about the body and the brain, its millions of neurological pathways and synaptic connections, but only now was he able to offer a hypothesis from his own experience that there may only be a limited space for memories, and that older memories were ousted by the newer ones, whether we wanted them to be or not. He was losing the feeling of her fingers woven with his beneath the blanket. He was losing the smell of her hair on the pillow. He was losing the shape of her neck which that sapphire blue dress had accentuated so well. He could blink images of her onto the backs of his eyelids like old photos, but he was losing the essence of her and he was furious. After everything they had gone through to cement their bond. After everything she had gone through to shift her faith. It had been more than a year since he had seen her. He clawed at the hole in his mattress and fished out the part of her letter he had kept from the Russians on the train the day Tim had been killed. He mouthed her phrases and diction; it helped him hear her voice again. Around the disembodied voice he tried to build her body, but instead he saw a black-skinned woman. A Madonna in fact. In a stained, warped picture. And found himself feeling under his blanket into his trouser pocket where there was nothing but that bloody cheap watch from Freiburg market.

Tick tick tick tick.

'Are you all right up there, buddy?' Edgar's voice sounded concerned, but slightly irritated too by his friend's unconscious fidgeting.

'Yes. Fine. Sorry. Edgar?'

'Ye-es,' he sung with barely concealed impatience.

'Did you bring any paperwork back from the hospital?'

'Can't say I did, no. I know reading material is severely limited round here but I haven't sunk so low as to use our medication stats for bedtime reading. Yet.'

So Max rooted deeper into his mattress and found a stub of a pencil and the letter from Tim's erstwhile lover. There wasn't much of it that wasn't charred or covered in words, except for the top of the yellow page where the beastly woman had decided it would improve the presentation of her adulterous words if she left a nice header space. Good girl! Good girl, Max chewed the appellation with his tongue as he concentrated on folding the blank area, scoring it well with a black-rimmed fingernail, then, with all the care and precision of a bomb disposal expert, tearing it off.

He found Paul awake on his bunk, but not awake in the way everyone else was – exhausted but prevented from sleep by the malicious squall – no, Paul was awake like a child is awake on Christmas Eve.

'Paul?'

'Dr Portner.'

'I have a favour to ask.'

'Like I said, Doctor, I owe you one.'

The war was over. Germany had surrendered yesterday. Erika was a married woman with a baby on the way. A Catholic convert who had relished her wedding at Freiburg cathedral and since seen the devastation her erstwhile party had brought to her country. Things could only get better now, surely, even under the occupation of the Allies. Perhaps they would help rebuild the country they had bombed to smithereens. Perhaps food would not be so hard to come by. The daily ration of fifty grams of bread, one potato, fifty grams of fat and one hundred grams of meat or sausage was getting rather tiresome, not to mention damned unhealthy she thought, as she watched her own skinny hand pull back the lace curtain at the sound of footsteps marching towards the apartment – Karl and Martha's apartment where she had lived for the past couple of months, where, despite the nurturing muliebrity of Martha, Karl still fluttered about her, as he had done on that indelible train journey from Neurode, convinced that she would give birth unsupported on the living room rug any second.

He had a point. The midwife from the neighbouring village, whom she had engaged for her birth, had fled when prisoners released from Dachau had pillaged the area. But Erika had a plan. She had heard that since the bombings in Munich, the University Orthopaedic Clinic had been relocated to Bernried Castle and she was going there today to talk to the doctors about letting her give birth there.

The frilly edge of the curtain between her fingers was a kind of braille relating stories of that wedding day: the long bridal gown her friend had smuggled out of her parents' shoe shop where a sign over the front declared *EXCHANGE A BRIDAL GOWN FOR SHOES!* Erika had nothing to exchange for the shoes, but her friend had pilfered a pair of white ones for her too and the outfit was complete. She was almost saddle sore after riding about the fields on her bicycle all afternoon the day before the ceremony, picking flowers to decorate the altar. But not as sore as she was after the wedding night, Erika

137

snickered to herself, as she recalled the uncorked passion of that night with Max, the percussion of the headboard against the wall of their hotel room and the sphincter-mouthed indignation of the middle aged woman at breakfast the next morning which was a sure sign to the young lovers that she had had the pleasure of reserving the room next to theirs. The hotel room was paid for by Erika's parents.

'No daughter of mine is going to spend her wedding night in student digs,' her father had announced deliberately in front of Max's parents, flexing his factory owner's financial muscles as they met for the first time at the Polterabend, the wedding-eve party. 'I'll arrange a room for you at the Zähringer Hof,' he said vaingloriously, his eyes fixed as he did on Erika so that she wasn't sure for a moment whether the room in question was meant for her new husband too.

'Well, it's good to see at least someone is prospering when the rest of the country is going to pot,' Karl said with no intention of malice and just in case it could possibly be received that way he punctuated the statement with a little laugh.

'Well, I don't suppose the country would be going to *pot* if all of its men did their duty and fought in this war,' Erika's father said with *every* intention of malice and just in case it could possibly be received any other way he punctuated the statement with a little laugh. 'I'll be going back to front as soon as we're done here.'

Done here! Erika despised the way he made her wedding, the most special day of her life, sound like an irritating bit of business that had to be endured before he went back to the really important business of killing in the name of the Führer. But then business, any business had always come before her, she thought shifting her foot with the scar on the sole from the time she ran barefoot from her deadening solitude in the villa.

'Captain of the Border Guard,' he said puffing up his chest as if on parade. 'I assume we're all in favour of defending our country against invasion by the Russians?'

'Invasion? Or retaliation?' Karl mumbled rubbing his wrist.

His counterpart might have chosen to ignore that or perhaps he didn't even hear it under the noise of his own convictions. 'I fought at the Battle of the Somme, you know,' he forged on. 'Wounded terribly.' He hitched up a trouser leg revealing an impressive scar.

'Oh dear,' Erika's mother groaned and took Martha by the arm. 'If you boys are going to start comparing the size of your... scars, then us girls will leave you to it.' And she grabbed her daughter too and went off to graze at the buffet they had miraculously conjured from their rations.

Erika looked back sympathetically as Max wobbled, poised to join her as soon as courtesy dictated he could.

'I fought in the Great War,' she heard her father bark and saw Karl's eye twitch in response to that horror's dubious epithet, 'and my greatest wish, when this present war came upon us was that we older generations would fight, and not our sons,' he said putting a hand on Max's shoulder, which stunned Erika not simply because it was so warmly done, but because it was almost the first time he had acknowledged his son-in-law all evening, 'so that they could have a better future'.

Karl glared at the hand on his son's shoulder as if it was riddled with leprosy.

Given the state of the transport system and the constant threat of air raids they couldn't have expected many more family members to make it to Freiburg, but Erika was more than happy just to have Edgar, Babyface, Horst and other college friends present to celebrate with and dilute the tensions her parents inevitably brought with them.

And I want to create a family of my own? She wondered, I've spent all my childhood trying to run away from family and here I am about to make another one. I've spent all my childhood watching my parents live out the kind of resignation they call marriage and here I am about to get married too. Am I mentally handicapped? She laughed as she gulped on the champagne, provided by her father, of course.

As tradition had it at the Polterabend everyone had brought some pieces of old crockery to smash at the end of the evening.

'I love this part,' Edgar's eyes had sparkled as he raised a plate and hurled it to the ground with all the force his maverick being could muster.

Erika could have sworn she saw Max flinch as the sound of the first item smashing resounded around the room. She went over to him and held his hand as the crashing and cracking crescendoed. It was true. With every item exploding on the floor a little pulse of terror was transmitted from his hand to hers. She squeezed his hand to smother the implication and looked into his face. He smiled broadly, raised a cup above his head and threw it at the floor with the kind of abandon he wanted her to see.

Babyface and Horst seemed to enjoy the licensed anarchy just as much as Edgar, whilst Martha and Helene threw their pieces with rather less vigour, almost reluctantly in fact and looked mournfully out over the floor of broken ceramics – such a waste of perfectly good crockery! Erika could see them itching to get the brooms and tidy up the porcelain snowdrift they had created by their destruction. But it was not their job. The entire point of all that mess was that the bride and groom were left to clear it all up as a symbol of their commitment to working together through the trials of life and Erika and Max grabbed the brooms with gusto.

'Look at him go,' Edgar heckled. 'He's going to be a very good boy around the house, isn't he?'

Max and Erika chuckled at Edgar's performance as required, but shared a clandestine grin knowing there was more to this ritual than housekeeping as far they were concerned and the jingle the shards made as they swept them across the floor was music to their ears.

'In my day,' Erika's father proclaimed, 'the groom had to clear this lot up all by himself, you know, to show his commitment to take on domestic duties in the marital home.'

'No, dear,' Helene said at a volume fuelled by plenty of champagne and Nussaschnapps, 'that was just what we all told you at our wedding. Shame it didn't have any effect in the long term, eh?'

Erika watched with a mixture of dread and delight as her father's florid face somehow became even redder and Karl guffawed.

'Max!' Martha's admonishing tone had both Max and his papa turning to her obediently, but Max junior quickly realised it was his father who was in trouble for laughing as Martha only ever used

Karl's actual first name when she was reprimanding him. And if he was particularly for the high jump she would use his full title: *Max Karl Portner!*

Erika twisted the lace curtain around her finger. There were two army officers heading towards the door. She panicked briefly. Before she realised they were American officers. Before she realised they weren't German ones coming to inform her of her brave husband's death perhaps, as he served his country on the Eastern Front. Nevertheless she twisted the curtain tighter, just as she had twisted the train of her wedding dress around her finger fearfully as Karl had staggered towards them outside the cathedral, his suit smeared with blood, his grazed hands clutching a dead goose.

'Papa, what on earth has happened?' Max ran to meet him, checking him over as Karl used to do to Max when he was a little boy returned home crying after some misadventure playing on the farm.

'I called up a friend who lives nearby. Franz, remember?' he appealed to his wife who had already deduced quicker than her doctor son, merely by his demeanour, that it was not Karl's blood on his suit, or even the goose's for that matter. 'He took me out on his motorcycle. We scoured the countryside for a farmer that would give us a good price on a goose. I bought it for your wedding breakfast. No son of mine is going to have a wedding breakfast without some quality meat on the table,' his voice quivered as he tried in vain to echo the braggadocio in Gunther's declaration last night concerning the hotel room.

'So what about this blood?' Max asked having now come more scientifically to the same conclusion as his mother.

'I'm not sure where we had driven to. Closer to enemy lines than I could have imagined I suppose. Or perhaps it was one of our own soldiers thinking we were the enemy.'

Erika's father sniffed loudly at the absurd notion of one of his comrades making such a mistake.

'What? What happened?'

'There was gunfire. I was riding pillion holding on to the goose and Franz was driving. He got hit. Lost control of the bike. We both came off. But he died from the gunshot wounds.'

'Where's Franz now? Are you sure he's dead?' Max demanded and Erika could see him instinctively gearing up to go and try to save Franz's life wherever he was. She felt the same medic's urge tightening the muscles in her white shoed feet, but the urge to have nothing spoil her wedding day was even greater and her eyes bore into the back of Max's head willing him to turn around and see her on the steps of the cathedral; the cathedral that she could barely stomach sitting in not so many months ago; the house of the faith she had sedulously studied and, with archaeological dedication, unearthed the relevance of to her own life, in order that she could share that life completely with him. And cathedral or no cathedral, Catholic wedding or not, she couldn't help but be relieved, as ashamed as she was to be, when Karl answered:

'He's dead all right. Some people rushed over from the nearby farm. They knew him. Better than I did. They brought me back to town and took the body on to his wife. Oh, Martha what a terrible thing for her to endure. We must go and pay our respects.'

'We all will. Later.' Martha rubbed pointlessly at the stains on his suit, smoothed his lapels and straightened his tie. In those few adoring, protective gestures and the unspoken end to her sentence *but right now we have your son's wedding to attend*, Erika knew she would be more than happy if she and Max ended up like Karl and Martha.

She opened the door to the American officers, both with riding crops in their hands. One yapped in rubbish German:

'Go from this apartment immediately. If you do not have all things out in the few hours next, you will not be able to come for them and they will be confiscated.'

That's all he said, gripping the riding crop as if he would not hesitate to use it on her should she be an uncooperative little filly. She was speechless, but she opened the door fully now to let them see her belly in the hope that the sight of her predicament may soften them, change their minds even.

They turned and left abruptly and a few hours later she sat on the doorstep with her shell-shocked in-laws and boxes full of their possessions, Karl's wrist almost visibly throbbing at the thought of more odysseys playing the porter.

'Doctor! Doctor!' Max barely had a chance to put down his bag when he arrived at the hospital before the private called him over with such urgency Max assumed the pain in his kidneys had returned.

'Are you OK, Manfred?'

'No, the captain just died. Look!'

The soldier was right. It was easy to tell when someone even as comatose as the captain had finally given up the ghost because all the bugs were finally abandoning his body. But now, on the hunt for fresh, living meat to feed on they were pullulating across the floor towards Manfred's bed.

'Do something!'

Just when the putrid caravan of Wanzen were halfway on their exodus across the gulf of rimy floor between their old home and their next terrified intended conquest, fire rained down from the heavens and incinerated every last one of them.

'Thanks, Doctor,' Manfred exhaled examining the carnage on the floor for any signs of survivors. But the trowel full of white hot embers Max had scooped from the fireplace had been effective. He only wished he could have been as effective when the captain was alive.

The captain was their first fatality so Max went back out to the gate where he had been counted through only minutes before that morning by Sergeant Volkov, the handsome guard who was, to ask where they were to bury the dead.

'Wherever you like,' he smiled with a laissez faire that Max was supposed to see straight through and did.

With more faux confederacy Volkov ducked into the small hut by the gate and brought out a shovel. 'Just make sure it's nowhere near the camp.' He held out the shovel to Max who felt like he was stepping into a snare by taking it, but took it nonetheless, reasoning that Volkov's amusement may simply lay in the fact that he was requiring Max to dig the graves himself.

Max enlisted Bubi's help and the two of them went up on the hill between the shore and the forest and began digging. Or rather they began jarring their own skeletons by ramming the shovel into the solid earth for a few futile moments before trying another piece of unyielding ground, and another, and another. Volkov loitered at a distance behind them, ostensibly to make sure the prisoners didn't escape, but they all knew it was for no such reason but for his own entertainment. Max looked over his aching shoulder to see Volkov's smooth face lacerated by a grin.

'Anywhere you like, Doctor.'

'The ground's too frozen,' Bubi called out, as exasperated as his boss, but a little less comprehending of the dynamics at work.

'OK,' Max put a tranquilising hand on Bubi's sinewy arm. 'OK,' he called out to Volkov, 'we can't bury the dead in the earth. I hope you enjoyed that little…'

'No, *you* cannot bury the dead in the earth, Doctor. Not *we*. Do not tar me with the same brush. *You* cannot bury the dead. It seems God is denying your kind a sanctified burial. But then what would Nazis want with such a ritual anyway? You lot eschew religion, isn't that right? Hitler is your God, no? No? Only, the last I heard Hitler was being blown to pieces as he cowered in a bunker somewhere like a rat underground. So how does that work? Your God is not very omnipotent, not very omniscient. He's not even immortal.'

'I'm not a Nazi,' Max's words were drowned out both by the sound of the waves slapping the shore and by Volkov cackling, but he didn't feel it was worth raising his voice to be heard. He knew this wasn't a debate, just a ridiculing.

'You dump the corpses at the bottom of the hill. Altogether in a pile. When we have enough human popsicles they'll be dragged up here for the foxes to feast on,' he marched over to them, snatched the shovel from Bubi and stomped down the hill back to the shelter of the gatehouse.

The captain was left at the bottom of the hill as ordered. But he wasn't alone for long. By the end of the week he had eighteen companions all of whom froze together like fish in a Baltic trawler's hull. Then rope was lashed about them and a horse that was so malnourished it was almost a corpse itself staggered up the hill dragging the bodies eventually to the top.

Edgar and Horst stood by the window that night, hugging a tin can each of Peter's gruel and looking up towards the hill. It was too dark to see anything, but the horrific screams of the foxes had the two doctors imagining the corpses had come back to life just in time to feel the vermin teeth ripping into their frosty flesh. Horst looked over his shoulder to see Max pouring over a patient's Bible.

'Should we say a prayer or something?' Horst's weak offer fell on the slippery floor and wriggled off under the nearest bed.

'What's the point anymore? If God has put us in this shit then praying is useless.'

Edgar's response hooked Max's ears and reeled him out of the warm morphinic waters of scripture. To Horst, Max hadn't budged, his head still deep in the Bible, but in fact Max was now spiritually thrashing and slapping himself around on the cold floor of doubt where Edgar's shocking words had just landed him. Edgar the church organist, the devout Catholic. Yes, he was cynical about most things, had indulged in a more licentious way of life than most, must have raised many a priest's eyebrows in the shadows of the confession box, but despite all this, or perhaps because of all this, Edgar always came back to his faith at the end of the day. But now here, where the days had no discernible end or beginning, if Edgar had decided prayer was pointless, Max was going to need a hitching post of incredible stability to cling to as the tide pulled at his feet and the wind howled through his head.

As Max was counted through the gate at the end of his shift he was met by Volkov, whose face was contorted in a confusion of emotions comparable with his own. But whereas those which disfigured Max's were qualm and conviction, Volkov's usual mask of spite sat awkwardly now over an expression that Max thought might be envy. But since Max could not imagine for a second how this could be, he blamed the eternal dusk on his misinterpretation of his captor's expression.

'After rollcall in the morning you will walk to Pechenga.'

Pechenga? That was the nearest town to Gegesha and Max had heard it was over six kilometres away. There was certainly no envy apparent as Volkov informed him of this.

'Some of our officers reside there and they and their families require medical attention. It is a long walk. You will need this.'

Now that apparent envy was crawling all over his face again, Max was sure of it this time, as Volkov thrust the long fur coat, which had been draped over his arm, at the doctor and followed it with a Red Cross armband.

'Where do I report to when I arrive in town?' Max asked, feeling at once weak under the enormous weight of this coat in his arms and elated at the sensation of the soft pelt his fingers sunk into, with all the promise of warmth for his entire body the garment held.

'The guards that accompany you will direct you where to go,' Volkov's eyes poked around in Max's face for disappointment. 'What did you think, we were going to let you walk all that way alone?'

That night Max slept better than he had in months wrapped in his new fur coat. Better in the sense that, for an hour or two at a time, he slept undisturbed by the draughts and the damp, whelmed in a warmth he had not experienced for so long it felt like the first time. But at intervals he awoke with such a violent start, as guilt and fear took turns to disturb him. Fear that another prisoner would be driven to murder him for a touch of that warm fur, or guilt that Edgar or Horst would come to bed when their shifts ended and notice him snoring contentedly like some hibernating bear. Assuming Ivan didn't spitefully take back the coat between visits to town, Max vowed right then, as his trapped body heat anesthetised him again, that he would take turns with them each night to have the coat.

After rollcall in the morning he set off on his six kilometre hike, a guard walking in front and one behind, as Volkov had told him, but unexpectedly he had a companion on his travels, a fellow prisoner and a Franciscan monk called Christoph.

'I have been given the task of walking into town every morning to fetch the mail,' Christoph simpered.

'Every morning?' Max looked at the monk, his robes covered in nothing but a layer of cement bag garments and thought about offering up his fur coat, but there was something about Christoph's manner that told him he almost revelled in this painful situation, as if it was some kind of self-flagellation. Besides, there had to be a reason why the Soviets thought he didn't deserve a fur coat and Max didn't want to rouse the wrath of the guards by undermining it.

'Yes, the Russians think it upsets me, but in many ways I have to say I prefer it to the heavy toil most prisoners have to undertake. This walk is actually very peaceful when the guards are not abusing me. It's a great time for meditation.'

Max took this as a hint to shut up and did a little meditating of his own as they walked on for a while without a sound but the crunching of four pairs of boots on the rough road. Either side of them was nothing but fields as far as the eye could see but he only knew this because the light from the moon lit them up like vast lakes as it reflected off the snow that lay there.

Volkov had been so delighted to tell Max that he would not be making this journey unaccompanied by guards, but he wondered, even if he had been alone, would he be tempted to run away over those fields? Would he even survive out there for as many weeks as it would take to get back home? Could he leave Horst and Edgar back there in Gegesha? He had this terrible realisation, as he contemplated the silver countryside, that after so long in captivity the place he was drawn back to at the end of each day, the place we usually call home, was now for Max a Russian prison camp on the shores of the Barents Sea.

The town was more several buildings dropped either side of the road than the exciting electrically lit urban sprawl Max had conjured for himself around the word.

'Well, this is my stop,' Christoph said brightly as they arrived at a wooden building serving as post office, general store and community hub.

'It was nice to meet you,' Max said holding out his hand for Christoph to shake.

But the monk didn't get a chance to take it.

'Move it!' one of the guards barked, kicking Christoph in the buttocks with a force that propelled him towards the store. 'You'd do well not to associate with traitors like that, Doctor,' the guard continued in Russian, aware of the doctor's linguistic skills.

'Traitors?'

'Yeah,' the guard beckoned Max on as his comrade stood guard outside the post office into which Christoph had scurried, 'He gave himself up to us at the first sign of war just so he could avoid the fighting. He is a traitor to your country. A disgrace to you and his church.'

Max nodded to appease the guard, but was in no way in agreement that avoiding this war was something his God would have disapproved of. He thought of his brave father putting a bullet through his own wrist – all those carpals and metacarpals, tendons and muscles that met there in biological and mechanical harmony splintering apart like factions of the same political party, severing each other, breaking down the powerful whole, disabling. A gust of freezing wind rushed across the fields and penetrated his fur coat carrying images of his father helping Erika through overcrowded stations. He hated the way the guard's denigration of Christoph seemed to simultaneously steep Max in honour and nationalism. He was here to help people, he wanted to scream down the silent street, he wasn't there as a soldier, he never was. He was no more a fighter than the monk.

'Here's your first stop. A Russian officer lives here with his wife. He's concerned she has diphtheria or something.'

The guard clomped up to the porch and knocked on the door of the little house. The obelisk of an officer answered immediately peering past the guard at Max.

'Are you the medic?' he growled.

'Yes, Colonel…?' Max said quickly observing the man's epaulettes.

'Utkin,' the Colonel informed him impatiently. 'Come in, come in,' he said indicating Max only.

Max left the guard on the inhospitable porch and followed Colonel Utkin into the living room, where a roaring fire had him quickly removing his coat. But the Colonel hurried on through to a bedroom at the back of the single storey home, where another fireplace was alight and candles burned by the bedside of a woman in her late thirties, Max guessed, though her illness, whatever it was, the unflattering light and the less than comfortable conditions could have put a few years on her.

Max set his bag down by the bed and began to examine the woman's neck.

'Could you open your mouth for me, Mrs Utkin, please?'

The woman did as she was asked.

'How long have you felt ill, madam?'

'It's been a couple of weeks now,' the Colonel answered for her. 'I think it's diphtheria. Is it diphtheria? Have one of my men brought some bloody disease into my house from those stinking prisoners?'

Max didn't know whether to be offended at the epithet or flattered that the Colonel didn't seem to tar him with the same brush as he used for the rest of the POWs, so he let the comment wash over him and concentrated instead on the symptoms of his patient.

'Her glands are swollen, but there is certainly no bull neck associated with diphtheria. No grey pseudo-membrane over the tonsils. Mrs Utkin, I think what you have is just a very sore throat and a touch of the flu.'

'Are you sure?' The Colonel sounded almost disappointed.

Max feared the officer might doubt his competency as a doctor so he made sure to deliver his prescription with utter conviction and confidence. 'I am sure, yes, sir. So all you need to do is...' He looked into his bag at a small tin of pulverised aspirin and thought of Horst diligently measuring out the hospital's meagre ration into doses small enough to make it last for all their 'stinking' patients. He closed the bag. 'All you need to do is warm up some salty water and get your wife to gargle with it three times a day.'

'And that will cure her?'

'I have no doubt it will. Do you have access to any aspirin?'

'They sell it at the post office.'

'Good.' Max maintained his composure though the thought of shelves full of painkillers in the little shop where Christoph was being handed the mail right now stung Max to his core. 'A couple of tablets every day will help with the swelling and the temperature too. I guarantee she'll be as good as new in a matter of days.'

'Really? You're sure?'

As sure as I can be with the terrible bloody resources you supply me with. He had to hold the words back beneath his vocal chords with such force he nearly developed a bull neck himself.

'Absolutely,' he smiled.

Utkin studied the doctor's face as he had countless prisoners he had tortured under interrogation. Then, convinced the doctor was telling the truth, his heretofore stony expression erupted with a volcanic joy. 'Well, that is very good, very good news. How can I ever thank you, Doc—? I know, I know.' He hurried out to the living room and the inelegant sound of things sliding around wooden shelves and cupboard doors being slammed accompanied perfectly the awkward tableaux of Max politely smiling at Mrs Utkin in bed and Mrs Utkin clutching at the top of her blanket wishing she could be left in peace.

'Here you go, doctor, take these as a token of my appreciation,' the Colonel said shoving a loaf of bread, a tin of pork and a bottle of vodka into Max's shocked grasp.

'Oh no really, that's not necessary.' Max's words were at total odds with the firm grip he now had on the treasures. A whole loaf of bread! Meat! And this vodka would make an excellent disinfectant at the hospital.

'Come!' the Colonel ushered Max back into the living room. 'We'll have a shot of that vodka now to celebrate the wife's recovery.'

'Oh no,' Max said putting his coat on and trying to find pockets big enough for each of his gifts, 'I really have to get on. I believe there are other patients for me to see today and...'

'Sit down,' Utkin barked with more slamming of cupboard doors as he located two small glasses before sitting too. 'Take off the coat and sit down.'

Max clutched his latent bottle of disinfectant but watched as the Colonel sat on the edge of his chair as if ready to spring up at any moment and throttle Max if he didn't join him in a drink.

'Well, I suppose, a swift one cannot hurt,' Max said slipping his coat off and sitting opposite Utkin, who snatched the bottle and began to pour.

'That's right it can't,' he said. '*Na zdorovie!*' though he threw the alcohol into himself in a way which made Max think he was trying to make it hurt. 'Ah, this is my medicine, doctor. Without it I would have never survived in this hellhole. I'll never forget,' he said pouring himself another shot, 'Sunday June 22nd 1941. I leaned out of my comfortable bed and turned the radio on as I always did. But the usual physical exercise program was not on. Instead it was incessant military march music. So you knew something was up, you know what I mean?'

Max nodded though he wasn't sure exactly where this was going.

'Then my papa came up and asked me to go for a beer with him and my little brother Alex. It was hot that morning so we sat outside the café. They had the radio on there too. I couldn't escape that bloody music until it was interrupted by Foreign Minister Molotov: "Citizens," he announced, "Fascist Germany has attacked us." And what did I do? I tried to get another round of beers in, tried to make that morning with my dad and my brother last as long as possible, because somehow I knew then that I would never see them again. We were all called up to the front the next day and both of them were dead by '42. To family!' Utkin raised his glass.

'To family!' Max toasted enthusiastically, but merely sipped at his drink.

The Colonel was having none of that. So shot after shot they fired into the back of their throats and soon Max stopped worrying about his dwindling supply of disinfectant and instead began luxuriating in the heat inside him and out. He began to relax into the chair, even stretch out his legs in front of him. The climate and the atmosphere in Gegesha had you in a permanent state of contraction. Max only realised this as he unfurled himself before the fire like a crocus before the spring sun – a crocus watered by rains of booze. He soon stopped worrying about getting in trouble for not seeing the other sick relatives of Russian officers. After all, he was here with Colonel Utkin. He was only following orders. Besides it was still early. Ridiculously early to be drinking, especially for someone who hadn't had a drink in so many months, but, yes, yes, that's it, it was early, so after this little drink he would still have time to see the other patients before walking home... walking back to the camp, he meant to say. It was a shame Horst and Edgar weren't here. They could have all enjoyed a drink together. God knows they deserved one. And this Utkin, he wasn't so bad. For a Russian. And his wife. She seemed... well, he was sure she would be very nice if she didn't feel so awful. But she'd be right as rain after a few gargles of salt water. My, what a fuss! It's not like her fingers were black with frostbite, or she had festering wounds awash with maggots. Not like her penis had exploded. Max, giggled to himself – not that she had a penis of course. At least he didn't think so, but if she did it would be an interesting case he could write up for the medical journals. Anyway, shouldn't he be encouraging Utkin to get some salty water warmed up for her to gargle? Perhaps he should have just prescribed this vodka instead for her to gargle. If there were any malignant bacteria in the back of his own throat they could not have survived the burning inundation he had subjected them to over the last few minutes, hour, whatever...

The next thing Max knew he was one of those bacteria being slapped with liquid, but his was not a fiery soaking. He was gasping and convulsing as bucket after bucket of cold water was thrown on him by the two guards where they had dumped him outside the barracks after bringing him all the way back unconscious from town.

'That should sober you up,' one of the guards snorted.

'OK, OK, that's enough!'

Max could barely see but he was relieved to hear the unmistakably fearless voice of his ally Edgar.

'The water is starting to freeze on his skin. We have to get him inside otherwise he'll die.'

He felt himself lifted by friendly, if not a little miffed, hands. He felt his clothes being stripped from him and the scratchy surface of his mattress beneath his trembling bones. He tried to speak, but his mouth was glued shut with an adhesive that tasted of sand. He felt blankets being piled on top of him. He only owned one so he gathered these were the charitable offerings from his friends' beds. He desperately wanted a drink of water, but as he tried to articulate this his bunk began spinning and it was all he could do not to be sick on this improbable and terrible fairground ride. On the banks of the Rhine he had once seen a soldier's eye protruding from his face because of the bullet which had entered his temple and pushed it out. Finally he knew what that felt like. But for Max, it felt like there were two zeppelin-like bullets pushing both of his eyes out of his skull and no death to save him from the pain.

It was all Erika could do to stop Karl escorting her to the makeshift hospital at Bernried Castle, but when she pointed out to him how Martha needed him more than she did right now, how the best thing he could do for all of them was find them a new home as soon as possible, and how it really was a very short journey before she would be surrounded by health professionals whose nerves would be a lot less 'frayed' by the presence of a woman due to go into labour at any time, he eventually capitulated.

'But this is a hospital for wounded soldiers, Frau Portner, not a maternity ward,' said the hairless and rather wrinkly doctor in charge with an apologetic brow that only added to his striking resemblance to a sphinx cat in a white coat.

'I don't mind, Dr...?'

'Löwe.'

'I really don't mind, Dr Löwe,' Erika smiled. 'You see, my midwife fled when all the looting took place recently and so this really would be the best place for me to be.'

Dr Löwe wrung his hands. 'But I'm afraid we really don't have the equipment for helping someone through a birth. I mean, if there were complications.'

'That's OK,' Erika said as cheerfully as she could, 'I'm a doctor too and I've even brought my own medical books and instruments specifically for birthing.' She pointed to the box at her feet on the steps to the castle.

The doctor's bright blue eyes became watery, as if he might burst into tears at any second. 'Well, the truth is, Frau Portner, erm, *Dr* Portner,' he attempted to lessen his own agitation by laughing at his little faux pas, 'we... no one here, me in particular, well, how can I put this... I've never delivered a baby before.'

The admission finally took such a great weight off the doctor's depilated shoulders that all his wrinkles were instantly, though momentarily, ironed out so that his head resembled a bar billiards ball. How such an "experienced" doctor could have gone through his career without ever delivering a baby, Erika could only wonder at, unless he was unusually late in coming to the profession. But this speculation had to wait, as Erika realised she needed now to pour all her resources into a display of coquettish femininity at a time when she felt much more slob than siren.

'Really?' she said with fluttering eyelashes. 'That does surprise me, a physician of such obvious experience and skill as yourself. But still, there is something about you that tells me no matter what situations present themselves you will always *rise* to the challenge and excel yourself.' She thought she might have gone a little too far having put such a ridiculous emphasis on the word rise, which had Erika desperately trying to blink images of the doctor's glabrescent wrinkly appendage from her mind under the disguise of more flirtatious eyelashing.

'Well...' Dr Löwe meowed, still unconvinced.

'And besides, the thing is,' Erika said suddenly clutching at her hips with genuine discomfort. I think this baby might be coming.'

'What do you mean?' the doctor blanched.

'I think it might be coming *now!*'

Max requested that Edgar or Horst go back to town instead of him on the next visit. Partly because he was terrified that he would bump into Utkin again and be subjected to another drinking marathon with all the nauseous, head splitting symptoms that proceeded from it, but also he wanted his friends to feel some of the austere luxury that came with donning the fur coat and getting away from the prison and the hospital for a while, albeit via a six kilometre hike to a village of maudlin and ailing Russians. But his captors were having none of it.

So he found himself trudging into town with Christoph again the following week. The monk was limping most of the way and his cheek was black with bruising.

'Come and see me in the barracks tonight,' Max whispered to him as they walked. 'Let me tend to your injuries.'

The monk cocked his head and attempted to hang a smile across his broken face, but Max wasn't sure if that meant he would come.

Thankfully Max's guard led him straight past the Utkin residence this time and on to a small apartment block, which might have afforded the tenants on the top floor some wonderful views in the summer, if the summer ever came. But everyone here was still groping their way through the Cimmerian winter. A winter which froze all the water in the officers' toilets, rendering them unusable, hence the stench and the obstacle course of turds Max had to negotiate in the street as he entered the block.

He knocked on the door of apartment number three. He had to knock a few times, each time harder than the last to be heard over the clamour inside. Eventually a child answered and stood staring up at Max for a moment. He beamed at the girl as he might have done at a long lost friend, after all it had been so long since Max had seen a child, the limpidity and guilelessness inherent therein so far from the world he had inhabited for the last few years. However, this little girl did not return his smile, nor did she appear to embody those ingenuous traits Max was yearning to see. After glaring at the alien for a protracted second she scurried back into the pandemonium of the apartment leaving the door wide open and apparently neglecting to announce his arrival to her parents.

'Hello?' Max called out edging his way inside and knocking hard on the open door as he went.

The girl and her three siblings were the main cause of the racket. That and the adults' harassed reaction to them. The kids played like any other kids would play, but cooped up in this pokey apartment, instead of out in the sun-drenched fields of a life their parents had to leave far away, the sound was amplified to distorting levels. The man and woman shouting the most at the kids Max assumed were the parents, but there were three other couples in the flat, the men in various states of undress so that it was difficult for Max to ascertain their rank, and the women in various states of pregnancy so that it was easy for Max to ascertain why he had been ordered to come here.

Eventually, as Max continued to shuffle politely further inside, one of the women sat at the table in the centre of the room, one of the few pieces of furniture there, noticed him despite her heavy eyelids.

'Are you the doctor?' she said her hand reaching weakly out for the man slumped next to her as if to rouse him to protect her just in case he was not the medic at all but an intruder.

'I am. How can I help?'

'A one way ticket to Moscow would help,' another woman sat on the floor piped up as she sewed a shirt as if she was trying to stab it to death.

Max snorted quietly and politely at her little joke and waited for a sensible answer from someone.

'My wife is in here,' the officer who had been leaning on the window sill since Max entered propelled himself forwards into an afterthought of a room attached to the main one, in which was barely enough space for a single bed, the only bed in the entire flat, Max noted.

On the bed lay a heavily pregnant woman with a white sheet under her blotted with blood.

'Hello, Mrs...?'

'Lagunov,' the woman sighed. In the dim light provided by a lamp from the other room this young woman's skin had the colour and texture of old paper. 'Am I losing the baby?' she asked without agitation, as if this was a regular occurrence in her life.

'Let me take a look,' Max said glancing at the officer for some kind of unspoken permission to delve between his wife's legs. 'When do you think are you due?'

'Not for another month or so *yet*,' Mrs Lagunov gasped the last word, her head and shoulders catapulting from the bed, one hand reaching out to clasp her abdomen, which felt as if it was about to split open.

'No, you're not losing the baby,' Max said, his own heart beginning to race to match the speed of his patient's.

'Then what's wrong with her?' her husband shouted over her cries.

'Nothing, it's just that she's having the baby. Now.'

As well as for its hairless wrinkly skin, the sphinx cat is also recognisable by its bright blue eyes, saucer-like on its little face. In this respect Dr Löwe resembled the cat even more as he urgently found a room in the castle for his newest patient recently gone into labour.

Where she sat on her bed unpacking her box of books and equipment, Erika could see out of the window over the acres of immaculate parkland that surrounded this early twelfth-century Augustine monastery. It was hard to imagine she was still in the same congested, crumbling country she had travelled through with Karl, the same devastated, incinerated country Benjamin had told her so much about as they rattled about in that windswept carriage full of displaced people. It was hard to believe she was even on the same continent with these ancient trees reaching up unencumbered, their cuckoo-sprinkled canopy out of sight. She opened the window and the simple room was suddenly adorned with the gentle croak of frogs, and perfumed with jasmine.

For a moment she felt guilty that her in-laws were combing the streets looking for a new home when she could quite happily have lived here forever, until a contraction yanked her back to her own precarious reality – giving birth in a hospital for wounded soldiers with no expertise in midwifery around her. And no husband.

She hadn't heard from Max now in eight months, since just after their wedding when he was ordered out to Breslau. She hadn't heard from her own father, who was commanding a regiment somewhere, for the same length of time too. She hadn't even had any contact with her mother in Neurode since she had left with Karl. If Max could not be here for the birth of his child she would have wished for no one else but her mother. She needed those zaftig arms around her now, her reassuringly commanding tone, her experience. Because Erika knew, she could read all the books she wanted to, pass all the medical exams she had, call herself a doctor, but her mama had one qualification Erika couldn't possibly have achieved yet – she had given birth successfully to two children.

There was a gentle pawing at the door and Dr Löwe's startled eyes entered the room before the rest of him. 'Shall I take your instruments for sterilisation?'

'Oh thank you, yes,' Erika handed them over. 'Contractions are coming a little more frequently now,' she informed him.

Consequently there was little room left on his face for those eyes.

'Is there a nurse that can come and assist?' Erika asked.

'All of our nurses are nuns,' Löwe said in one of his eternally compunctious cadences, 'so they are not allowed to be present at the birth, I'm afraid'.

'Praise be!' Erika muttered sarcastically.

'I'm sorry, what did you say?'

'Nothing.'

'But anyway I have asked Dr Becker to keep an eye on you.'

'Oh yes,' Erika brightened at the news. 'Who's he?'

'An orthopaedic surgeon.'

'Great,' she deflated again.

'Lots of passion for his vocation, Dr Becker. I'm sure you'll like him.'

Erika read between the lines here quickly as if the facts were spelt out by the furrows on Löwe's pale skin. 'So when did he qualify?'

'Oh, I, erm, don't know, one... or two years ago.'

Erika lay back on the clean sheets and began leafing through her Stöckel with even more focus than she had the night before her exam when, crammed in that musty armchair with Max, they had tested each other till the early hours.

The room suddenly got even darker as the doorway filled with nearly every other member of the household who had heard Max's announcement.

'Can you bring the light in here, heat up a bowl of water and bring as many sheets or towels as you have?' Max ordered the rabble at the door hoping that might disperse them a bit. But no one budged.

'Nearly all the sheets and towels we have are here on the bed already,' the husband said.

'Where are the other beds? Where does everyone else sleep?' Max asked curtly.

'This is the only bed we have. We usually take it in turns to have an hour in it through the night, but last night with Klara in this state we had to leave her there.'

Max looked incredulously at the officer, a lieutenant as he soon discovered. Officers of similar rank, pregnant women and children living in conditions in many ways worse than their own prisoners'. His very own bunk in the draughty heights of the mouldy barracks suddenly seemed bizarrely desirable. The wooden seat over the hole in the ground they had in Gegesha also seemed to him almost decadent compared to crapping in the streets as the Russians did, despite the rats, sitting atop the pyramid of shit which grew out of the hole, waiting to nip at the buttocks and scrotums of the prisoners trying to relieve themselves there.

'Well then, how about newspaper? Bring as much newspaper as you can. And soap. Well, give her some room to breathe!' Max said as firmly as he dared to the audience crammed in the doorway. 'And let's have that light in here! Please.'

The lieutenant dispersed the sorry crowd as he crashed through it on his way to bring the items the doctor had requested whilst Max dumped his coat in the corner of the little room, rolled up his sleeves and said delicately to his patient, 'That was a contraction. Now when the next one comes make sure you breathe through it. Do not push. You are not ready to push just yet, OK?'

'Hmm,' Klara said through tightly clamped lips, anticipating more pain.

Max pulled out his pocket watch, laid it on the windowsill and kept an eye on it until the next contraction came. The lieutenant soon returned with soap and water and a rather emaciated pile of paper.

'It's all we have,' he said apologetically.

'It's OK. Just lay it under the sheets. If you can try and shift a little, Mrs Lagunov?'

Whilst the lieutenant and his wife performed the awkward dance necessary to remake the bed as instructed with her still on it, Max washed his hands thoroughly. More thoroughly even than he needed to perhaps, as it gave him time to think, to recall the procedure and work out how he was going to do it with such limited resources.

'OK,' he said shaking his hands dry when he saw the state of the towels on offer, 'I need to, er, check, erm, inside, to, er...'

'Yes, yes,' Klara saved him. 'Whatever you need to do.'

He pulled his stethoscope from his bag and looked around for her husband who was hovering just outside the door now, looking half desirous to be with his wife again, but glad of the duty of keeping the rabble away as his excuse for staying sentry by the door.

Max inserted two fingers into the woman's vagina.

'That's what you need to do!' Erika bellowed at Dr Becker as the contractions came harder and faster. 'Two fingers in and check for the position of the baby's head, the presentation, the dilation.'

Dr Becker, who looked but a few years older than a baby himself did as he was told.

'What do you find?' Erika said in a tone that reminded her of her own teacher Dr Stöhr when the class were up to their elbows in the innards of a cadaver.

'Head well down,' Max told himself, but made sure it was loud enough for Klara to hear too since the news was good, 'Anterior presentation, only a thin rim of cervix remaining. Have your waters not broken yet?'

'I don't think so. I didn't expect to be having the baby yet.'

'That's OK. In fact that's good,' he said listening with his stethoscope to the baby's heart. 'A hundred and thirty beats per minute. That's good. Strong and steady.'

His own heartrate wasn't far behind the baby's now and the trauma of the next few minutes was only going to increase it and everyone else's in the room. Max had assisted on a number of births during his training but never had he led, let alone been the only medic present.

Another contraction tore through Klara and Max checked the watch. Contractions every three minutes.

'My waters have broken now. At least I hope that's what just happened,' Klara visibly blushed despite already being red with exertion.

Max checked and confirmed her suspicion. 'Let me pull out that wet sheet,' he said as Klara hauled her hips about. 'I can see the baby's head now, Mrs Lagunov, so when that next contraction comes you can push. But not too hard, do you understand?'

As he delved in his bag for more tools – the pliers that he used to cut Paul's frostbitten fingers off, the clamps made by the ex-engineer from Heidelberg from wire stolen from the perimeter fences – he wondered whether to elaborate for his patient that if she pushed too hard and split her perineum he didn't really have the appropriate tools to sew her up again.

'Check the heartrate,' Erika ordered Becker, blinking the sweat from her eyes.

She felt his hands shaking as he held the stethoscope to her flesh.

'About a hundred and forty beats per minute,' he said.

'Good. Just pant through it, pant through it, it's not time to push yet,' Erika instructed herself although she could have sworn Becker began panting too as she said that.

Another contraction ripped through her. She roared. She reached out for someone to grasp. Her mother. Max. All she got was a fistful of wet sheets. She tried not to imagine the worst, about the baby or Max. She refused to give birth to this child unless its father would be there for it as it grew. But the baby didn't seem to be waiting for permission. Then as the pains rent her body she started *hoping* for the worst. Well, death was the only excuse that bastard could have for not being here with her holding her hand right now, wasn't it? How could he leave her at a time like this? Have his way with her and then flounce off to the front and play doctor with all those nurses swooning over him and all those whores telling him to forget the wife, live for now, after all you might not be alive tomorrow so what was the point of waiting faithfully?

'Just pant through it, you know, in and out,' was all the information he chose to offer Klara as Max took hold of the baby's crown to try and stop it shooting out if she didn't follow his instructions. 'On the next contraction the head will be born.'

Attached to mother via baby in this way he felt the next mutilating wave surge through them. The accompanying yell from his wife had Lieutenant Lagunov stepping in and out of the lamp-lit room like a vampire into the day. Impossibly, in this fridge of a room, Max was sweating now almost as much as Klara, and then, eased out on Max's terms much to the frustration of Nature, the head appeared. Blue and puckered as if furious to be out in this world. And Max didn't blame it.

A head poked through the doorway. Blue and puckered. It was Dr Löwe.

'How are things going in here, Dr Becker?' his voice quivered as he laid a pair of freshly sterilised forceps on the table by the bed.

'Well, everything is OK,' Becker chewed on the words as he leafed through Stöckel, 'But I am starting to think that things are taking a little longer than they should.'

They both looked at Erika, who had to agree with him, but there was no way she was going to let either of them loose on her or her child with those forceps.

'It's fine,' she gulped. 'Just a little more time, that's all we need.'

'But the baby's head is very low now, Frau Portner...'

'*Dr* Portner,' Dr Löwe simpered.

'... And I'm not sure time is what we have.'

'OK, Mrs Lagunov, you're doing great. The head is out. Now,' he mumbled the rest for his ears only, reciting from his university's recommended manual on childbirth by Stöckel, the book he and Erika had tested each other from for the paediatric exam. He may have been able to coach her when it came to Latin, but when it came to childbirth she was clearly the better student. And in a way he wouldn't let himself be better than her in this subject. They all knew Babyface was a natural when it came to paediatrics, but Max thought it was impossible to be more knowledgeable than a woman when it came to pregnancy and birth. After all, how could a man ever know what it really felt like to have another human being tearing its way out of him? How could he ever know what you would really need in that situation? Sure, Max knew where to clamp and cut, but that wasn't what he meant. This was a heaven-sent miracle, but it was also one of the most brutal things he had ever seen, and he had seen some brutality since arriving at the front. He had no idea how he would ever deal with seeing Erika in this situation, if and when the time came for them to have a baby together.

'Observe the restitution of the head through one eighth of a circle. The presenting shoulder can then be delivered from under the pubic arch,' he recited from Stöckel. 'Now, Mrs Lagunov when the next contraction comes you can push as hard as you like, OK?'

Klara nodded furiously, her sweaty hair whipping her face as she did so. Then a sound rose from her like that of his old motorbike accelerating through the desolate streets back in Breslau, her entire being shuddered—

'Push!' he cried.

She pushed with every reckless, visceral, fading pulse of power she had left in her body, spurred on by the sight of Becker reaching for the forceps. Dr Löwe let out a yelp, Erika heard the clattering of forceps against the other instruments on the table, she heard the call of a cuckoo somewhere out in the garden, then a high, furious wail drowned it all out and she felt something soft wriggling against her knees. Becker had dropped the now redundant forceps—

 nd he held a little boy in his hands.

 nd he held a little girl in his hands.

For a moment Max marvelled at the sight and the soft slimy heat. Then he remembered there was work to be done and he applied two of his clamps to the umbilical cord and cut in between them with the pliers. He held the baby boy upside down by the ankles to ensure he inhaled no mucus and listened for breath.

The room was so quiet now he could almost hear the five deutschmark watch, which languished in his pocket jealous of the quality timepiece lording it up on the window sill.

Tick tick tick tick.

Then the baby cried and Max wrapped it in a stained towel and gave it to its elated mother, who cooed over it as if it was a thing of serene beauty. But covered in mucus and blood, purple and raging, to Max it was ugly. It even sent strong recollections his way of horrors he'd seen on the Maginot Line. Yet the mother doted and seemed to be suffering from a joyful amnesia from the agony her body had just endured. He was suddenly aware of his own malnourished, aching, abused form and wished he could experience that forgetfulness new mothers have for pain every morning when he woke in that abominable hut alongside a thousand other tortured souls. But then, he reasoned, perhaps men do have amnesia when it comes to pain and suffering, the pain and suffering associated with war at least. Otherwise surely the First World War would have been war enough. And he found himself seeing the ugliness of the baby in Klara's arms not just in its temporary physical state, but in its immutable gender too.

But his job was not over yet. He needed, she needed, to deliver the placenta, and it needed to be delivered whole. If any pieces were left behind there would be a great risk of infection or haemorrhaging which in these conditions with these tools and medicines would be undoubtedly fatal. But, as with his thoughts on her perineum, he thought it was best not to share this with the patient either.

Twenty minutes passed during which Max leant on the mildewed window-sill trying to recover the strength the delivery had taken out of him, whilst Lieutenant Lagunov, an officer who had fearlessly lead troops into some of the most bloody skirmishes on the Eastern Front, finally found the courage to perch on the edge of the bed, comfort his wife and greet his new son. One of the other women stepped inside too and helped wash and dress the baby in the smallest clothes they had – his big sister's cast-offs which looked ridiculous not in their femininity but in their sheer size on his minute body. And then the placenta released itself from the womb. Although the parents could hardly have cared less what was going on at the other end of the bed, Max examined the organ with as much care as he had the baby itself. He held it near the lamplight and prayed it was intact.

Lieutenant Lagunov shook Max's hand and sent him out into the street with nothing but his thanks, which was fine by Max. He was worried for a moment there that Lagunov, like Utkin, might have pulled a bottle of vodka from somewhere and insisted on wetting the baby's head, but it seemed Lagunov didn't have access to the same provisions as Utkin, or if he did he didn't want to share them with the German, doctor or not.

Max floated home pleasantly intoxicated on the part he'd just played in the successful delivery. The wind that had molested him on his walk into town this morning was gone and the atmosphere now was halcyon. Even the Northern Lights put on a brief show for him and he would have stopped and bowed at the green dream cloud saluting him had he not been flanked by two moaning guards completely ignorant of the miracles going on all around and above them that day.

The guards left him at the gatehouse and Max walked back toward the barracks alone, unaware of Sergeant Volkov aiming his rifle at the back of his head.

She was perfect.

Her little Netta blinking in the light of this puzzling world. Despite everything, Erika thought, I did it. Despite having to endure this birth not just without her husband or family, but without anyone she remotely knew present. Despite the presence of Doctors Tweedledum and Tweedledee who were currently delivering her placenta, though she had stopped worrying about their competencies as soon as Becker had lowered Netta into her arms. Despite being displaced from her family home by circumstances and then turfed from her temporary home by two American officers wielding riding crops. Despite the risk of being bombed or shot at at any time throughout her pregnancy. Despite having to keep herself and her baby healthy on such meagre rations. Despite the trauma she had put her body through travelling the length and breadth of the country in those horrid trains – and once on the outside of one. No! These thoughts – flowing through the bottom of a dark gorge in her mind while her senses above were incandescent with the new life before her – dammed themselves up momentarily and took another course: *she* had not put her body through that trauma. *He* had put her body through that trauma. Hitler and his cronies. And deep in that gorge of her mind there was fury at the Führer that could have put her in such danger; that could have put everyone in the country through such pain and loss. But she buried it, for now at least, held her daughter just that little bit tighter, and thought her heart might explode when Netta's tiny hand grasped her little finger and all her child's vulnerability and all the journeys that awaited it, her desire to protect it and the Sisyphean enormity of the task tsunamied over her.

As the waters receded she became aware of Dr Löwe's gentle purring, 'There's someone here to see you, Dr Portner.'

She looked up to see a large bunch of lilacs at the door with Karl peeking out from behind them. 'Is it OK, to come in?'

'Of course,' Erika said crying almost imperceptibly. 'Come and meet your granddaughter.'

She had wanted so much, had rehearsed it even as she lay in bed every night in recent weeks, for that sentence to be *Come and meet your daughter* as Max appeared breathless at the door, back from the front, just in time, unharmed. And though it wasn't to be she could never begrudge Karl the honour of being the first relative to meet little Netta.

'Oh my Lord,' he huffed waving the lilacs about until Dr Löwe took them from him and went in search of something resembling a vase. 'It's... she..?' Erika nodded, smiling through her tears. 'She's here already? I... I had no idea it would be so soon otherwise I would have come...'

'It's OK,' Erika reassured him and laughed at the sight she had been spared of two doctors *and* her father-in-law flapping around the room whilst she was trying to deliver her baby.

'Do you want to hold her?'

'Me?' Karl said rather pointlessly as Becker had also long since left the room.

'Yes. Her name's Netta,' she said holding the baby up to him.

After visibly steeling himself for his most precious porterage of recent times, he took Netta in his arms and held her for much longer than he had ever managed any of those damned suitcases without so much as a twinge in his damaged wrist.

'Oh, I almost forgot,' Karl said to Erika though he was unable to take his eyes from Netta, 'a man came to the flat, just while we were putting the last of the things on the cart. Said he had a message for you. He insisted upon giving it to you personally, so I brought him along. He's waiting outside. But I said I'd only bring him in if you were up to it and now you've... well, perhaps I should tell him to come back another...'

'A message from whom?' Erika said arranging her hair and making sure the sheets were covering her in a manner which told Karl she had already decided to receive the messenger; that she had already decided whom the message was from. As Karl had. As they both hoped.

'I don't know. For sure.'

'Is he German?'

'Oh yes.'

'It's OK. Let him come in.'

Karl handed Netta back to her mother and disappeared for a minute. Erika told herself not to get too worked up speculating. After all, the last time she received an emissary a couple of days ago it was those callous American officers kicking her out of her home. At least this time she knew it was a fellow countryman. But was that a good thing or a bad thing? And if it was bad news, about Max, was this really the time to receive it, postpartum, with her baby in her arms. How would her own vulnerable physiognomy react to grief right now? And Netta shouldn't be present, shouldn't feel her mother wracked with grief at such a tender age; who knows what repercussions it may have on the child in the future? No, don't let him in, not now, not today.

'Karl?' she called out weakly at first then she found more vigour, more volume in her urgency. 'Karl? Karl?'

'Yes,' he was there again. 'Is everything all right?'

'Yes, but...'

'This is the man I told you about.'

It was too late, the man was there. Yet his face seemed benign. Or was that just the humility all men project in the presence of a new mother and the tribulations they know she has just surmounted? This man though, Erika observed, was clearly the survivor of his own tribulations. The dark circles around his eyes, his skin and his clothes hanging loosely from him, the two missing fingers of his left hand, which along with the other toyed with a scrap of yellow paper.

'Hello Erika. My name is Paul,' he said. 'I am a friend of your husband's, Max. Max Portner?' he asked just to be sure as the woman had glazed over somewhat as if she wasn't recognising the name.

Eventually she nodded and he watched as she closed the blanket tighter around her child and let her little finger dangle near one of the baby's hands until it gripped it instinctively.

'Well,' he continued, 'we were both prisoners of war. Captured in different places, but we both ended up in a camp called Gegesha on the Russian border near Finland. He was the camp doctor...'

Was? She thought, he used the past tense. Why did he use the past tense?

'... and he treated me well when I needed it. He saved my life, in fact,' he said holding up his left hand just long enough to make his point without making the lady uncomfortable. 'And he asked me to give you this.' He handed over the piece of paper. 'I hid it in my shoe when I was released. In the heel,' he beamed. 'I made a little compartment in there for smuggling things about the camp, you know. We had to be resourceful like that. And your husband. He's one of the most resourceful people I know. He's doing such a great job for his fellow prisoners up there, taking such good care of them, when there's so much sickness and injury.'

Erika had stopped consciously listening the moment the paper had touched her hand. Those gorges of her mind channelled the sound of Paul's voice, absorbed the plaudits, took comfort from them, but, up above, her senses were overcome. One arm cradling Netta, the other hand stroking the rough surface of the besmirched paper as if it were her husband's skin, her eyes blinking away the tears urgently so she could examine the handwriting thereon. It was his all right. Because it was hers. Just like hers. There was nothing on it but an address, the address of the little store in Pechenga where the monk Christoph trudged to every day to pick up the post. But at last she knew he was alive, she knew why he had not been in touch (not that she doubted him for a second, she thought wryly, recalling some of the curses she had hurled at his image during labour) and she knew how to contact him.

Volkov was jamming the barrel of his rifle into Max's back with unnecessary and vindictive force, shepherding him away from the barracks, away from the hospital, away from the kitchens, away from any part of the camp Max was familiar with to the row of squat wooden huts downwind of the cesspit where the rats partied atop pyramids of faeces.

'Can you explain to me, *please*, what this is all about?'

Just like the baby boy he had delivered earlier, Max felt traumatised and furious at being pushed into a new world he was not ready for, that he would never be ready for.

'You have failed to follow orders, Portner.'

'Concerning what? What orders?' He wracked his brains desperately trying to think of a situation that Volkov could have possibly misconstrued as him not following orders. If only he knew what Volkov was talking about he could explain the misunderstanding. But somehow, Max thought stealing a glance over his shoulder, judging by the delight on his aggressor's face, Volkov had no intention of yielding to any explanations no matter how convincing.

'I specifically told you when you began your *work*,' he laced the word with as much sarcasm as he could to show how he rated their respective occupations, 'that should you allow more than nine per cent of the camp's population to be off work due to illness at any one time you will be held responsible'.

'I don't believe more than nine per cent of the camp's population *is* sick right now. We keep rigorous records, you've seen them for yourself.' He turned again and saw that Volkov had stopped outside the little huts, which up close could more accurately be described as boxes.

'Get in! Solitary confinement. That was the punishment stated for sloppy medical practise, was it not?'

'Look, let's just go back to the hospital and I can show you the figures, you can count the patients for yourself if you like. I am sure that there are less than nine per cent sick,' Max insisted. And then a thought struck him like the moonlight glinting on the tip of Volkov's gun. 'At least there were this morning before I left.'

Volkov giggled like a schoolboy. 'Amazing what a difference a day makes. I guess you should have been paying more attention to your patients here than hobnobbing with the officers in town.'

'Hobnobbing? They are my patients too. Because I was ordered to tend to them. By you!'

'Get in!' Volkov was no longer grinning. 'And if I have to tell you again you'll be shot.'

Max had to crouch to get in the doorway and once inside the windowless cage it was only shards of moonlight, slicing through the gaps in the logs that made up the roof, which showed him the cell was a square, just long enough for him to lay down in either direction. There was nothing in there but a bucket in the corner. This he assumed was his toilet. He guessed because of the stench coming from it – the guards weren't thorough when it came to cleaning the cell between guests.

Volkov slammed the door and Max heard him slide the bolts with exhalations of great satisfaction.

'Nighty-night, Portner,' he called and Max listened to the fading crunch of his boots on the frosted grass.

Just before the sound was completely muted Max was filled with a claustrophobic panic that had him wishing he was standing outside being stabbed by the barrel of Volkov's rifle again rather than being locked in this box alone. He shouted, 'How long? How long do I have to stay in here? How long? *How long?*'

There was no answer. Volkov was gone. And Max had the feeling that even if he was right outside the door, the Russian wouldn't deign to furnish him with an answer to that question.

Summer had finally clawed its way up to the Arctic Circle. That was the only way Max could have any idea how long he'd been inside. For a few hours every day in March, light – not moonlight, not lamplight, not candlelight, not light from the fire – but real strong sunlight made the gaps in the roof of the cell glow. The first sunlight he'd seen for almost five months. Despite his new environment, it brought such an overwhelming shift in the atmosphere at first he couldn't quite believe it. He feared the camp had been set ablaze and it was the light from flames gorging on the wooden buildings that burnished the air, but the slowly rising realisation that it was sunshine transported him to his boyhood playing on the farm, squinting up at the bright sky.

'I'll be Old Shatterhand and you be Winnetou,' he said to Horst reclining next to him in the hay.

'Why can't I be the cowboy?' Horst grumbled.

'Because Winnetou is the big Apache chief. The hero of the story. And you're much stronger than me.'

Horst contemplated this for a moment. The hero? Big and strong? Sounded good. But he could have sworn Old Shatterhand got his name because he could knock any opponent unconscious with a single punch to the head. Surely that was big and strong and more like him!

'Come on!' Max jumped up and the rustling of the hay beneath his feet was the swish of his horse's tail as he raced off across the range.

He mounted the cart outside the stables and balanced there on the shaft as if he was perched on a precipice looking out heroically over the Wild West with his blood brother Winnetou by his side.

And then he fell. Landed awkwardly and screamed in a most unheroic fashion. Horst ran to help but was nearly sick when he saw his friend's forearm bent in a way forearms should never bend. One of the farm workers rushed from the stables and hurried little Max to the doctor's surgery, only a stone's throw from the farm.

Dr Acker offered no pain relief to the boy, but instead, after pronouncing his diagnosis of a broken arm, he gruffly ordered Max to remove the leather braces holding up his shorts, which he tied around the boy's broken arm at one end fastening the other to the door handle of his room.

'OK, deep breath, young man,' Dr Acker squinted at Max and promptly slammed the open door.

'Old Shatterhand all right,' Horst mumbled with a giggling guilt, glad he had taken the role of the Apache after all.

The pain for Max from this improvised traction was indescribable but the results were quite astounding. He was back playing out with Horst and running errands for his Papa in no time, despite the cast.

'Go to the hairdressers and get your old man twenty Eckstein, there's a good boy,' Karl said handing him the money.

'You'll have to cut down on those cigarettes if we keep getting bills like this one from the doctor,' Martha huffed dropping the invoice into his lap for services rendered to one Max Portner Jnr.

Max scuttled off as Karl took in the figures on the bill and, though he was already halfway down the street in seconds he could still hear his father cry, 'A hundred and twenty deutschmarks?!' as he raced towards the bakers.

The bakers was where he always paused on his errand because it was in the window of that shop that dangled little sacks of Bruchwaffeln, broken waffles, sweet and golden and only five Pfennigs a bag. But when your Papa always gave you exactly the right money for his cigarettes there would never be any change from which you could ask to buy a treat like that.

'When I grow up,' he said to one of the tantalising bags, one palm flat against the window that might as well have been six inches thick for all the chance he had of ever feeling those scrumptious chunks in his hand – and even less chance now with that enormous doctor's bill lolling in his Papa's lap like a vicious cat, 'I'm going to earn so much money that I'll be able to buy a lorry load of you whenever I want.'

He slouched off, head down, to the hairdressers and just outside, his nose full of the odour of Brilliantine hair oil so he knew he was there, he got it: the solution to all his problems.

'If the doctor charges that much just for fixing my arm, just think how much he earns every day. Every week.' Max's eyes bulged. 'That's what I'm going to be when I grow up. I'm going to be a doctor. And I'll be rich.'

As with all little boys, the vow was soon forgotten in the eternity of a few summer days, until he was sixteen and faced with that carnage outside the theatre.

Max chuckled weakly at his six-year-old self. Twenty-five and a doctor now and yet still he would give anything for a bag of Bruchwaffeln because a piece of bread, three hundred and fifty grams of watery soup, and a cup of water was all that was shoved into his cell every day, although, since he was an officer, he was also treated to twelve cigarettes per day too. Never a big smoker he decided to save most of these – valuable currency in a prison camp.

Thanks to the arrival of the sun, Max saw the days turn into a week. Without it he wouldn't have known how long he had been in there. With just his watches to rely on it could have been four in the morning or four in the afternoon. How would you know in the polar night?

Tick tick tick tick.

And then when the sun went down he started to see things in the shadowy corners of his cell. Things moving, crouching, lurching, crawling, slithering. His mouth hurt for wanting. Wanting food – even some of his patient's stolen porridge or a handful of juicy cranberries from the barrel. And wanting a kiss.

It hadn't occurred to him until now with nothing to do but focus on his senses just how parched his lips were, not from lack of hydration, but from lack of affection. He closed his eyes, licked his lips, trying to ignore the cracks a recurrence of scurvy was making since he had been in the cell without cranberries and pine needle water, and rolled them together as he had watched Erika do so many times after applying some lipstick before they headed out for the evening. She said she hated him watching her, scrutinising her like that, but she always said it with a flushed giggle that made him think otherwise. He loved examining her, her deliberate confident actions at home, her careful uncertain ones in the laboratory. Alone in his digs whilst doing something as mundane as slicing a tomato he found himself imagining how she would painstakingly remove all the seeds and pulp from hers before she judged them ready to eat. Sometimes he tried to do that too. Most times he couldn't be bothered and wolfed it down seeds and all, but just imagining her there doing things her way was narcotic to him as much then as now.

He was watching her eating the perfectly prepared red fruit. He was watching her prepare her perfectly painted red lips. And he was kissing them. Kissing her. And it wasn't perfectly prepared or perfectly painted, it wasn't perfectly executed or perfectly finished.

It was clumsy and slightly off target sometimes, occasionally there were too many teeth or too much saliva, but it was an elegant awkwardness, just like that ballet by the banister after the summer ball. And each time thereafter that he had to inhale sharply through his nose because her lips were still passionately sealed around his, always felt like the first breath he'd ever taken on an alien planet with a superior atmosphere.

Tick tick tick tick.

He stroked the damp crumbly earth he sat on as if it were her hair.

Tick tick tick tick.

He heard her voice outside the door, over his head coming through the gaps in the roof.

'Goodnight,' she said.

'Goodnight,' he said.

'Nighty-night, Portner.' Now her voice was ricocheting inside the bucket and it sounded awfully like Volkov's.

And then there was silence. Silence except, as ever, for that bloody watch.

Tick tick tick tick.

He ripped the cheap timepiece from his pocket and threw it at the wall.

TICK TICK TICK TICK.

He groped around till he found it again, still quite intact, and he beat the ground with it, stamped his heel into it. And eventually the irritating thing shut up and he threw the pieces into the bucket where all the other shit goes.

Six weeks Max spent in solitary. Volkov was the one who released him. He wouldn't have missed the sight of Dr Portner emerging from that cell blinking in the sun for anything. Max felt like he had 100lb weights strapped to his feet. His face was swollen, his feet and ankles too. Standing should have been a joy after all that time in a box, but having to report immediately for rollcall, where the men swayed like crops in the breeze, being counted and recounted and herded and re-herded, he soon longed to lie down again.

In the mess-hut the sight of Horst and Bubi was more nourishing to Max than the skilly could ever be, but he bolted it down nonetheless as they filled him in on the missing weeks.

'We're losing so many every week,' Horst sighed, 'there won't be any prisoners left in the camp soon'.

'And that's why, with the population going down, I was even surer that we couldn't have exceeded our nine per cent quota when Volkov put me in the hole.'

'We hadn't exceeded it. Volkov knew that. He ordered me to show him the figures the morning you'd gone off to town to deliver that baby. And then the next thing I knew we had two new admissions. Both shot in the foot. Both had no idea why.'

'And guess who shot them?' Bubi said running his finger round his bowl to get every last drop of broth from it.

'Volkov?' Max said, doing the same.

Bubi nodded. Horst and Max shared a furiously helpless glance.

'How long did you spend in the hole, doc?' The ex-engineer from Heidelberg shoved his shoulder into Max's to get his attention though their elbows had already been vying for space at the long crowded table since he sat down.

'Six weeks,' he muttered

'Six weeks! That's tough. But you know what I hear? I hear that Ivan intends to keep all German POWs here in Gegesha for ten years.'

'No way!'

'They can't do that!'

'I'll go off my head.'

Max had heard gossip like this before. They all had, so they took it with a pinch of salt, but the truth was none of them had any idea how long they might be here for. And right now ten years was as likely as one, so he merely said to his engineering comrade, 'Could you take a look at my glasses sometime today. I think they need a new arm on the right. Could you work some of your magic?'

'Sure,' the man from Heidelberg said, picking at his teeth with a long yellow fingernail.

'We better get to work then, boys,' he said to Bubi and Horst.

'*We* better had,' Horst said in warmly reproachful tones. 'But *you* are being admitted as a patient today, my friend.'

'What?'

'You are clearly suffering from oedema,' he said gesturing to Max's swelling face, 'and so it'll be bed rest for you today. OK?' He rose in a way that brooked no discussion of the matter and Max loved his brother more than ever for it.

Within a day Max was up and about despite the oedema still partially present, but Horst knew it would be impossible to make his brother lie there and watch his patients suffer around him without lifting a finger so he allowed him to work.

As Bubi brought his attention to Christoph limping onto the bridge to the hospital, Max felt a flush of guilt at not being around for the past six weeks since he had told the monk to come have his injuries tended to the afternoon after they had last gone into town together, the afternoon Max was thrown in the hole.

Christoph's limp was more pronounced than it had been on their last meeting – no doubt exacerbated by the punishing walk he had to do every day – and it took him so long to cross the fifteen metre gangway Max marvelled at how he still walked six kilometres to town and back every day too. But he did. He could tell by the handful of mail he had for the patients today. And that was when Max realised that Christoph, in his ridiculously contrite way, was not here for treatment at all, but just, as usual, to deliver the mail.

He held three letters in his hand. Including the doctors on shift there were thirty-one men in the hospital out in the Barents Sea that day; the little infirm island of freedom where Ivan wouldn't dare to tread, with its icy spaces under beds crammed with contraband. In short, a kind of haven, and yet twenty-eight men would shortly feel like the unluckiest men on earth as yet again the letters from their loved ones didn't get through. And then their injuries would smart more than ever, the infections gnaw at their insides with renewed intensity, they would feel the cold throbbing in their bones more than usual, all accompanied tauntingly by the ravenous ripping of letters from envelopes already opened by Ivan, the satisfied rustling of paper being read and the contented coos of the readers. Max studied the faces of this majority of men in his hospital that afternoon and realised that despite them all being crammed in here together these men were as much in solitary confinement right then as he had been for those infernal six weeks.

'And last, but by no means least: Dr Portner.'

Max registered his name being spoken and shook himself from his musing to see Christoph's perpetual smile and his thin hand holding out an envelope to him.

'Excuse me?' Max said still groggy from pondering.

'This one's for you, sir,' the monk extended his arm from its cement bag sleeve until the letter almost touched Max's sternum, at which he could feel his heart pounding as if it was trying to get at the letter itself.

But still he wouldn't take it. Just in case there had been some mistake and then the disappointment would be even greater than that of the rest of the men looking enviously in his direction. He looked down first and saw the address handwritten on the envelope. It was his own handwriting. His own and not his own. It was Erika's handwriting.

'Oh,' he said eventually and gently took the letter with a trembling hand. 'Thanks.'

'You're welcome,' Christoph chirped and hobbled out over the bridge, back to shore.

After examining the envelope for so long as if the address on the outside was all Erika had written to him he heard Horst call out, 'Well, are you going to read it or not?'

Max looked up and saw his brother grinning as much goodwill towards him as he could muster through his envy.

Poor Horst, Max thought as he flopped onto the chair by his desk. But hopefully he'll hear from Eva soon. I mean, look how long it took for me to hear from Erika. I'm sure Eva's letter is just a few days behind hers.

His sympathy for Horst was endless, but his empathy was about to be obliterated. He had delayed long enough. He eased the pages from their torn wrapping, making sure to ignore the sense of

182

violation which attended the notion that Ivan had read his wife's words to him before he had, and began.

Dear Max,

My husband! I have rarely had the occasion to call you that since our wonderful wedding day and loving wedding night. I miss you and I am so sorry to hear that you have been taken prisoner, but don't worry, your friend Paul told me all about it so at least I know where you are and that you are alive.

I hope you got my letter about travelling to Bernried with your father. He was such a great help on that harrowing journey and, although we lived happily in Bernried for a couple of months, we were evicted by the Americans soon after the war ended. But we found a new house in Mengede, where your father is teaching at the primary school. The house came with the job. It's a three-storey red-brick terrace where we live now with your Aunt Bertel. I have the attic room which has the most beautiful Tiffany window. It reminds me of the rose window in Freiburg Cathedral when the light shines through it. Oh, I know you'll love it as much as I do. And at last we are slowly able to furnish the house since the Americans confiscated most of our possessions.

I will be applying for a license to set up as a practising doctor with the National Health Service when the time is right. Which brings me to the most important and exciting piece of news. Right now I am not able to work as I am very busy looking after our new baby daughter Netta. She is only a few weeks old as I write this (perhaps she will be a few months older by the time you read this if Paul was correct about the length of time things take to find you up there in the North), but she is beautiful and healthy despite me having to give birth without a midwife and just a doddering old quack and a newly qualified orthopaedic surgeon to assist me! But don't worry, Stöckel was there to offer his guidance too!

I hope it is not long before you are allowed to come home and see her. I show her photos of you every day and tell her all about you. She has your blonde hair and your green eyes. Your father spoils her rotten. He dotes on her of course and I know you will too.

I will write again soon. I do hope Edgar and Horst are still with you and that they are well. Please send them my love and send me a letter soon if you are allowed.

Love always,

'Dorothea'

He was a father. Yet he'd had no idea Erika was even pregnant. Her sickness in the fragment of letter he'd retrieved from the monastery garden in Breslau, the symptoms he'd assumed were due to her persistently low blood pressure, the reason for her schlepping across the country with his father, all made sense now and during the following months those missing pages would often write themselves in the frost on the floor of the hospital, in the mildew on the roof of the barracks, in the wisps of cirrus cloud as he walked into town, on the back of the prisoner in front of him at roll call as he sat on the stool he had fashioned for himself from three off-cuts of wood he found discarded in the street. Bending over patients on low non-adjustable beds all day and the occasional relapse of oedema was starting to take its toll on his back and legs.

'You've got to hand it to those Germans for their ingenuity,' he understood one of the guards saying, as the others fumbled over counting heads at the front as ever. 'If you throw a hundred empty tins at them they will come back with a tank.'

'Ingenuity?' a more familiar voice growled. 'I call it insubordination.'

And suddenly Max felt his stool kicked out from under him and he fell painfully to the unyielding ground.

'Jesus!' Edgar spat in Volkov's direction as he went to help up his friend.

'Leave him on the ground or he'll never walk again,' Volkov bawled and the guard counting heads lost his place yet again.

'The man has got some medical problems which makes him unable to stand for long periods.'

'*The man* should have been standing like everybody else.'

'Well, he could probably manage it if you lot could learn to count to a hundred in less than an hour.'

'Edgar,' Max warned, nursing his back, fearful for his pal's safety if his vehemence continued.

But Edgar's patience was wearing as thin as his faith. 'What is wrong with you? What is it that makes you think it is acceptable to treat people this way?'

'I don't treat *people* this way,' Volkov sneered. 'I treat Nazis this way. And it is small reparation for the way you have treated us. In your concentration camps. In the villages, raping and pillaging.'

'I am not a...'

'I have seen it with my own eyes,' Volkov shouted Edgar down. 'I have served on the Front too and I'll never forget looking down from an embankment at a derailed train carriage full of dancing Germans, firing their pistols at the ceiling, bragging about their little victory and how they had ransacked the houses in the village just east of Minsk of food and booze. How they had shot any civilian who had got in their way. And then I saw one of those civilians among them. A Russian woman. They stripped her naked, rubbed boot polish over her breasts and made her dance for them. They poured booze into her throat until she gagged, but they didn't stop until she was as drunk as they were so when they took her outside to rape her she could not have fought back even if she had dared to.'

Max could not tell if the drops on Volkov's chin came from his rancorous mouth or his mournful eyes.

'Earlier that day before we'd fallen back, when we were making some progress along the embankment I caught sight of a figure crouched, wounded apparently, three metres in front of me in the middle of the pounded hollow of the road. I saw him start at the sight of me so I knew he was the enemy. Saw him stare with wide open eyes as I strode up to him holding out my revolver, pressing it to his forehead. His response was to snatch a photograph from his pocket and hold it up to me in his trembling hand. It was a picture of him surrounded by his wife and kids. Lots of kids I seem to remember. And I so I forced down my anger and walked on.' Volkov drew on the chilly air as if it were the first cigarette he'd had in years, 'He was there in the train carriage later that night. Dancing and celebrating with all the other rapists. I'll never make the same mistake again.'

He glared at Max on the ground at his feet as he might have glared at that soldier. For a moment Max thought Volkov was about to make good on his promise as his hand hovered near his holster. But with characteristic volatility he turned on his heels and marched across the parade ground as Max could imagine him striding across the black and torn up ground of the railway embankment.

Netta would soon be three years old. She had been weaned and was surrounded by three doting relatives, so Erika had sent off her application to work with the National Health Service.

It was rejected.

'Why on earth would they reject you?' Karl said with his usual paternal loyalty, arms crossed, leaning on the door frame to her attic room.

'They said the area already has three medical practitioners covering a population of twenty thousand.' Erika sat with Netta on her lap in the window seat below the Tiffany pane which cast a rainbow of colours for the child to play with.

'So nearly seven thousand patients per medic is OK, is it?' he ranted at the absent powers that be.

'Apparently so,' Erika said with a lot less fervour than her father-in-law, sedated as she always was by the light from the stained glass, and the connections it made in her head to Freiburg, the cathedral and her wedding day.

'Well, we'll see about that!' And he stomped away down the stairs leaving Erika only mildly concerned about what he meant. She had a lot less energy than she did even when she was heavily pregnant and, although she imagined Karl would be right now marching into town to go and (almost) bang his fist on the desk of those Health Service cronies, just as he had to with the NSV ones back in Neurode all those years ago, she had no intention of chasing after him to calm him down. Besides, you never know, he might actually convince them to give her a job. He could be very persuasive, she smiled to herself.

'Especially if you like cigarettes or chocolate,' she giggled at Netta, the cushion of time allowing her to see that diabolical journey of theirs through rose-tinted glasses these days.

She sat for a long while in the window as her child played at her feet. It was times like these that she missed Max more than ever.

189

Times of rejection, of feeling inferior, when she needed to feel him wedge his slim body next to hers under the blanket, see the pages of a textbook confidently leafed through and hear him say, 'I'm doing nothing for the next two days, except helping you to cram this Latin and that's final, OK?'

'*Trapezius, trapezii*,' she murmured at Netta.

'Bapeeziuh, bapeezii,' Netta sang back.

Erika laughed and felt her *trapezii* loosen.

A couple of hours later, she carried Netta downstairs to find out what all the banging coming from the living room was about. She was shocked to see everything covered in dust sheets and the living room divided in two by the enormous piece of Gypsum Board Karl was hammering into place.

'What's going on?' she called out over the noise.

Martha appeared behind her and informed her, 'Karl has decided that if the Health Service won't give you a job then you should start your own practice right here.'

'In the living room?' Erika turned wide-eyed to her mother-in-law who instinctively took Netta from her tired arms. 'I am so sorry, Martha, I never asked Karl to do this.'

Her mother-in-law hushed Erika just as she did Netta when the child was colicky. 'It's OK, I know that. This is typical of him,' she said and they both watched him as he took a break to rotate and flex his left wrist, aching from pressing on the gypsum, 'and I think it's a great idea'. Martha blinked at Erika in slow motion, like a contented cat, and all Erika's anxiety was demolished and instantly reconstructed as excitement.

Whilst Karl was busy putting the finishing touches to the partition, Erika hurried to a carpenter he recommended who could help her out with some specialised furniture for her new surgery. His workshop was nothing more than a shed behind a display room on the edge of a tiny village near Mengede, but the intoxicating smell of wood shavings and the sophistication of the items on display convinced her that Karl was right in sending her there.

'A table, you say?' said the carpenter brushing the woodchips from his dark hair and his shirt front when he finally stopped focusing on sanding his latest project and was immediately enthralled by the young woman before him with beautifully sculpted cheekbones and penetratingly polished eyes.

'Yes, but not a table table.'

'Not a table table?' the carpenter repeated patronisingly, though he had hoped to sound more beguiled and amused.

'No. Not a table for dining or coffee or, erm, writing.'

'Like a desk?'

'A desk?'

'A table for writing. Otherwise known as a desk.' His attempts to appear charmed and charming were failing miserably.

'Yes?'

'You don't want a desk?'

'No.'

'Right. So what is it you need?'

'A table to examine people on.'

'Oh.'

'I'm a doctor you see.'

'Ooohhh. An examination table!' he exclaimed as if the carpentry skills needed to create *an examination table* were completely different from those needed to create *a table to examine people on*.

'Exactly,' she said. Her irritation with him would have been greater if she wasn't so uncomfortable with herself trying to describe her requirements, and her embarrassment might not have been so acute had she not found the carpenter rather attractive.

'I think I could manage that for you,' he said. 'You'd need it to be so high,' he suggested demonstrating the necessary height by flattening his palm in the air in front of her waist. 'And as long as your tallest patient I suppose,' he laughed.

She managed to chuckle too before adding, 'With an adjustable back and foot rest.'

'OK. I'm sure we could manage that.'

'Good. But it needs other things too.'

'Other things?'

'Other features.'

'Features?'

'Yes, specifically, erm, stirrups.'

'Stirrups?'

'Yes, two adjustable arms coming out of the end with stirrups for the feet.'

'Like on a saddle?' he asked genuinely unsure.

'Yes, but these stirrups keep the patients… the *female* patients…' she was hoping she didn't have to go on; that he'd get it and save her the trouble. She could see the cogs turning behind his gradually widening eyes but as yet no light had turned on. 'Their knees up and their legs spread so I can examine their—'

'OH!' he roared, 'I see.'

'A gynaecological examination table,' Erika said.

'A table for examining people with gynaecological, er, problems,' he elucidated, since *a table for examining people with gynaecological, er, problems* clearly required a much more specialised set of carpentry skills than a mere *gynaecological examination table*.

'Exactly,' Erika confirmed.

'That shouldn't be a problem.'

They both stood there, slightly breathless and flushed for a moment – Erika was sure it must have been the dust from the wood shavings affecting her lungs – until he said:

'Now, with regards to payment.'

'Oh yes,' she said. 'Do you have any idea how much it will cost me?'

'Well, I do, but I was wondering if we could come to some arrangement whereby you paid me by some other means than money.'

Erika's heart changed gear. She couldn't say that a lustful signal or two hadn't flitted across some portion of her brain, as yet unnamed by psychologists, since she had laid eyes on this carpenter and the muscular forearms bulging from his shirt sleeves. Perhaps it was also memories of her parents sending her off to live with Frau von Geröllheimer in Berlin as a result of her affair with Richard, the son of a 'mere' carpenter in Kunzendorf, which set deliciously rebellious feelings stirring in her loins. But she had never for a moment considered acting on such thoughts or feelings, let alone whoring herself to pay for her surgery furniture.

'Oh my God,' the man said, devastated as the look on her face related her most recent thoughts to him. 'I did not mean...'

'No.'

'Of course.'

'Of course.'

'I would never dream of...'

'Of course.'

'Of course. What I meant was: could you supply me with alcohol instead of money?'

'Alcohol?'

Things were going from bad to worse! The man she was entrusting with the job of constructing her specialised furniture was a drunk. How could he guarantee the work would be done on time and to the necessary standards if he was out of his head on booze or hungover? And he was asking *her* to supply the liquor; be the agent of her own downfall!

'Yes, you being a doctor and all I believe you can get your hands on pure ethanol from the chemist at a good price, can you not?'

'Well, er, yes, I can, but—'

'Oh that would be so good. It is so hard for me to get it and so expensive too these days and without it my brushes get ruined so quickly,' he said gesturing to a large glass jar on his workbench crammed with paint brushes crying out for some ethanol to clean them of the paint and the varnish that clogged their bristles. 'And I use it to get paint off the woodwork too. It really would be a godsend if you could get some for me.'

'Oh, I see,' Erika laughed a little too loudly to sound rational, but she didn't care – her relief demanded it. 'Yes, yes, I'm sure we can come to some arrangement about that.'

Max was doing his rounds. It was the middle of the afternoon and it was the middle of winter. But this winter was nothing like the last three he had spent in Gegesha. It should have been dark and it should have been cold, but the hospital was as bright as if were noon in June. No more trying to attend to wounds whilst squinting in the murky glimmer from candles improvised from empty rifle cartridges filled with industrial oil and a strand of cotton for a wick. No more skating about precariously on icy floors, no more hands and feet, backs and bones throbbing with longing for the sensation they used to call warmth. This was a gilded age, life was good. Electricity had finally reached this outpost of the Soviet Union.

Max trailed an eight metre long cable behind him as went from bed to bed, which was attached to a Heizkissen, a heat pad strapped to his back, a present made for him by a grateful patient. The first time he tried it Max could barely concentrate on his work, his ecstasy was so great. And there was a general air of quiet bliss throughout the camp these days as so many men learned how to build Heizkissen or little radiators, or traded cigarettes or food for one from the technological types manufacturing them from the wires and asbestos the prisoners stashed under the hospital beds. The barracks steamed with the heat radiating from each man's bed. The electricity cables strung from building to building glowed red in the eternal dusk from all that demand upon them. So it wasn't long before the guards noticed and confiscated all the Heizkissen and Wärmestrahler. They shouted at the prisoners, smacked a few about as they reprimanded them for these misdemeanours, but they knew that as soon as they left them alone, those resourceful Germans would start making more – and that suited the guards just fine as they would have even more heaters to confiscate and sell at the market in town.

With lightbulbs hanging from the ceiling of every building where once only bayonet-sized icicles did, the men were more inclined to outbreaks of festivity. By stashing away twenty grams of bread from your daily ration for a mere three weeks you'd have four hundred grams which when mixed with a gram of sugar and a load of berries from the barrel would cook up a treat over the fire into something akin, if you imagined hard enough, to Silesian Streuselkuchen.

'Happy birthday to you!' Max beamed at Horst presenting him with the cake which was the cue for all the occupants of the hospital, who were fit enough, to burst into song with him. Max watched his friend's eyes sparkle, in the glow from the now redeployed rifle cartridge candles, with all the childlike coyness which that simple melody has the power to induce in someone of any age and any nationality, any race or political persuasion. And Max was sure in that moment he could see his own daughter's eyes. The eyes that he hadn't yet seen, bewitched by the candles. The little hands that he hadn't yet held, palms pressed together in anticipation. The lips he hadn't yet kissed bejewelled with crumbs and smacking with the sweetness of the cake Erika had baked for her. Behind the cake he saw a bouquet of flowers on the table picked by Erika and his aunt Bertel from the garden of that red-brick terraced house, which he hadn't yet stepped foot in, but where they all thrived as a family without him. He saw his parents, Netta's Oma and Opa, showering her with congratulations and gifts on her birthday. Each birthday. Each of her two birthdays he had missed.

He'd kept a biscuit in his mattress after eating the rest Mrs Lagunov had given him in return for treating her for a bout of constipation.

'Take them as a token of my appreciation,' she'd said from the corner of her mouth without the cigarette in it, one eye closed to the smoke curling out of her nose, waving with one hand to the table whilst in the other she held little Oleg to her sagging breast so he could feed.

He'd kept the biscuit for weeks, until Netta's birthday. Then he'd told himself he was tasting the birthday cake that Erika had made as he nibbled on the cookie. Told himself the tears he quietly cried were tears of joy at seeing his family again, not tears of anguish trickling down his cheeks into his mouth and tainting the sweetness therein.

'Happy birthday, little darling,' he mumbled.

He was standing at the window, hands deep in his pockets, cable trailing out from under his coat like a monkey's tail. He was looking out at the sea, as black as ever in the Arctic afternoon, but uncommonly still. In all the time he had worked in this odd hospital standing in the water, he had been able to hear the waves slapping and flopping around the stilts, hear them grinding at the shore, see their whitecaps catching the moonlight on the horizon, sense that static soundtrack to his work even when he was back in the barracks. But today the sea had been stretched smooth like a gigantic piece of black leather pulled tight over the earth. So solid did it look that Max thought he could jump down from the bridge and run out across the surface. Run for miles. Run away. But to where? If he kept running straight he would be at the North Pole in no time, he huffed, and shortly after that he would be in Canada perhaps. Canada! Such a quicker route via the North Pole than travelling across Europe and then all the way over the Atlantic. On his stretched leather sea he could be in Canada in a matter of imaginary moments. Free of the Russians and this bloody prison. And then what? He demanded internally. What happens then? Then you are further away from your family than ever. What use is that?

The unusual stillness outside meant that even his billowing thoughts within could not deafen him to the sound of Horst's tattered boots slapping the earth urgently even way over by the perimeter fence where he'd resumed his sprint after being counted through the gate. He smiled at the unmistakable sound of Horst's loose sole flapping about as he ran. He smiled because he had another birthday gift for him.

'I knew it would come in useful one day,' he muttered to himself, reaching under the bed where amongst many other things was stashed the single boot the soldier had left in his hand as Max hoisted him out of that cattle train in Poland. It was the same foot as the one Horst desperately needed a replacement for and a little too big Max guessed, knowing his brother's measurements almost as well as his own, which would be easily packed to fit, much better than being too small. And most importantly it was in good condition and would keep his friend from getting trench foot.

Max turned towards the door long before Horst's feet hammered across the bridge and finally stopped as he closed the door behind him.

'What's the matter?' Max whispered since most of the patients were napping.

'Christoph just came back from town,' Horst followed Max's lead and lowered his panting voice. 'Said the Red Cross were there. Said they had told Ivan they would take letters from the men, deliver them back home.'

'Our letters?'

'Yeah, at last! Finally I'll have a way of getting in touch with Eva. And you can write back to Erika. Finally. Isn't that great news?'

Horst still hadn't received a single note from his wife and, although Erika had written many, only one other had got through to Max since her news about Netta.

'That is,' Max said looking over his shoulder dismissively at the solid sea, for now he had a much more direct way of getting home; a way he had almost given up dreaming about. 'That is really great news.'

*

'Have you heard the catch, though?'

Trust Edgar to piss on their picnic. So many of the men were looking forward to sending letters home that Max couldn't help but wonder if Edgar, having no family or someone special to write to, was enjoying explaining Ivan's proviso as much as Volkov enjoyed explaining it to him.

'The letters home are not allowed to be more than fifteen words.'

'Fifteen words?' Horst stopped admiring his new boot and sat up on his bunk. 'You mean fifteen lines.'

'No I don't mean fifteen lines, buddy.' Edgar remained supine on his bed, hands behind his head, enjoying the new Heizkissen under his back. 'I mean what I said.'

'Fifteen words?' Max said through his legs which dangled over the edge of his bunk above Edgar.

'Is there an echo in here?' Edgar sighed.

'What the hell can you say in fifteen bloody words?' Max wasn't sure if he or Horst said this out loud but both of them were thinking it.

Edgar's response came swiftly as if he'd planned it earlier. '*Wish you were here. Well not exactly, but I think you know what I mean.*'

'Shithead,' Horst grumbled whilst counting on his fingers to see if Edgar had used too many words in his oh-so-witty response, so that he could win a little victory back from his smart-arsed sparring partner.

Of course Edgar hadn't, but Horst didn't dwell on that – he had far more pressing things to consider, like how to fill in the three-year-wide gap in his relationship with his wife using no more than fifteen words.

The surgery was taking shape. Shelves that used to contain novels and a tea set had been cleared by Martha and now five glass jars stood on the top shelf in a row, each containing a human embryo in formaldehyde, each at a different stage of development. Netta stood, head back, mouth open, staring up at these rather ghoulish decorations. The little unfinished humans distorted by the glass around them and yellowed by the chemicals preserving them were there to demonstrate to pregnant women seeking an abortion in this Catholic stronghold just how murderous their intentions were, as far as Karl and Martha were concerned anyway. But for Erika, whose scientific vein still ran deeper than her religious one, they were there to inform her patients so together they could decide upon the most practical course of action.

Below the jars, and equally fascinating to young Netta, was a jar full of leeches used to suck the blood from the varicose veins of patients, their red sphincter-like mouths stuck to the glass had Netta unsure whether she wanted to kiss them or run away. And whilst her daughter was occupied with the jars, Erika was admiring the examination table Rodrick the carpenter had just hauled in, before which she had been admiring Rodrick's strength at hauling such an extremely heavy thing around. Although Karl had insisted on helping him with it Rodrick seemed to find the idea of a middle-aged grandfather with a dodgy wrist helping him as emasculating, and each time Karl tried to get a grip on the thing the carpenter had shoved it another few metres along the hall. And this was no ordinary examination table. Rodrick had taken it upon himself to fit cupboards on either side and drawers at the end below the metal stirrups. A panel even slid out from under the headrest to provide a surface for instruments during operations.

'I thought, you know, since you told me how your folks had partitioned their living room off for you that space would be at a premium, so all these additions should help with that,' he said opening the cupboard doors proudly.

Erika admired the mahogany spaces the carpenter revealed as well as the hands that revealed them.

'It really is amazing,' she gushed, 'and you're right, it will be so helpful.'

Rodrick demonstrated the adjustable backrest accompanying himself with short little hums like the revving of an engine as he sought further approval from his customer. He smoothed his hand along the leather upholstery from top to bottom until he came to the stirrups and with a quick little wiggle of one he thought better of further demonstration.

'Try it out for yourself,' he said before quickly adding, 'the head rest, I mean, not the, erm…' and he turned to inspect the plasterboard partition in order to conceal his blushes.

Erika was overwhelmed. It was the crowning glory of her new little surgery. Her first foray into life as a professional doctor.

'Who did this partition for you?' Rodrick enquired with a hint of scepticism.

'I did,' said Karl coming in from the kitchen and puffing his chest out proprietarily.

'Oh,' Rodrick said, running out of places to hide himself. 'It's erm…'

Erika saved him, 'It really is the most splendid table, Rodrick, thank you. I'm not sure a few bottles of ethanol can be payment enough for this.'

'Nonsense. It's what I asked for, wasn't it. And to me that stuff is priceless anyway.'

'But all the extra features you've added. It's so thoughtful of you.'

'We agreed a price already. The extras were just that. You didn't ask for them so I'm certainly not going to charge you for it. Consider it a good luck gift.'

'Well, at least let us offer you a coffee and a piece of cake before you go,' Martha said from the doorway where she'd been quietly standing for sometime.

'Well, thank you very much. That sounds like something I would happily agree to there, Mrs Portner.'

Erika and Rodrick smiled at each other. Then they smiled at the examination table.

'Karl,' ordered Martha, 'a hand please'.

This snapped Karl out of his rather stern scrutiny of Rodrick ever since he'd got a whiff of the carpenter's disapproval of his partitioning, not to mention the young man's approval of his daughter-in-law. He followed his wife into the kitchen where she was yet to decide whether to rebuke Karl for his suspicions (and in doing so rebuke herself) or add to them by voicing her concerns to him as she stood by the sink with the tap running to mask the words.

Erika and Rodrick were still smiling at the examination table. Then they smiled at each other.

'If there's any other jobs you need doing, then you don't hesitate to call me, OK?'

Erika wanted to touch the forearms exposed by his rolled up shirt sleeves as a show of gratitude, perhaps even secretly stroke the hair there lightly as she did so, but found herself instead saying, 'I appreciate that. My husband is in a POW camp in Russia at the moment, but I'm sure he'll be back soon.'

'Oh, carpenter too, is he?'

Erika wasn't sure if this was one of Rodrick's genuine questions or one of his attempts to show how indispensable he was to her.

'Well, no, but, I mean—'

'I bet it's hard having him away for so long.' Rodrick lowered his voice and flicked his eyes towards the door before letting them settle on her face again absorbing every nuance in her expression as he spoke. 'All I'm doing is offering you some help, if you want it, if you need it. There's no shame in asking for help. I know a strong intelligent woman like you may not want to ask, but I'm telling you not to worry about that.'

She couldn't resist any more and put a hand on his forearm which he immediately secured there with his free hand.

Erika started ever so slightly as the sound of water gushing furiously from the tap in the kitchen reached her. She looked down to see Netta by her side, head back, mouth open staring now at the carpenter with all the fascination and suspicion she had earlier heaped on glass jars of nullified children and wriggling blood suckers.

Max spent the first half of his next six kilometre walk into town discussing with Christoph the stipulations Ivan had put on their writing letters home, and the next half in many silent and abortive attempts to fit everything he wanted to say to Erika into fifteen words. As he walked, his fingers tapped out the words of his latest composition from deep in his fur lined pockets, often many times over as he thought he may have counted incorrectly and if he just counted one more time, a little more carefully, perhaps seventeen words would become sixteen, and sixteen words would become fifteen.

They weren't allowed to say anything about the war, their treatment as POWs nor the conditions in the camp, which Max found liberating – it meant all he had to do was concentrate on letting Erika know how much he loved her and Netta.

only allowed fifteen words so: don't worry, everything is fine here, I will be home

Idiot! You wasted five words telling her you're only allowed fifteen words, Max thought grinding his teeth as he walked.

Don't worry, everything is fine here, I will be home soon. Sending my love to you and

Way over! Way over!

Sending my love to you and Netta. So happy to hear you are both fine.

That's fifteen words, bang on. But does it sound like I'm gadding about here having a ball, *so happy*, whilst she struggles at home with the baby on her own? Damn it! Damn it all! Damn the Soviets and damn their bloody rules!

If only he could make Erika feel how much his heart ached to be with her and to see little Netta the fruit of their love.

'In there,' one of the guards was saying to him.

He had been so engrossed in his frustrating attempts to compose a message he had barely noticed when they had arrived in town and that they were standing outside the apartment block next to Lieutenant Lagunov's. The guard waved him inside with his rifle and Max found himself knocking on the door of a flat identical to the lieutenant's and equally crammed with people. But this time they were all adults – just about – and all females. This was where the prostitutes lived who serviced the Russian soldiers and today it was Max's job to check their health and disinfect where necessary, just as he used to in Breslau at the convent. However, there was no chance of a nun answering the door this time. What with the stench from the shit-lined street, the ice on the inside of the windows and thirteen girls crammed into a room not much bigger than Sister Hilda's cell back in Breslau, bitching and scratching and gnashing at each other, the place was more like a circle of Dante's hell than anything remotely divine.

'Which girl have you booked?' the young but haggard woman answering the door sniffed through her running nose as if she might be able to tell just from his scent who this guy in the fur coat had chosen.

'Oh, no,' Max stuttered, 'I'm not here to see a woman. Well, not just one.'

The woman's severely plucked eyebrows arched upwards towards her hair net and her already twisted lips coiled around themselves in amusement. Max quickly deduced the cause of her reaction and added:

'No, not like that. I'm here to see all of you.'

'Oh, better and better,' she cackled.

'Hope he's got a big fat wallet then,' another woman draped herself over the first one's shoulder, speaking to her in German.

'Are you German?' Max switched from Russian to his native tongue.

'Are you?' the women chorused with a sudden air of excitement.

'Yes.'

'So are we!'

The partially open door was now swung wide open and Max was welcomed into the room by a gaggle of German voices and the not displeasing sight of young women in various states of undress.

'But I'm not a client,' he had to insist over the clamour. 'I'm a doctor.' He patted his Red Cross arm band to draw their attention to it, though they were far more interested in admiring the cut of his coat and feeling the quality of the fur. 'I'm here to examine you all.'

Max quickly noticed that not all the girls were German. Some were local girls and so he felt he needed to maintain an extra standard of detached professionalism for them; show he was not enjoying too much the music of his own language played on these precious female pipes. He didn't need any negative reports about him getting back to the guards – and Volkov in particular.

As in the Lieutenant's flat there was just one small bedroom off the main room where he arranged with the girls to set up his surgery for the morning, after they had tidied it and removed all evidence that this was, inevitably since there was nowhere else, the room the girls worked in if they weren't called out to an officer's residence.

One by one he checked the girls, secretly revelling in the treble of their voices, their gentle teasing of him and their often caustic gossip. He handed out condoms, just as he had to the Russian soldiers though most of the men just tied them over the barrels of their rifles to keep the snow and water out. It worked a treat and they didn't need to fiddle about taking it off if they needed to use their guns – they could simply shoot through the rubber without any loss of accuracy.

'Some of the married officers have been following the boys' lead when it comes to protecting their guns with rubbers,' Isabel, the girl who had answered the door, giggled as they all sat round the table feeding Max coffee and biscuits after his work was done, 'but then their wives find the packets of condoms in their pockets and kick them out of the house for having affairs'.

'You can hear them arguing from the other side of town,' another more blowsy girl chimed in.

Max had to laugh along with his new friends.

'Some of the wives even end up coming round here, trying to smash down the door, screaming about how they're going to scratch our eyes out for sleeping with their men, silly cows,' Isabel cackled showing everyone a mouthful of half-chewed cookie.

And then one of the Russian girls sitting on the floor behind Max said just loudly enough for him, but perhaps not everyone in the room, to hear, 'But the thing is some of the wives are right.'

A furious knocking on the door made Max jump. He wasn't sure why he should feel so nervous all of a sudden. Perhaps he expected it to be one of those incensed wives. Perhaps he expected it to be a guard raging at him for taking so long – after all, he was here to work, not have a tea party with a load of whores. But it wasn't a guard or a wife, though he stood anyway, feeling like it was a sensible juncture at which to take his leave.

'Would you mind, lovey?' Isabel said to Max waving at the door, far too full on coffee and biscuits now to get up again.

Happy to oblige, Max stepped over the Russian girl and opened the door.

It was Jenny.

'Max?'

'Jenny?'

'Max!'

'Jenny!'

'You two know each other by any chance?' Isabel squawked.

Max didn't even turn to acknowledge her question. He was far too entranced by the apparition before him on the threshold. And in the second it took him to accept that Jenny was here in front of him, alive and well, it was all he could do not to throw his arms around her. Jenny, however, possessed none of the same boundaries when it came to decorum and hugged him with such affection it felt like he had his Heizkissen strapped to his back again. Yet it was much more than that. At first it was a shock to Max. He hadn't been embraced in this way, embraced by a woman since... well, since the last time he'd seen Jenny in Breslau that day in the convent when she'd congratulated him on his Iron Cross. So it took a moment for him to allow his body to receive such a gesture, but at the welcome end of that paralysed period he melted and reciprocated with a fervour and duration that almost had Jenny feeling self-conscious in front of her "sisters".

'I thought you were dead,' he exhaled into the shoulder of her coat, fur like his. 'I was sure you had all been killed when the convent was bombed.'

'So did I for a moment there,' she said pulling away but patting his arms and chest to show she wasn't rejecting him. 'Is there any of that coffee left?' And she walked into the room.

Max had stood on the doorstep for a minute hoping his guards were not loitering outside, hoping they hadn't seen him embracing Jenny or thought he was ready to go back to camp. He wasn't ready. And he'd hovered about in the doorway as Jenny poured herself a drink until she said:

'There's a right old draught with that door open, Max. Are you going or have you got time for another coffee?'

He had time, he said. He had nothing but bloody time. And he passed it for a bit longer with the girls, chatting, gossiping, though all he really wanted to do was get Jenny alone somewhere and talk like they used to talk. As friends, as confidants. Although he couldn't be sure at first with her nonchalant attitude around the table, it seemed she wanted the same thing too and eventually, after she had shared him with the rest for long enough, she led him by the hand into the little room and sat him on the bed.

'Sister Hilda dragged me down to the crypt as the bombing started,' she said finally answering his query. 'All of us who got down there survived.'

'But some didn't?'

'Mother Superior, Trudi,' she shook her head so slightly that Max wondered if he hadn't mistaken it for her trembling.

'Oh dear.'

'But it was out of the frying pan and into the fire,' she said getting on her knees and reaching under the bed for a small suitcase. 'We eventually clambered out of the ruins and the Russians were all over the place. They sent the nuns off to labour camps and girls like me off to Russia to entertain the troops.'

Volkov's account of the German soldiers raping that Russian woman had Max thanking God the likes of Volkov seemed to be taking their frustrations out on the POWs and not the girls. Or were they?

'And how are you?' he asked suddenly concerned, as her doctor and her friend. 'Are they treating you badly?'

'I'm OK. I mean, it's not exactly the convent here, is it,' she sneered at the dank room, 'but it could be worse, couldn't it?'

'What do you mean?'

'For you too. Well, look at us. A couple of Germans in the middle of nowhere, captured by Russians with a hell of a lot of axes to grind. But you and me we're alike, aren't we? '

Max didn't want to disagree, though he couldn't think how they were alike, so he kept his mouth shut and watched her as she finally fished something from the case and sat up on the bed next to him.

'We both provide a service that the enemy needs. And they're willing to give us some perks for providing it.' She stroked her own fur coat, stroked the lapel of his, then put her arm out to encourage him to stroke it.

He did.

'It's fox,' she informed him proudly. 'Yours too, eh?'

'I suppose so,' he said, though he'd never really thought about which animal the fur came from. He was far too busy enjoying the warmth it provided to ask incidental questions like that.

'Yeah, it's fox,' she sighed. 'The soldiers eat fox round here. Then they sell the pelts or have them made into coats like these for us lucky buggers.'

Max caught his breath, his nose suddenly filled with the stench of the bodies he routinely put at the bottom of the hill, the bodies the maggots had done with, the bodies that froze like logs until the skinny horse hauled them up to the top of the hill where the foxes fed on them howling ghoulishly between rotten mouthfuls. Were the Soviets so sick or desperate for meat that they ate the animals that had feasted on decaying Germans? They're cannibalism by proxy had him almost heaving. And his complicity in it by wearing the fox fur had his skin crawling. He slipped off the coat.

'Warming up again,' he mumbled.

'I was putting away the spare trousers you'd borrowed when the bombs started falling,' Jenny said showing him what she'd pulled from the case. 'That was when I found this in the pocket and I was convinced *you'd* been killed.'

It was the picture of the Black Madonna and child.

'I told you to keep it with you always for protection, you dumby!' she smiled as she slapped the air between them with the picture and for a moment he thought she might cry.

'I know. I'm sorry,' he laughed a little harder than he might have, to try and keep her tears at bay.

'If you'd kept hold of it you might never have been captured and ended up in this Godforsaken place.'

'But then I never would have met you again, would I,' he said as lightly as he could, 'so you see Mary must be looking after us anyway'.

'What, God moves in mysterious ways and all that?' she scoffed.

He shrugged. He really wasn't sure anymore.

'Have you got a pen?' she said with a pantomime tut.

'In my bag,' he said ducking into the other room where he'd left it and where the girls sprang into stilted conversation as if they hadn't been trying to eavesdrop the entire time.

He smiled politely at them, retrieved his bag and went back in to Jenny.

She snatched the proffered pen, scrawled on the back of the picture and without letting him see it she buried it deep in the inside pocket of his coat.

'You won't forget it this time,' she said.

'No,' he said, although if it wasn't so cold outside he would have gladly abandoned that fox fur coat for good.

'Now,' she said buoyant again, 'when was the last time you washed those trousers?'

Max looked down at his lap gormlessly, 'Er...'

'No-oh!' Jenny cried in mock disgust.

Max showed his teeth in a guilty yellow grin.

'That's, what, three years since I last washed them?'

His nod mixed mock shame with the real thing.

'We don't exactly have the facilities at Gegesha.'

'Get them off!' she ordered.

And he heard tittering from the room next door as he did as he was told.

As his trousers recovered from the shock of their own cleanliness, lying on top of the stove and gently steaming, Max, having to cover his legs out of modesty with that dreadful coat of his, and Jenny, examining her prune-like finger tips and reapplying her nail varnish, joined the others for more coffee. There were a few less ladies than before as duty had called them off to work, but Max was quite comfortable with any number of these women, as long as his friend was among them. And Isabel was just one of her comrades who had noticed that Jenny's being had seemed to lose all its angles and edges since Max had been around, which compelled her to ask:

'So how long have you been a POW, Max?'

'Three years more or less. Since Germany surrendered on the last day of the war.'

'Three years is a long time to be away from family. From loved ones,' she added slyly.

'It is.'

'There *are* loved ones then?'

He looked at her squarely in the face, not entirely sure what she was getting at and stated, 'Yes.'

'Max's got a wife back in… Freiburg, isn't it?' Jenny announced, well aware what Isabel's game was and determined to show her that her friend was not like the Russian officers round here with their sordid little secrets.

'It was, yes, but she's living in Bernried now with my parents.'

'Oo, cosy,' Isabel said into her cup.

'We've got a daughter now too,' he continued proudly.

A few of the girls gasped with delight.

'Really?' Jenny said. She had to respond. He was looking straight at her when he said it. It was her he wanted to share his news with more than anyone else in this room full of strangers. But she allowed the delicate operation that is the application of nail varnish to keep her eyes from his for as long as possible, so there was no way he could register her disappointment; her sense that after all this time without him and after such a short time reunited, it was all over. Because when it came to babies it couldn't go on. With clients it was a whole other story. No, she couldn't give a damn if they were fathers or not. Christ, a girl has to make a living, right? But when it came to the others, potential lovers – even if they were married at first, even if they said that it made no difference about the kids – as far as she was concerned it did make a difference and men with kids were out of bounds when it came to finding a partner.

'Yes, her name's Netta,' he beamed.

'Netta. That's a nice name, isn't it, Jenny?' Isabel said. 'Jenny?'

'I'm sorry,' Jenny said. Her nail varnish had never been so badly applied. 'What was that?'

She could barely look up from the table, since it was only a few moments ago – that moment when he had unwittingly declared himself eternally unavailable to her – that she first realised she wanted him.

'The doctor's daughter. Her name is Netta.'

'Oh. Nice name,' she threw a smile across the table for Max to catch. He was keeping his hands warm under the coat on his lap. One hand had ferreted its way into the inside pocket where it was gratefully caressing the old picture of the Black Madonna, its unseeing thumb gliding over the words newly inscribed on the back:

My dear brave Max. May you never lose me again! With admiration always from Jenny. x x

The surgery was empty. It had been empty since the day it had opened. It was full of things. The glass jars still stood on the shelves, the examination table still stood in the middle of the room, its cupboards and drawers now full of instruments and equipment. But the surgery was empty of patients. Not a single one had made an appointment. Twenty thousand people in the area, only three National Health Service doctors to go round. Why weren't they flocking to the door, Erika said through chewed lips to the window where she stood endlessly, hands on hips like a mannequin advertising white coats. Perhaps Rodrick was right after all. Perhaps she did need some help and this proved she was too bloody stubborn to ask for it. And she didn't just need furniture made for her by a man like Rodrick, she needed a breadwinner like him. What was she thinking? She knew for a fact that those other medical practitioners in the area were all men. She felt the buzz of exclusivity at being the only girl in her group of friends at university rush through her, then felt it instantly chased out of her by the male chauvinism of the medical world. That buzz hit the window with her breath and evaporated. Being a doctor was a man's game, it always had been. She watched as the shiny new plaque on the wall by the front door caught the attention of passers-by:

DR ERIKA PORTNER

They registered the female name and moved on swiftly. That was what they were doing, she was sure of it, men and women alike. She should have had the sign made with just her initials.

DR E. G. PORTNER

Then by the time they had got through the door and realised she was not just the secretary or the nurse they would probably be too polite to turn around and walk out, they would have to go through

211

with it and then they would realise she was a bloody good doctor, tell all their friends and she would have to find new premises to handle the enormous influx of patients, leaving those other three medics twiddling their insensitive thumbs and wondering where all their business had gone.

Rodrick had nice thumbs. Nice fingers. Nice hands. They were hard, calloused, enormous compared to hers. She felt so precious when he put her hand on hers that time over there by the examination table. Precious because she felt as if that rock of a hand could crush hers with ease, but she knew it never would, it would only be gentle, only be sensitive, only be protective, only make her feel—

These wild thoughts shot through the window, cavorted about on the pavement and darted across the road where they were instantly ran over by a bicycle already out of control, which promptly crashed into the kerb right outside Erika's door.

The rider was hurt. The rider was whining with pain. The rider needed a doctor.

Erika's eyes slowly rose to the clear blue sky above the terrace across the road.

'Thank you,' she mouthed.

Was her gratitude for the distraction or for the patient? Probably for both. She grabbed her bag and hurried outside.

The fallen rider had a nasty gash on one leg, which was bleeding profusely. She was also clutching her right arm to her chest which Erika recognised as the symptom of a broken clavicle. She bound some gauze tightly to the wound on the leg and helped the woman inside.

Once sat up on the examination table with her leg elevated, aspirin administered for the pain, the woman found the breath to speak:

'This is your surgery?' she winced as she focused on her surroundings properly for the first time.

'Yes,' Erika said, examining the woman's collar bone which was already swollen and purple where the break was. 'Are you having trouble breathing at all?'

The woman took a deep breath to test herself. 'No, it just hurts in my shoulder.'

Erika was encouraged by the depth of the breath and explained the pain was just from the broken bone itself. It had clearly not penetrated the lung. 'We need to get a sling on that and keep it elevated for at least four weeks.'

'Oh, no,' the woman grumbled, 'I can't be out of action that long. I'm a writer you see. And I'm right handed.'

'A writer, eh?' Erika's interest was piqued, hoping she had Germany's answer to Virginia Woolf in her midst.

'Yes, a journalist with the *Mengede Zeitung.*'

'Oh, how interesting,' Erika said, pulling out a folded square of bandage from the cupboard under the journalist and proceeding to turn it into a large triangle which she lay gently over the woman's shoulder.

'It can be,' said the woman gradually letting go of her arm and entrusting it to the doctor when she felt how deftly she turned the triangle of cloth into a comforting and supportive sling and how respectful she was of her body as she worked so closely around her chest.

'Oh, that feels a bit better already,' she said.

'The painkillers are probably beginning to take effect,' the doctor said missing the compliment the journalist paid her on her sling and her manner.

'Now let's see about this wound,' Erika said peeling back the gauze sloppy with blood.

'Is it bad?'

'Not too bad, but I could put a couple of stitches in there just to help it stay together as it heals if you like?' she said pulling open a drawer at the journalist's feet where she kept her sterile tubes of catgut.

'OK,' the journalist said paying more attention to the stirrups protruding from the table above the drawer. 'You're well equipped here,' she observed recalling the cold table of her own brusque doctor and his rough fingers poking at her insides, 'for women, I mean'.

'I specialised in gynaecology during my training,' Erika said. 'Not that that seems to count for much now,' she muttered as she found the appropriate needles.

'What do you mean?'

'Well, you are my first patient. And I've been open for over a week.'

'Really?'

'Yes,' Erika sighed. 'I suppose people around here are just not ready for a female doctor yet.'

'Not ready? They just haven't got a clue what they're missing. A woman being treated like a woman by a woman. Instead of having our breasts and genitals mauled by these condescending apes,' the journalist winced and smiled in quick succession as Erika introduced the sutures and looked up at her patient to check her reaction. 'My friend has mastitis that needs surgery and she's terrified about the state her doctor might leave her in after the way he's maltreated her boobs so far. I know what she means. He's my doctor too.'

'Well, send her to me,' Erika said appalled.

'Oh I will and I think you'll be getting many other women through that door very soon when they read my next piece about you in the newspaper.'

'No writing till that collarbone has healed!' Erika chastised her patient warmly though the thought of a glowing piece about her in the paper right now challenged her allegiance to the Hippocratic Oath to the utmost extreme.

'I can type with one hand,' the journalist grinned as they both admired her now neatly closed wound.

Erika had so enjoyed the solidarity this fellow female had shown her; was inflated by the compliments paid her; grateful to her for pointing out her advantage over the other doctors, which, no matter how hard they studied, how many papers they published, they could never match: her femininity. But whilst the writer railed against men and despaired at *having our breasts and genitals mauled by these condescending apes*, Erika couldn't help but notice a rush of blood to her own loins at the thought of her breasts being mauled by apish hands. It had been so long since she had felt another man's hands running over her skin and squeezing her breasts in the naïve way they do. The writer, she guessed, had a husband at home who took his fill with such mundane regularity the woman could discern no difference between their doctor and the husband anymore. But Erika, though appreciative of the sisterhood, did not see herself in the same tired category as her first patient. Erika was young, passionate and, for all she'd heard in the last couple of years, a widow. Or in other words, single. Alone. And that is why, having waved the writer off, she found herself making an excuse about catgut to Martha, parrying her mother-in-law's concern for the surgery with a snappy comment about there being no patients anyway, and hurrying down the street smoothing her dress and prodding her hair between its clips.

When she arrived at Rodrick's workshop she was breathless, from the speed of her journey and the anticipation of the destination. He was up to his ankles in sawdust, sweating profusely as he sawed relentlessly at an enormous plank of spruce. In only his vest, Erika used the sight of his thick engorged arms pumping to tell herself she was in the presence of a mythical specimen, the kind of Nordic superhuman she used to tell her wide-eyed girls about as they sat around the Hitler Youth camp fires, and so this was an opportunity no one could blame her for seizing.

Rodrick looked up as her shadow moved across his light. He stopped sawing, as breathless as she was, and asked her what was the matter, grabbing modestly at his shirt which was hanging on a nail in the wall. Without a word she stopped him from unhooking the shirt, slid her fingers up his moist muscular arms and, finding the back of his head, her eyes now glazing over in fear and ecstasy, she pulled him down to meet her fast drying lips.

The workshop was open. Anyone in the village who chanced to look down the alleyway, or even worse, came to the workshop to request Rodrick's services, would be able to see. But that made it even more thrilling to Erika. And Rodrick was more than happy to be seen, like this, thrusting into a woman such as Erika, as she lay half naked on his workbench, her hair now unclipped and full of sawdust; her hands frantically insisting he mauled her exposed breasts in a way in which he was more than happy to do.

She didn't feel guilty afterwards. She told herself it was simply natural. Nature reigning supreme again. Just as in the Swiss Alps all those years ago. She revelled in her animalistic side and on her next rendezvous flayed her arms and legs around in Rodrick's bed in celebration when he was out using the toilet. She felt more annoyed than guilty. Annoyed that she had to sneak out of her own home to be with him, tip-toeing about like her four-year-old self trying to escape her parents' villa for the mystique of the factory beyond.

She could barely think her husband's name when she was lying in the carpenter's bed, but when she did she tried not to compare Rodrick with Max. She tried. And sometimes she failed. Rodrick was so much more masculine than Max and in many ways so much easier to love. She talked about the Nuremburg Trials with Rodrick, and about how good life was in the thirties under the National Socialists. They agreed on everything and they never talked about religion. In fact Erika found him a little boring. Intellectually he was not the sharpest tool in the workshop, but she wasn't there to talk, she told herself, and besides sometimes Max could be so bloody minded. *You're going to have to convince me of your faith. Or I have to convince you of mine. Otherwise we'll have to separate.* He threatened her! That's basically what that was, wasn't it? Max bullied her into converting, talked her into marriage. They were all there at Freiburg, pursuing the same scientific goals and yet somehow he managed to make her feel like she was in the wrong for following that science to its natural conclusion: atheism. But there is nothing wrong with a natural conclusion; a tangible, corporeal reality. As doctors they knew that better than anyone. So nature it was. And natural she felt, if not bloody feral flailing her arms and legs around in those sheets and giggling uncontrollably.

They were in the barracks when Christoph delivered the mail. It was much later than his usual delivery, but then in retrospect Max contended if it had been at the usual time, when all of the doctors were likely to be in the hospital, Volkov could not have been there, still prevented from entering the hospital like all the other guards by his blessed paranoia. Volkov had clearly engineered this delivery, having been one of the guards to read the prisoner's mail before it was handed out, so that he could be there to enjoy the fall out when Horst read the first letter of Eva's that had got through in all the years he had been away.

'I'll read it later,' he said eyeing the lingering Volkov and pushing it under his pillow.

'No, doctor,' Volkov said coolly, though his hand on his holster said he was anything but cool, 'you will read it now'.

All the prisoners were on edge with Volkov hanging around and each of them in the vicinity of Horst's bed, Max included, sat themselves up on their bunks. As Max's eyes darted about the hut the expressions he saw had him recalling the passers-by at the tram crash outside the theatre when he was sixteen, not helping with the wounded, just gawping at the carnage.

Horst read. There was no sound in the barracks save the constant eerie song of the wind wheezing through the gaps in the shoddy structure. Max examined his brother's face as closely as Volkov did. Saw his slack open jaw gradually clamp itself shut. Saw the masseter muscle flex in his cheeks as he ground his teeth. Saw him grip the paper in his hands just as Mrs Lagunov had gripped the stained sheet on her bed as her baby forced its way out of her. It wasn't a long letter and less than a minute later, after having to re-read the first sentence three times to make sure he hadn't misread it, his hand shot upwards and delivered the paper to Max for his brother's opinion.

Before Max began reading, Volkov's smug voice stopped him. 'Aren't you going to say thank you, doctor?' Volkov always laced the

217

word doctor with such distaste it was obvious to Max he envied their skills and the status it gave them in the camp. He looked up from the paper. Volkov and Horst had locked eyes. Volkov gloating, Horst glaring.

'*Thank you for delivering my mail personally, Sergeant Volkov, thank you for making sure it got through to me this time,*' the Russian instructed in condescending tones.

This time? Max wondered if Horst had noticed that phrase too. There was something in it which, intentionally or not, gave Max the impression that Eva had written on many other occasions and that Volkov was aware of this, or even directly responsible for the letters not getting through. Yet now, when her letter contained bad news, which even without reading it was perfectly obvious to Max, Volkov made sure it was delivered and that he was there to relish the fruit of his sabotage.

And then Horst was launching himself up from his bunk and Max was launching himself down from his to stop his brother attacking the guard which would surely result in his being shot.

'No, Horst, no!' Max was barely able to hold him back until Bubi threaded his way between the beds from his bunk further down the hut and provided another bulwark between the enemies.

'Thank you, Sergeant Volkov for delivering the mail, now would you kindly leave,' Max spat over his shoulder as Horst continued to rage.

Although he tried to hide it behind his bravado, Volkov was shaken by the ferocity of the prisoner's outburst. Horst had always been more brawny than his friends and despite the years of malnourishment, he was still capable, especially with his current motivation, to pulverise his slight tormentor as finely as he ground coal for treating diarrhoea in the hospital.

'You should keep your little bulldog on a tighter leash, Dr Portner,' Volkov said trying not to hurry from the barracks, 'otherwise he'll have to be put down'.

The chloroform was administered by a mask held over the face. When unconsciousness was evident the cutting began. 'Great job, darling,' Erika said to Netta, 'but you have to hold the mask over the lady's face like that the whole time until I'm finished, OK? Can you manage that?'

'Yes, Mama,' Netta said teetering on the stool at the side of the examination table, her little hands gripping the mask which delivered the anaesthetic gas from the canister on the floor to the woman with mastitis who had come to Erika on the journalist's recommendation. Even though she had a four-year-old girl as her assistant – perhaps because she had a four-year-old girl as her assistant – the woman was infinitely more comfortable here than in the hands of Dr Frankenstein as she and her friends liked to call their family doctor. Ex-family doctor.

Having made an incision over the abscess, Erika inserted her finger into it to break down the fibrous tissue there and release more of the pus, which came oozing out much to Netta's disgusted enchantment.

'Keep your eyes on the mask,' Erika said noticing it slip from the patient's face. 'We don't want the lady waking up during this, do we?'

Netta was sure she wouldn't like to see this if it was happening to her so she concentrated as much as her young butterfly brain could on the task in hand.

Business was booming now since that article had appeared in the *Mengeder Zeitung* and she couldn't thank the journalist enough for it. But all these patients and all these procedures had their downside too. She knew she shouldn't complain, but she was exhausted. She had had to extend her surgery hours as it seemed that every one of the ten thousand women in the area was now coming to her for treatment. She needed a slightly more experienced assistant than her four-year-old daughter and her four-year-old daughter should be playing in the garden or learning piano with her Opa not watching her mother digging about in a lady's pustular breast...

There was a knock at the front door.

Erika huffed.

… And she needed someone to answer the door when Max's parents were not around. She couldn't rely on them forever. They had done so much for her already.

Luckily, this time Martha was on hand to answer and she opened the door to Rodrick. Erika was too busy draining the abscess and making sure this woman's breast was not defiled by the extent of the wound she had to make to hear their conversation. She didn't hear Rodrick ask for her. She didn't hear Martha say she was busy. She didn't hear him ask when she would be free. She didn't see her mother-in-law simply point to the plaque on the wall by the door.

DR ERIKA PORTNER

She didn't hear Martha tell him how Karl had made that plaque.

'Despite his handicap, despite his age,' she said, 'he is still very good with his hands and we don't need any more help thank you very much. *Erika* doesn't need any more help thank you very much,' she said pointedly and stared at him until he wrung those big calloused hands and meekly turned from the door.

Erika glanced up as the front door was shut firmly. She caught her breath as she recognised the dark hair on his bowed head, free of woodchips, washed and waxed, passing the window. She heard the stool dance on the wooden floor as Netta nearly toppled off it and snapped:

'Netta, will you concentrate!'

Although she might just as well have snapped at herself.

The infection seemed to have been removed. Now all she had to do was make sure the wound was sutured in a way that would leave minimal scarring.

After surgery closed, she made yet another excuse to the raised eyebrows of her in-laws and hurried to the village to apologise for not being available when Rodrick called.

Thank God for Martha, she thought as the sound of her heels

ricocheted about the quiet street, although she knew it was terrible to think so. Thank God she is always there to look after Netta.

She didn't give Rodrick a chance to speak when he opened the door. She stopped his mouth with hers, led him to the bedroom, stripped him, as he did her, and pulled him down on top of her, enjoying the way his weight crushed the breath from her.

'Your mo... Martha told me to sling my hook basically,' he said later picking at a patch of peeling varnish on the bed post.

'Basically?'

'Told me you didn't need any more of my help. Told me Karl could take care of everything.'

Erika stared at the ceiling deciphering the words for a moment.

'She knows!' Erika said to herself with a surprised naivety which astounded even Rodrick.

'I suppose she wouldn't be too happy about you becoming Frau Rodrick Gerlich then?'

The carpenter's thinly veiled proposal fell on ears only half-aware of what was being said. Erika was too concerned right then about the repercussions of her actions at home. If Martha knew, then Karl probably knew. Perhaps Aunt Bertel too. What did they think of her? Were they about to throw her out of the house? What would become of her and Netta then? Perhaps she should have thought of that before she left her daughter with her husband's parents so she could run to another man's bed? She smothered this chastising voice with a pillow and told herself it was fine. They obviously understood, otherwise she would be probably on the streets already. As long as it stopped here.

'Damn them!' She sat up and hit a bewildered Rodrick with the pillow. I suppose they expect me to go to confession now, do they? To stay at home, she fumed inwardly, work my fingers to the bone and be a nun for as long as it takes for my husband to come home? If he ever does.

Hang on! What was she thinking? She didn't need to worry about being thrown out on the streets. There was a big strong man here offering her a considerably smaller, but very well maintained roof over her head. His construction skills were second to none.

Adding another room for a surgery onto the workshop would be no great stretch for him. She looked at Rodrick's bovine mystified expression. She grinned, flashed feline eyes and straddled him.

Later that day she sat at her desk, rubbing her tired eyes, yawning incessantly, a blank piece of stationery before her, her patients' notes finally updated and stacked neatly to one side. She picked up a pen, looked over at the window where that dark, clean, waxed hair had passed earlier, clenched her incisors together behind pursed lips and began to write a letter.

Dear Husband,

This is the last letter I am writing to you because on June 24th I am going to marry another man. Then I don't have to work any longer. I have already been working for three years since you've been away from home. All the other men come home for leave, only you POWs never come. Nobody knows how long it will take until you come home. That's why I am going to have a new husband. I will give the child to the orphanage. I have to. I cannot stomach this life any longer. There is no way to survive with these few pfennig benefits. At work they have a big mouth when it comes to the women. But now I don't need to go there anymore, ~~my now~~ *the other man is going to work for me. All wives whose husbands are POWs will do the same thing and they will all get rid of the children. Three years of work is too much for a woman and 20 Mark for benefit and 10 Mark child benefit is not enough. You cannot live on that. Everything is so expensive now. One pound of bacon costs 8 Mark, a shirt 9 Mark.*

Your wife.

When Max had read and re-read the letter he sat down on the edge of the bunk where Horst lay. He was furious at Eva on behalf of his brother. How dare she rant about the cost of a shirt when her husband was right now wiping his tears with the filthy cuffs of the same shirt he'd been wearing for the past three years! Three years of interminable nights when he dreamed of nothing else but being back with her; when, had he ever been free to go, had the gates been left wide open for him, he would have run and run for as long as it took to get back to her and the kid. How dare she rant about the cost of bacon when her husband had nothing to eat but watery broth and black bread every day of this miserable existence!

'She knows you're a prisoner.' Max tapped at the paper. 'Whatever happened to loyalty, till death do us part, in sickness and in health?' He figured the best way to console his friend now was to encourage him to rave against his wife, since pity might only push him further to despair.

'The war. That's what happened to loyalty,' Horst replied with surprising equanimity. 'She has a point. She's had to work God knows where, suffer all kinds of abuse and try and look after Lisa at the same time. It's a pragmatic decision. And I can't blame her.'

Horst caught Max looking at him with a fair degree of horror.

'It's true, Max. If I showed up at home tomorrow I know she'd forget all about this... other man. Look!' He snatched the letter back. 'She doesn't address it to me, to *Horst*, and she doesn't sign off *Eva*. She says *Dear Husband* and *Your wife*. She can barely bring herself to call that other bloke her new husband. Look!' He flapped the letter at Max desperately – as desperate to convince his mate as himself. 'She crossed it out there and put *other man*. That's all he is. A practical solution to a dire predicament.' He lay back on the bunk again, hands behind his head, contemplating the canvas of the bunk above. 'I have to get back to her. That's all. And when I do everything will be fine.'

Max sat, head in hands looking down the tunnel of bunks before him, full of snoozing men, many of them husbands too. He hadn't heard from Erika in a while. Perhaps she was beginning to struggle too, perhaps she will soon seek solace, financial or otherwise, in an *other man*. He wasn't sure he could be so level-headed about it if he received a similar letter.

All wives whose husbands are POWs will do the same thing and they will all get rid of the children.

How could Eva be so sure? Erika wouldn't go to such extremes. She had the support of his family. She was going to apply for a license to practise medicine in Bernried, she said. She would be working for the National Health Service and making more than enough money to look after Netta. No daughter of his was going to end up in an orphanage! His inner tone sent memories of Gunther's voice echoing down the tunnel of beds:

'*No daughter of mine is going to spend her wedding night in student digs.*'

He laughed quietly at himself and gave Horst's leg a concerned but supportive rub as he got up onto his own bunk. There was a theory – wasn't there? – that women tended to marry men that resembled their fathers.

'God forbid,' he said shaking his head at the ceiling as he pulled his blanket over him.

Netta was already clutching her book of Grimms' *Kinder und Hausmärchen* when her mother came into the room to tuck her in.

'Which one shall we have tonight?' Erika asked perching on the edge of the bed and taking the book from her daughter.

'*Aschenputtel*, Mama. Will you read me *Aschenputtel*?'

Erika cradled the book and let the big pages peel off from her thumb as she searched for the tale, but before she found it, she stopped.

'No. Let's not have *Aschenputtel*,' she said. 'It's so... violent,' she grimaced and Netta began to sulk.

'What about *Die Wichtelmänner*?' Erika tried to buoy up her little wretch. 'Yes, let's have *Die Wichtelmänner*!'

And as her mother began the tale of a poor shoemaker and charitable elves, Netta was longing for the other story where the heroine's mother watched over her from heaven, dropped beautiful gowns and slippers in her lap so she could go to the ball and made sure that eventually, no matter how unlikely it seemed, the prince would find her and they'd live happily ever after.

It wasn't long, however, before Erika's story was just a string of soothing sounds, the words themselves irrelevant, and Netta was soon asleep.

Erika closed the book on her lap and leaned on it with such force it would seem to someone entering the room that she was suffering stomach pains. She squinted at the Tiffany window, mesmerised by the evening light diving through the stained glass and landing on the floorboards in pools of sapphire blue and cherry red.

Voices downstairs disturbed her tussled thoughts. Karl's voice. Martha's voice. And a man's voice. The voices were raised to a degree of animation, excitement, commotion even. Despite the fear that told her to hide away up here in the attic, she found herself checking her appearance briefly in the mirror before hurrying downstairs. She had to hurry, as there might still be time, she realised, to stop him saying anything stupid to her in-laws.

In the ever-fluctuating intensity of light emitted from the bulbs which dangled from the beams of the hospital, Max, having completed his rounds, pored over the papers on his desk with such absorption one might have assumed he was auditing the sickness figures or checking the stock levels. But in fact he was still trying to concentrate everything his heart and mind had to communicate to Erika into fifteen words – and with more urgency now than ever since Eva's letter to Horst had Max itching with paranoia. After yet another growl of frustration and the furious scratching of his pencil over an unsatisfactory attempt, Edgar appeared at his shoulder.

'Think of it like a song, buddy.'

'What on earth are you talking about?' Despite the crossings-out, Max instinctively put his hand over the page self-consciously.

'Think of it like swing,' he said clicking his fingers to the tune in his head.

'Swing.'

'Yeah. And think of a full length letter like an opera.'

Max loved the opera. Well, Erika loved the opera and she had taken Max on a few occasions after which he was hooked himself. It was one of the things he missed most about being in prison here. He had not yet become as enamoured with swing music as his best friend.

'You see, that's one reason – I think – why the Nazis had such a problem with swing. It is a threat to classical music because, in just a three minute song, it can take the spirit to heights an opera takes three hours to reach.'

Max looked at his bohemian friend suspiciously and said, 'But don't tell me you don't appreciate classical music now. You played organ in the church for God's sake. You were the first one to buy a ticket for *Madame Butterfly* or *Carmen* when they came to town.'

'Uh!' Edgar slapped a hand over his heart, '*Carmen* – such a triumph of melody and orchestration. And as for that fiery gypsy. Enough to turn a homo hetero.'

Max had to smile.

'No, I love classical music, but the Nazis were probably worried if everyone fell in love with the music of the *nigger*,' he mouthed the word with pantomime disgust, 'and fell out of love with the interminable racist rants of Wagner and the likes, then the country would go to pot. And *we* know better than most where that policy got us, don't we.'

Max removed his hand from the page and examined the clouds of graphite he had scratched there.

'A song, you say?'

'Exactly. Right now you need to think like a swing musician.'

'But I don't exactly have the music of Vince Lopez and his Smooth Swing Orchestra behind me to elevate the words, do I?'

'Suave Swing Orchestra.'

'Eh?'

'It's Vince Lopez and his *Suave* Swing Orchestra. Not Smooth Swing Orchestra,' Edgar said with listless disapproval, before snapping back into his effervescent role as Max's lyrical guru.

'Well, think of yourself as a poet then.'

'A poet.'

'Yes, a poet,' he cried. 'Trim off all that unnecessary fat from the sentences chattering away in your little head and charge the remaining words with meaning to the utmost degree.'

'But how?' Max recalled watching with gaping awe as Reinhold Schneider took to the stage in the basement of The Golden Bear and recited his beautifully encrypted antiestablishment pieces.

'Only those who pray may still be able

To stop the sword over our heads...'

Max felt the confluence of emotions again when these glorious opening lines accompanied Erika's unreasonable stomp from the bar. He knew he had to follow her. He wanted to. He wanted her to be happy. He wasn't happy if she wasn't. But just a few more lines first. He had to hear a few more life affirming lines from the mouth of the poet himself before he went back to real – as yet uncertain – life outside The Golden Bear, in the streets where the Bächle trickled like tears on the face of the city.

'Only those who pray may still be able
To stop the sword over our heads...'

There's fifteen words there, Max counted, but I'm no Schneider, he told himself.

'Think of the Japanese masters of haiku,' Edgar was pontificating now. 'In a mere seventeen syllables, or should I say *on*,' he bowed, 'they managed to capture the physical and spiritual world in a highly refined and conscious manner.'

'Edgar,' Max said from beneath unamused eyebrows.

'No, you have to try. Come on.' He nudged Max from the chair and took his place. Pencil poised, he thought for a moment then began to write:

Ice and unceasing snow

'No that's six syllables. It has to have three lines of five, seven, then five syllables.'

Ice and drifts of snow

'There we go!'

Freeze my dreaming but every day

'Well that's eight syllables,' Max pointed out, getting dragged into the game.

'I know, I know.'

Freeze my dreams, but each day

'Better,' Edgar told himself sucking on the end of the pencil, 'but too much cold, ice snow and freezing'.

'And what's this got to do with Erika anyway?' Max grumbled.

'You'll see, you'll see, give me a chance, old boy.'

A few more rejected words, much rapid counting of syllables and then finally Edgar recited his masterpiece:

Ice and drifts of snow
Blight my dreams yet Erika
Still I rise for you.

'Uh!' That hand was clamped to his breast again. 'How's that? And, one two three four five six... fifteen! It has fifteen words exactly. I'm a genius! Send that to her and melt her heart, mister. I've clearly missed my calling. I should have been a poet not a bloody doctor.'

'I'll attest to that,' groaned the prisoner in the nearest bed who'd had to endure irrigation of the gaping ulcers on his leg by Edgar that afternoon.

Unlike his patient, Edgar was back on his feet, admiring the words on the desk as if it were a painting in the Louvre.

'It's... lovely, er, I think,' Max sighed, 'but it's not me, is it? I mean, she'll wonder who the hell wrote this. Think it's a prank or something.'

'A prank? A prank?' Edgar squeaked. 'Erika appreciates literature. She would see the craftsmanship in this even if you can't.' And he stomped off to pointlessly poke the fire.

Max sat staring at the flamboyance Edgar had left on the page until his eyes saw nothing, but his ears tuned into the ebb and flow of the waves on the shore outside; to all the memories they brought like bottles breaking on the stones and unfurling their messages to float on the surface of Max's trance.

'Take care,' Erika had ordered Edgar before they left for the Rhine, 'of him and you. And if you come back dead, I'll kill you'.

Fifteen words. Most of which made no sense. And yet they said it all.

I know it is not the same, but would you be my adopted
brother, brother?

Fifteen words from his dear friend Horst sewed up a wound in his soul he thought could never be repaired when Sepp was killed.

My dear brave Max. May you never lose me again! With admiration always from Jenny.

Those fifteen words from Jenny were like a Christmas gift to a child when he discovered them many days after she'd written them, and he felt they gave the talismanic picture even more power to protect him from the rigours of life in Gegesha.

All prosaic indeed compared to Edgar's outpouring, but Max knew exactly what he wanted to write to Erika now as he blinked himself back to the present and pressed his pencil into the page with a secret smile.

'Max, Edgar!' Bubi's voice was so cracked with grief as he entered the room that Edgar dropped the poker and rushed over to the boy.

Max kept his eyes on the page, but the pencil had stopped after only one letter, a long confident *L*.

'What is it, Bubi? What is it?' Edgar hissed.

Max waited for the word that he both knew would come and prayed would never do so. In the ever fluctuating intensity of light emitted from the bulbs which dangled now from the beams of the hospital like little luminous nooses, Bubi said:

'Horst.'

Transcription of covert recording made at Gegesha labour camp 16 June 1948.

Meeting commenced 0830hrs

Utkin (Colonel): Explain to me what happened.

Volkov (Sergeant): Yesterday afternoon, the afternoon of June 15th, I was alerted that a prisoner had escaped.

Utkin: How had he escaped?

Volkov: He was counted out of the gate in the morning but failed to return after his shift at the hospital.

Utkin: He's a doctor then?

Volkov: Yes, one of them.

Utkin: How did you know he wasn't tending to a patient somewhere; to one of our officers in town for example?

Volkov: This particular doctor never does go into town. I have personally seen to it that only the chief doctor is sent to treat our officers, sir. The medic in question is just his subordinate.

Utkin: That may be so, but where did you eventually find the doctor?

Volkov: The prisoner was caught up with on the road west of Pechenga heading for the border. He was spotted by our men at the checkpoint ducking off the road. I was already in pursuit at this time anticipating the prisoner's move.

Utkin: How very insightful of you, sergeant. How did you know he was going to make a run for it?

Volkov: Well, he had just received some, er, devastating news from Germany. Sad really. His wife was marrying some other man apparently. I expected he might do something rash.

Utkin: So you were there when he was apprehended?

Volkov: Yes. I was radioed from the checkpoint. The prisoner was attempting to go cross country to avoid our vehicles, but our armoured car had no problem with the terrain and he was apprehended without further incident.

Utkin: Without further incident, you say? You are joking surely, sergeant?

Volkov: Well, without further incident until he attempted to grab at my pistol, sir, but luckily I got there first. That's when there was a bit of a scuffle for it resulting in the gun going off.

Utkin: Going off?

Volkov: Yes, sir. The prisoner was shot.

Utkin: Did you attempt to treat his wounds?

Volkov: Of course, sir, but without a medic present there was only so much we could do.

Utkin: But there was a medic present wasn't there, Sergeant?

Volkov: I beg your pardon sir, but there wasn't.

Utkin: There was. And he was writhing about on the ground no doubt due to the bullet wound in his..?

Volkov: Oh, I see, in his stomach sir. It appeared to be in his stomach. Of course it was likely to be, what with the scuffle and everything. But it was difficult to tell, the light being what it was.

Utkin: It's the middle of bloody June, Volkov,

you can't blame it on the dark this time.

Volkov: It was, erm, raining sir.

Utkin: [unintelligible] So now we're one medic short in a camp already overrun with death and disease, where even our own men are dropping like flies.

Volkov: But he was trying to escape, trying to attack us, sir and so I simply—

Utkin: You simply went by the book as you always do, sergeant, right? Well, very well done. Very well done.

Volkov: Thank you, sir.

Utkin: Oh, get out!

Meeting adjourned 0840hrs.

Max saw his feet first. Two odd boots. One pretty worn, the other in great condition, the one he had given to Horst not that long ago. That was when he knew it was true. The unbelievable truth that his brother was dead. The body dumped at the bottom of the hill with all the others from the hospital. Except Horst hadn't ever been treated in the hospital. He never stood a chance at surviving the bullet wound. And Max never stood a chance of trying to help him.

'You stupid bloody idiot, Horst. Running away on your own like that. Without even telling me. Not that I would have let you go, of course, but at least if you had insisted I could have made sure you took... I don't know... some things in case of emergenc—' Max's body was seized by spasms of grief.

He felt Edgar's hand on his shoulder. Heard Bubi's shivering lips utter, 'Oh God,' and tried to get a grip on himself as he always did when the boy was present. Not that Bubi was a sixteen-year-old boy anymore. Bubi was a twenty-year-old man, but Max still felt an overwhelming desire to protect him from grief and horror, and be a bastion of confidence and strength for him, which no boy should ever have to provide for himself. From Mrs Lagunov's little Oleg to Bubi to his own daughter Netta, none of them had asked to be born and certainly not into a world as desecrated as this one. They owe us nothing, Max cried out inwardly. Not even after a lifetime of rearing them, when we are old and infirm can we demand they look after us in return. No compensation is great enough for what we did by bringing them here in the first place. The very least we selfish adults can do, Max riled at himself, is soften the blow of existence as much as possible.

As his weeping eyes took in the rest of his friend's body and blinked at his face, Max realised what he was looking at was Horst, but not Horst. That was Horst's face – despite the blue skin and frost on his eyebrows, which made him look aged, it was clearly his face. But it wasn't *him*. Because his spirit had gone, hurrying back to wherever it had first been dragged from when he was conceived, and left the body unrecognisable.

To cocoon himself in the arms of his wife was the only thing that could even begin to ease the sting of his loss, yet he didn't even have Erika's body with him here, spirit or no spirit within it. How was he supposed to recognise her anymore, keep her in his mind? Every time he thought of her it was a struggle to see anything now. And he wondered if it was the same for her. She's receding from view, he sobbed to himself, like the unscathed Germany did at the end of a tunnel as he watched from the back of a train passing into Romania. She was a voice on a radio, a radio that couldn't be tuned. A ghost among the static. A face in a movie, a movie reel burnt in the bombing of the cinema where the audience slept in their seats with cherry red faces from carbon monoxide poisoning. Put the reel through the projector once more and some frames would have survived, but the images would flash across the screen too quickly to be identified, especially by an audience of suffocated corpses. The letters she wrote no longer got through. She waited invisibly for word from her vanishing husband.

He sat up on his bunk, clawed his stub of a pencil from the mattress and his as yet unwritten postcard from his bag and wrote his fifteen words to Erika at last:

I am in hell. There is no God. Live for the moment and forget me.

Edgar looked for hours at the empty bunk next to him and heard the scratching of the pencil above him. When Max finally stopped thrashing about and slept, Edgar got up and read the words on the postcard Max held to his chest in the light of the Midnight Sun burning through the rotting roof.

Erika burst into the living room to find him standing there facing Karl and Martha. She still knew so little about Rodrick. She didn't even register as she almost slid down the stairs, that the third voice in the living room was far too trebly to be his. It was a man's all right, but not the heavy lowing of her lover. Rather the gentle yapping of an old friend.

'Babyface!'

Most of the apprehensions he'd had at seeing Erika again after all this time were blown away by the huff of relief that shot from her gaping mouth. And if any remained thereafter they were squeezed out of him by the arms she clamped so firmly around him.

'Hey!' he said, partly as greeting, partly in shock at the intensity of her welcome.

'What are you doing here?' she squealed, releasing him for a moment so she could examine him. It was no surprise to Erika, or anyone else that knew his nickname, that the years had been kind to Kurt Bayer. He didn't look any different from the last time she saw him in Freiburg and she couldn't help a snort of envy, especially given the tut she'd just aimed at her own drawn reflection upstairs moments ago.

'Kurt is staying just the other side of Dortmund,' Karl beamed, delighted to have a male acquaintance of Erika's in the house whom he didn't consider a threat to the stability of his household or his absent son. 'I was just saying the last time we saw him was probably on your wedding day.'

'I think that's probably true,' Babyface said, just as he'd responded the first time Karl had said this minutes ago.

'What an eventful day that was!' Karl chuckled. 'What with the goose and...' He flushed and looked suddenly sad, '... and poor Franz.'

Martha put a hand on his arm to let him know she could take it from here and she did: 'We had to beg, borrow and steal to make that wedding day a success, rationing being what it was at the time.

237

It was quite some challenge, wasn't it! But all worth it in the end, eh?' She looked straight at Erika, as if daring her to disagree.

'Oh, I remember it well. Great party. Great day. Good times,' Babyface sighed.

Each of his short sentences seemed to bring the sun a degree lower behind the rooftops. The four of them stood trying to fill the growing silence with little coughs or chuckles until Martha said:

'Well, I will make you two a nice cup of coffee as I'm sure you have so much to catch up on.'

'Oh thank you, Mrs Portner, that's very kind.'

'No trouble,' Karl said following his wife into the kitchen. 'Make yourself at home. Any friend of Max and Erika's is a friend of ours.'

Erika felt the barb in that last statement, intentional or not, and scowled at Karl's back as he disappeared. Babyface, perceptive as ever, noticed.

'Trouble with the in-laws?' he whispered.

'Oh, no, no,' Erika ushered her friend into the most comfortable armchair and pulled another close enough so she didn't have to speak with any volume to be heard. 'It's just that... well, sometimes they seem to handle Max being away so much better than I.' Before she receded into an unsociable reverie on the scene she thought she was descending the stairs into a minute or so ago, she slapped her knees and chirped, 'So, what *are* you doing here anyway, Babe?'

'Your letter?' Babyface said to his unfocused friend, 'the one you wrote to me recently?'

'Oh! I did, yes. Yes, of course. Oh, I'm sorry if it sounded so dramatic, but, you know...'

'I know. I understand. It's not dramatic to feel depressed when your husband has been away for...'

'Three years, nine months and eight days... roughly.'

They both smiled knowingly at this and it sent Erika's mind racing back through summer balls, nights in crowded basement bars and intellectual sparring in a draughty room filled with friends all trying to keep warm on a winter's day; the kind of cerebral stimulation she'd almost forgotten was possible now her life consisted of talking about fairy tales with her daughter or explaining pustules to patients.

'But as much as I love you,' Erika squeezed her friend's knee, 'I'm sure you're not staying in Dortmund just because of me.'

'How could you say such a thing?' Babyface pantomimed offence. 'Actually you're right, I was sent here to help out at Dortmund paediatric unit, and thought what a perfect excuse to come and see old Erika.'

His grin only seemed to make his smooth face smoother. Erika thought of the lines she had noticed around her eyes recently and a pulse of paranoia told her that was why he had just used the epithet *old*. But the paranoia quickly transmuted to envy again.

'I wish Max had chosen paediatrics,' she said through gritted teeth. 'I wish all of us had, then the boys might have never had to go to the front and they wouldn't all be stuck in some Bolshevist hellhole right now.'

The guilt that Babyface was about to endure for having stayed in Germany throughout the war was quickly obliterated by the memory of Erika's passion for fascism, which her venomous enunciation of the word Bolshevist told Babyface was yet to be fully extinguished.

'Any more news from the camp?'

'Nothing, since that man came and gave me the address Max had written down.'

'I can ask around at the hospital if you like. You never know. Someone might know someone who knows something.'

'That's very sweet of you, darling.' She rubbed his knee now, and to Babyface it felt like there was both warmth and irritation in the action. 'But perhaps,' she lowered her voice and darted her eyes towards the kitchen, 'perhaps we have to face reality. Perhaps they are never coming back'.

'Oh, but...'

'No, Babe, surely it's only sensible to face it at some point. Netta is growing up fast. She needs a father in her life. What if I wait only to be told eight years from now that Max has died or been executed?'

Babyface had come to help, but right then confronted with perfect logic and probability, branches of science he entrusted decisions to every day, at home and at work, he felt powerless to do so.

'You're feeling desperate, tired, I understand,' he offered. 'That's why I'm here. You can talk to me. We can even think about some medicine to help you through.'

'Like what?'

'Benzedrine, methedrine. You must have read about them. Our lot and the Allies were all using them to get through the war. Doctors are using them now to keep going on long shifts too. It can help lift your spirits, Erika.'

'How do you know? Are you using them?'

She perceived his almost imperceptible hesitation before he replied, which told Erika it was not the answer to her problems.

'Yes,' he said, 'sometimes. Look, you need help. Try it and see if it works for you.'

'You're right, Babe, I do need help. But what I need is a friend...'

'You have that...'

'I know and I love you for that, but I mean I need a partner, a rock, a man around full time. So perhaps I should be... trying that instead of drugs first?'

'Here you go!' Martha came in with a tray adorned with coffee, biscuits and even napkins.

We *are* honoured, Erika sneered inwardly at the display, but said nothing until Babyface had thanked her profusely and Martha had retreated to the kitchen.

They sipped on coffee. He munched on a biscuit and studied her face as she studied the ripples her tapping finger made in her cup. Eventually he dared to say it.

'Have you been... tempted? I mean, is that what this is all about?'

'What *what* is all about?'

'All this talk of finding someone else. And your letter, it was like you felt the need to get something off your chest, but you didn't know where to turn.'

Erika nodded at the dark waves and tapped so hard now on the edge of the cup some of the coffee nearly spilled out.

'You can tell me anything, you know. We're *buddies*, as Edgar would say.' He tried to lighten the mood with memories of their flamboyant friend. He knew he was so close to a confession that he was more thrilled at the idea of getting one than actually dealing with any fallout from it.

'There is a man,' she told her cup. 'A carpenter in the next village.'

'Oh. OK,' Babyface felt sick with triumph.

Erika might have been saying something else about this man, about what he looked like perhaps, what they had got up to together even, but the only thing he heard as he tried to digest this information, as the feelings it provoked foamed up inside him, was: 'He'll do.'

'*He'll do?*' Babyface quickly drank the remainder of his coffee and put down his cup, freeing his hands for the gesticulation necessary to ram home his point. 'You mean to tell me you're going to spoil everything between you and Max for someone who will merely *do*? Jesus Christ, girl, if you're going to stab Max in the back at least do it with someone who's not second best.'

Erika was rocked by this outburst despite the hushed tones it was executed in. If she had thought about more than just herself for the next few minutes, she would have realised that Babyface was not just worried about her relationship with Max being spoiled, but the destruction of their neat little gang – Horst, Edgar, Max, Erika and Babyface – the five musketeers, whom he was so looking forward to reuniting with when all this mess the war had left was finally behind them.

'I'm not stabbing anyone in the back, Kurt,' Erika whined. 'I'm just trying to move on with my life, and do right by my daughter.'

'Max's daughter too.'

'He might be dead!'

'He wasn't when that man with the missing fingers came to see you.'

'That was three years ago. Three years in a labour camp.'

'But he was a doctor there. He'll have more chance of surviving than most. And if anyone will survive it's those three. Together they're a pretty formidable bunch, don't you reckon? Come on, Erika, what were you thinking?'

'I'm thinking I might let you prescribe me some Benzedrine after all,' she giggled briefly, uncontrollably.

'Oh, grow up, Erika! God knows where you'd be now if it wasn't for Max.'

'What the hell is that supposed to mean?' she hissed.

'He saved you.'

'From what?'

'From being an outlaw right now, for one thing. From being one of Hitler's mindless sheep. From thinking this is OK,' he said ferreting about in his pocket and pulling out a flyer, which he handed to her.

At the top of the flyer were the English words REMEMBER THIS! Beneath were five photos. Appalling pictures of emaciated naked bodies piled in long rows being prodded by the barrels of German soldiers. Women picking the clothes off corpses in barbed wire cages. Men in striped pyjamas huddled in the snow in a gateway with a sign forged from wrought iron, incontrovertibly in German, above their heads, which read WORK SETS YOU FREE. Death and abuse on a scale even she as a doctor had never seen. And at the bottom of the page the English words DON'T FRATERNISE!

'What's this?' she asked as steadily as she could.

'What the British and Americans are posting around town for their soldiers to read.'

'Is this supposed to make me feel more positive that my husband is in a camp like this, because I'm afraid you're way off, Babe.'

'Those aren't pictures from Russian camps, Erika. They are German camps. The kind your heroes sent all the Jews to. The kind they would have sent Edgar to for being queer if they had got to him before the Russians did...'

'This is propaganda, darling, you must know better than to be fooled by fake images like this.'

'... and these are the kind of places they would have sent Professor Hass to for speaking out against the Nazi euthanasia programmes.'

'Who?'

'Oh, don't give me that, Erika! Professor Hass, remember? The gent that *someone* poisoned in the café on campus. Was that a fake? No, it was very real, wasn't it? I mean, you know better than anyone how real that was, don't you?'

Investigatory Interview Record
University of Freiburg

STRICTLY PRIVATE & CONFIDENTIAL
FILE NOTE Minute Taker's original covert copy before official amendments were made: deleted section marked by red{}

Name of witness/employee interviewed	Stefan Eckstein
Job title	Laboratory assistant
Department	Medicine
Allegation/Issue	Use of university resources for illicit purposes
Date of interview	1st December 1942
Interview Venue	Rector's office
Name(s) of other attendee(s)	Jana Tillmann — Minute taker
Horst Seckler – Rector, Chair and Investigatory officer	
Gregor Brotz – Professor of Biochemistry	
Interview Started	16:10

Introduction

Mr Eckstein has been asked to attend this interview to assess how cyanide solution from the university laboratories was used to allegedly poison Professor Hass on 29th November 1942.

Note of Discussions

Horst Seckler (H.S.): Mr Eckstein, I am sure you are aware by now that Professor Hass was poisoned using cyanide solution.

Stefan Eckstein (S.E.): Yes I am. Terrible. Just terrible.

H.S: And are you aware that an amount of cyanide solution was taken from the university supplies the day before Professor Hass was poisoned?

S.E: Well, it wasn't taken so much as I gave it to someone. I mean, legitimately. I mean, they came like any other student does, showed me their Identification card and told me what the substance they were requesting was for. They signed for it and I gave it to them.

H.S: And who was it that came and asked you for cyanide on the 28th November?

S.E: I don't recall their name, but they showed me their card.

Gregor Brotz (G.B.): You don't recall their name, but they showed you their card! Did you even bother to read the card then? Because what the hell is the point of looking at someone's ID card if you don't bloody well read it?

H.S: All right, Professor. Perhaps then Mr Eckstein, you can describe the person in question.

S.E: I can yes. She was—

H.S: Ah, it was a woman, was it?

S.E: Yes. A woman. She was young. She certainly looked of student age. Dark hair, long dark hair, just to here [S.E. puts his hands on his shoulders]. Not particularly tall. Average height for a woman I would say. Brown eyes, I think. And a purple coat. A dark purple coat. Long. With a red scarf.

G.B: And she just asked you for cyanide and you gave it to her.

S.E: She asked for a small amount of cyanide solution to use in a study concerning its toxicity in rats. It hardly sounded groundbreaking, but there was nothing unusual in her request. She signed for it anyway. I can easily bring you the records and then we will know her name.

G.B: Do you really think, Stefan, that someone who intends to use a substance to poison someone else would sign for it using their real name?

S.E: I don't know.

H.S: Well, it shouldn't be too difficult to identify the woman in question if she is a student at the university. There are so few in the department of medicine. And your description has been very helpful, Mr Eckstein.

G.B: Have you discussed this incident with anyone else, Stefan? {No need to minute this bit, Jana.

S.E: No. Well, nobody except my friend Kurt.

G.B: Kurt?

S.E: Kurt Bayer, he's a student in the department.

H.S: You know him, Gregor?

G.B: I do, yes. Shouldn't be a problem.

H.S: So, Mr Eckstein, it is vital that you do not discuss this matter with anyone else. And you can tell Mr Bayer the same. Both your positions at the university will be in jeopardy if you do. As you can imagine, this is a very serious matter. And in order to catch the culprit we rely on your utmost discretion.

S.E: Of course. But, Rector, am I in trouble for giving the cyanide to this woman?

H.S: Not at all, not at all, we understand you were just doing your job. The most important thing now is that you forget about the whole business, all right?

S.E: All right.

H.S: Thank you for coming and for your co-operation. Professor Brotz will be sure to let the laboratory head know how helpful you have been and I'm sure that will be most advantageous to you in your career.

S.E: Oh, well, thank you, sir. [leaves the meeting].

H.S: Sorry about dragging you over for that, Gregor, but we have to be seen to be doing something, don't we?

G.B: Unfortunately, we do.

H.S: Jana, please type up only the pertinent parts, as Gregor indicated. The rest you can… misplace. Heil Hitler!

G.B: Heil Hitler!}

Additional Information

I confirm that this is an accurate record of the meeting held on 1st December 1942

Interview finished	16:30
Signed by Investigatory Officer	
Signed by Employee	S. Gibb
Date	1st December 1942

E rika and the boys were going to the Gauleiter's speech. The first snow was yet to fall, but everyone could feel it coming. She re-wrapped Max's scarf around his neck before they left their digs.

'You'll feel warmer this way,' she said, enjoying fussing over him, whilst he enjoyed being fussed over. He might as well enjoy something about the next hour, he thought to himself. He certainly wasn't going to enjoy the rant which would inevitably blast from the little dictator Hitler had appointed to the region, as he had to each region of the country. But since attendance was mandatory, Max went along finding the spectacle both terrifying and yet fascinating, in the way he did the dissection of a tumour on a brain.

A shrill whistle shot up from the street outside and ricocheted off the wet window. It was Horst letting them know they were waiting.

'Hang on!' Max grinned as Erika hurried to the door. 'What about you?' And he fiddled with her scarf which was actually so neatly tucked into her coat he could not improve on it, but it was a great excuse to touch her once more and to secretly and mischievously enjoy delaying her as he knew how keen she was to hear the Gauleiter speak.

'There's nothing wrong with *my* scarf,' she said slapping his hands away. Although she did so gently and with a smile he was suddenly shot through with resentment for its colour, the red of the National Socialists. In order to expel this feeling he focused on her coat instead, which was of a colour he could find something positive in.

'I love this old coat on you,' he said.

She jiggled about at the door impatiently.

'You look lovely in purple. So... regal.'

She softened a little. Another whistle penetrated the glass.

'We have to go,' she said and pulled him from the room.

'Come on, Max and Dorothea!' Edgar blasted as he strode off ahead of the others, looking up at the lecture hall as he passed with the words THE TRUTH WILL SET YOU FREE carved in gold above the great windows; the lecture hall where the illustrious Professor Hass would be speaking in a couple of days time, and Edgar couldn't wait.

The Gauleiter's speech took place in the Platz right in front of the cathedral. It was no coincidence. As Max, Edgar and Horst were to find out soon enough at the convent in Breslau, Hitler enjoyed such symbolic gestures when it came to the church. Not that the Gauleiter, peacocking behind a swastika-clad lectern, was merely going to rely on symbolism today. His words were flagrant, unequivocal.

'The Bishop of Eichstätt said in a... subtle, but unmistakable way that the Church had sole claim to the worldview education of baptised Catholic youth. He proclaimed the same right with regards to Catholic organisations. He was just as sly but unmistakable in objecting to a ban of political activity on the part of priests. He said that the political revolution was over and that "the National Socialist movement's battle for people's minds" was an attack on the Church, on Catholic bishops, priests, indeed on Catholicism in general.'

'Of course it is,' Erika heard Max mumble to Edgar. 'Hitler wants to be God. He wants the divine right to say who lives and dies. He expects blind faith from everyone.'

'Well, the church insists on devotion even if you doubt,' Erika said keeping her eyes firmly on the Gauleiter, her head up, her arms folded, against the cold, against doubt.

'But it doesn't do so by threatening you with imprisonment or worse otherwise,' Horst said louder than the others were comfortable with.

Erika's response was ventriloquist-like. 'No, it just threatens fire and brimstone. Come on, Horst, you know the church should clean up its own act before casting aspersions on the National Socialists.'

'What on earth are you talking about?'

'You've heard the stories,' she hissed. 'Priests sexually abusing children in their congregations. Is that the alternative to National Socialism? Please!'

'Resistance movements. Ha!' the Gauleiter shrieked. 'Medical students in universities around the country...' Max, Babyface, Edgar and Horst suddenly stiffened as if the Gauleiter was talking directly at them. 'Spoiled brats who foul their own nest while others are dying for them on the front. Their kind shamelessly abuse their privileges. They can study in wartime thanks to *our* money. The Treaty of Versailles gave us nothing but poverty, inflation and unemployment. Our Führer eliminated all that.'

Erika luxuriated in the boys' silence and nodded along with the cap perched on the bald head in front of her. However, her stomach growled as if to contest the Gauleiter's statement. She thought of her sparse, damp room, her box for a table, her meals of bread and jam. Then she thought of the money her parents sent each month, which allowed her to eat better, splash out a bit, for a week or two at least, yet she saw that allowance as she saw the fence around the villa when she was small.

'Our daily worship is going to our workplaces to build the German nation. And our daily prayer is work for that nation.'

After rapturous applause for this final statement, the crowd dispersed. Max, Babyface, Edgar and Horst made for the café, hands shoved deep in their pockets, huddled together so tightly as they chattered away that to Erika they looked like a four-headed beast. She followed them nonetheless, until, that was, the bald man in the cap held her by the arm.

'Can I help you?' she said offended.

'I think we can help each other. You're from the university I suspect?'

'I am,' she said shoving her hands deep into her own pockets now.

'A student of medicine?'

'Yes,' she said fingering a large hole in one pocket she hadn't noticed before.

'I completely agree with your thoughts on the church. I completely agree that the National Socialists are the solution for our nation. But even in your university the threat to all that is good is festering as we speak. However, I can eliminate it for you. As easy as wiping out an infestation of rodents. If you just supply me with the chemicals to do so, *doctor*!'

'What *chemicals* do you mean exactly?'

'A small amount of cyanide, the kind you students use every day for one experiment or another. That's all.'

'Oh… I don't really use…'

'A hundred Marks,' he said shoving the cash into one purple pocket.

She didn't dare look. She just rubbed the notes between her fingers as if she could count them that way. They felt warm after being in the bald man's pocket.

'You don't have to worry about what I do with the stuff. Just see it as a simple purchase, which doesn't only help you out financially, but helps the nation we both so love.'

As she hurried to the café she caressed the notes in her pocket and it was all she could do not to insist on buying everyone a round of schnapps to celebrate.

It was two o'clock in the morning when Max was dragged from his bed for interrogation. The first he knew of it was the collar of his shirt cutting into his neck as he was yanked onto the floor. In the struggle the entire bunk nearly toppled, waking Edgar below who shouted after them:

'Where are you taking him? What are you doing, you bastards!'

Max had barely had chance to focus his bleary eyes on who was doing this to him, but his ears picked out Edgar's words clearly enough. Not just because they were shrieked down the barracks after him, but because the fear in them was so new it penetrated even Max's molested being. Long gone was the caustic wit and the sarcasm that had always been his armour; now his words were raw and naked, the words of someone that has lost so many friends. And when your family *is* your friends there is nothing left when the last one is taken too.

The two mute guards, whose orders it seemed were to drag Max so fast that he couldn't find his footing, bore him like he and Edgar had done so many wounded soldiers from the churned up waters of the Rhine or the battered streets of Breslau, but when it finally came to set him down it was not gently onto a hospital cot – he was dumped with unnecessary force into a chair before a desk in an office which he had barely had occasion to set foot in since the day he arrived at Gegesha all those years ago.

Now more alert, but still spluttering from the way his shirt had been used as a leash, he tugged at his collar and found his watering eyes settling on the unlikely vision of a window box bursting with radishes, their ripe red heads just poking through the soil beneath a healthy little jungle of leaves above, making the most of the all night sunlight in this Arctic summer. Which of the officers that inhabited this building was nurturing little root vegetables and yet had no idea how to treat a human being? Max found the sight of the neat, well-tended window box hilarious in his tousled state and, as he watched the leaves leaning towards the sun, he knew that there couldn't be a more perfect environment on the entire planet to break a human spirit: months and months of soul destroying darkness only to be followed by a short enticing spell of so much sun that you couldn't sleep, before it ducked below the horizon again for another eight months. Then on the rimy edge of the world, the colourless sea stretching off into infinity, it was easy to feel abandoned by God and, when you had given up on God, feel abandoned by humanity. It was just surprising that the Russians deemed it appropriate to subject their own men to the same conditions and not expect them to break too, or go about breaking each other in response to such confounding circumstances.

Max shoved his eyes along from the radishes to find Sergeant Volkov standing to attention by the wall. Guarding the radishes, Max giggled inwardly, drunk on the pain inflicted on him so far and on the anticipation of more. No seriously, he told himself, if he's standing like that, there must be a superior in the room. So he turned to look at the desk where Lieutenant Lagunov sat.

The lieutenant looked almost as dishevelled as Max felt, ragged as he was from still sharing that stinking flat and the one foul bed with three other families and their ever increasing broods. He had actually stopped taking his turn in the bed at night. It wasn't worth the disruption to his hip-bruising sleep on the floor. Besides, just an hour in the sagging but soft bed was as tormenting to him as the brief Arctic summer was to Max.

Max thought about asking after Mrs Lagunov and little Oleg, to remind the soldier, if necessary, of the service he had been to his family in case it would help mitigate his plight – whatever his plight was – but since the lieutenant looked as unprepared to be here at this hour as Max, he thought better of it. Still slumped in his chair, hardly moving his lips, the interrogator began:

'Gunther Jordan.'

'I beg your pardon, sir?' Max's question was a genuine one. He could have sworn Lagunov had just uttered the name of Erika's father, but he must have been mistaken. This is what such *sehnsucht* did to a man's brain, Max reasoned. He was hearing things now. His mind was making any little connection to Erika it could from the most tenuous of links.

'Gunther Jordan. I know you know the man. So how about you tell me all of his movements since the war began.'

'It is true I know the man,' Max chose his words carefully, just in case they didn't know *the man* was his father-in-law. He was suddenly terrified that something bad was going to happen to Erika because of this. 'But how could I know much about his movements since I've been stuck here for the past four years?'

'But before that you were in Germany. We picked you up in Breslau, I believe.'

'You did but my… everyone I knew…' He had a feeling they knew all about his family already but nevertheless he refused to acknowledge his relationship to Gunther yet and tempered his description of their location. '… everyone I knew was over the other side of the country. I rarely heard from them thanks to your guns blowing our planes out of the sky'. Max knew he had snapped a little too soon, but the image of those remnants of letters snowing down on him from clouds of smoke and flame, of all that affection, that effort to connect ripped up and scattered to the wind by a few dumb artillery shells, pushed a button in him.

Lagunov barely had the energy to be riled by this, but he did sit up a little before saying, 'So tell me what you do know from those *rare* occasions you heard from or about him.'

Max saw a great threat in the soldier's little movement. Lagunov wasn't at home now among the kids and the women, the pregnancy and the illness, where he was constantly out of his depth; he was here in his office where the rules and the pecking order were as clear as the Arctic air.

'I know that he spent time in Greece in the early part of the war, then some time in '44 he went to serve as an officer in Caucasus,' he said recalling Gunther's boasts directed at his own papa the last time he saw them both at his wedding. 'Apart from that I know nothing about him or his movements.'

Lagunov shifted again, always in short, slight moves – a pawn on a chessboard. Now he was leaning forward slightly. 'I think you saw our radishes over there. I am more than happy to give you some if you just tell me what I need to know.'

Radishes! Were times so hard, Max thought, that he would sell his own father-in-law down the river for a handful of root vegetables?

But nevertheless Max's mouth went about trying to imagine the peppery burst those little red bulbs would make in his mouth when bitten, but it was so long since it had consumed something of such flavour it was struggling to recreate the effect. Meanwhile Max's eyes were mesmerised by the warming steam rising from the cup on the desk, which was devoid of anything else except Lagunov's peaked cap and an enormous bunch of keys so big it must have opened every single lock in the entire camp and beyond.

'I would love some radishes, sir,' Max eventually said in utter earnestness, 'but I honestly do not know more than I've told you already'.

He heard the scuff of Volkov's boots on the wooden floor behind him, saw Lagunov's eyes dart up over his head, then nothing. Nothing happened for a while, except Max became aware of how hot it was in this office. So much hotter than any room he had ever been in during the last four years.

'Gunther Jordan is being detained in one of our other labour camps, you know.'

Max didn't know and Lagunov could see this from the way his prisoner's face twitched at the news. 'He's been sentenced to twenty-five years hard labour.'

Twenty-five years! Max reeled, not just at the possibility of staying here in Gegesha for another twenty-one years, but at the fact that poor Erika must now be dealing with losing her father as well as her husband to the war.

Lagunov continued, 'I know Gunther Jordan is a relation of yours—'

'You're right,' Max cut in reasoning that he should quickly offer up more information on his relationship to Gunther, even though it was clear now they already knew about it, but at least it would *look* like he was being cooperative if he told them before they told him. 'He is a relation of mine, in fact he's my wife's father, but we have never been particularly close and I don't know much about what he gets up to. However,' he added with a bitter sarcasm he seemed to have inherited from Edgar, 'if perhaps you'd allow me to write to my wife using more than fifteen bloody words, I could ask her to enlighten you'.

The boots behind him were on the move again, but this time Lagunov chose not to impede their progress across the room with his tired eyes and a second later Volkov's hands were clamped around Max's neck forcing his head down to his knees.

'You know more, Portner. You know where he was during the war and you're going to tell us.'

Volkov had come to be synonymous among the men with brutality but his filthy murderous hands on Max's skin now, after what he'd heard about Horst's demise, was too much for him to bear. He twisted himself out of Volkov's grip and stood up facing the sergeant spitting the words, 'But then, Lieutenant, you'd have to make sure your sergeant let my wife's reply through otherwise you'll never get the information you want. You see, he has a tendency to confiscate letters and murder prisoners too, did you kn—?'

Volkov grabbed Max with both hands at the back of his neck and yanked him down towards the ground bringing his knee up to Max's face as he fell.

Max heard himself squeal with pain and Volkov hiss. 'Don't forget your place, you Nazi cockroach. You're in my Empire now and you will tell us what we want to know.'

There was a jangling and scraping above as that huge bunch of keys on the desk was grabbed and brought down on Max's head.

'Tell us the truth!'

Ch-mp.

'Tell us the truth!'

Ch-mp.

'Tell us!'

Ch-mp, 'Tell us!' *Ch-mp, ch-mp.* The keys bit into the ball of human on the ground.

Max had put his hands over his head until they curled up, bruised and bleeding. Then only his skull was left to protect him from death as the keys thumped into him again and again. The barracks key, the office key, the solitary key, the kitchen key, the key to the storerooms, the key to the locksmith's workshop, the key to the armoured car, the key to the main gate, the keys to freedom – that's what each and every one of them were. Where once he thought the guards brandished them to keep him captive, now he realised that all together and wielded like a multi-headed mace, rapped over his head until his skull caved in, they were in fact the keys to freedom, because death was the only road to freedom now.

Somewhere in his fading consciousness Max felt a cooling rush of air on his raging scalp, heard another set of boots scuff the floor and felt a pause of such welcome length between beatings he thought that he had finally died. But the pain was not gone. And in the afterlife there was no pain, isn't that so? But that was the afterlife he used to believe in, not the afterlife he'd come to accept now, the one that bore a diabolical resemblance to the present. Yet despite this acceptance, the notion that the pain you die in is eternal too sent a contraction of panic through him that made him long perversely for the sensation of metal pounding on his skull again. There was the sound of the chair toppling and of someone bawling, 'Get off of him, get off, you idiot!' Then the smell of bad breath and vodka as two big arms sat him up. But having sat him up the arms did something extraordinary – they embraced him, cradled him and a voice apologised to Max for the behaviour of his subordinates.

'This man helped my wife,' Colonel Utkin roared. 'And yours, you bloody fool. What do you think you're doing letting this animal loose on him?'

'I-I-I didn't—' Lagunov began wearily.

'Go and get the other medic from the barracks! Quickly! This man needs attention.'

Utkin had spoken with his eyes fixed on Max's bleeding head, dabbing at it with a handkerchief he'd pulled from his pocket and leaning the doctor against his broad chest as they sat on the floor. Lagunov looked at Volkov. Volkov looked at Lagunov. Both unsure who was just ordered to get help, so neither budged. Until Utkin looked up appalled and howled, 'You!' to Volkov who scampered from the office and across the parade ground to the sound of foxes crying up on the hill.

Max's wounds were not as bad as Edgar first feared. There was no evidence of serious concussion, but a few days in a bed at the hospital to be sure was in order with round the clock observation by the only functioning doctor left until he was too tired to observe anything, then Bubi took over under strict instructions to wake Edgar should he notice any vomiting, convulsions, sensitivity to light or sound, slurred speech or confusion in the patient.

Bubi, wide-eyed, had parroted Edgar as he listed the symptoms to look out for and the young man recited them constantly under his breath in between prayers for his mentor's quick recovery as he sat by Max's bed rocking ever so slightly on his chair.

The patient woke at intervals relieved to see empty beds in the room. The sickness figures were reasonably low, he tried to reassure himself, although since the population of the camp had dwindled so much due to death and the occasional release, it took a much smaller number of patients to reach the nine per cent quota allowed. Those who were on the mend toiled away using the bounty stored under the beds, making heaters, fashioning tools better than the ones they were given to work with in the factories or the forests, making extra clothes from cement bags or cooking porridge on the stove.

Max slept and when he woke again Bubi had turned into Edgar. He slept some more and when he woke again Edgar had turned into Jenny. But that could have been a dream. He was still a little disorientated from all that beating around his brain. He slept again and when he woke he saw Edgar out on the bridge buying cigarettes from a prisoner who worked in the cement factory. The factory worker handed over the cigarettes and Edgar handed over something in return which winked in the sunlight before disappearing into his pocket.

'What did you trade for those?' Max said through sticky lips nodding at Edgar's handful of smokes as he sat down again.

Edgar looked at his purchase in silence for a moment as if weighing up whether he had got a good deal or not. Then, deciding he had, he looked at Max, tossing his eyebrows as casually as he could and said, 'My Iron Cross.'

They hadn't had a chance to send them home after receiving them from the CO back in Breslau what with the attack on the monastery and their subsequent capture, so the medals had sunk to the depths of their bags, not the most practical of possessions, and remained there ever since. Yet no matter how hard Max tried, and despite the fact it was an accolade bestowed on them by a regime they didn't support, he couldn't help but be proud of his Iron Cross and he couldn't wait to show Erika and Netta.

'Don't look at me like that, Max!' Edgar whined, putting one of the cigarettes up to his mouth with a trembling hand. 'I don't need a bloody medal right now, but I really, really need a fag.'

He slept a little more and when he opened his eyes the next time he saw Jenny again. He tried to blink the apparition away but it remained, it reached out, it squeezed his arm gently. He felt it. She was real. She was there.

'I thought I was dreaming,' he said clearing his throat.

'Well,' she gave a sweet snort, 'I know I'm what most men dream of, but no, this time I'm really here.'

'Do you?' he asked.

'What?'

'Do you know that? That men look at you and dream that they were with you?' She cocked her head so he clarified, 'I mean, do you know how desirable you are?'

There was something about lying in bed in her presence, despite his injuries, that made him feel strong and confident to ask such things, as if they had actually just made love and were lying there together alone, not in a hospital surrounded by patients with a grinning Edgar watching from the desk.

She blushed, 'Well, I don't think I'm desirable.'

'Of course you do, otherwise you'd never have believed you could make a living out of it.'

She looked a little deflated, miffed even, that he had referred to her profession. And she was. Miffed that he had brought it up before she'd had a chance to say, 'And what if I stopped making a living out of it?'

'Are you?' he said beginning to sit himself up, but thinking better of it when he felt the blood start thumping through his sore head. 'Stopping?'

'I thought I might. Since the right man came along.'

Max felt suddenly nauseous, but he couldn't tell if it was his concussion or the thought of Jenny falling in love with someone. And when he dived a little deeper into that sea-sadness he could just make out that it was the thought of Jenny falling in love with someone other than himself that made him really sick.

So he had to ask, 'Have you found the right man then?'

'Well, I thought I'd bloody well lost him for a moment there,' she chuckled, mopping his brow with a handkerchief and staring directly into his eyes in case he missed her meaning.

When he had so proudly talked about his daughter to her and the girls in the apartment, she knew, as far as her own rules went on the subject, that he was now out of bounds to her. However, when news of Max's brush with death reached her, her own response – the way she grabbed her fox fur coat and found herself persuading one of the officers to drive her into the camp within minutes of hearing about it, fluttering her lashes and flashing smiles at the Soviet despite being out of her mind with worry – told her that her own rules were a load of rubbish, and that rules meant nothing when it came to matters of the heart. The fact that Lagunov was in the room when this violence was meted out on Max, made her resentment for her profession even greater as she tried to scratch images from her head of the Lieutenant straining and grunting over her whilst his wife was languishing in the shitty apartment next door breastfeeding little Oleg.

Her words and her touch were better than any medicine Edgar could have prescribed Max, even if he had all the resources of his once prosperous homeland at his disposal. As she leaned over Max and kissed him full on the lips, Edgar would not allow himself to see it as an adulterous act to Erika. He envied the fiery rush of emotion his friend must be feeling and wished him well. Who knew if they would ever get out of here! And anyway, since in this place or at home Edgar was doomed to a string of furtive fumbles down alleyways and could never sit in the Platz and kiss his partner in the full blaze of the summer sun, he enjoyed an even greater kinship with his friend now than ever before.

Tears rolled down Max's face as he luxuriated in the sensation of her lips fusing with his. Jenny saw them and wiped them away with a questioning smile, but no words. He reached up to her face to initiate another kiss and she obliged. Again the tears came. The tears of a lottery winner, of an Olympic gold medallist, of a freed man, or simply of a man who hasn't felt the lips of a woman on his for years and years; and of a man who knows from bitter experience that this rapturous beginning may one day require an agonising severance, a heart-breaking ending.

I t was too much having this girl squealing in the kitchen when there were patients sitting in the hallway waiting to be seen. Karl was at work, Martha was out and Erika could hardly keep leaving the patient she had, to tell her daughter off – how unprofessional would that look! So as soon as the asthmatic woman had left her surgery she marched out to the back of the house grabbing Netta by the scruff of her neck as she went through the kitchen and shoved her into the cellar where Bertel kept the chickens.

'No, Mama, no!' Netta wailed as the door was closed on her and she found herself in a dark cramped hovel that stank of chicken shit. 'How long? How long do I have to stay in here? How long? *How long?*'

'Until you can learn to be quiet,' her mother said in that nonsensical ways adults do when they don't know the answer to a question.

Erika tried to compose herself as she entered the house and approached the next unimpressed patient sitting in the corridor, desperately blinking images from her eyes of her four-year-old self with a bleeding foot being locked in her bedroom at the villa where she was imprisoned like Ash Fool until the Hitler Youth broke her out nine years later.

She wasn't just furious with Netta. She wasn't really furious with Netta at all. She was seething because Babyface had exposed her like a common criminal last night. She was angry at him for not understanding, not seeing the whole picture. His face had never looked so wrinkled as her explanations did nothing to assuage his suspicions. She told him she had no idea what the bald man would actually do with the cyanide; told him to remember how strapped they all were for cash at the time. She even told him she asked purposefully for such a small amount that nobody could do any real harm with it, but, in truth, she didn't know enough about its properties to have a clue just what could be done with it. She could tell Babyface even doubted the existence of the mysterious bald man, since none of the boys had seen him that day in the Platz.

But it was just that they hadn't noticed him as they were too busy criticising the Gauleiter and hurrying to the warmth of the café.

'Just because you didn't see him, it doesn't mean he never existed. You should understand that concept better than me!' she had quietly ranted at Babyface. But it was Max she really wished she'd said that too. Babyface was never a devout Catholic, and so she was even angrier now at him for not being devout; and at Max for not being around to hear her argument about believing the unseen; and at herself for being neither devout nor sure of her National Socialist principles anymore. This grey middle ground she paced about in these days was utterly infuriating to her. And what was more annoying, she could only compare it to some kind of Catholic purgatory. Perhaps the purgatory in Dante, she winced, that intimidating, sheer-sided grey, grey mountain. And then she found herself on the edge of a mountain and the mountain was Walmendinger Horn, up in the Allgäu Alps. Hans, the tall blonde Swiss boy, was there, holding her red booklet with one ungloved hand and telling her to be careful. Telling her:

'I like you, Erika. I like you because you are clever and strong. Just take care of yourself and look around you at all the other sides of the story before you make up your mind.'

What a patronising fool, he was! Of course she would look at all sides before she made up her mind. She saw the eagle riding the thermals far below their feet, its wings spread out like the eagle which sat atop a swastika on the book she snatched back from Hans. She saw herself clambering to her feet. Heard her thirty-year-old self bellowing through the wind at the back of the boy's head:

'It's listening to all sides of the story that has got me in this mess, you idiot. If I had just stuck to my guns things would be as clear as the sky and as pure as the air up here. But now it's all grey. Grey grey grey. And it's all your fault!'

She saw her boot on his back. Felt his moment of futile resistance. And then she turned away quickly, hoisted herself back onto the plateau, telling herself that it didn't really happen. She didn't see it for sure. So it couldn't have happened. Not in *that* way anyway. The last time she *saw* Hans he was fine. He probably held on just fine, despite the shove she gave him with her foot. Only later, when she was long gone, did he lose his balance, as he tried to get up off the ridge, and fall. Yes, that was how it must have happened.

'But you just said yourself, just because you can't see something, doesn't mean it doesn't exist,' Babyface's disembodied voice was whistling in the Alpine winds blasting through her skull. 'And you can't deny you saw your boot on his back. You saw that, didn't you? You felt yourself push him, didn't you?'

Her next patient was telling her all about her various ailments, but Erika didn't hear a word. She was too busy raging inwardly at Max, wishing he had done something terrible too so she didn't feel so bloody toxic next to him all the time.

In the gelid jaws of January the cables hung from hut to hut glowing brighter than ever against the black sky, as if it was intentional, like neon in the cities, and not the result of poor rigging and excessive current. Such shoddy and overused infrastructure often had dire repercussions and Max and Edgar had had their fair share of patients with burns and electric shocks. So as they trudged into the camp for dinner and saw the cable above the mess hut in the distance snap with a firework flourish and lash itself to the man smoking below they were not surprised, but ran to administer to what appeared to be the worst case of its kind yet, whilst Bubi ran to the office to tell them to cut the power.

By the time the doctors reached the man the electricity was off and the men in the mess hut had crowded outside to see what those lightning flashes and the sound like a massive and tightly tuned drum being beaten two or three times were all about.

The patient was black, his clothes and his skin, much of which had fused into one grotesquely new substance which covered his bones. It made him hard to recognise and until one of the guards shouted, 'It's Volkov,' even Edgar and Max, who were face to face with him assessing his airway, had no idea who it was.

Bubi arrived with some burning tapers for light in which Max saw Edgar sit back on his haunches, clench his teeth and take his eyes from the patient.

'What are you doing, Ed? The patient has burns inside and out, his airway is closing up as the swelling begins.'

'Exactly,' Edgar shrugged. 'There's nothing we can do for him now.'

Max looked around him at the crowd comprised of prisoners and guards, and told Bubi to move them back to give them space to work. Then, when he felt he could hiss at his colleague without being overheard, he continued:

'You mean you're refusing to treat him?'

'Of course I'm refusing to waste my time on a dead man, especially when it's him. And you should be too. Have you forgotten what he did to you? What he did to Horst? What he's done to so many men in here since the day we arrived?'

'Bubi, get me a pen. Not a pencil, it has to be a pen, and a knife from the kitchen. Quickly! His heart is still pumping, he just needs some air,' Max said blowing into Volkov's lipless mouth.

'He's the enemy, buddy, why help the enemy?'

'Because I help people. That's what we do, as doctors, right? And, if you didn't know, the war was over four years ago.'

'Really? I hadn't noticed,' Edgar said looking down his nose at the smouldering sergeant gently fizzing in the snow beneath him.

Bubi arrived with a pen and a knife as ordered.

'Hold the light near his face, Bubi, so I can see into his mouth.'

'For God's sake, Max,' Edgar scoffed.

'His upper airway is swollen shut. A tracheotomy is indicated.'

Max took the knife, which had been used to slice potatoes not many minutes before, and made a vertical incision below Volkov's well-defined Adam's apple. Then he fumbled with the pen, discarding the lid and the cartridge inside leaving him with a metal tube which he forced into the Russian's windpipe. Immediately his chest expanded as Volkov took a breath of Arctic air through the tube. His incised windpipe bubbled as he tried to moan from the unimaginable pain his incinerated body was enduring. His eyes grew wide in the light from the tapers Bubi held as his body sucked gratefully at the air but his mind realised that the maintenance of consciousness the air brought only meant the perpetuation of the pain his nervous system registered. Max sat back to reassess the situation and Bubi leaned in and whispered to Volkov:

'Serves you right.'

Max heard Bubi and grief crawled over his skin like maggots over the floor of the hospital. If only I hadn't lost control in front of him when Horst died, Max sighed inwardly, mourning the boy's early discovery of the human capacity for vindictiveness.

'So now what, boss?' Edgar sneered. 'That was a nifty little trick with the pen, but with burns this severe the rest of his airway will close up eventually and we have no resources to deal with a patient like this.'

'Get a stretcher, Bubi,' Max asked gently and then answered Edgar, 'We make him as comfortable as possible until the end.'

'With what? We have no morphine. We've hardly got any aspirin left, not that aspirin would touch him in this state.'

Volkov's still blue eyes moved around in his blackened skull indicating how he was taking in everything said over him and how he wanted so desperately to beg for help, to plead with these resourceful Germans to come up with a solution, like they had for every other predicament in this hellhole, to save him or put him out of his misery.

'Carry him to the hospital,' Max ordered as he helped Bubi lift him onto the stretcher.

'He doesn't want to go to the hospital,' Edgar said with thinly disguised mockery. 'He's afraid of catching something in there, remember?'

Max surprised himself by hesitating even though he knew Edgar's protestation was absurd now.

'Then take him to the office,' another officer said slipping through the crowd; the crowd that was already thinning – well, some of them had left their food on the table and it needed to be eaten before it got cold or before someone else took advantage of the distraction and stole it.

Bubi and a strong-stomached guard carried the stretcher to the office. Max followed. Edgar remained by the mess hall – it was dinner time after all – and called after Max:

'You were right, Max, sorry. This is a much slower more painful death for him. I see there was method in your madness after all. I like it.'

Volkov more than anyone else in Gegesha had made it clear to Max how he resented him for the 'perks' he was afforded for being a doctor – if you could call a coat made from man-eating vermin, a twelve kilometre round trip on foot in shabby boots, near alcoholic poisoning from an excessively grateful Colonel and delving your hands into unsanitary and festering parts of humans perks. But

Max never persevered in his vocation here because of the perks. Or even because of fear of punishment if he lost a Soviet patient. It never occurred to him all the time he went into town that he should be anxious about that; that he would be punished for it if he did lose one. He simply hoped for the best for everyone not to save his own skin, but because that's what he hoped for all his patients – as all doctors should. And he was as proud of this as he was of his Iron Cross.

When the officers had left the room repulsed by the sight of their charred colleague and the guard who had carried the stretcher had hurried outside to throw up, not so strong-stomached after all, Bubi and Max were alone with Volkov. That was when Max put his finger over the end of the pen protruding from Volkov's throat and told himself, as he locked eyes with his Polish comrade, that he was shortening the patient's inevitable suffering and that he took no satisfaction whatsoever from being the one with his finger over the hole.

She had hoped her letter to Babyface would bring him to see her, just as it did. Somewhere in the maelstrom of emotions she now constituted she wanted him to stop her seeing Rodrick, but when he spoke to her so condescendingly, with such surprising censure, she felt like a child, locked behind the villa gates, or admonished by a handsome Swiss boy, and it made her seethe. It made her want to kick against the gates Babyface was once again closing on her. It made her want to slap the disapproval from the faces of parents; however, whereas once it was her own, now it was Max's. And the only way to kick against all this disapproval was, of course, to do the very thing that they all disapproved of.

But, perhaps equally as predictable, was the lack of pleasure she found in Rodrick's bed this time. As the beast of a man mauled her breasts and poked at her genitals his weight on her was oppressive, his words afterwards nothing but dumb mooing to her now. And that was exactly how she wanted it to be. Then, instead of being told what not to do all the time by everyone, she, for once, would enjoy some control and tell another adult what they couldn't do.

'I don't want to see you anymore, Rodrick,' she said coldly, standing next to the bed where he lay as she dressed.

He was speechless.

'We had some fun. It was... nice. But I'm too... busy with the surgery and everything.'

She almost lost some of her poise as his silence sucked these pathetic excuses from her, which only made him more repulsive to her.

'But what about all we talked about?' he managed as she grabbed her coat. 'About us getting married, about you living here?'

'Here? Really?' she said with all the contempt she could muster, as if he'd just asked her to move into a cow shed. 'Besides, I'm already married, Rodrick.'

She hurried out before he could say it, but his cry of, 'Erika!' reached her on the stairs just as Hans' voice had when she had kicked him as mercilessly from the outcrop, and she clamped a hand over her mouth so her sobs could not be heard as she fled into the street.

The banging and the shouting started around midnight. She had been asleep, or at least lying in bed with her eyes screwed shut, for more than an hour. It was Rodrick's voice moaning and wailing in the quiet street outside. It was his big fist pounding at their front door.

'I love you, Erika,' his words were slurred with boozing. 'You cannot do this! You come back to me this instant! Open this door! Open this door!'

Erika scrambled from her bed and out of her room in a bid to quieten him down before not only her in-laws and her daughter, but the whole street heard. Karl and Martha were already stood on the landing. The looks on their faces! Erika didn't know what was worse: Martha's disgust or Karl's sadness.

'It's over. It's finished,' she hissed at them both in a tone which suggested she was not responsible for the lunatic making a scene at their front door.

'Does that sound like something that's finished, Erika?' Karl winced as he massaged his wrist.

269

The clumsy thunderous clanging of trucks driving into camp was a sound so alien to the prisoners they were out of their bunks and puffing clouds of vapour into the early morning gloom even before they had to. So many trucks could only mean one thing. A new cohort of prisoners, freighted in from another Siberian camp no doubt. One that was ailing as much as this one. One that had lost as many inmates as Gegesha. It made economic sense to combine the two dwindling populations on one site and close the other. At least that was what the ex-engineer from Heidelberg was saying through chattering teeth to Max as the doctor quietly hugged himself and looked into the back of the first truck to swing around on the parade ground honking its horn festively before grinding to a halt.

The truck was empty. And so were all the others.

Max hugged himself a little tighter and stroked the quilted jacket he had been bequeathed by a dying patient, with his fingertips. It was much more preferable than the fox fur coat which he'd traded for a lot of cigarettes and a horse blanket stolen from the stables now sewn into his new jacket as a lining to help him through the winter.

'Perhaps it's us that are being taken to another camp,' he muttered to the ex-engineer with a sudden flush of concern for all the relationships he'd forged here in Gegesha (what if he was separated from the ex-engineer? Who would make his vascular clamps and surgical instruments then?) and the supplies they'd amassed under the hospital beds (they could hardly load the trucks up with all that contraband right here under the guards' noses). He gripped his coat so tightly now he pinched his own skin beneath all the layers. His heartrate was up, his breathing faster. He should have stayed in bed like Edgar, who was convinced there was no good reason to get up whatever the racket outside. When was there ever a good reason to get up before you had to? But as the guards ran to meet the drivers descending from the cabs and the backs of the trucks were dropped opened with a bass drum boom, Max felt inexplicably protective of Gegesha and everything about it. The idea of going to another camp, even one in more clement latitudes, was to him unsettling.

The open ends of some of the trucks now revealed the vehicles to not be completely empty, but rather carrying a number of crates in which were bottles that the drivers and the guards began handing out to the prisoners who had drifted, in the shadowy way all of them moved these days, closer to the trucks.

'This is how we treat you,' cackled one of the drivers. 'You get a bottle of champagne to take home.'

Fifteen words. Some of which might have made sense in another time or another place, but right now, even though they held the meaning Max had ached to hear for so long, he did not hear the last word. Or if he did his body, having consumed it, could not keep it down and vomited it into the snow. Instead he held a bottle of Ukrainian sparkling wine in his hands.

This is how we treat you?

Indeed this is how they had treated him for four years. That hideously cosy fur coat. Those agonisingly brief letters home. A skull bashing followed by a cuddle from his captors. The wonder of electricity with all its burns and electrocutions. Should he be so surprised that they were now handing out bottles of Krim Sekt? They'd probably be smashing him over the head with them in a minute. Or, if they all started glugging down gallons of this stuff now, he'd have more patients with gastric problems than he knew what to do with tomorrow. Then his nine per cent quota would surely be surpassed and he'd be back in the hole for another six weeks.

'We're going home, we're going home!' The ex-engineer from Heidelberg, soon to be simply an engineer from Heidelberg again, danced weakly about brandishing his bottle of plonk.

'We're going home, we're going home!' Others joined in the chant until it reached the timbre of a football crowd, despite there being only a few hundred prisoners left in the whole camp from the thousands that had been captured.

Max backed away and shuffled inside. He knelt by Edgar's bunk. His friend had one eye open, clearly irritated by the commotion outside, but by now curious about what he thought he was hearing.

'What's going on, buddy?' his words were muffled by his pillow.

'We're going home,' Max's words were muffled by his doubt.

271

Not doubt that what the guards said was true, but doubt that he *could* really go home. That he could handle the transition. After all this time. He could barely believe his own emotions, but he was scared to leave Gegesha. Scared to go to Mengede. Back to his Mama and Papa. To his wife and child. That was it! Some part of his brain argued with another as his body got on with gathering his belongings and shoving them into his bag. That was it: he wouldn't be going *back* to his child. He had never even met her, so had never even left. He had spent virtually no time with his wife too since they had been married, so the concept of going back to a wife was a false one too. OK, OK – one thought buffeted another – so you're not going back to your wife and child if you want to indulge in such semantics, but you're going back to Erika. The love of your life, remember? The Dorothea to your Max, the person you couldn't bear to be without throughout your student life. Joined at the hip, as some said. And he felt his hip pressing with delightful discomfort against hers as he wedged himself in that tattered armchair under his blanket in her digs. In fact it was the hip of Edgar on one side and the ex-engineer's from Heidelberg on the other as they crammed themselves in the back of one of the trucks. The ex-engineer from Heidelberg, soon to be simply an engineer from Heidelberg again – until, that is, his tremors lose him his job and his mood swings lose him his wife, and he becomes just an ex-POW in Dossenheim.

Funny how, as the last of the gaunt men hauled their light bodies into the truck, Max was thinking about going home to Erika at all. He never for a moment stopped to think that she might not be waiting for him anymore. And he never once thought about Jenny and whether they had a life together beyond Gegesha.

The truck rattled out of the camp and shook a terrible thought to the forefront of Max's teeming mind.

'Oh God,' Max said.

'What is it, buddy?' Edgar said.

'The letter I sent Erika.'

'The what?' Edgar shouted over the noise of the engine.

'The letter,' Max raised his voice too. 'The last letter I wrote to her told her to forget me, forget her faith... Oh my, what if she believed me?'

'Impossible,' Edgar said with more surety than Max had heard from his friend in a long time.

'She might have done. It's been so—'

'It's impossible, because she hasn't read the letter,' Edgar grinned.

'How do you know?'

'Because,' Edgar sighed dramatically, 'I knew you would one day regret what you'd written so that's why I took the liberty of intercepting Christoph before he took the mail into town. I destroyed the letter. So no need to worry.'

Whilst feelings of indignation at his privacy being invaded brawled with his gratitude to Edgar, another far more pragmatic thought was allowed to articulate itself:

'How did you persuade Christoph to give you the letter? He takes his duty as postman very seriously. *Took* his duty as postman very seriously.'

'Everyone has their price.'

'How many cigarettes did that cost you?'

'Oh, no cigarettes at all. Seems the dirty little monk had other predilections and I was only too happy to oblige,' Edgar winked. 'Anything for my buddy, eh!'

Bubi, who had been both shocked and entertained by this little story, giggled, a sound that reminded both doctors of the boy he had been when they had met.

'If you need somewhere to stay, Bubi,' Edgar said what Max would have, had he been more sure of his own domestic arrangements in Mengede, 'you know you've always got a place with me.'

'Thanks,' Bubi looked as uncertain as Max felt, 'but I'll be going back to Poland. Mama and Papa will be waiting'.

There weren't many years between the two, but Max felt so envious of Bubi then for having such a simple, youthful life waiting for him; despite being in his twenties now, and despite not knowing yet how his time as a POW would affect both him and his parents, Bubi clearly had every intention of picking up his childhood exactly from where it had been so rudely interrupted.

Max smiled warmly at the boy until his attention was caught by the view beyond Edgar's beaming profile of Gegesha receding so unceremoniously from view as Germany had from the back of that train that took him through Romania. It had been a train full of wounded and sick soldiers he'd been charged with transporting from the Eastern Front before his posting in Breslau. The train had to pass so close to the Southern Front the Romanian driver and his stoker were petrified that they'd be attacked and they were threatening to jump off leaving the Germans to the mercy of the Russians. That was when Max had pulled his gun on them and ordered them to keep going. He never had any intention of using it, but luckily the Romanians didn't know that. So throughout the entire duration of the war he had never used it and then it was taken from him as he stood with a mouthful of brick dust in the rubble that once was the monastery before the Soviets began to herd them like cattle around Breslau.

As the truck swung past the path that led to his hospital out on the Barents Sea he was suddenly furious at the Russians for taking his gun because right now he wanted to shoot every single one of them. In the face, just like they did to the one-legged soldier in pyjamas outside the bombed monastery. He wanted to see them suffer, see the fear in their eyes as he held the barrel to their foreheads, because he was furious that they had taken his burgeoning adulthood from him, enraged that they had taken his daughter's early years from him, but what he was more incensed about than anything else was the bewildering yearning he had for Gegesha as it disappeared among the pine trees.

'It's over,' Edgar was saying tearfully. 'It's finished.'

And all Max could think of was the guard prodding them into the isolation truck when news had reached them all of the end of the war. Max had said the same thing to that guard back then in '45: 'But it's over!' And the guard had just replied, 'So?' because he knew, as Max did now, that this was far from finished.

The truck was soon lumbering slowly through the potholed roads in town. Jenny and Isabel, who were chatting by the road, had to hop onto the grass bank to avoid the slaloming vehicle. They looked into the back as it passed and, among the excited faces there, Max's morose one stood out for her. She shrieked his name and ran after the truck.

'Where are they taking you? Max! Where are you going?'

He suddenly found himself on his feet, hanging on to the steel skeleton of the roof and shouting with no great enthusiasm, 'Home! We're being released! We're going home!'

'Where's home?' she was barely able to keep up now.

She saw him shrug and the last thing she heard was, 'Mengede? I'll be in Mengede, Dortmund. Look me up!'

Even Edgar had to raise an eyebrow at the recklessness of that. The thought of the fireworks, which would ensue should she ever take Max up on his offer and turn up at the front door of the house he shared with his parents and his wife, both thrilled and alarmed Edgar, and set him tapping out a frenetic swing beat on his long bony thighs.

Netta was playing the piano when the man arrived. There was a commotion outside on the doorstep. Her mother and grandparents all rushing out with whoops and cries to meet him. Although the doorstep was only a few metres away from her across the living room, Netta allowed the chords her little fingers stretched to play and the gentle roar of flames from the stove, which the piano was snuggled against, to muffle the little riot outside.

She couldn't make out if her mother was crying or laughing. The same for Opa and Oma. And this confusion told her to stay at the piano where everything made sense: the fairy dust sound her right hand produced on the high keys; the unblemished perfectly polished black of the instrument before her; the warmth from the green tiles of the stove which towered over her all the way to the ceiling; a carapace of comfort and familiarity.

Yet in no time curiosity had her using the reflection in the glassy wood, just above the lid where the word Blüthner was etched in gold flowing letters, to peek at the scene behind her. The adults were silhouettes in the square of ghostly white light the open door shone onto the piano. Sometimes the silhouettes were separate, but mostly they merged into one or two bigger ones and Netta knew this meant there was a lot of hugging going on. People hugged when they were happy or in love. But they also hugged when someone was upset, so this didn't help at all. And then her mother called out to her:

'Netta, Netta! Come and see who has arrived!'

She turned on the piano stool to see her mother's face, almost unrecognisable – she hadn't smiled so broadly in a very long time. But she was trembling too as she presented the man to Netta and Netta to the man.

'Darling, this is Netta.' Erika's hands hovered at his arm as he carefully stepped over the threshold, as if she expected him to fall at any moment. 'Netta, this is your father.'

Erika heard her own voice quivering, saw her own hands

fluttering, but it wasn't for fear that Max might fall. She was afraid of him for the first time in her life. Afraid of who he might be now. Afraid in case he had heard from Babyface about the distant past, or heard from anyone in the town about the recent past. But also she was afraid that her husband wouldn't be proud of the part of him she had nurtured and crafted over the last four years; she was desperate for him to love Netta. As desperate as Max was that his parents were enchanted with Erika the first time he introduced her to them all those years ago, in the world before the war.

Netta slipped down from the piano stool and assessed the stranger before her.

Max marvelled at the little human before him.

Netta saw a man who looked like he may be sharp to the touch for his collar bones stood out through his open jacket and his hands looked more like the skeleton's in her mother's medical books than those of a person with skin and muscles on top. His jacket was quilted and seemed to sit oddly on his frame, as if it had been made by a very bad seamstress. The inner lining looked to Netta more like part of a horse blanket than the usual material. He held a relatively new looking *ushanka* (relative to everything else about him) and wrung the furry hat in his bony hands as he knelt in front of her.

Max smiled at the little girl who had lived so long already in this world without him; who could stand up on her own two little feet without his support; who it seemed had even started to play the piano without his tutorage. It would have been hard enough for him, even with all his medical knowledge, to have come to terms with the miracle of holding his own new-born child in his arms. But to have missed that and be faced now with this new miracle sent his soul grieving and celebrating in a fusion of emotions that was more than his scientific brain could handle – the only physiological result of which could be, apparently, tears.

Max hugged his daughter though she kept her arms firmly by her sides, flinching as those collar bones and equally dangerous looking cheekbones came hurtling towards her like spears. He smelt funny. She couldn't say *what* he smelt like, but she knew for sure he didn't smell like Mama, or Opa, or Oma, or even like Tante Bertel. He didn't smell like family. And he didn't look like the wonderful man her mother had told her all about. He didn't look as strong or as clever. He didn't even look like the photographs she had seen of her father, so how could this be him? Father was in a land far far away. And could never be reached. This had been the way things were for her whole life. To try and change that now seemed mean, a cruel joke.

She wriggled free from the man's embrace and cried, 'Mama, Mama!'

Erika instinctively wrapped her distressed daughter in protective arms, all the while fighting an equally powerful urge to push her back into her father's. She has to love him, Erika thought. She *does* love him. He's her father. She must! I must mend this broken picture, Erika told herself. This was not how it was meant to be. Not what she had envisioned every night when Netta had fallen asleep, photo in her little hand of the strong jawed, high foreheaded gentleman, his bright eyes magnified by his round glasses, leaving Erika to doze with the dream that they would be reunited as a family one day.

Netta unburied her face from her mother's shoulder and looked back at Max. This is it, Erika thought, this is the moment all is mended. It was understandable. The poor little girl. Her first reaction was bound to be one of fear. I mean, she had never actually met the man before in person and here we are insisting she accept him as her father. She felt Netta's tiny lungs inflate against her breast and knew it signified she was about to say something. Erika was all ears:

'She's *my* mama,' the little girl yapped at Max with surprising venom. 'She's not yours!'

Erika let out a rather limp laugh to let Max know that it was just one of those silly things children say sometimes, and jiggled her daughter about in her arms as if to expel any more silly things lurking in her throat the way she used to burp her after breast feeding. Karl and Martha added their own unconvincing giggles to the accompaniment of this excruciating moment and Max could not seem to find a place or person in the entire room to rest his hollow eyes on.

Netta stayed strategically on her mother's lap all evening, between Erika and Max. The two adults sat by the Tiffany window in the attic room for hours, glancing bashfully at each other, occasionally talking quietly, occasionally reaching out and touching the other's arm with wonder, as if it was their own arm miraculously grown back after an amputation – but only when they noticed Netta's tired eyes closing again. Yet Netta's eyelids would frequently pop open and each time she would realise the unsettling dream she was having about the strange man in her house was actually true.

'Someone's ready for bed,' her mother whispered into Netta's hair.

'Mmm,' Netta agreed with an involuntary cat-like stretch of her entire body, then addressed the man for only the second time in her life, this time in sleepy tones, but they were equally hard for Max to hear:

'You have to go now,' she yawned. 'It's getting late. My mama and I live here. But you can sleep out in the shed,' she said with all the genuine generosity her drowsy spirit afforded her.

The words stung his soul more than any abuse had his body during his time in Siberia, but Max clung to that absurd little olive branch, the offer of accommodation in the outhouse, and it emboldened him to respond:

'Oh, that's very kind of you, Netta,' he spoke in pantomimic style, 'but I really really would rather move in here with you and your mummy.' Before Netta could protest or rouse herself further from her slumber he fished two brown paper bags from his rucksack and went on, 'So I've got a deal for you. How about this? Can I move in for two bags of sweets?'

Erika clucked gently. It was a conditioned response to any talk about sweets with Netta at this time of night. But it was only a half-hearted cluck. She knew, in this case, the possible magic Max was working far outweighed any detrimental effects on her daughter's molars.

Netta's drooping lids were drooping no more. 'What kind of sweets?' she ventured, looking down her nose at the treasure in her father's hand. The sweets weren't in a small brown paper cone, like the boiled raspberry-shaped fruit drops she bought from the witch at the corner shop whenever she'd saved up enough money. Opa gave her a penny every time she went to the shop for him to buy his cigarettes and when she had saved ten pennies she could afford one little cone full of those delectable sweets. The witch, who stood behind the counter with her crooked nose, warty skin and long grey hair, could not even frighten Netta into speeding up her purchase. Netta would have to marvel first at the neat rows of big glass jars, shelf upon shelf of liquorice twists, aniseed balls, pear drops, lemon sherbets, every flavour, every colour imaginable, even though she and the witch knew very well that in the end she would always chose the raspberry ones. And when the sweets were finally eaten Netta would put the paper cone on the head of one of her dolls and a twig from the garden between its legs and pretend it was the witch flying home from the shop on a broomstick.

Max unravelled the top of one of the bags. Netta thought she must still be dreaming. The bag contained enough sweets to fill three paper cones. And the bag was full of raspberry fruit drops. She smothered a grin by rubbing her itchy nose with the palm of her hand and snuggled back into her mama's chest.

'Do we have a deal?' Max said softly.

'Er... OK,' she sighed. 'It's a deal.' And she closed her eyes knowing, deal or no deal, there was no way her mother would let her have so much as one of those sugary treats this late at night. But tomorrow, she told herself, she would remind the adults of this bargain, because adults had a naughty way of changing the rules day by day.

Max smiled triumphantly at Erika. Erika returned one of relief whilst trying not to stare at her husband's brown teeth. When she'd overcome her shyness around him and finally kissed him on the mouth, after Karl and Martha had left the room, his halitosis was overpowering. She told herself not to be repelled by it or any other aspect of his somewhat decaying physical appearance. It could all be repaired with a little time and care. And a lot of home cooking. The important thing was that he was home and he was Max.

But this wasn't home.

Max had never lived in this house before. Everything about it was unfamiliar to him, even the furniture inside since the Yanks had 'confiscated' everything his parents had furnished their previous house with. Familiarity to him was the mildew-dappled roof of the barracks on waking; the direction and speed of the mischievous wind at rollcall which was the most reliable calendar in the dark months; the warm embrace of a Heizkissen on his lumbar; the soppy flop of the chilly waves around the stilts which held the hospital above the sea. His hospital. Where he was in charge, where he was trusted, not feared, not pitied, not different. Where, despite the impossibility of helping many given his appalling resources, he had helped some. Where he practised medicine as was his dream since he was sixteen. As Erika had done, it seemed, very successfully downstairs for some time now. As he was not allowed to, he'd been informed by a demob officer, until he had gained a year's civilian experience in a local hospital.

Civilian experience?

As if *civilian experience* was going to present any problems to him as a doctor! What did they think he was going to do to his patients in Mengede? Start hacking away at them with pliers from the tool shed? Start trying to clamp severed blood vessels with bits of the garden fence? He'd have all the wonderful equipment that modern medicine could afford at his fingertips coupled with all the resourcefulness he'd had to cultivate as a POW on the edge of the world. As if *civilian experience* was going to present any problems to him as a doctor!

Yet *civilian experience* as a man, as a husband, as a father, as a son. He could already see that was going to be an entirely different matter. That was so much more difficult to envisage, despite its relatively pretty frame, like the view through a stained glass window of a church.

So he found himself wondering instead about his previous home. What was happening in Gegesha now? Was his carefully maintained barrel of pine needle infusion just sitting there becoming stagnant? Were the cranberries slowly rotting with grubby hands no longer delving in and shoving fistfuls of them between healing lips? Had the snow begun edging its way inside, squatting in the barracks, the hole and the office with no one there to shovel it away? And what about all those illicit treasures stashed under the beds in his hospital? The beds where his grateful patients used to lay, dependent on him, like children; children who greeted him whenever he arrived at their bedside, despite their woes; who had no mother to flee to whining, 'She's *my* mama! She's not yours!'

He swallowed the sneer that threatened his face as Erika returned with a towering plate of steaming food, the sight of which made him want to vomit.

He shivered.

Shivered in a way he had never done in all the time he had spent north of the Arctic Circle.

They had encouraged him to have a bath, found him a change of clothes, but afterwards he had slipped his jacket with the horse blanket lining back on and went back to the window in the attic, looking out through the red and blue glass.

'It's not cold in the house tonight, darling, why don't you take that old thing off?' Erika laughed, stood behind him and went to slip it from his shoulders.

'Leave it,' he snapped feebly.

She snatched her hands away, convinced his next utterance would contain the name Rodrick or Professor Hass, but nothing came and she told herself not to be so silly; told herself he just needed some space. Of course he needed some space. All this excitement in one day, it was more than he was used to in the prison camp, she assumed. Not that he'd said much about it yet. But when the time was right she was going to get him to tell her *everything*. Yes, yes, when the time was right, but not until then. Not now.

She backed off and left the room, turning at the door to see him silhouetted in the streetlight streaming in through the window. He was looking out through the stained glass, despite its translucence, his eyes focused beyond, across the rooftops, towards the North, in the manner of one who is longing.

Acknowledgements

Warren Fitzgerald for his indispensable help in writing the novel and without whose support and constant pragmatic advice the novel would not exist.

Demi Quinn for putting me in contact with all the people that mattered in the process of writing and producing the novel.

Gareth Howard leading the production team effectively

Kate Appleton and Josh Hamel my publisists in the UK and USA

My husband for his love , support and patience when the writing of the novel distracted me from my other work.

The love of my children and grandchildren which inspired me to keep going when things got tough

Lightning Source UK Ltd.
Milton Keynes UK
UKHW01f0625050618
323752UK00001B/196/P